MORE GUYS AND DOLLS

MORE
GUYS *and* DOLLS

Thirty-four of the best
short stories
by

DAMON RUNYON

With an introduction by
CLARK KINNAIRD

Garden City Books

GARDEN CITY, NEW YORK

Contents

RUNYON A LA CARTE

Introduction

AFTER Alfred Damon Runyon (which was the name with which he signed his first short stories) departed into the shades, his ashes whirling down among the passersby in Broadway, it was recalled that one evening he offered to bet he would return after his death. No takers.

Runyon is back with us, as we knew him before, in this new book. It is an Event with cap E for reasons which are obvious to those who already are admirers of his literary works, but which may require some explanation to others. The collection has six of his Broadway stories not previously found between book covers, all of them from the period of 1931 to 1939, the years when most of the best of his Broadway stories were written. With these are more than two dozen others of his best, including "The Idyll of Miss Sarah Brown." That was the tale, as one and all should know by now, from out of which Runyon materialized anew on Broadway, amongst his "Guys and Dolls" (some who also appear in other stories in this volume).

It perhaps should be mentioned at this point, for the benefit of newcomers to the Runyon scene, that the "Guys and Dolls" of the Broadway stage also derives in part from another story, "Pick the Winner," the chronicle of the long-distance romance of Nathan Detroit (called Hot Horse Herbie in the original) and his ever-loving fiancée. Also that the master himself had a direct hand in two earlier Broadway shows, "A Slight Case of Murder" and "Saratoga Chips."

Four other stories in this collection are particularly noteworthy. "Blonde Mink" and "Big Boy Blues" were the last of all the Runyon Broadway tales. "Nothing Happens in Brooklyn" and "A Call on the President" are the stories in which Runyon introduced what I believe were his favorite characters.

It has been suggested repeatedly that Runyon "glorified" the murderers, dope-dealers, rum-runners, thieves, kidnapers, bookmakers, horse-players and parasitical hangers-on who comprised most of the principal protagonists in his Broadway stories. The impression may be due to too hasty or unperceptive reading, or lack of understanding of the background of the stories. When Runyon began his satiric Broadway saga, a new phenomenon was making itself felt in the American press. This was the Broadway columnist who sought all his news, or what passed for it, in speakeasies, and came to see gunmen, smugglers, and white-slavers in the likenesses of Rolands, Robin Hoods and Galahads. Runyon began by making gay with the Broadway columnists. He delineated the type as a "hundred per cent sucker," a two-timer, a craven. He went on to poke fun at the outlaws and bums about whom the columnists wrote with such awed or reverent hyperbole. As J. C. Furnas observed, Runyon made "a hard-boiled enemy of society behave like St. Francis of Assisi, demonstrating for all and sundry that the softest hearts beat beneath the latest fashions in bullet-proof vests." It was not a new device, for Western outlaws had been treated in similar fashion by Alfred Henry Lewis and other humorists, but Runyon used it skillfully and distinctively. The result was that he captivated readers of *Cosmopolitan, Saturday Evening Post,* and *Collier's* (and the subsequent collections of the stories in book form) with his humor, his realistic reporting of human nature, and his argot.

Runyon had no illusions concerning the stuff of which his Broadway characters were made. In one of his own newspaper columns of the time he remarked, "There are only three men in the night life of Broadway whose word is worth a nickel." Similar realistic views of the habitués of Broadway and the sporting fraternity run through the verse of which he produced a large quantity in the Thirties, verse in which he evidenced the gift for metaphor which Aristotle defined as the supreme power of the poet. "Just a Good Man," "The Three Cheers Boys," "Ghosts of the Great White Way," "The Manly Art," "The Old Horse Player," are among Runyon poems that leave us without doubts about his feelings. From the last-named came that tag-line that became the title of one of the stories in this book, "All Horse Players Die Broke."

The proof that Joe and Ethel Turp, whom we meet in these pages in "Nothing Happens in Brooklyn" and "A Call on the President," were his favorite characters in his later years, is that he made them the principals in a long series of his daily columns and in his weekly contributions to *Pictorial Review,* in which he had complete freedom in choice of subjects. He wrote several dozen stories of the Turps after "Blonde Mink" and "Big Boy Blues," which were the end of his Broadway saga. The Turps he delineates are basic Americans with all the homely and broad virtues, and without anything in common with the persons of the narrow world of Broadway. In several stories in which he has the Turps visit that small world, he makes them feel out of place and glad to get away from it. He endows them with the traits of which he wrote with sentiment in his earliest fiction. They obviously were folks he cherished, as he did My Old Man, the most frequently recurring character in the earlier fiction.

Understanding this, we may enjoy the gargantuan humor of the *comédie humaine* he lays in Broadway, without any after-feeling of shame for having laughed at the crimes, violence, dissipation and predatory worthlessness of most of his Broadway people. We may begin to appreciate the quality of his craftsmanship. As W. Somerset Maugham is quoted (by Leonard Lyons) as saying, there is another good way to memorialize Runyon. It is to buy Runyon's books and give full recognition to his talents as a writer.

Runyon had pride in and appreciation of his craftsmanship. Once he called my attention to the fact that he was represented in more anthologies with more different stories than any other writer of the time. But he lacked confidence in his ability to produce longer works. He did not believe he could write a novel. He rejected proposals that he work on one, as he passed off suggestions that he give up his daily newspaper work to concentrate on fiction. Yet he maintained interest in a single character through hundreds of thousands of words, more than the average novel contains.

I submit that one of the most artfully delineated and fascinating characters in modern American literature is this character, who tells us, "names make no difference to me, especially on Broadway, because no matter what name a man has, it is not his square moniker," and offers us no square moniker, or any shape moniker at all, for himself. Namely, and nameless, the narrator of most of the stories in this book and the other Broadway tales of Runyon.

Here he is again, The Guy of guys among the guys and dolls, still nameless, but a man unforgettable, as Runyon was and is.

Damon, you win that bet.

CLARK KINNAIRD

MORE GUYS AND DOLLS

Ransom . . . $1,000,000

———————◆◆◆———————

I SAID to Dan the Devil: "What am I going to tell Francesca?"

He said: "Say, you never have to tell Francesca anything. She knows enough to mind her own business. That's the way she was brought up. Anyway, she isn't at Shadow Island just now. She is still in Macon. She has been in training there to be a nurse ever since I went away."

He meant since he had been in prison.

When a fellow is in prison, you always say he is away. When he gets out, you say he is back. Then nobody's feelings are hurt. A lot of people hate the word "prison."

So we headed the Bumble Bee south, a million-dollar cargo stowed away in the hold where we used to hide the Scotch, and the same mob that we used to have when we were running stuff up out of the Bahamas years ago, all except Dan and One-eyed Conroy.

Dan the Devil cooled off Conroy in 1927 for turning stool pigeon. So Conroy was not with us, but we had Black Angelo, Innocence and Fatso Kling and me. Dan the Devil stayed behind in New York to look after the business arrangements.

Black Angelo was navigator of the Bumble Bee. He was a sawed-off, hammered-down Wop out of Brooklyn, who had been a pretty fair welterweight in his time. Innocence was a moonfaced, sad-looking fellow who always seemed just about to break out crying, while Fatso Kling was a big Heeb from up in the Bronx.

I went down to take a look at our million-dollar cargo when we were a day out. His name was John Withington White III. He was six feet two, and weighed 190 pounds. It was nearly all muscle. He got it rowing at Yale. He lacked three months of being twenty-three years old. He was a nice-looking young fellow. I think he should have been a heavyweight fighter. I still had a big lump on my jaw where he nailed me.

He was stretched out on a bunk Innocence had fixed up for him, and the adhesive tape we had put over his eyes was still there. He couldn't take it off himself because he was handcuffed and leg-ironed, and chained to the bunk. He had on evening clothes, now all crumpled up. I pulled the tape off his eyes. It must have hurt, but he made no complaint.

I said: "How do you feel?"

"Rotten," he said. "Where am I, and why?"

"You are at sea," I said. "You have been kidnaped. We're going to hold you for a million dollars ransom. You are not going to be hurt if you are a nice boy, and you'll be returned home as soon as your folks pay you out. But you must be a very, very nice boy."

"Kidnaped?" he said. "Why, that's exciting! I remember now. A gang jumped on me in front of our house. I got in a couple of pokes at them, and then one of them held my arms, and another stuck something under my nose, and I must have faded out."

I said: "Yes, we had to give you the pencil. That's a gag that looks like a pencil, but it's really a syringe, and squirts plenty of sleepiness. You were hard to handle. Look at my jaw."

"Oh," he said, "I'm sorry! Kidnaped, eh? Say, I've read of such things happening to other people, but I never dreamed it could happen to me. It doesn't seem real. It's like a movie."

I said it could happen to anybody in this year of 1933.

"Why all these chains?" he said. "Why not let me loose so I can look at the scenery? And I want to get a message to my mother that I'm all right, so she will not worry."

I said she probably knew by this time. I said our New York agent had probably contacted the family, and that they understood the situation. I said I was sorry I couldn't turn him loose, but we did not dare take chances on a prize like him making a get-away. Furthermore, I said we did not care to have him get a line on where we were going.

I said: "You may not know it, but you're the biggest sneeze in history. You ought to be proud. Nobody was ever held for a million bobs before."

"Well," he said, "suppose my people can't raise all that money, what happens then?"

"Why," I said, "then we just drop you in some nice hole in the ocean with plenty of weight around your neck." I wanted him to understand thoroughly that he was in a tough spot.

"I feel sick," he said, turning over in the bunk.

That night I went down to take a look at him again, and he seemed sick, sure enough. I thought at first it was only from seasickness, or maybe from the stuff that Black Angelo made him inhale out of the pencil when we were taking him.

Then I felt his forehead, and found he was burning up. He seemed to be having trouble breathing, too. I listened to his chest, and it sounded like a sawmill inside. He talked wild. I said to myself, This fellow is getting up some kind of fever.

We had not bothered to put any medicine on board the Bumble Bee, but Black Angelo had some aspirin he used for headaches, and I got some mustard out of the galley and made up a poultice for young White's chest. I had the chains taken off him, and then I undressed him and made him as comfortable as I could, but I could see he was pretty sick, and thinking of what Dan the Devil would say about this made me very nervous.

I was mighty glad when we sighted Shadow Island.

It is a chunk of land of a hundred acres or so, heavily wooded, off the coast of Georgia, a couple of hours' run by motor boat from the mainland. Some rich old Southerner had it for a summer home many years ago, and Dan the Devil bought it for a hide-away for himself when he was in the money.

A narrow, shallow creek took you in for about a quarter of a mile to a dock in front of the house, an old frame bungalow with trees all around it.

Francesca was down at the dock when we pulled in.

She was wearing a man's polo shirt and khaki pants, with sneakers on her feet, and no stockings. She was as brown as an old saddle. Her black hair was hanging loose. She was tall and thin, and very pretty. I had not seen her for several years, but she did not seem at all surprised at the sight of me.

She said: "Hello, Pally. Where's Dan?"

I said he was back in New York cleaning up some business.

She said: "How does he look?"

I said he looked all right, except his hair was getting gray and he was thinner.

"Poor old dear," she said.

Then she saw Black Angelo and Innocence and Fatso on the boat.

She said: "There's something wrong with this picture."

"Hi, Francesc'!" Black Angelo said. "We come to catcha da feesh."

"Yes?" she said. "Now, isn't that nice!"

She knew Black Angelo and Innocence and Fatso as well as she did me, and she had known me all her life. She knew all about them. She knew all about Dan the Devil, too. He never made any secret of his operations to her, and anyway, she could read, and anybody who could read knew about Dan the Devil. He got as much publicity in the past ten years as any man alive.

I said: "Dan didn't know you were here yet."

"No," she said. "I was not supposed to come here for a month, at least. He wrote me just before he left that place and said he thought he might come down to Shadow Island right away for a rest. I wanted to surprise him, so I got a leave of absence from the hospital in Macon where I am training and came here ahead of time. I'm anxious to see Dan and to be with him awhile. I'm going away this fall for good. I'm going abroad."

It had been her plan since she was old enough to realize who her father was, and what he was. She had often talked it over with me in the old days. Not many people knew that Dan the Devil had a daughter. She never used his name; she called herself Francesca McGarry. But she had a great affection for Dan, just the same. I think she felt that circumstances over which he had no control made him what he was, and she was sorry for him. She was the only person I ever knew who was not afraid of him.

Old Mike McGarry and Bridget, his wife, came out of the house to say hello. They were Dan the Devil's uncle and aunt. They were nice old people who belonged in New York, but when Dan got in his big trouble, they moved to Shadow Island, mostly on Francesca's account. She had always escaped the newspapers, and Dan didn't want her around where they might dig her up and make it unpleasant for her.

Mike told me that they had been on Shadow Island only a few weeks after Dan went away when Francesca got the idea of going to Macon to learn to be a trained nurse. It was all right with Dan. Anything Francesca did was always all right with Dan.

I had not let on to Black Angelo and the others, but I was mighty worried. Finally, I got Francesca off to one side. I had a lot of confidence in her good sense, even when she was just a little girl. She was always calm and cool.

I said: "Listen. We've got a sick kid on the Bumble Bee. I've been doing the best I could for him, but he seems to be getting worse. It would be a tough thing for Dan and all the rest of us if this kid should happen to put his checks back in the rack."

She said: "I thought it a bit peculiar that you gentlemen should come here in that boat. Where did you get this kid you are talking about?"

"Well," I said, "it's a sneeze. That's the story. The biggest in history. He is worth a million bobs to us."

She said: "Ah, kidnaping. Somehow, I never thought Dan would come to that. It's not very high-class. I don't think I care for it."

I said: "A million makes it very classy. You aren't thinking of hollering copper, are you, Francesca?"

She slapped my face with her open hand. This was for suggesting that she might be thinking of calling the police.

She went aboard the Bumble Bee and took a look at John Withington White III. I think she expected to see a child. She became very indignant because we had left him in the hold. He seemed in a daze and paid no attention to Francesca as she examined him.

She said: "Move him to the house. He may have pneumonia."

"He may have double pneumonia," I said, "but he doesn't go into the house."

I felt a little sick myself that night when I thought back over the years that had passed since Francesca's old man and I had first known each other.

Dan Dubois and I went to public school together in West Forty-seventh Street when we were kids. Later on, we started out hacking at about the same time around the old Garden Café at Fiftieth Street and Seventh Avenue.

This was along in 1913—twenty years ago. Dan was a fine-looking young fellow in those days, with no more harm in him than a baby. But he was too smart to be driving a taxi. His mother was a West Side Irish girl named Flaherty, who married a Canuck. They were both dead.

One of the dancers in the Garden liked Dan. She called herself Francesca D'Orsay. He used to take her driving in the park between her shows and after hours. She was a cute little black-eyed, black-haired girl with lots of zip. I think she was French.

Anyway, early one morning Dan got hold of me and made me drive the two of them down to the City Hall, where he got a marriage license and married Francesca, right there. I was a witness.

Dan took Francesca to live with the McGarrys over in West Forty-ninth Street, right back of where Madison Square Garden is now. The McGarrys had raised him. Aunt Bridget was Dan's mother's sister. She cooked ham and cabbage better than anyone I ever knew.

Francesca kept on working until a baby started coming along, and then she had to quit. She didn't like the McGarrys, and it made her tired waiting around their house for the baby. Finally the baby turned out to be a girl, and they named it Francesca, and as soon as she was able to be up and around, Dan's wife skipped out on him, leaving the baby. They say she went back to France.

I think this changed Dan Dubois a lot. He had always been good-natured, but now he suddenly turned sour and mean. He was sour and mean to everybody except little Francesca. I can remember him hacking all night, and then putting in the morning up to noon riding Aunt Bridget and the baby around in the air. He liked to play with the baby, and was always buying her little toys. Dan was about twenty-one then.

He picked up a drunk one night with over three thousand dollars on him, and Dan clipped the drunk for the whole roll. After that he quit hacking. He was around gambling awhile, and then I heard he had joined up with a mob of heavy men, or safe blowers. They made a specialty of robbing country post offices and small banks up the state. Dan was getting a reputation as a tough fellow when the war came on.

He enlisted in the infantry and went to France, and was decorated for something he did in the Argonne. No one ever doubted Dan's gameness. I was in the war a little bit myself, but I was back hacking when Dan came home from France and got a job as a sort of doorman and bouncer at the old Golden Slipper night club. He used to hire me once in a while to take Francesca and him out riding.

She was about six years old at this time, and the image of her mother, except that you could see she was going to be much taller. She talked as serious as a grown-up. Dan always called everybody Pally, and Francesca got to calling me that. He treated her like she was sixteen instead of six, and like he was her best beau instead of her father.

One night Dan killed a fellow called Charley the Clutch, outside the Golden Slipper. He shot Charley right through the heart with an army automatic. Everybody said Charley had started to pull a gun on Dan first, so Dan was acquitted right away. Charley was a tough fellow, and nobody was sorry to see him out of the way.

I've always thought that next to his wife skipping out on him, the killing of Charley the Clutch had the most influence on Dan's life. A few months later, he shot and killed Shanty Ahearn in a gambling row. Shanty had a knife in his hand when they found him, and Dan was acquitted again on the grounds of self-defense, though afterwards some reliable parties told me Dan deliberately picked a row with Shanty. You see, the first time Dan killed a man, it was more or less by accident. The second time it was on purpose.

He had now established a reputation as a killer, and he seemed to be trying to live up to the reputation. One day he slugged a harmless small-time gambler by the name of Max Goldfarb, and Goldfarb afterwards died of his injuries. Dan had a lot of trouble getting out of that, and it started people calling him Dan the Devil. I think he liked the title at first.

He got hold of some money in 1920, and at a government auction he bought a fast little boat that had been a patrol boat during the war. It could be handled by a couple of men if necessary, and it could fairly sizzle through the water. He changed the name of the boat to the Bumble Bee, and painted it up nice, and then he started on the run up from the Bahamas, which was where nearly everybody went after liquor in those days. I went with him, because hacking was not so good about then, and everyone else was making money hand over fist in booze, so I thought I might as well give it a try.

I was with Dan Dubois on half a dozen trips, including the one when we ran into a big storm and got kicked all over the ocean, finally winding up on what turned out to be Shadow Island. It was a nice spot, and after we had been there several days fixing up the boat, Dan fell in love with the place.

He said: "Some day when I get plenty of potatoes, I'm going to have a spot like this for a home for Francesca and me and the old folks."

He meant the McGarrys.

Dan said: "You know, it is coming on time for me to commence thinking of putting Francesca in school some place where nobody will know who she is."

It was not long after this that he told me he had put her in a school in Montreal, and sent the McGarrys there to live.

I quit Dan about the time he commenced moving into the important money. I went back to hacking. I could see that he was going far, and he liked me as much as he liked any man, and I could have had a nice piece of his play, but I didn't have nerve enough.

Black Angelo and Innocence and Fatso, who first started with him on the Bumble Bee, stuck with him, and afterwards were his right-hand men for certain jobs. In three years, Dan the Devil was the top man in booze in the United States, with a whole fleet of ships on the water, and a tremendous organization.

He had plenty of trouble on his way up. There were fifty different combinations in the field, large and small, when he started, but Dan ripped right through all of them. He mowed down his opposition like a farmer mowing hay.

The Devil was a good name for him now. Human life meant less than nothing to Dan, and he was very careless with his own. He was in alcohol and beer, as well as in booze, and he controlled a raft of other rackets, like gambling and phony labor unions. He had plenty to say in politics. He went eight or nine years full tilt, and then Uncle Sam stepped in on him one day and wanted to know about his income taxes.

Dan the Devil didn't know anything about his income taxes. He had never paid any. He thought the government was kidding. He laughed when he was indicted by a Federal grand jury. Nobody thought the government would get anywhere with him because he had so much money and so much power.

The government proved that he had had an income of ten million dollars in three years, without saying anything whatever about any other years. It came out at his trial that he had bought Shadow Island for twenty thousand cash, and had spent quite a bit more fixing up an old house there, which was something I didn't know before, although I knew Dan had a hide-away somewhere where he used to go now and then when he wanted to get away from everybody. It brought back to me what he said the time we were piled up on the island.

The government afterwards seized everything it could belonging to Dan, but it couldn't seize Shadow Island, because it seemed that Dan had transferred ownership of it to the McGarrys.

Dan hired half a dozen of the best lawyers in town, but it didn't do him any good. He must have spent close to a million on the trial. Any man on the jury could have got rich just by forcing a disagreement, but they must all have been honest men, because they found Dan guilty in an hour.

Then the judge sentenced him to three years in Leavenworth prison, and fined him two hundred thousand dollars. Dan spent a world of money trying to get a new trial, but in the end he had to go. Then he laughed right out loud.

He said: "I've robbed and killed and brought in booze and bribed and corrupted, and done about everything else you can think of, and I could have been convicted on any one of a dozen tough raps, but the G-guys finally lag me for not paying the government its share of wrong money."

He was a model prisoner, and got out in a little over two years. A lot of reporters met him at the station when he came home, and he gave them a long interview that got big headlines in all the papers next day.

Dan said: "I'm through with my old life. I'm going into some legitimate business and live down the past. I'm thinking of taking a long rest with some relatives of mine who have a place off the coast of Georgia where I can lay around and fish and get my health back. There is nothing in fighting the law. Crime does not pay. There are no handholds to a wrong dollar."

Two weeks later, Dan the Devil sent for me.

I was glad of it. I wanted to tell him something I thought he ought to know. He was staying in a little apartment in Fifty-sixth Street, just off Ninth Avenue.

I thought he looked old, though I knew he was only about forty. His shoulders were humped over, and his face had big, heavy lines. A couple of years in the can takes a lot of gimp out of anybody.

Dan the Devil never really looked his part, even in the days when he was running around with a gun in each hand. Most killers are a little crazy, and generally show it in their eyes, but Dan had quiet, slow eyes.

If you did not know him, you would never have picked him out for a tough fellow.

He was sitting in a chair by the window looking out into Fifty-sixth Street when I came in. He said hello. Then we talked about different things. He went back to the days when we were hacking together, and once or twice something he brought up made him laugh.

I said: "What's become of Francesca and Uncle Mike and Bridget, if that's a fair question, Dan?"

Then he told me about them moving to Shadow Island when he went away, and about Francesca training to be a nurse. I said Francesca must be quite grown-up by now. He looked at me, as if thinking my question over.

He said: "Francesca is all right, Pally."

It was the first time in years I'd heard him say anything sort of tender about anybody.

I was a little surprised when Black Angelo, Innocence and Fatso Kling came in. I hadn't seen any of them for a long time, though I had heard about them, and what I'd heard wasn't anything complimentary. Night-hacking keeps you in touch with what is going on.

It was like a reunion of old soldiers, but I knew that our being there at the same time was not altogether an accident, and I wondered what Dan the Devil had on his mind.

Dan said: "You guys may not know it, but I'm broke." He stopped and looked at us, one after the other.

"Well, Dan," I said, when his eyes came to me, "hacking is not the best business in the world, but I've got a few yards saved up, and you're welcome to all or any part of my taw."

"Oh, I don't mean broke that bad," Dan said. "I've got a little left, though it's mostly snowed in. I mean broke as far as real dough is concerned. I was a millionaire several times over once. I knew the racket couldn't last, so I got smart. I went in for the legit. I went into Wall Street. I built the Regality Hotel. I backed a few musical shows. I was in worse shape than anybody knew when my trial came up, and the mouthpieces finished me. I'm clean."

Innocence said: "I'm clean, too. I always am." Black Angelo and Fatso nodded, as much as to say they put in with Innocence.

"Everybody I know seems to be broke," Dan said. "I've been looking around a bit since I've been back. Conditions are very bad. I wonder where all the dough went? The guys who would help me if they could are out of action. Some guys who could help me if they would are giving me the back of their necks. Well, I'm not beefing. I'll just remember them.

"Booze is a dead issue," Dan said. "I've got a piece of three ships that are rotting in Halifax, and three or four speeders that cost a hundred *G*'s laying at City Island that anybody can have for the asking. I understand I've been declared out of the Red Legs Brewery over in Jersey since beer was made legit, and they got a government permit. I'll take that up later. What I'm getting at is that I've got to get hold of some ready. I've got to make a good big score somehow, so I can go into real action again."

He stopped and looked at us again, one after the other. I started to tell him something I thought he ought to know, then I decided to wait.

Dan got up and started to walk up and down the room. He dropped his voice.

He said: "Fatso, I know what you and Innocence and Angelo have been doing since I went away. That's one reason I sent for you. You've got experience. Another reason is, I know you're okay. Pally, I put you in because I want somebody that can do a little thinking at the right time." He said: "Listen. We're going into the only thing there's any quick scratch in now. We're going in on the sneeze."

"It don't cost much," Innocence said. "All you need is a basement."

"I know some parties that done right good," Fatso said. "I know of one score of twenty *G*'s."

Dan the Devil said: "A lot of petty-larceny guys have been monkeying with it all over the country the past couple of years. They think if they get twenty or thirty or even fifty *G*'s they're doing great. You know I wouldn't waste time on anything small. We're going into this on a big scale."

"I gotta da pens'," Black Angelo said.

He showed us. I had seen one of these squirt-gun things before, but Dan examined it with some curiosity. They call it a pencil, though it looks more like a fat fountain pen. I think it originated in Brooklyn. Some doctor over there figured out a mixture that flattens in one whiff if you spray it into anybody's nose, and a mob got hold of it and passed it around.

Black Angelo explained that it beat a blackjack or choking, or putting a bag over a person's head when you were taking them, as it knocked them out so quick they couldn't put up a fight or yell. Black Angelo seemed to know a lot about the business.

Dan said: "The trouble with most of these cheap guys who have been around on the sneeze is they have had no real organization, and no business system. They've been grabbing anybody they thought had dough, without first finding out if they really had it, and how much, and how soon they could get it on the line. In nearly every case you've

read about, they've had to come down from their original price. That's
not good business. The first thing you've got to get in every case is a
first-class finger man to pick out the right party for you."

I could see Dan the Devil had something definite in mind already.
I said: "Well, Dan, no dolls and no children."

"Have I ever been a sap?" Dan said. "They're both poison. Do you
know Skunky McLarnin?"

I knew him well. He was a wizened-up, ratty-looking fellow who had
been running night clubs and speak-easies around Broadway for years,
and was now running the Boulogne Club in West Fifty-second Street.
He had been a customer of Dan's in the old days.

I always had an idea that Skunky might be a stool pigeon at heart,
but it was just an idea. I never really knew of him being out of line
anywhere. Few people liked him, but that made it dead even as far as
Skunky was concerned, because he liked few people himself.

I said: "A wrong gee."

"Maybe," Dan the Devil said. "The world is full of wrong gees right
now, as I've been finding out since I came back. But Skunky is not going to be wrong with me, because he knows I'd guzzle him like a turkey.
Anyway, Skunky has dug up a finger for the biggest touch in the world.
Listen to the story."

It seemed from what Dan the Devil said that this finger had called
on Skunky and told him that under the terms of a father's will, there
must be paid to a young fellow named John Withington White III on
his twenty-third birthday, the sum of one million dollars in cash.

It was some peculiar idea of the father's to test the boy. He wanted
him to have that much cash in hand, to do what he pleased with, when
he got out of college.

The father's name was John Withington White II, and he was a big
man in his day. He had been dead six or seven years, and his widow
had remarried a Wall Street broker by the name of Adrian Aiken. I
knew who Adrian Aiken was. I had often seen him along Broadway, and
I'd had him for a fare lots of times. He was a tall, thin, well-dressed,
gray-looking fellow, with cold eyes, and he was a big spender.

I sometimes saw him with a woman I judged was his wife. She was
not a young woman, but was nice-looking and very quiet. According to
Skunky's finger man, the way Dan told it, she had charge of the young
fellow's estate, and he would be twenty-three in three months, and she
had already put a million dollars away to pay him on his birthday.
There was a lot more to go to him from the estate later on.

John Withington White III had just graduated from Yale and was
now playing around New York, Dan the Devil said, and Skunky's finger

had put the proposition to Skunky of digging up a mob to grab the young fellow and hold him for about two hundred and fifty thousand dollars ransom, because the finger told Skunky the boy's mother would pay that kind of money like breaking sticks, especially if she thought he was in danger of being hurt.

Dan the Devil said: "It only shows you what small ideas guys have, when they talk about two hundred and fifty *G*'s for a sneeze worth a million. That's what we want—the million."

I said: "Who is the finger, and is he reliable, and how did Skunky come to think of you? You know he's got reason not to love you if his memory is good."

"Well," Dan said, "I guess I was responsible for Skunky thinking of me. I was in his place the other night and I happened to mention that conditions were bad, and he said he didn't suppose I'd be interested but he knew of a proposition worth a million. I told him for that kind of dough I'd start an earthquake, and then he laid it out to me.

"Then," Dan said, "I got to thinking that with this for a starter, and with the right organization, I could make a big business out of the situation. I'll shake this country before I get through. As for the finger, I don't know who he is, and I don't care. Skunky says he is a hundred percent, and I hold Skunky responsible. He knows what that means.

"Skunky and you guys and his finger will cut the two hundred and fifty *G*'s—that was their idea of a price. I'll take the rest for mine," Dan the Devil said. "That's my own idea, but of course you'll also get a bonus from me, and a better cut the next time."

Then for a while Black Angelo and Innocence and Fatso and I talked over where we would hide the young fellow after we had grabbed him.

Black Angelo and Innocence held out for a basement. Fatso said an apartment house up in the Bronx was always a perfect hide-away.

I said some quiet farm in the Catskills would be better. We had quite an argument, with Dan the Devil sitting there thinking. He finally settled it. He said we would take John Withington White III to Shadow Island. It sounded like a good idea, the way Dan explained it.

He said: "If there's any beef in the papers about this, which I'm going to try to prevent, nobody is apt to connect me with the case in the first place, and in the second place, if they do, Shadow Island is the very last spot in the world they'd look for him, because I've said I'm going there for a rest, and no one would figure me chump enough to try to hide a sneeze where I was going to be myself."

He said: "Pally, you hop over to Chester, Pennsylvania, tomorrow

and hunt up old Pop Waddings and see what kind of shape the Bumble
Bee is in. You remember I gave her to him for helping me out in that
jam when the G-men chased us up the Delaware. Tell him I want to
borrow her back for a while."

So I went over to Chester, on the Delaware, and found Pop, and
sure enough the old Bumble Bee was in pretty fair shape. She was
painted a different color than when we used to ride her back and forth
to the Bahamas, and needed cleaning and a lot of new supplies.

When I got back to New York, and saw Dan the Devil alone, I told
him the something I thought he ought to know.

I said: "Dan, there's been a big change around here since you've
been away. A new combination is in charge in this town. When you
went away, everybody split out and got to fighting among themselves."

"Well?" Dan said.

"Well," I said, "overnight a fellow came up out of Brooklyn with a
new mob of red-hots, all young kids. They call him the Peacemaker,
because his idea of stopping the heat was to cool off the old mob leaders,
and then take over their business. Very few people know him, and
nobody seems to know any of his rods. They move fast and mysterious,
and they've filled a couple of cemeteries already. He's got a sort of
Ku Klux Klan of the underworld."

"Well?" Dan said.

"Well," I said, "there have already been rumors around since you've
been back that you are planning on going into action, and I know this
fellow won't stand for you in his territory. I'm only telling you, Dan.
This is a strange mob. I hear they've got a council that meets every
so often and votes on who is to be cooled off next. Dan, what I'm getting at is that I hear they've voted on you."

Dan the Devil looked at me for at least two minutes without opening
his mouth. Then he said: "Why?"

He meant why had they voted on him.

"Dan," I said, "the Peacemaker's name is Goldfarb. Abie Goldfarb.
He had a brother."

"Goldfarb?" Dan said. "Goldfarb? I remember. So they voted on me,
did they? Well, Pally, you now hear me voting on Goldfarb, brother of
Goldfarb. I hereby cast my vote in favor of cutting Goldfarb's heart
out and throwing it in his face. But first I must get this other matter
out of the way. Goldfarb, eh? The Peacemaker, eh?" And Dan the
Devil laughed.

I said: "Well, Dan, I've told you."

He laughed again, but twice in the next three days, right on Broadway, shots were fired at him from passing automobiles, and Dan realized I had told him the truth and took to laying low.

About a week later, we grabbed John Withington White III in front of his house in East Sixty-seventh Street, taking a longer chance than we wanted to, but getting away with it very nicely. We were lucky. You have to have a little luck in these things.

Skunky McLarnin pointed him out to Fatso in the Boulogne Club one night, and for a week hand-running we had Fatso casing him, day and night, so we would get a line on his habits. We generally knew where he was going to be every night, because Skunky seemed to be getting information from his finger man and passing it on to Dan.

We made half a dozen different plans to take him in half a dozen different places, but we had to give them up one after the other, because they didn't seem practicable. Fatso really decided it. Fatso said that John Withington White III never used a private car, but always a taxi in going around at night.

Fatso said no matter where he went, John Withington White III generally got home around two o'clock in the morning, and after paying the driver off, he would let himself into the house, which was an old-fashioned five-story residence, by way of a door on the ground floor, and that between the time young White paid the driver and got to the door, the taxi would be pretty far up the street.

Now this was important, and it showed the value of an experienced hand like Fatso. He said he timed the performance by his watch several times, and it took about six minutes from the moment John Withington White III paid and dismissed the taxi driver for young White to get into the house.

Fatso said it was very rarely anybody was in the street at that hour, but Dan the Devil was afraid of that little off chance that somebody might accidentally bob up. We wanted young White to disappear without a trace. Then one night Fatso reported that he had tailed John Withington White III to the Casino in Central Park, and that night it came on a steady rain, so Dan the Devil said this was the night.

Fatso said young White had taken a girl from a swell apartment house on Fifth Avenue to the Casino. They had gone in a taxicab. So Fatso watched the apartment house, figuring that young White would take the girl home.

We had hired a limousine as big as a hearse, and we had a phony license plate for it. Innocence did the driving. Along toward two o'clock we drove over into East Sixty-seventh Street, and parked the car up the street from the White house, which was one of a row of houses that looked pretty much alike.

If anybody came along they could see Innocence dozing in the seat, as if waiting for his boss in one of the houses. Black Angelo and Dan the Devil and I got out of the car before it parked, and Dan went one way and Angelo and I the other way, but never getting far away.

Pretty soon a taxicab stopped in Sixty-seventh Street about half a block off and near a street light and we saw Fatso get out, so we knew John Withington White III had left the girl's apartment house. Now of course he might not have come direct home. He might have gone any one of a thousand places, but we were playing the only line on him we had. That was Fatso's observations.

The rain had stopped, but the street was deserted. By and by we saw another taxi coming, and it pulled up in front of the White house, and a young fellow in evening clothes got out. We had all been moving toward the house as we saw the taxi's lights, and Fatso gave us the office that this was our man.

Black Angelo and I were walking toward the young fellow, arguing about the fight between Max Baer and Max Schmeling. Fatso was coming along behind us like a fellow hurrying home, and Innocence and Dan the Devil were coming slowly the other way, also talking. We walked just fast enough to be pretty close to John Withington White III as he finished paying the taxi driver.

It was just as well for the taxi driver that he kept on going about his business after he got his money, because Fatso was ready to jump on the running board and take good care of him. There was nothing unnatural about the general set-up, especially to a fellow who was not suspecting anything.

John Withington White III was walking toward the door of his house, taking his keys from his pocket, when I stopped and asked him if he had a match. He started to fumble in his pocket, and I must have made some little wrong move.

He said: "What is this?"

Then he tagged me on the chin with a nice right-hand drive. He was a game kid. He never thought of yelling. He saw Black Angelo in front of him and he took a punch at Angelo, but the next instant Fatso had his arms pulled back behind him, and Black Angelo had the pencil in his face, and John Withington White III went out like a light, and was in our car quicker than you can say scat, with never a soul outside of us to see him go.

We drove over into Jersey by way of the tunnel, and across Jersey to Philadelphia, and through Philadelphia out the Chester Pike to a spot below Chester where a little stream called Darby Creek empties into the Delaware. It is a tough spot to get to unless you know all the roads.

We used to run the Bumble Bee in there years ago when things got hot. That's how we first met Pop Wadding.

Dan the Devil had telephoned Pop to have the Bumble Bee there, and there she was, all ready to go when we got there about seven o'clock. Pop was no hand to ask questions, and he said nothing when he saw us lug John Withington White III on board and put him in the hold. He only shook hands with Dan the Devil, and the two of them stood on the shore watching us as we dropped out into the stream. Dan had a very short talk with us before he left.

He said: "I'm allowing about three weeks to this situation. Pally, at the end of that time, if you haven't heard from me, get in touch with me by phone from Brunswick. If this fellow's people haven't paid every dollar by then, you're to get rid of him. That's positive."

He said: "I want no chicken-heartedness about this, now. If we don't get paid, and nothing happens to him, we may as well quit. But if something does happen to him for failure to pay, then we'll always collect promptly in the future. Keep him in the hold and chained up. If there is a beef in the papers, get rid of him. If you don't hear from me in three weeks, get rid of him. That's all."

Dan the Devil drove back to New York, and by noon he had sent a letter by messenger to the home of John Withington White III.

Dan said in this letter that young White had been kidnaped, and that it would cost the family one million dollars to get him back safe and sound, and if they did not pay up, they would never see him again. He said he knew they had that kind of money in cash, and he wanted it.

Dan said if they notified the police or the newspapers it would be the same thing. They would never see John Withington White III again. This is what Dan the Devil meant when he told us he was going to try and prevent any publicity. He said in his letter that the wisest thing for the family to say was that John Withington White III had been called out of town on business.

He told them to wait quietly a week, and that they would then hear his exact terms from him, and that, in the meantime, John Withington White III would not be harmed. Skunky McLarnin was working with Dan on the negotiations, and he wanted Dan to demand the ransom at once, but Dan said no. Dan said it was best to be patient, and if they waited a week and no heat started up, it would be a sign that the family was willing to negotiate quietly.

Dan said the trouble with most of these deals was that the sneezers got too impatient. Then, too, he wanted to give the Bumble Bee time to reach Shadow Island.

He said in the letter that an ad in the morning papers saying "Okay John" would be notice to him that the family understood, and every morning paper in town had this ad the next morning. Of course Dan the Devil did not sign any name to the letter.

Then a week later, Dan sent another letter to the house saying he wanted two hundred and fifty thousand in currency in denominations of anywhere from ten to one hundred dollars put in a suitcase, and left in a certain spot in Central Park as evidence of good faith. He said he would arrange with them later for the payment of the balance in batches of two hundred and fifty thousand each, to be delivered in the same way in spots he would designate over a period of a week or so, and young White would then be sent home.

Skunky asked Dan if he wasn't afraid they would mark the bills.

Dan said: "Let them mark. There's a lot of marked money that was paid in cases of this kind floating around the country, and no harm done. If you wait long enough before you start circulating it, no one will remember to look for marks. Besides, one reason I sent young White so far away is to give us time to change the money into new money before we deliver him."

Dan said he was distributing the payments over a period of time because a million dollars in one gob would be too bulky.

Dan sent the young fellow's cuff links and his monogrammed hand-kerchief and a monogrammed wallet to the White home to prove that he had John Withington White III, and he also said in a letter that went with this package that if the family kept him waiting for any length of time he might send them one of John Withington White III's ears.

Now I learned all this afterwards, of course. I am patching this story together from what I saw, what I heard and what I believe, for I was on Shadow Island, having troubles of my own.

John Withington White III did not have pneumonia, single or double, but he was pretty sick for a few days. He was so sick one day that Francesca talked of sending to Brunswick for a doctor. Of course I wouldn't stand for that.

She said: "But suppose he should die?"

"Then he dies," I said. "We'll give him a nice burial. It may save us a lot of bother, at that, in case his people don't settled for him."

She said no more about a doctor, but started working on the young fellow herself. She kept trying to persuade me to move him to the house, but I said no I didn't want him getting a line on his surroundings. I made Francesca promise not to talk to him any more than was absolutely necessary. I didn't think Francesca would be indiscreet, but when a young girl and a young fellow get to chatting, you never can tell what they'll say. And I didn't like the fact that Francesca had quit wearing her khaki pants and put on skirts.

In a few days John Withington White III was sitting up taking plenty of nourishment, and I put the irons back on him again. Francesca made quite a row about this to me in private but I held out against her.

I had Black Angelo sleeping in the hold with John Withington White III every night, and Fatso on guard in the daytime. Black Angelo was very fond of Francesca. I have often wondered since just how much talking Francesca did to young White when only Black Angelo was there, and what about.

I took many a trip around the island in a motor boat, more to be doing something than anything else. Shadow Island stands off by itself, and out of the track of shipping, and it isn't once a month that you ever see a boat passing that way.

So a little over a week after we got there, I was surprised to see a launch cruising around not far off the island, wtih four young fellows on board. One of them hailed me and asked the way to Brunswick. They said they had been fishing and had drifted off their course.

I pointed out their direction. Then I said it was a hot day.

One of them said: "Yeh, it's berling."

I waited around until they were out of sight, then hurried back to Shadow Island. "Berling" for "boiling," "erl" for "oil," or "oil" for "earl," that's Brooklyn and nowhere else in the world. I called Black Angelo and Fatso and Innocence together and told them.

I said: "They must be some of Goldfarb's red-hots. They must think Dan is here."

"Well," Fatso said, "then they won't monkey around here much when they find it ain't so. Goldy don't want nobody else in this bunch, does he? We ain't important enough."

This seemed reasonable. After all, Goldfarb wasn't going out of his way for small fry like us.

Two mornings later, we found Innocence dead as a mackerel in the woods not far from the house and close to the shore. He had been on outside guard that night. He had been stuck in the back with a sort of dagger made out of an ice pick, and pinned to him by this dagger was a note addressed to Fatso. The note said:

Hello, Fats. I want that White kid. I've got ten guys down here with me. We will call for him tomorrow morning. No use trying to duck out in your boat because we fixed the channel. Sorry about Innocence but he got tough.

Goldy

I did not know then, of course, that Dan the Devil had been visited in New York by a fellow named Shoes McGlochlin, who used to work with Dan in the old days.

Shoes said: "Dan, I don't want you to hold it against me, but I'm carrying a message from Abie Goldfarb. Dan, your number is up. You're a sure thing to go unless you round yourself up with Goldy. He knows you've got a big score in sight. He knows you've made a fat sneeze, and he's willing to call everything even if you cut him in. He wants fifty percent."

Dan was somewhat startled, but not by the demand. He was startled that anyone knew of the taking of John Withington White III. Not a line had appeared in the papers about it. Not a whisper, as far as he knew, had been breathed about it by White's family.

He said: "Shoes, I'm not going to spit in your face like I would if I thought you were anything but a messenger boy. Go back and tell that mockie that nobody cuts in with Dan Dubois on anything. Tell him I wish he had come to me himself, that's all."

Shoes, who told me this afterwards, smiled at the answer. He said: "Dan, I wish I was ten years younger, and didn't have a wife to look after, if you know what I mean. But protect yourself in the clinches, Dan."

It was that night that Goldfarb the Peacemaker went South by train with a picked crew of his red-hots.

About this time, Dan the Devil seemed to weaken a little bit. He seemed to feel that he needed help at his end of the line. Skunky McLarnin wasn't much use to him, because Skunky was too well known to too many people to take any chances. Maybe Dan didn't rate Skunky's moxie very high if it came to a tight fit.

It is my own opinion that Dan commenced to see that he was a little rusty himself in spots, now that he was trying to take everything on his own shoulders. He wouldn't have admitted it to anybody, but I think he saw how times had changed around him, and realized that he was getting old.

I'll tell you something about propositions like the one we were working on. It takes youth, like any other business. Youth has recklessness and nerve, and will run all kinds of chances. Youth doesn't stop to think of obstacles or consequences, or to study things out. When a fellow gets along toward middle age, no matter how desperate he may have been when he was young, he thinks more, and slower.

Dan the Devil knew this better than anybody else. When he was going big, Dan always had a lot of young fellows around him. He got to the top by taking advantage of the slowness of old guys who stopped to think. Maybe he suddenly realized that he was working with a lot of old men, for Black Angelo and Innocence and Fatso and I were all about the same age as Dan the Devil, and Skunky was ten years older.

The reason I think Dan must have got to thinking this way is because he sent to Boston for a young fellow by the name of Speedy Cesare, and brought him into the thing. Speedy Cesare was a little, brown-looking fellow with plenty of sense, and all the nerve any one man is entitled to have. He had been with Dan the Devil a short time before Dan went away, but long enough for Dan to get a good line on him.

After Dan went away, Speedy got mobbed up with a Boston outfit, and was doing just so-so up there. He was a restless, lone-wolf chap, always looking for adventure, and when Dan got a message to him he hustled to New York at once without knowing just what Dan wanted. He wasn't quite so enthusiastic when Dan laid out the proposition.

He said: "Say, there's an awful beef everywhere about the sneeze just now. I see they're going to top a guy out West for it."

He meant they were going to hang a man for kidnaping.

Dan the Devil said: "What do you want them to do? Give him a medal? I'd top him, too, if I was on the other side and wanted to teach a lesson. But if I was on that side, I'd have guys like you and me swinging from every tree and telegraph pole like scarecrows, to remind everybody that if you live by the rope you croak by the rope."

Dan told Speedy Cesare he was going to get twenty-five *G*'s if everything went all right. It was a good thing for this story that Speedy was in, at that, because he helped me a lot when I got down to piecing things out.

He told me how Dan the Devil got the suitcase in Central Park.

In a letter he sent to the White home, Dan fixed nine o'clock sharp in the evening as the hour the suitcase was to be left for him. Dan always liked to work when there were apt to be plenty of people in the streets. He claimed they made good cover for a get-away.

In Central Park, in a direct line across Fifty-ninth Street from the Athletic Club, which is at the corner of Fifty-ninth and Seventh Avenue, there is a little short bridge over a tunnel that runs under one of the most generally used roadways in the park. A path to the carrousel where the kids ride the phony ponies runs through the tunnel.

This path comes winding down the hump of high ground on the Fifty-ninth Street end of the park to the tunnel, making a little ravine just where it disappears into the hole under the road.

Between the bridge and the stone wall that runs along the Fifty-ninth Street end of the park is a short distance of ground covered by grass and bushes. Dan the Devil had a car with the engine running parked at the curb in Fifty-ninth Street and was leaning up against the stone wall just before nine o'clock on the evening he had designated. There is nothing unusual in fellows leaning up against this wall at any time.

Speedy Cesare waited inside the park under the bridge in the little ravine I have mentioned. There were people scattered around inside and outside the park, because it was a hot night.

Speedy stretched out on the grass until a couple of minutes before the car was due. At nine o'clock on the dot, a big open roadster came roaring down the road, hugging the right-hand side. From his spot beneath the bridge, Speedy couldn't see who was in the roadster, and of course Dan couldn't either. But whoever it was, he remembered Dan's instructions to a *T*. As the roadster hit the bridge it slowed down a trifle but never stopped, and the driver chucked a suitcase over the right-hand railing.

In two snaps of your fingers, the suitcase was on the end of a long rope that Speedy hooked to it, and was hopping through the bushes like something alive as Dan hauled in the rope. Two minutes more, and Dan's car was tearing away.

Speedy laid down on the grass again. If it was a trap and the cops came, all right. He was broke and hungry, and sleepy, and had gone into the park to grab a few winks. He wouldn't know anything about a suitcase. He hadn't been around New York for a long time. He wasn't very well known there anyway, and had no police record there. Who would believe the cops that a man had thrown a suitcase containing two hundred and fifty thousand dollars over the bridge, and it had suddenly evaporated?

Speedy told me this was the way Dan the Devil reasoned. If it wasn't a trap, and anybody saw the performance, they might puzzle over it awhile, but would let it go at that. New Yorkers are great people for minding their own business because they're always afraid of getting in a jam, Dan told Speedy.

Dan said: "That's one reason why you can get away with more in broad daylight in New York than you can in darkest night anywhere else."

But no one seemed to notice the affair. Speedy waited around awhile, then walked out of the park. He dodged around in subways and taxicabs for the next hour, and about eleven o'clock he went over to Dan's apartment in West Fifty-sixth Street. Dan let him in and pointed to a suitcase open on the table.

The suitcase seemed to be filled with old newspapers and magazines. A paper sack of walnuts was on top. That was all. There wasn't as much as a two-dollar note in real money in sight.

Dan the Devil looked at Speedy. Then he looked at the suitcase. Then he looked at Speedy again. Speedy said he felt the hair on the back of his neck crawling. Speedy said he probably never will be as close to the meat house again and still be alive. That's the morgue. For one solid half-hour Dan the Devil stood looking at the suitcase, as if he couldn't believe what he saw.

Finally Dan the Devil spoke one word. He said: "Bilked!"

By and by he talked more. He never outright said he had any thought that Speedy might have had anything to do with the bilking, but Speedy always believed that for a few minutes his price was about a hundred to nothing.

Dan the Devil recalled Shoes McGlochlin's visit to him. He said maybe young White's people had taken the matter of the kidnaping to Goldfarb and asked him to help them. It had often happened that parents and others interested in someone that has been grabbed by one underworld outfit got another underworld bunch to try and make contacts for them, which was the worst thing they could do.

Dan said if John Withington White III's people had gone to Goldfarb for help, apparently the first thing Goldy did was to try to double-cross them by attempting to shove in on Dan. Dan said if they hadn't gone to Goldfarb, how did Goldy know about the taking of young White?

He said: "Maybe Goldy told them to play this trick on me. But why? Even Goldy must know that it's just the same as signing young White's death warrant, so how does Goldy profit? White has got to go now, or everybody in the country will be laughing at Dan the Devil. I'll take care of Mr. Goldfarb later."

It was just at this time that I got Dan on the telephone from Brunswick. He didn't wait for me to do any talking.

He said: "Come back, all of you, as quick as you can, but first carry out the original orders I gave you."

I said: "I wish I could, Dan, but Goldfarb and company are here and Francesca has sneezed our friend."

After I had explained as best I could over the phone, Dan said he would hop a plane and get down South as quick as possible. But he didn't start at once.

He went looking for Skunky McLarnin to see if Skunky or his finger man had any theory about the suitcase and its strange contents. Dan made Speedy go along with him. Speedy could see that he hadn't received a hundred-percent acquittal in Dan's mind yet.

Dan hadn't been taking direct routes to anywhere or going through lighted streets for some days, to keep Goldfarb's red-hots from getting a good crack at him, but Speedy said he seemed to have forgotten caution, except to the extent of taking one peek out into the street in front of his apartment before stepping out the door. There was nobody in sight but a kid across the street whistling "Stormy Weather."

Dan the Devil took Speedy to Skunky's Club Boulogne, but they said Skunky hadn't been around as yet. Dan and Speedy were going out when the doorman stopped them. He was a gray-haired fellow in a night-club uniform.

He said: "You remember me, Meest' Dubois?"

Dan looked at him and said no.

"I Tony," the doorman said. "Black Angelo's brud'. I weeth you on da ol' ferraboat."

Dan the Devil had a ship in the old days called the Mary Ann that everybody knew as the ferryboat because she used to make runs from St. Pierre right up to a dock in the East River, loaded with booze, as regular as a ferry.

"You remember?" Tony said. "You ver' nice to Tony, Meest' Dubois. Also my brud', Black Angelo. You ask for Meest' McLarn'. He go away early tonight weeth Meest' Aiken. You know Meest' Aiken? A fina da man. Spenda da mon'. Geeva da teep."

Some drunks coming in to the Boulogne interrupted. Tony and Dan waited until the doorman had bowed them inside. By and by Tony came back. He dropped his voice to a whisper.

He said: "Meest' Dubois, thees I theenk is for you to know. It is import'. I, Tony, Black Angelo's brud', and weeth you on da ol' ferraboat, will speak."

He looked up and down the street. A few taxicabs were standing in front of the Boulogne, the drivers half asleep. Somewhere up the street someone was whistling "Stormy Weather."

Tony said: "Meest' Dubois, when Meest' McLarn' weesh not to be found, always he go to apartamenta he keep in Sevent' Avenue. I know thees, because many times I take theengs to heem there. Always he have tell me sh-h-h about thees places, because he say it is there he meet his womans. Meest' Dubois, lasta week I tak' to thees place, sanawitch and bottla Scotch, and there is weeth Meest' McLarn' the man by name Peace-a-mak'."

Speedy said he couldn't bear to look at Dan the Devil's face.

Tony said: "Meest' Dubois, thees man, the Peace-a-mak', and Meest' McLarn' mak' mooch talk. They do not know Tony hears, but they speak-a you name, Meest' Dubois. Danna da Dev'. They mak' beeg laugh, ho, ho, ho, ho, ho! I say to myself, 'Tony, thees laugh is not good for Meest' Dubois. I will tell Meest' Dubois of thees.' But I do not see you until now, Meest' Dubois."

Dan said: "What's the number of that joint, Tony? Laughed, did they?"

Tony mentioned a Seventh Avenue address. "Numb' Nine-B," he said. "Eight' floor back-a, on Sevent' Avenue side. Oh, yes, Meest' Dubois. Beeg laugh. Ho, ho, ho, ho, ho, ho, ho! Tell-a Black Angelo when you see heem, his brud' Tony say 'allo. Beeg laugh, Meest' Dubois. Beeg!"

It was one o'clock in the morning, and Dan the Devil called a cab and had the driver take him and Speedy Cesare to the house in East Sixty-seventh Street from in front of which we had taken young White. Despite the hour, lights were burning all over the house.

Dan rang the bell, and a butler appeared after a considerable wait, and Dan asked if Mr. Adrian Aiken was at home. The butler said no, and then Dan asked for Mrs. Aiken. The butler hesitated, and while he was hesitating, a woman appeared behind him. She was pale and haggard, and looked as if she had been ill. She said she was Mrs. Aiken.

Speedy said he believed Dan went to the house on some impulse of revenge against the family, but the sight of the woman changed his mind.

Dan said: "Lady, if I can have a word with you in private, I think I have some information that may interest you."

She did not answer, but motioned the butler away and led Dan and Speedy into a living room. Dan handed her the wrist watch that he had taken off of John Withington White III, along with his other knick-knacks. She stood trembling, the watch in her hand, looking at Dan the Devil, but not saying a word.

Dan said: "Lady, that's to show you I'm not here as a phony. What I want to know is, have you paid any money to anybody for your son's release, and if so, who did you pay it to?"

"Who are you?" she said. "How do you know anything about my son?"

"Never mind," Dan said. "Did you give anybody any money?"

"Only my husband, Mr. Aiken," she said. "He has been taking care of the dreadful affair for me. Do you know where my son is? Is he safe?"

"How much?" Dan said. "Two hundred and fifty thousand?"

"More," she said. "A million. That is what they asked. Oh, sir, if you know where my son is, please speak. Is there anything wrong? When is he to come home?"

Dan the Devil stood looking at her awhile. At last he said: "Lady, I think you're on the level in this. Don't worry about your son, and don't tell anybody about this visit. Not even your husband. Promise me that."

"I promise," she said.

Then Dan hurried Speedy Cesare from the house.

They went by car back to Dan the Devil's own apartment, where he sat, scarcely saying a word, until a little after three o'clock in the morning. Then they walked over to Seventh Avenue to the address given Dan by Tony.

It was a big apartment house on a corner of one of the Fifties, one side on Seventh Avenue, the front on the cross street. It was one of the swellest apartment houses in town when it was first built, but that was years ago.

It was so old-fashioned it had fire escapes leading from the roof almost to the ground on the Seventh Avenue side. They don't put these fire escapes on modern buildings in New York, but all the old-timers have them.

From across the street on the Seventh Avenue side, Dan the Devil and Speedy Cesare could see that the back apartment on the eighth floor was lighted up. The windows were down from the top and up from the bottom for air, because it was a warm night, but the shades were down. Occasionally, however, they could see the shadow of a man pass the windows inside the apartment.

Dan the Devil and Speedy took up a position opposite the entrance hall of the apartment house in the side street from where they could watch a colored boy in uniform. He was evidently the elevator boy, but as is usually the custom in these old-time houses, he also seemed to be looking after a telephone switchboard that was in the hall, so it was a sure thing he was the only boy on duty.

He sat dozing in a chair at the switchboard, and Dan and Speedy watched him for half an hour. He got a couple of telephone calls in that time, but none from the elevator, and Dan was suggesting that Speedy go up the street to an all-night delicatessen store, look up the number of the apartment-house telephone in the directory and give the elevator boy a phony call, when the boy plugged in on his board, talked awhile, and then got up and went outside, and started up the street toward the delicatessen. He had evidently been sent on an errand by some hungry tenant.

Almost as soon as his back was turned, Dan the Devil and Speedy ran across the street and into the apartment house. Dan led the way up one flight of stairs after another, on the jump, until they reached the seventh floor.

Then Dan, followed by Speedy, went to the end of the hall on this floor to the Seventh Avenue side, climbed out the hall window onto the fire escape, and climbed up the fire escape to the eighth floor. Between the fire-escape landing to the first window of the lighted apartment across the face of the building, there was a gap of perhaps six feet.

Dan the Devil never hesitated. He yanked off his low-cut shoes on the fire-escape landing, and as Speedy did the same thing without knowing why, Dan suddenly swung himself from the landing across the wall to the window ledge.

As he landed on the window ledge, he grabbed the top of the open window to steady himself an instant, then flipped up the lower part of the window and went into the room. He had his gun out of the shoulder holster under his left arm the same instant he went through the window, because when Speedy came flying through himself, to fall in a heap on the floor, there was Dan covering Skunky McLarnin with his gun. Skunky had his hands up. He was in his shirt sleeves. There was blood all over his shirt and trousers.

Dan said: "Hello, Skunky. We didn't bother to knock because we wanted to surprise you."

It was the bedroom of the apartment, and Skunky was standing beside the bed. On the bed were two big suitcases of yellow leather, both open, and both apparently filled to the brim with packages of money. A couple of other suitcases stood on the floor full of clothes. Skunky evidently had been packing.

His face was as white as a fresh collar. His eyes were popping half out of his head. Finally he tried to smile.

He said: "Hello, Dan. Say, I was just going to get in touch with you. Well, I've got the dough. The entire million. We can cut it up right away. I'm glad to see you, Dan. I thought something had happened to you."

Skunky sat down as if too weak to stand any more. He sat down on the bed between the suitcases full of money. Dan stood looking at Skunky. Skunky didn't seem to see Speedy Cesare, who also had him covered with a pistol. Skunky looked all shriveled up. Suddenly he jumped up from the bed.

He said: "All right, all right, all right! To hell with you, Dubois! No wonder they call you the Devil. You aren't supposed to be alive, and here you are. Yes, it's the two-X. It's a cross. You know it, and I can see you know it. What's the difference? I'm a goner, anyway. Go ahead, Dubois, and give it to me. What are you waiting for?"

"Take it easy, Skunky," Dan said. "Take it easy. Let's talk this over. Maybe I might get big-hearted. I want to hear all about you and Aiken and Goldfarb. I love to listen to stories. Sit down, Skunky, and tell me all."

"I knew you knew," Skunky said. "I don't know how you found out. I guess you just ain't human. Well, all right; I'll tell you."

He sat down on the bed again and started to talk. Probably he thought that by talking he gained time. Speedy had a good memory. He remembered almost word for word what Skunky McLarnin said, and repeated it to me afterwards. It was a long story.

Skunky said: "Adrian Aiken was stuck on Beth Robare, a chorus doll at the Boulogne. She's been around, and is smartened up to everything. She'd been a sort of sweetheart of mine, off and on, for years. Aiken was always a sucker for that kind ever since I've known him, and I've known him a long time. He was broke. Any time he wanted dough, he had to get it off his wife, and she was commencing to shorten up on him. Maybe she'd heard he was spending his potatoes on Robare.

"Aiken knew about the million dollars that was to go to his wife's son, and he got the idea of clipping her by having some mob kidnap the boy and hold him for ransom. He figured two hundred and fifty thousand was about the right figure. He knew his wife would turn the matter of negotiation over to him, and that he could keep it so quiet there wouldn't be any police investigation.

"He was going to get the dough off her and hold it out on the mob, but give them a bilking in a way that would make them sore enough to put the boy out of the way for good and all. For the terms of old man White's will provided that if anything happened to John Withington White III before he was twenty-three years old, the estate would go to the mother. And Aiken figured that if something also happened to White's mother later on, Aiken himself would come in for plenty of her estate."

Skunky said: "You can bet all the corn in Kansas something would have happened to Mrs. Aiken if he got rid of the boy. He tipped his duke to Robare, and she told me. Aiken was going to marry her in the wind-up. He was a low-down guy.

"When you asked for the million, it was water on Aiken's wheel. It made the touch all the bigger for him. I was to get a hundred *G*'s of the original amount for digging up the mob. I was surprised when you fell for it, Dan. I didn't think it was in your line.

"Well, Aiken got the money off his wife, all right. He kept her from going to the cops. Then we framed up that phony suitcase he delivered to you in the park. I thought that would set you on fire. I figured you'd have the kid guzzled in about two minutes after you opened that suitcase and found the nuts. Or have you?"

Skunky said: "Now a hundred *G*'s was all okay with me on the original plan, but when Aiken got a million and still wanted to hold me to a hundred, I felt I was taking the worst of it. Besides, I just couldn't see a rat like that get away with all that sugar. He brought the dough here to hide it, and when he paid me off, I told him I'd have to have about half.

"Well, he balked and put up a beef, so I let him have it with a knife. That's why I'm all mussed up. He's in the next room if you like unpleasant sights, but I guess they're no novelty to you."

Dan said: "I see. So you've pushed your finger man. And who told Goldfarb this touch was coming off? And what's his mob doing down around Shadow Island?"

"Well, Dan," Skunky said, "I knew you were going to be greatly annoyed when you got to figuring things out quietly. I knew you'd be looking for your old friend Skunky. So I told Goldfarb what was doing, and I was going to cut my end with him in return for him taking you out of the play at the right time.

"But Goldfarb got hoggish. He first tried to declare in with you; then he said that if young White's mother would pay one million, she'd probably pay two. So he hustled South with his guys, figuring to snatch the kid off you and hold him for a new ransom if the first was paid, besides collecting off of me if he shoved you."

Skunky said: "I guess I've been X-ed by Goldy. When I made the deal with him he told me he'd have Stormy Weather, the greatest cooler in this town, on you, and that you'd positively be gone by six o'clock on the morning of the fifth. That's this morning, and you're still alive."

Dan said: "It's only a little after four now, Skunky. Give the guy a chance. Well, I think that's all."

Skunky begged just a little. "Take the whole million, Dan," he said, "and let's call it all even."

"Oh," Dan said, "I've got the million. I'll be saying good-by, Skunky."

"To hell with you, again," Skunky said.

Dan the Devil gave Speedy the twenty-five *G*'s he promised him, taking the money out of one of the suitcases; then they left by the door, stopping to get their shoes off the fire-escape landing. Each carried a suitcase.

They walked down to the third floor and rang the elevator bell. When they heard the elevator coming, they ran down the stairs, and out into the street without seeing a soul, except a young fellow going down Seventh Avenue whistling "Stormy Weather."

After they had walked about a block Dan the Devil said he would relieve Speedy of the suitcase he was carrying. Then he shook hands with Speedy and said he might as well return to Boston.

The papers made a big sensation of the killing of Mr. Adrian Aiken, the broker, and Mr. Montgomery McLarnin, the famous night-club operator, by thugs bent on robbery, who forced their way into Mr. McLarnin's apartment where he and Mr. Aiken were discussing a business deal. Nobody knew Skunky's first name before.

Some people who read that besides the slugs found in his body, Mr. McLarnin had a notch in his upper lip, laughed about the robbery story. That's the Sicilian brand for a squealer. Speedy Cesare was a Sicilian.

It was true that Francesca had kidnaped John Withington White III, as I had told Dan the Devil on the phone.

We tried to keep the killing of Innocence and the presence of the Goldfarb mob from her and the McGarrys at first. Then old Mike Mc-Garry tried to go outside in the motor boat along toward noon, intending to make a trip to Brunswick, and found the mouth of the creek blocked. An old boat loaded with rocks had been sunk in the clear water of the creek, which wasn't very deep at any time.

Now even the motor boat, which drew very little water, couldn't get through, and besides, Mike said a launch with several fellows in it was cruising off the mouth of the creek, and one of the fellows whistled a slug past Mike from a rifle. Old Mike was very much upset, and he told Francesca about it, and Francesca came to me.

She said: "What is it all about, Pally?"

I explained to her that Goldfarb seemed to have decided to take John Withington White III away from us and collect the ransom that we were entitled to get. I told her who Goldfarb was, and all about the situation. I said I couldn't understand how he knew we had young White.

Francesca said: "You mean he wants to re-kidnap this boy you kidnaped?"

I said that was about the size of it.

"Well," she said, "would the boy be better off with Goldfarb than with you?"

I said I didn't know how he would be with Goldfarb, but that it was a cinch he couldn't be any worse off than he was going to be with us, the way things were looking.

She said: "What do you mean, Pally?"

I said the next thing we knew all this hullabaloo would be attracting attention from the law on the mainland, and that we were not going to be found with John Withington White III in our possession if there was any spot on the island where I could dig a six-foot hole.

She said: "But what if these other fellows make an attack on you?"

I said I thought that was the very last thing Goldfarb would undertake, because he was like us, he didn't want to run the risk of attracting any outside attention. I said he probably figured we would give up young White without a struggle, and he was giving us plenty of time to think things over.

"Anyway," I said, "even if they come on the island they won't bother you or the McGarrys. Maybe the best thing we could do is give the guy up, but if we did that, what would Dan say?"

I talked it over with Fatso and Black Angelo. Neither of them thought we ought to give the young fellow up alive after we had gone to so much trouble. They didn't think Goldy would risk a battle.

We couldn't arrive at any decision, and we heard no more from Goldfarb's crowd outside, though by sneaking down through the woods to the shore, we could see the launch cruising around. They must have known that we had only the one motor boat on the island, though there was a tiny little lifeboat on the Bumble Bee. I spoke of this to Fatso, and suggested that it could get past the obstruction in the creek because it didn't draw any more water than a cake of floating soap.

Fatso said: "Well, if it could, what then? There ain't any of us could row it anywhere, and besides, we ain't got anywhere to row it to. Was you thinking of going to Brunswick and asking the gendarmes to help us keep our guy?"

Francesca was listening to us at the time. She didn't seem to be disturbed by the situation. And later, I saw her taking some food to the Bumble Bee for John Withington White III.

It was when I was having a very sweet dream about being back safe on Broadway that Fatso came in and shook me. He was much excited. He said: "I see Francesca and that young guy going down the creek in the little boat off the Bee. What am I supposed to do?"

I was off the bed in an instant and started out of the house on the run, with Fatso waddling after me. I thought he must be out of his mind, but when I hopped aboard the Bumble Bee and went down into the hold, I understood what had happened, and what I didn't understand then, I learned afterwards, because Francesca loved to tell the story.

Black Angelo was stretched out on the bunk where John Withington

White III had been chained. He was unconscious. Francesca had given him his own pencil, taken the keys to the handcuffs and the leg irons out of his pocket and turned young White loose. She had even hand-cuffed and chained Black Angelo to the bunk.

Then Francesca and young White had dropped the little boat over-board. It was always lashed on top of the cabin, and it was so small a baby could lift it.

It was a still, hot night, and I could hear the oarlocks from far away. I ran down along the bank of the creek a short distance before I realized they were out in the open water. As I thought, the little boat had no trouble sliding past the channel obstruction.

There was nothing I could do until late that morning when Fatso and I got a line under the sunken boat in the creek and pulled it to one side, so the Bumble Bee could get through, and we tore for Brunswick, where I called up Dan the Devil.

When I got back to the dock where I had left the Bumble Bee, it had disappeared. Black Angelo and Fatso must have suddenly dogged it and decided they had enough of the situation.

I always tried to excuse them in my own mind by figuring they may have seen the bunch of Goldfarb's red-hots who loaded into a big motor boat while the Bumble Bee was at the dock, and went out to Shadow Island to reinforce Goldy, and later to scare the McGarrys half to death. I always said to myself that maybe Black Angelo and Fatso intended returning to the island ahead of the motor boat.

But this excuse never seemed to fit, because the Bumble Bee was afterwards found floating upside down a hundred miles off that coast. It had run into a hurricane away out, and if Black Angelo or Fatso escaped they never came back to say so. I guess the eels got them.

Now it seems that in the launch that was cruising off Shadow Island was Abie Goldfarb, the Peacemaker himself, and four of his crack red-hots. A red-hot is a fellow who is especially handy on the trigger.

Abie was a small, blond fellow, with a big hooked nose. He came up out of the Red Hook district in Brooklyn, and had lived there most of his life. He was a smart fellow, and he wasn't trusting any million-dollar scores to anyone else.

John Withington White III was at the oars as the little boat came slipping out of the creek. It was a dark night, and you couldn't see far across the water, and young White rowed as quietly as he could, but Abie's bunch heard him just the same and started their launch toward the noise of the oarlocks.

But Abie had been laying well out for fear we might chuck a few slugs at them, so the little boat got a jump on them at the start. Francesca knew the general direction of the mainland and young White rowed that way, though they had no real idea where they were going. They could hear Abie's boat coming on steadily, though of course at first Abie didn't know who he was following. All he knew was that somebody was trying to get away from Shadow Island. He had some local fellow out of Brunswick running his boat, and the fellow knew the waters in that neighborhood.

John Withington White III was pretty stiff from being chained up in the hold so long, but after rowing awhile, his muscles loosened up, and he made the little boat skip along like a water beetle. He kept changing his course to fool the mob in the launch behind him.

From Shadow Island to the mainland in the direction Francesca and John Withington White III went, it was around six or seven miles. They got a good break, because the water was fairly smooth, and there was no moon. But they could hear Goldy's launch putt-putting behind them, and by and by it commenced to get light because dawn comes early down there in the summer.

Then the fellows in Goldy's boat could see what they were after, and while I don't know that any of them had ever seen John Withington White III before, and I know they had never seen Francesca, they couldn't have helped suspecting that these were people worth interviewing. A couple of shots were fired at the little boat. Francesca said she didn't think they were intended to hit anything because they went wide, and Goldfarb's red-hots seldom missed.

The shore was still about two miles away, and Francesca and John Withington White III had about a quarter of a mile lead on the launch when it got light enough to see real good, and John Withington White III had been rowing around quite a while. I've heard fellows who claim they know say that a man can't outrow a motor launch, but that's what John Withington White III did. He must have been a natural-born rower.

It was broad daylight when the little boat bumped against the shore of the mainland. The last few hundred yards, John Withington White III had a cinch in his race against the launch, because the water shallowed off, and the launch had to take it easy to keep from going aground, while the small boat could ride a goldfish bowl.

Where Francesca and John Withington White III landed, the pines run almost down to the water, and as soon as they piled out of the boat they started running for the trees. The launch stopped about a hundred yards offshore, and Goldy's bunch hopped out into the water and started wading ashore. In a few minutes, Francesca and John Withington White III were well back in the pines, but also in one of the toughest stretches of swamp in the world, with plenty of water underfoot, and the cypress trees standing thick and close.

They ran and ran, and kept running, floundering and falling, but still struggling on. They were going hand in hand like a couple of children. They could hear Goldy's bunch right behind them. I wish I could have seen those city fellows running through the swamp, especially Goldy. Occasionally they fired a shot, just at random. I guess they were convinced now that the fellow ahead of them was young White.

Finally, deep down in the woods, John Withington White III and Francesca came to firmer ground, and made better time. Then Francesca played out. She couldn't run any more. She stopped and began to cry. Of course John Withington White III stopped, too.

Francesca said: "Go on. They'll not bother me. They won't know who I am, but they're bound to recognize you."

John Withington White III picked her up in his arms and kept on running. He must have been a powerful fellow.

At last he came out of the swamp to a small clearing out in the sun and was about to run across this clearing, because there was thick undergrowth on both sides, when there came a peculiar noise. John Withington White III stopped dead in his tracks, then turned and lunged into the undergrowth, and struggled through it for another quarter of a mile.

Francesca told me that at this moment the pursuit was so close behind that it seemed a sure thing they would be overtaken. They could hear Goldy's crowd floundering and swearing just a few yards away. Then suddenly Francesca and John Withington White III heard a strange scream. It was a man's scream, and Francesca said it was the most terrible sound she ever heard.

Then there were other screams, and then yells from different voices, and the pursuit seemed to be turning behind them and going back the other way.

But John Withington White III, carrying Francesca in his arms, kept plugging through the woods, until at last he came to a clearing, and saw in the distance the buildings of a plantation.

He stopped and listened, but there wasn't a sound in the woods behind them. Then young White sat down on a log, still holding Francesca in his arms as if she was a baby, and began kissing her.

But nothing ever surprised Francesca. She said: "Why?"

"Because I love you," he said.

"You won't when you find out I'm the daughter of Dan the Devil, the man who kidnaped you, and one of the most disgraceful characters in American history."

"I know it already," he said. "Black Angelo used to keep me awake at night entertaining me with stories of your illustrious parent."

"And you don't mind?" she said.

"I once looked up the inside history of the Whites," John Withington White III said. "Especially our line. One of my ancestors was hanged in chains for piracy. One of my great-great-grandfathers was run out of San Francisco by the Vigilantes for swindling the forty-niners. Another great-great-grandfather wrecked two banks. My grandfather on my mother's side stole five railroads from the stockholders. I suspect that my father was a profiteer during the late war." He added: "If you can stand for my family, I can stand for yours."

Francesca said: "I'll try."

It was an hour or so afterwards that Francesca wondered what had happened to their pursuers. They were still sitting on the log. At least, John Withington White III was doing the sitting.

He said: "Maybe they ran into something I was lucky enough to avoid."

He never explained to Francesca, but that night several of Goldy's red-hots wandered into a small settlement on the edge of the pine woods babbling like a lot of crazy men, and when a searching party went out into the woods they found what was left of Goldy some distance from the little clearing in the sun, where he had stumbled right into a whole family of rattlesnakes that John Withington White III had seen in time to avoid.

There wasn't too much left of Goldy, at that. The buzzards had been busy. Everybody said that was a queer way and a queer place for Goldy to wind up.

A milkman by the name of Marcus Stromberg, delivering his milk at dawn, saw a man who was afterwards identified as Dan the Devil, get out of a taxi near the corner of East Sixty-seventh Street and Fifth Avenue, dismiss the driver, and then start walking through East Sixty-seventh. The man was carrying a big suitcase in each hand.

This Stromberg also saw a young fellow walking along the street with his hands in his pockets and a cap on the back of his head, not far behind the man with the suitcases. Stromberg said the only reason he noticed him at all was because the Strombergs were musical and it annoyed him to hear the young fellow whistling "Stormy Weather" off key.

Then Stromberg heard something go pit-pit-pit, and looked around and saw the man stretched out on the sidewalk between his suitcases. The young fellow was walking away rapidly. He was still whistling "Stormy Weather." The cops were greatly astonished to find nine hundred and seventy-five thousand dollars in cash money in the suit-cases.

I've always had a sort of an idea that maybe Dan the Devil got to thinking about Francesca kidnaping John Withington White III, and putting two and two together, and figuring why, and that he was taking the money back to young White's mother. But I've never mentioned that idea to anybody that knew Dan the Devil. They'd never believe he would have softened up that much.

I saw an item in a newspaper the other day that said that Mr. and Mrs. John Withington White III were spending their honeymoon at Shadow Island, the private estate of the bride's uncle, Mr. M. Patrick McGarry.

Francesca put in a good word for me. She said I'd always been a little off. So I'm back hacking.

Maybe a Queen

IF YOU go to Sixth Avenue and Forty-second Street and take a peek at Bryant Park behind the Public Library, you are bound to say to yourself, well this is a terrible-looking spot for a romance, because nowadays Bryant Park looks somewhat seedy and out at the elbows, and generally it is filled with guys who are also somewhat seedy and out at the elbows sitting around on benches. In fact, some of these guys are nothing but bums.

However, a matter of maybe twenty years ago Bryant Park is a much more pleasant-looking spot, with green grass growing all around and about, and it is there that a romance starts that finally becomes the oldest romance anybody ever hears of in this town, and very historic. In fact, it finally becomes such an old romance that everybody considers it practically incredible. It is the romance between a doll by the name of Ida Peters, and a guy by the name of Jack O'Donahue.

Now of course everybody that reads the newspapers the past twenty years hears of Ida Peters, because at one time she is getting more publicity than the Prince of Wales, what with being married to some rich guy about every Monday and divorcing him early Tuesday, and wearing more diamonds than Boston has beans. But very few hear anything whatever of Jack O'Donahue, because he is nobody much in the beginning, and he is still nobody much at the finish.

He is a tall, skinny, good-looking young guy of maybe twenty-five twenty years back, and at this time he is clerking in a haberdashery store on Fifth Avenue and is rooming in a joint on Sixth Avenue not far from Bryant Park and it seems that of an evening he is fond of sitting on a bench in the park and smoking cigarettes and thinking of very little, and the reason Jack O'Donahue thinks of very little is because he is such a guy as cannot think of very much.

Anyway, it is while he is sitting in the park one evening that he meets up with Ida Peters, who is then in the chorus at the old Hippodrome, and who happens to go over to Bryant Park this particular evening after a rehearsal to take a load off her feet, which become very tired, indeed, from standing around at the rehearsal. And it seems she sits down on the same bench with Jack O'Donahue, and one word leads to another, and the first thing you know they are well acquainted.

But Ida Peters does not hang out in such places as Bryant Park as a rule. Generally during her spare time she is hanging out in the Beaux Arts Restaurant across from Bryant Park, or in Bustanoby's over in Thirty-ninth, and in Murray's, and other spots where they have what they call tea dansants in the afternoon, although a tea dansant is nothing but dancing and personally I never hear of much tea being connected with such propositions.

But these spots I name are swell spots a matter of twenty years back, and some very swell guys and dolls patronize them, and it is by no means usual for a chorus doll from the Hippodrome to be hanging out in these spots. In fact the chorus dolls from the Hip are more apt to be hanging out in Jack's, where no one ever hears of such a thing as a tea dansant, especially the tea part, or in the back rooms of the beer joints along Sixth Avenue, for I am now speaking of the days when beer is to be had without fear of mortification setting in immediately after drinking same.

But you will never catch Ida Peters in a beer joint, for from the minute she hits New York from her home town, which is a town in Pennsylvania by the name of Allentown, Ida Peters declares herself as out for nothing but the old do-re-mi, and her idea is to hang out in spots where the old do-re-mi is apt to be found. She especially declares herself one evening to Jack O'Donahue when they are sitting on a bench in Bryant Park, which is the first night he tells Ida Peters he loves her, and wishes her to be his ever-loving wife.

"Listen, Jack," she says, "I am in this town long enough to tell the difference between a guy who is on the level with a doll and a guy who is just on the make, and I think you are on the level. I think you really love me, at that, Jack, and," she says, "I am going to tell you something else. I like you. But Jack," she says, "you are poor, and I size you up as a guy who will always be poor. It is no crime to be poor," Ida Peters says, "but personally I am sick and tired of being poor.

"I am raised in poverty and despair back in my home town," she says. "My mother is dead, and my old man is a drunken bum. My three brothers are drunken bums. I am twenty-two years old," she says, "and I never have a new dress in my life until I come to New York two years ago and earn it myself. I never have a plaything when I am a kid. I never have enough to eat. I get little schooling. I do the family washing and ironing and cooking, and the best I get is a smacking around now and then from my old man. I never have a sweetheart. I never have anything whatever.

"Now," Ida Peters says, "I wish nice clothes and diamonds, especially diamonds. I wish to live in fine hotels, and have servants and automobiles, and all this and that. I look in the mirror," she says, "and I see I am no worse-looking than a lot of dolls who have these things, and there is no reason why I shall not have them, too. They call for money. Well," she says, "who has the money? Guys have the money. All right," she says, "I make up my mind long ago that I will get the money off these guys, for guys with money are mostly saps, anyway. But," she says, "I will get this money legally and honestly. I will marry these guys with money.

"I wish to go to Europe," Ida Peters says. "I wish to have a château in France and a villa in Italy. I even wish to be a countess, or a duchess. Yes," Ida Peters says, "maybe a queen. I know I am talking crazy," she says, "but other dolls get these things and why not me? Why not Ida Peters? I like you a lot, Jack," she says, "because you are nice and sweet and clean, but you are not for me. Now," she says, "if you wish to keep on seeing me you must never speak of marriage again to me."

Well, of course, these are most astonishing sentiments to hear from such a young doll, and as she says more or less the same things to other parties, it finally gets around that Ida Peters is nothing but a sharpshooter, and is taking dead aim at rich guys. Of course many dolls around this town are doing the same thing, but they are not so outspoken about it and many citizens claim that Ida Peters is entitled to much credit for her frankness.

However, Ida Peters does not always remain so frank, especially about her family, because in later years I hear her say her family is of old Revolutionary stock, and that her great-great-grandpap freezes his toes when he is with Washington at Valley Forge, and once when someone speaks of Allentown to her and asks if she ever hears of the place she wishes to know if it is in this country.

Of course the idea of a doll who is nothing but a chorus doll at the Hip saying she is going to grab herself a rich guy is very laughable indeed to one and all, especially such a doll who is no better than Ida Peters, for Ida Peters is by no means a raving beauty. Many a time in later years I try to figure out why she has such a power over guys, but I never seem able to find the answer.

She is about medium height, not very tall, and by no means short, and she is thin and flat all the way up and down, with very thin legs. She has soft blond hair, and a lot of it, and her skin is white and smooth, and always looks as cool as polished marble. Her eyes are blue and cold and never seem to change expression. She very seldom smiles, and when she does she shows plenty of nice teeth. Furthermore, she has a nice nose, and small hands and feet, and in their time these hands and feet cost more dough than the German war debt.

I once hear a guy say Ida Peters looks mysterious, although personally I figure she looks a little dumb, but of course I am not much of a judge of dolls. In fact, if I am looking for a doll I will never choose Ida Peters. I will choose a doll who has more zing in her. As far as I am concerned Ida Peters has no appeal to me whatever, but then maybe I have no appeal to Ida Peters either, if anybody ever asks her.

But other dolls tell me that Ida Peters has what they call style. Other dolls tell me that she is always what they call a clothes horse, claiming that when she is hanging around the Beaux Arts and Bustanoby's and other spots in a little tailored suit that may not cost her more than fifteen bucks, tops, she can wear it better than most dolls can wear something that may cost a couple of C's.

Furthermore, other dolls tell me that Ida Peters' strength with guys is playing the old hard-to-get, looking them over out of her cold blue eyes in such a way as to make them feel about two feet high, no matter how high they may really be, and also causing them to wish to have some truck with this faraway doll. Other dolls do not care for Ida Peters personally, and are always putting the blast on her behind her back, but they all admit that she has a certain something which makes guys a little dizzy in the head, and also makes them wish to send her orchids, and so forth.

But Ida Peters will have no part of any guy unless she thinks he has plenty of potatoes, and she drops him in a second if she finds out she is wrong. Furthermore, she has no sympathy or any consideration whatever for such a guy, even though he may spend plenty on her for a while, and even though he may be caring about her more than somewhat, and she always drops him in as cruel a way as she can think of, such as looking right past him the next time they meet as if she never seen him before.

Afterwards when I read about guys scragging themselves over Ida Peters I can see how this can be. And while many citizens claim that Ida Peters is nothing but a guy-hater in her heart, I can see how she is only sticking to a campaign she maps out in advance. Anyway she always gives me a nice hello, so I do not have any kick coming. In fact, I always claim other dolls have a right to be giving three cheers for Ida Peters at all times, because the way she chucks guys around gets a lot of dolls in this world even for the way they are chucked around by guys.

Nearly every evening at seven o'clock she meets Jack O'Donahue in Bryant Park and sits there on a bench talking to him for an hour before she goes to work at the Hip, and even after she leaves the Hip and gets a job with Ziegfeld and becomes a famous show doll, she keeps on meeting Jack O'Donahue, for cold and hard as she is, Ida Peters is now in love with Jack O'Donahue, and there is no doubt about it.

But from the first night he mentions it, she will never again let him talk of marrying her, although she does not mind him talking to her about how much he loves her, and in fact she encourages it, because such talk is always very pleasant to any doll's ears. Then when it is time for her to go, she kisses Jack O'Donahue on the mouth, and this is all there is to it until the next time. She never lets Jack O'Donahue take her places, because she says she knows Jack O'Donahue cannot afford it, and she must not waste time going places with a guy who cannot afford to take her places, no matter if he does love her and she loves him.

Now of course Jack O'Donahue does not believe Ida Peters means what she says about marrying for the old do-re-mi, figuring that she is only talking to hear herself talk as dolls will do, and that some day she will haul off and become Mrs. Jack O'Donahue, because he is such a guy as believes in the power of love, and is probably the only guy in this town in the past fifty years who does believe in this. In fact, if you ask me, Jack O'Donahue never in his life has any real understanding of Ida Peters.

He is personally somewhat innocent about one thing and another, and I always figure he must be a little simple because if he is not a little bit simple he will tell Ida Peters to go and take a jump in the East River for herself, and find himself a doll who is not so daffy on the subject of dough, if there are any such dolls left in the world, and if he simply must have a doll. But Jack O'Donahue lets Ida Peters chuck him around to suit herself as she chucks every guy she meets around, when she wishes, and as far as anybody knows he never complains of the arrangement.

Now then it is seven o'clock of a Thursday evening on September 10, 1912, after Ida Peters is meeting Jack O'Donahue in Bryant Park nearly every evening for over a year, that she shows up there and speaks to him as follows:

"Jack, dear," she says, "I have something to tell you, and I am not going to stall around with you in telling it. Jack," she says, "I marry a guy by the name of Watkins this afternoon in the Little Church Around the Corner, and we are going away tonight on our honeymoon. He is a rich wholesale grocer from Minneapolis," she says, "and we will live there."

Well, as Jack O'Donahue sits looking somewhat confused as any guy must do when such news busts right in his pan, she begins crying and throws her arms around his neck and states as follows:

"But Jack, dear," she says, "I will never love anybody but you, and every year on this same date and at this same time I will meet you here for our little hour together."

Then she kisses him on the mouth, as usual, and goes away, leaving Jack O'Donahue sitting there quite dumfounded, and this is where the romance really starts making history.

Now no guy in his right mind will ever figure Ida Peters means what she says about this once-a-year business, and no guy in his right mind will accept such a proposition anyway, because this comes under the head of being chucked around by a doll more than somewhat, and everybody who hears of the matter has a good laugh and forgets all about it, although one and all admire Ida Peters for sticking to her ambition to grab a rich guy.

But as I tell you, Jack O'Donahue must be a little simple, for who is sitting on a bench in Bryant Park at seven P.M. on the evening of September 10, 1913, but Jack O'Donahue.

Well, maybe it is just an accident that she is in New York this day, and maybe it is only a doll's curiosity that takes her around to Bryant Park at seven P.M., but this is also where Ida Peters bobs up, and naturally the meeting between her and Jack O'Donahue is very pleasant indeed, especially for Jack O'Donahue, as he winds up with a big kiss on the mouth.

Ida Peters is looking very prosperous, and wearing plenty of large diamonds, and it turns out that this Watkins guy out in Minneapolis is a very fair score indeed for any doll, as he is worth maybe a million bobs. But it also turns out that he is only a start for Ida Peters, for in a little over a year she gets a divorce from him, and when she shows up in Bryant Park on the next September 10th, right on time, she is now Mrs. Caleb Grimes, of Chicago, and her diamonds are twice as big as when she is Mrs. Watkins.

Well, in the course of the next ten years, Ida Peters marries three other guys and divorces them one after the other, and every time she marries a new guy he is a guy who has more potatoes than the last guy and generally more of a social position, except once when she marries a guy by the name of Marchbanks, who is an Englishman, and who turns out to be quite a bum. But of course any doll is apt to make a mistake now and then in her marriages when she is marrying as freely as Ida Peters, and anyway this marriage is by no means a total loss as she catches an English accent off of Marchbanks.

I will say one thing for Ida Peters, she never has a lick of scandal in connection with any of her divorces. They are always very clean, indeed, because generally she charges her husbands with nothing more serious than cruelty, and usually she even parts good friends with them, although some of them complain that she is very tough about the financial settlements.

And in all these years she never fails to arrive in Bryant Park at seven P.M. on September 10th to meet Jack O'Donahue and spend an hour with him. She is living in Europe when the war breaks out, and three times she makes trips across the ocean to keep her date, paying no attention whatever to submarines, although some claim that the submarines are more afraid of Ida Peters than she is of them.

For the first few years, Ida Peters' annual date causes some gossip around and about, as it is considered quite unusual indeed, but as the years roll on, and times change quite some, and many citizens who knew about it in the beginning go lay down and die, it is forgotten, and even when Ida Peters arrives in this country from time to time loaded down with her diamonds, and all this and that, no one ever seems to remember about her date, and she never mentions it herself.

The newspaper scribes write more about Ida Peters in her time than any other doll in the world, because in between her marriages some guy is always falling in love with Ida Peters and knocking himself off when she refuses to give him a tumble, and she provides much good news for the scribes in other ways. So it is very strange that Jack O'Donahue's name never gets into any of the stories about her, but by this time Jack O'Donahue becomes a sort of religion with Ida Peters and very sacred to her, indeed, and her date with him is one thing in her life that she does not wish brought up.

Now Jack O'Donahue is one of these guys who just do not seem to gather any potatoes or to get anywhere in particular as he goes along through life. He goes from one job to another, and generally they are nothing but clerking jobs and pay very little, and he is steady and behaves himself good, but he never manages to lay up anything. I see him once in a great while as the years go on, as he occasionally drops into Derle's billiard academy where I hang out, and he will sit around and watch a game by the hour, never saying much of anything, and every time I see him he seems to be thinner than the last time.

He always has a sad and lonesome look and he never seems to have any friends, although naturally many guys know him by sight and say hello. He is still living in the joint on Sixth Avenue, and he still sits around on the benches in Bryant Park smoking cigarettes, and while he is always neat and clean-looking, I notice his clothes are getting pretty shabby the last time I see him. Afterwards I hear that Ida Peters often tries to make Jack O'Donahue take some of her potatoes, but he will not listen to such a thing, and in fact he says she is insulting him, so she stops trying.

By this time of course Ida Peters has plenty of potatoes, and her diamonds are famous all over the world, so it does not seem as if there can be anything more that Ida Peters can wish, but it seems there is one more thing, at that. It seems that Ida Peters wishes a title, even though titles are not worth a dime a dozen anywhere.

So after she gets rid of a husband by the name of Raoul something, who is a big newspaper publisher in Paris, Ida Peters hauls off and marries a guy by the name of Prince Podubny, who is a fat guy, and has a very large mustache, and is by no means young, but he has more potatoes than any guy Ida Peters ever marries up to this time, besides his title.

Furthermore, it seems that Prince Podubny is very much in love with Ida Peters and gives her bigger diamonds than any of her other husbands, and also pearls and emeralds and one thing and another, and when Ida Peters is dressed up to go anywhere she is a more pleasant sight than a trip through a Fifth Avenue jewelry store.

And it is a good thing for Ida Peters that she finds Prince Podubny, for what happens but she loses all her own potatoes that she accumulates after years of hard work and saving off her other husbands in the blow-up of the Waggenstaff Bank in New York, and in blow-ups of several other matters in which she has potatoes invested. But of course losing these potatoes makes no difference to Ida Peters now that she has Prince Podubny, who seems to be a prince in a country over in the Balkans with some kind of claim to being king if he gets the right break.

Now as showing you how smart Ida Peters is, she never fails to tell any of her husbands in advance about her annual date with Jack O'Donahue, so she will not run into any complications in case a husband happens to put a private dick on her, as husbands sometimes do, but most of her husbands are very broad-minded about the proposition, figuring it is nothing but a passing fancy, until the prince comes along.

Well, it seems the old prince is very jealous indeed of Ida Peters, and can scarcely bear to have her out of his sight, but he loves her so much that at first he does not complain about her annual date, and in fact he comes to the United States with her two years hand running so she can keep this date with Jack O'Donahue, and furthermore the old prince is gentleman enough not to try to find out who Jack O'Donahue is, or anything else about him. But then it seems the prince commences to brood on this mysterious guy in Ida Peters' life, and to be very jealous of him.

It seems the old prince pictures Jack O'Donahue in his own mind as maybe a very dashing, romantic guy, although if he can only get a slant at Jack O'Donahue he will never worry about him any more, for by this time poor Jack O'Donahue is a very sorrowful spectacle, indeed. He is so thin you can scarcely see him when he is standing sideways, and he is stoop-shouldered, and his hair is quite gray, and his eyes are now away back in his head, and he is by no means dashing, and by no means romantic. He is only sad-looking.

But it comes on September of 1930, and on the morning of the ninth Ida Peters, who is now the Princess Podubny, arrives in New York from Europe with her ever-loving husband Prince Podubny and a raft of servants and luggage, and they go to a swell hotel to stay in about nine rooms, and it seems that in the evening they go to eat dinner with some very rich friends on Park Avenue, and then they go to a show, and naturally Ida Peters puts on as much of her jewelry as she can carry without help, including the Podubny pearls, which some guys say are worth a million bucks, and a lot of bracelets, and large diamond rings and one thing and another.

Well, they get back to the hotel about midnight, and there are many cablegrams waiting for the old prince, and he reads them as soon as they get to their rooms, and he says to Ida Peters like this:

"Well," he says, "I always tell you I will make you a queen some day, my darling. Now the time arrives. I just receive news that a revolution starts in my country in my behalf, and my advisers wish me there at once to take command. There is no time to lose. We will sail the first thing in the morning."

"Why," Ida Peters says, "this is very glad news, indeed, because if there is anything I wish in this world it is to be a queen. But," she says, "you know I cannot sail in the morning, because of my date tomorrow evening."

"We cannot wait," Prince Podubny says, very cold, indeed. "We must go early in the morning, because every hour is precious. There may be no other ship for several days."

Well, Ida Peters says if it is so important for him, to go ahead and sail, and she will follow after him as soon as possible, but the old prince has his neck bowed now, and he speaks to her as follows:

"You must go with me," he says. "It is my wish, and as I am now practically a king I must be obeyed. Anyway," he says, "much depends on showing my people their new queen, and furthermore I make up my mind it is time for you to forget this old foolishness."

But Ida Peters says she will not go until she keeps her date with Jack O'Donahue, and then the old prince starts to rave at her, saying he always suspects there is more to this old romance than just an annual meeting in a park and he gets very tough, indeed, with her, but he forgets that he is talking to a doll who is used to having pretty much her own way.

"Well," Ida Peters says finally, "I am going to keep my date, and if you continue speaking to me in such a harsh tone I will walk out of this room."

Well, then the old prince gets very, very angry with her, and says to her like this:

"All right," he says, "but if you walk out of this room now you walk out of my life forever. Look at yourself in the mirror," he says. "You are forty if you are a day, and the chances are I am giving you the best of it, at that. You are not as young or as good-looking as you used to be and you will never again be able to hold guys in the hollow of your hand.

"Look yourself over," he says. "The way you stand you represent over a million dollars in American money, but you do not have a dime to your name any more. Well," he says, "if you walk out of this room you are going to leave every diamond and pearl you have on and walk out of here with nothing but your dress on, for they are all mine, although," the prince says, getting big-hearted, "I may let you take a coat, at that, as it is getting chilly outside and I do not wish to see you catch pneumonia.

"Ha-ha-ha," he says, laughing like the villain in a play, "how will you like this general idea? I know you well enough to know you love diamonds and clothes and luxury too much to toss them all away for an hour with an old sweetheart, no matter how much you think you love him, which is probably not much," he says, "because you are not capable of much love. So forget it, and call your maid, and start packing," the prince says.

Well, Ida Peters stands there looking at him a minute, and then she begins stripping off her pearls and her diamond rings, and her bracelets, and one thing and another, and when she gets a good handful of them she hauls off and lets them fly at the old prince, and then she turns and walks out of the door in nothing but her evening dress, and the prince sails the next morning, and in two months is king of his country, and has a divorce from Ida Peters without giving her a nickel's worth of alimony.

Personally I hear that what makes the prince especially sore about the whole proposition is that when Ida Peters chucks her jewelry at him one of her diamond rings hit him in the mouth, and the diamond is so big it knocks out a lot of brand-new bridge work that costs the old prince plenty of potatoes.

But it is now a few minutes to seven o'clock the next evening and generally Jack O'Donahue is in Bryant Park waiting when Ida Peters arrives, but he is not present this evening and Ida Peters stands looking all around and about in a dress she borrows from the friend in Park Avenue, when all of a sudden she sees a bunch of guys coming along a path in the park from the Forty-second Street side, and these guys seem to be carrying something among them and what are they carrying but Jack O'Donahue.

Furthermore, they have very little trouble carrying him, because Jack O'Donahue is now two pounds lighter than an old sponge, and as they carry him up to where Ida Peters is standing, one of the guys takes off his hat and says to her like this:

"Madam," he says, "this poor guy is just hit by a taxicab out there in Forty-second Street. He is trying to cross the street, but," he says, "he seems to be somewhat sick, and is so weak that he falls down right in front of the cab. I am a doctor," the guy says, "and I wish to call an ambulance, and take him to a hospital, but he asks us to bring him over here to the park, saying there will be a party here he wishes to see.

"Well, Madam," the guy says, "I do not wish to speak of bad news, but if you know this poor guy and wish to talk to him you better do it fast, because he is pretty badly hurt, although," the guy says, "if the taxicab does not get him, the t.b. must in about another week."

Then Jack O'Donahue opens his eyes, and looks at Ida Peters standing over him and crying more than somewhat, and he whispers as follows:

"I love you, Ida Peters."

And as Ida Peters kisses him on the mouth, Jack O'Donahue hauls off and dies and the oldest romance anybody ever hears of in this town winds up where it starts.

Well, of course, you are wondering how it is I am able to learn so many details of this old romance, but I can prove everything I say by Ida Peters herself, who tells it all to me on different mornings when I am waiting for my cakes and coffee.

"But," I say to Ida Peters, "do you not sometimes regret your hasty action when you learn how the old prince is indeed king, and you will be his queen if you use a little judgment? And especially," I say, "do you not regret it as long as Jack O'Donahue has to die anyway?"

"No," Ida Peters says, "I have no regrets, because the way I figure it, it is no great trick for any doll to marry a prince and maybe become a queen, as princes are very great chumps for dolls at all times. In fact," she says, "the chances are you will find several dolls sitting around on thrones here and there who starts off by marrying princes.

"But," she says, drawing herself up very proud, indeed, "I will guarantee that you will have a tough time finding another doll who tosses off a chance to be a queen for nothing more than the memory of an old romance, especially a romance with such a guy as Jack O'Dona-hue, who is a guy who is practically no dice, any way you figure him."

"Well," I say, "I can see where you may be right, and it is all most unusual, and very strange. In fact," I say, "I do not recall ever hearing anything like it before in all my born days, and I am around and about Broadway quite a spell now."

"Furthermore," Ida Peters says, and her voice is as cold and haughty as it ever is in the old days, "you can bet all the grapefruit in Florida that I am the only head-waitress in the world who tosses off a throne just to hear a guy say 'I love you,' although," she says, "personally I consider it worth it.

"Now," she says, "if you wish another cup of hot java, I will get it myself."

Burge McCall

BURGE MCCALL hated his wife.

That made it 50-50 between them.

They lived together most unpleasantly for three years and four months.

For a year and two months, Burge McCall didn't like the way his wife looked at him. It made him nervous.

His wife, Mrs. McCall, was a tall, thin woman with black hair and big black eyes. She always wore her hair parted in the middle, and smoothed down slick on each side. She never had much to say.

She was the kind of woman that other women always called Mrs.

They never used her first name. It was Venita. Her family lived in Peppersauce Bottoms, just south of the Santa Fe yards. Her father was a switchman.

Her sister, Anola, was married to Sled Sather, the druggist.

Burge McCall met Mrs. McCall at an Elks' picnic. Burge was a big Elk. He had been married twice before, but his other wives ran away from him and got divorces.

What they said about Burge was a caution. It interested everybody in town.

Burge McCall thought he was quite a lady killer.

He didn't know that most of the women in our town said they wouldn't touch him with a ten-foot pole.

They said Mrs. McCall married him to get away from the noise of the Santa Fe switch engines. Some said they didn't blame her, at that, although others thought Burge McCall would be much worse than a switch engine.

He was a short, heavy-set man with a loud voice. He put grease on his hair and perfume on his handkerchief. He had a habit of sucking his teeth with his tongue, and making a peculiar sound.

Burge McCall was chief clerk of the District Court, and made a good salary, but he was very stingy with Mrs. McCall. He liked to spend all his money on himself, and on other women.

He undoubtedly was a bad husband. Some said he was the third worst husband in our town, but this was probably rating him too high.

Burge McCall never could understand his wife, Mrs. McCall.

When he called her names, she never answered. Burge McCall was accustomed to women who called him names right back when he called them names. Burge McCall said his second wife knew more names than he did.

But Mrs. McCall would only look at him.

That started him to hating her within two months after they were married.

Then one day, after they had been married two years and two months, Burge McCall slapped Mrs. McCall in the face. That is why for a year and two months Burge didn't like the way she looked at him.

She wiped the place where he slapped her with her hand. She said, "McCall, you are a big rat. Some day you are going to regret what you have done."

Burge McCall was somewhat disappointed in her. His second wife threw a flatiron at him for slapping her. He had a notion to slap Mrs. McCall again for calling him a big rat, but he didn't like the way she looked at him.

One hot day Burge McCall dropped into Sled Sather's drugstore to have a drink, and Sled said, "Hello, Burge. Your old woman was in here this morning and bought a pound of rat poison."

Burge said, "What did she want with a pound of rat poison?"

And Sled said, "Well, she said she wanted to poison a big rat."

Sled said it must be an awful big rat for her to want that much poison.

Burge McCall thought nothing of this at first.

Then he got to thinking that there never had been any rats around his house. He got to thinking that, as a matter of fact, rats are rather unusual in our town. He got to thinking that Mrs. McCall had spoken of him as a big rat.

Burge McCall put two and two together. He went home very nervous.

He thought some of asking Mrs. McCall about the rat poison, but decided it would do no good. He figured she would only say she got it to poison a rat, and what of it, and Burge McCall would have no answer to that.

But he felt sure there were no rats around his house.

He did manage to bring up the subject of rats in an offhand way once or twice, but Mrs. McCall paid no attention to his remarks. She just looked at him.

Burge McCall sneaked all over the house when he thought Mrs. McCall wasn't noticing, looking for the rat poison. He never found it. He never found any rats either.

He began worrying terribly.

He went to see Doc Wilcox and asked him how arsenic tasted. Doc Wilcox said he didn't know. He said he had never tasted it. He said he would bet it tasted awful.

Burge McCall got so he wouldn't eat a smitch at home. He always had some excuse for taking his meals downtown, and this was a great break for Mrs. McCall, as it relieved her of a lot of work.

She hated cooking, anyway.

Burge McCall wouldn't even take a drink of water in the house, but would go to a neighbor's, half a block away, when he was thirsty. He quit liquor, because he figured it would never do for him to go home intoxicated. He wanted to be in full possession of all his faculties at all times.

This was another good break for Mrs. McCall, because when Burge McCall came home intoxicated, he was always very mean. He was even meaner intoxicated than when he was sober.

Finally Burge McCall decided that the safest thing for him to do was to keep Mrs. McCall in sight as much as possible. He got to taking her to the movies, and to Elks' picnics. He always spoke nicely to her, because he didn't want to irritate her.

The other women in our town began envying Mrs. McCall the attention she got from her husband, especially when he bought her a sealskin coat in the winter of 1933.

One day Burge McCall looked at Mrs. McCall and noticed she was not looking at him with the look that made him so nervous.

He noticed her eyes were smiling at him. He took her in his arms and called her Hon.

When Burge McCall died of apoplexy in 1935, his wife, Mrs. McCall, openly shed tears.

Sled Sather afterward said he never could understand why Mrs. McCall had once asked him to tell Burge McCall that she had bought a pound of rat poison to poison a big rat, when she never bought any at all.

Lou Louder

LOU LOUDER was a bartender.

He tended bar in the Greenlight saloon.

He was tending bar there the night Shalimar Duke was killed.

Lou Louder was very tall, and very thin, and very pale. He said he was sent to Our Town by a doctor in Buffalo, N. Y., to die. Lou Louder had t.b.

Lots of people used to come to Our Town to die. The doctors in other parts of the country highly recommend the climate.

Shalimar Duke was the owner of the Commercial Hotel. He was a short, fat man. He was one of the most popular citizens of Our Town. His books showed that more than twenty-eight thousand dollars was owing him on old accounts when he got killed.

Shalimar Duke married a Mexican girl half his age, named Pabalita Sanchez. Her people had a big sheep ranch. She had beautiful black eyes and black hair and an awful temper. She was like her mother, Juanita Sanchez. She was like her aunt, Maria Gomez, too.

Pabalita was pretty fly, but how could Shalimar Duke know that? He was forty-seven years of age.

The two Baker boys, Joe and Sid, had a fight about her and quit speaking to each other. This made it inconvenient in their business. They were partners in the B. B. coal yard.

Each thought Pabalita loved him. She told them so.

Shalimar Duke went into the Greenlight saloon one night and was talking to Lou Louder when Sid Baker came in. Sid had a .38-caliber revolver in his left hip pocket. Sid was left-handed.

Shalimar Duke asked Sid to have a drink. About that moment, Joe Baker came in. He had a .44-caliber revolver stuck in the waistband of his pants.

Shalimar Duke asked Joe Baker to have a drink. Shalimar Duke didn't know the Baker boys weren't speaking to each other. Shalimar Duke didn't know about the Baker boys and Pabalita.

He was the only man in Our Town who didn't know.

Joe Baker and Sid Baker were gentlemen. They accepted Shalimar

Duke's invitation to have a drink, even though they didn't speak to each other.

Joe Baker stepped up on one side of Shalimar Duke, Sid Baker stepped up on the other side. They were all as close together as your first three fingers. Lou Louder was in front of them behind the bar.

It was a hot night. The side door of the Greenlight, directly opposite the bar, was standing open to let in a little breeze. The breeze brought in the perfume of some roses growing at the side door of the Greenlight.

It was a strange place for roses to grow.

Roses were always growing in strange places in Our Town.

There was no one else in the Greenlight saloon at the time.

Shalimar Duke and Joe and Sid Baker all called for straight bourbon. The Greenlight served good bourbon to its regular customers.

Shalimar Duke stepped up on the footrail of the bar, so he was up higher than the Baker boys, and Lou Louder, too. He raised his glass, and said "Here's how," and they started to drink when Shalimar Duke fell to the floor dead.

A big-bladed knife with a very heavy handle was sticking in the back of his neck at the base of the brain.

His blood ran out in funny little rivulets on the floor.

He never said a word.

Joe Baker was arrested by Sheriff Letch and taken to the county jail. Sid Baker was arrested by Chief of Police Korn and taken to the city jail. The jails were about a mile apart.

They found a .32-caliber revolver in a side pocket of Shalimar Duke's coat. Some said maybe he had learned about Pabalita and the Baker boys, and was out looking for them when they beat him to it.

There was much indignation in Our Town.

Lou Louder was questioned by Coroner Curley. Lou Louder said he had turned to the back bar after serving Shalimar Duke and the Baker boys with their bourbon, so how could he see just what happened?

Coroner Curley said, "That's right, Lou."

A number of citizens went to the county jail and broke down the door and took Joe Baker out and hanged him to a telephone pole. Joe said it was all right with him. Joe said he was the one who stuck the knife in Shalimar Duke. Joe said he wanted to get rid of Shalimar Duke so he could have Pabalita to himself.

Joe said, "Boys, I deserve my fate."

The telephone company afterwards complained because the hanging broke some of its wires.

Joe Baker really thought Sid killed Shalimar Duke. Joe was trying to save Sid by taking the blame on himself. Joe remembered that Sid was his brother.

He didn't know that about the time they were hanging him a different crowd of citizens was taking Sid out of the city jail and stringing him up to a girder on the Union Avenue bridge, and that Sid was confessing that he jabbed the knife into Shalimar Duke.

Sid said he did it so Pabalita would be free to love him alone.

Sid Baker really thought Joe killed Shalimar Duke and was trying to save Joe as Joe was trying to save him. Sid remembered that Joe was his brother. He remembered what fun they had together when they were little kids.

It was all very confusing to the citizens of Our Town when the stories were compared after the funerals.

Some said it showed that blood is thicker than water.

There were many arguments about which of the Baker boys really stuck the knife in Shalimar Duke. Sheriff Letch had a fist fight with Chief of Police Korn about it. Sheriff Letch said his prisoner, Joe Baker, was the more truthful of the Baker boys, and must have done it, because he said he did.

Chief of Police Korn stood up for Sid Baker.

Pabalita Duke ran the Commercial Hotel for six years after Shalimar Duke's death. She died of pneumonia contracted while keeping a date with a traveling man in a snowstorm.

The first thing she did was to try to collect Shalimar Duke's old accounts.

She never was very popular in Our Town.

Lou Louder lived thirty years longer. Before he passed away he told Doc Wilcox that when he turned to the back bar after serving Shalimar Duke and the Baker boys with their bourbon, he saw, by the back bar mirror, Pabalita step to the side door of the saloon and throw the knife that killed Shalimar Duke.

The knife wasn't meant for Shalimar Duke. It was meant for Lou Louder. It would have got him, too, if Shalimar Duke hadn't stepped up on the footrail of the bar as Pabalita let fly.

If Shalimar Duke had remained standing on the floor, the knife would have cleared his head and hit Lou Louder kerplunk in the back between the shoulders.

Lou Louder said he had quarreled with Pabalita and had written her a note telling her he was through with her. She got awful mad about it. Shalimar Duke found the note and went into the Greenlight saloon to kill Lou Louder.

He was mentioning his intention to Lou Louder when the Baker boys came in, Lou said.

Shalimar Duke stepped on the footrail to get up high enough to have a freer crack at Lou Louder, so Lou thought.

The Baker boys had also gone into the Greenlight saloon to kill Lou Louder, so Lou told Doc Wilcox. They didn't know each other's idea because they weren't speaking. Pabalita had told them, separately, that Lou Louder had insulted her, and made each of them promise to kill him. They both mentioned to friends that they were going to kill Lou Louder, and the friends warned Lou.

Pabalita had no confidence in the Baker boys.

Lou Louder remarked to Doc Wilcox just before he died that he always felt he had rather a narrow escape that night.

He didn't die of t.b.

He died of old age.

The Chamber of Commerce of Our Town often pointed to Lou Louder during his life as an example of what our climate will do for a man.

Joe Terrace

JOE TERRACE killed his wife, Mrs. Terrace.

He never liked her very much.

Joe Terrace was a linotype operator on the Morning Chief.

He was a mighty good man at his trade.

He rarely made a typographical error. He was so accurate that Bob Frater, the proofreader on the Morning Chief, seldom bothered to read proof on Joe Terrace.

Bob Frater once won five dollars from Saul Letch by betting him Joe Terrace wouldn't make a typographical error in six months.

This was when Saul Letch was a printer on the Morning Chief and before he was elected sheriff. Mr. Cleve Van Dusen, Sr., owner of the Morning Chief, got Saul elected sheriff. Mr. Cleve Van Dusen, Sr., always liked to have his own man in the sheriff's office. He liked to have his own men in all the other offices, too.

Joe Terrace thought he was pretty slick about the way he killed his wife, Mrs. Terrace.

He planned it for twenty years.

The first ten years he couldn't think of how to do it. He was a slow thinker. The second ten he got it all worked out.

Every Sunday and holiday when the weather was nice Joe Terrace would take his wife, Mrs. Terrace, on a little outing into the hills northwest of Our Town.

Mrs. Terrace hated outings. She hated hills. The sand fleas got into her stockings.

She was a short, fat woman, and very good-natured. She always tried to please her husband, Joe Terrace. He called her Tubby. She went on the outings because she thought he liked them. She didn't know he was planning to kill her. It would have upset Mrs. Terrace.

Joe Terrace always took her to a place in the hills called Lover's Leap because a couple of lovers were supposed to have jumped off the cliff to their death years ago.

There are fifty thousand Lover's Leaps in the United States, and the story about them all is exactly the same. It is very strange that so many lovers jumped off cliffs together.

On Memorial Day, Joe Terrace took his wife, Mrs. Terrace, out to Lover's Leap and got her to look over the cliff. While she was looking, he hit her on the head with a rock and knocked her off the cliff down into the creek bed.

Nobody in Our Town ever thought of doubting Joe Terrace's story that it was an accident. He put a mourning band around his hat and looked sad.

Everybody remembered what a faithful husband Joe Terrace had been, and how he took his wife, Mrs. Terrace, on those outings. Everybody said Joe Terrace must miss her apple strudel.

One Monday morning Sheriff Saul Letch was having his breakfast at his home on South Catalpa Street. It was over a year after Joe Terrace killed his wife, Mrs. Terrace.

Sheriff Letch had the Morning Chief propped up against the sugar bowl in front of him. His wife, Mrs. Letch, was hiding in the kitchen until Sheriff Letch left the house. She knew he would be in bad humor. He generally was.

An election was coming on, and the church people of Our Town were hot after Sheriff Letch. They were led by Rev. John S. Clee, pastor of the First M. E. Church, South. Rev. John S. Clee was giving Sheriff Letch fits. He said Sheriff Letch was no good. He said Sheriff Letch was leagued with the forces of evil. Rev. John S. Clee meant the saloon-keepers and the gamblers.

He didn't mean Mr. Cleve Van Dusen, Sr., owner of the Morning Chief.

Things looked pretty bad for Sheriff Letch.

He got up from the breakfast table after drinking only two cups of coffee, and put on his hat, and went to Joe Terrace's house on West Eighth Street.

Sheriff Letch usually drank four cups of coffee with his breakfast. His wife, Mrs. Letch, made wonderful coffee.

Sheriff Letch knocked on Joe Terrace's door for ten minutes. Joe Terrace worked nights on the Morning Chief, and slept until noon. He was a sound sleeper.

He finally came to the door with just his pants and undershirt on. He was holding up his pants with one hand. Sheriff Letch said, "Good morning, Joe, come with me. You're under arrest for killing your wife, Mrs. Terrace."

Joe Terrace said, "All right, Saul. Wait till I get my suspenders." He said, "I'm not sorry to be arrested. It's been on my mind." He said, "Yes, I killed her, Saul. I wish I hadn't. How did you find out?"

Sheriff Letch said, "I read your confession in this morning's paper, Joe."

Joe Terrace said that couldn't be, because he hadn't made any confession; and Sheriff Letch showed him Rev. John S. Clee's sermon in the Morning Chief. The Morning Chief always published all the sermons delivered in the churches Sunday in full. Mr. Van Dusen, Sr., said it was good for business with the church people.

In the middle of Rev. John S. Clee's sermon, where he was talking about the Lord forgiving sinners, was a line that said, "Please, Lord, forgive me for what I did to Tubby."

This line had no relation to the rest of the sermon.

It didn't make sense.

Joe Terrace pleaded guilty to murder in the second degree, and Judge Dixony gave him fifty-five years in the penitentiary.

Some said it wasn't enough.

When it came out how Sheriff Letch discovered Joe Terrace's guilt by reading Rev. John S. Clee's sermon, the church people of Our Town said Sheriff Letch couldn't be such a bad man if he read sermons.

Rev. John S. Clee took back what he said about Sheriff Letch being leagued with the forces of evil, and went around making campaign speeches for Sheriff Letch.

He said Sheriff Letch was all right.

Mr. Cleve Van Dusen, Sr., put an editorial in the Morning Chief, saying that it was a wonderful thing for Our Town to have a man in office of the high spiritual character of Sheriff Letch.

Sheriff Letch was re-elected by a large plurality.

He never mentioned that he knew Joe Terrace always set up the sermons for the Morning Chief, and of course Sheriff Letch never made it public that he had been reading the sermons every Monday morning for two years only because he was always hoping to catch Joe Terrace in a typographical error so he could win his five dollars back from Bob Frater.

Sheriff Letch told his friends that he figured a linotype operator's attention was more apt to wander when he was setting up sermons than on any other kind of copy, and especially Rev. John S. Clee's sermons because they were so dull.

It is a curious thing that nobody else in Our Town noticed that typographical error before Sheriff Letch brought it up, not even Rev. John S. Clee.

Leopard's Spots

———————◆———————

ONE NIGHT I am sitting in Mindy's restaurant on Broadway reading the sports news in an early edition of a morning blat when I am surprised more than somewhat to see where an unknown prize fighter by the name of the Louisiana Leopard wins a ten-round decision in the city of Philadelphia, Pa., over Chester Nubbs, the leading contender for the heavyweight championship of the whole world.

What is more, I see that the manager of the Louisiana Leopard is nobody but Spider McCoy, who is a personal friend of mine, and this also surprises me no little because the last time I see Spider he is getting ready to go to Philadelphia, Pa., with a prize fighter who is called Pigsfoot Groody to fight Chester Nubbs, although of course nobody expects Pigsfoot to fight Chester very long or very much, and especially very much, not even Spider McCoy.

In fact, Spider does not expect Pigsfoot to fight Chester Nubbs past Chester clearing his throat, because the idea is Chester is up there in sight of a million-dollar match with the champion of the whole world for the heavyweight title, and in the matches his manager, Jack Keegan, is taking in between, all he requires is large guys to just make believe to fight Chester, for naturally Jack Keegan is too smart to be taking chances on Chester getting outfumbled by some sausage and losing the title shot.

So for the Philadelphia match, Jack Keegan orders such a guy from Spider McCoy who generally has a stock of large guys on hand for emergencies of this nature and Spider selects Pigsfoot for the assignment because Pigsfoot is not only very sure-footed in these matters but moreover he appears with Chester Nubbs before in other spots under other names and they are very good friends and understand each other.

Spider is getting one thousand boffoes and two round-trip tickets for Pigsfoot for the fight in Philadelphia, Pa., and counting his cut and what Pigsfoot owes him in dollar touches this will be about seven-fifty net for Spider, which is considered a very good depression score, especially as all Spider and Pigsfoot have to do to earn the money is to look serious.

Well, I continue reading what the blat says and it seems that the Louisiana Leopard is a substitute for Pigsfoot because it seems that Pigsfoot is taken down sick some days before the fight and that Spider brings the Leopard on very hastily to take Pigsfoot's place and there the Leopard is with a decision over the leading contender for the heavyweight championship of the whole world, although the blat says it is without doubt the dullest fight in all history and that the customers are complaining no little and quite some before it is over.

In fact, it says that instead of trying to fight the Louisiana Leopard, the contender acts as if he wishes only to avoid him and this is considered very strange conduct, indeed, for a guy such as Chester Nubbs, who is supposed to hit so hard that it requires a medical operation to wake them up after he nails them.

However, there is a long statement by Spider McCoy to the scribes at the ringside immediately after the fight in which Spider says Chester Nubbs undoubtedly receives private information before entering the ring that the Louisiana Leopard is already a fugitive from nine states for crippling opponents with his terrible blows and that the contender is afraid to take a chance with him. Furthermore, Spider challenges the champion of the whole world on behalf of the Louisiana Leopard to a contest for the title and Spider says all he wants for the Leopard's end is a hundred thou.

Naturally I am delighted at this news as I can see where Spider is in the money again because a guy who can bob up overnight taking a decision from Chester Nubbs is just the same as wheat in the bin and I can scarcely wait until Spider gets back to congratulate him and also to get a peek at the Louisiana Leopard.

But it is several weeks later before Spider comes into Mindy's again and then he seems quite despondent and looks white and peaked and, what is more, he has fresh scars on his nose and around his eyes that I can see may be the leavings of a pasting and when I start to tell him how glad I am he finally connects, he shakes his head very sadly and says to me like this:

"Wait," Spider says. "Wait until you hear the story. But first I will order a salami sandwich on pumpernickel with a glass of domestic beer to come along. And listen, insipid," he says to Charley the waiter, "get a shuffle on those big flat dogs of yours, too."

"Why, Spider," I say, "you are speaking very crossly to an old pal such as Charley. What is the trouble?" I say.

"I despise waiters," Spider says. "If you do not despise them too by the time I get through, you are no friend of mine. I despise nurses, also. In fact," he says, "I despise everybody."

Well, I can see that Spider is in an unreasonable mood at this time so I wait until he knocks off his sandwich and his beer and then becomes much calmer and finally he gets around to telling me the story, though he stops in the telling every few minutes to give Charley the waiter a mean look until after a while he has Charley in such nervous condition that he spills an order of cold borsch down a customer's neck and causes Mindy to use language that you will scarcely believe.

Now then (Spider says) no sooner do I arrive in Philadelphia, Pa., with this Pigsfoot than what happens but he says he is sick and he begins carrying on in a most exasperating manner. I get him to a hotel and call in the house croaker and he takes one look at Pigsfoot and says that what ails him is his appendix and unless I get him to a hospital and have same extracted I will have a dead prize fighter on my hands.

Well, personally I will rather have a dead one than one with something the matter with his appendix but Pigsfoot seems in such great pain and yells so loud that he finally touches my heart so I take him to a hospital and the last I see of him they are making him unconscious with ether and when I tell them they can save all this bother by just waggling a boxing glove under Pigsfoot's beezer they think I am making light of a serious situation and request me to go away.

So there I am with a sick fighter on my hands and a fight ten days off and this is a most deplorable predicament to be sure, especially as I can see that I am morally bound to pay Pigsfoot's hospital bill. I return to my hotel and send for Jack Keegan to break the bad news to him that Pigsfoot will be unable to fight Chester Nubbs, and this Keegan acts as if it is his own appendix that needs something done to it and as if I am personally responsible for the matter.

But of course Jack Keegan is an old head in the fight game and he knows that things can happen to a fighter that can never happen to anybody else, so he finally says to me like this:

"Well, Spide," he says, "the only thing to do is to send for another ostrich at once and then we will get hold of Ike Clonsky the promoter and have him announce the substitution. This show is a sellout and," Keegan says, "we do not want to postpone it. Get anybody you can," he says, "only be sure he is as big as Pigsfoot and knows his job as well."

"Nobody knows his job as well as Pigsfoot, Jack," I say.

"I guess you are right there," Jack Keegan says. "I never see a better hand than old Pigsfoot, but," he says, "let us make this a quick one. My guy is always very nervous when he is in there with strangers. He will be all upset when he hears about Pigsfoot as they are such good friends. In fact," Jack says, "the chances are he will commence imagining there is something wrong with his own appendix. Chester is always imagining there is something wrong with him."

"Well, Jack," I say, "as long as he only imagines it, what difference does it make?"

"Why," Jack Keegan says, "it makes the difference that he keeps us broke half the time paying for doctors to look him over. Who will you get to take Pigsfoot's place, Spider?"

Well, I tell Jack Keegan I wish to think this over a while before I decide and that I will telephone him a little later and tell him the name so he can give it to Ike Clonsky, for the truth of the matter is I do not have another such a guy as Jack Keegan desires available at the moment and I want time to figure out where I can get one.

In the meantime, I go back to the hospital to see Pigsfoot because I get to thinking that maybe after a few days rest from the operation he may be able to go in there with Chester Nubbs after all and save us the expense of bringing in another guy and anyhow the way I look at it, Pigsfoot may just as well be lying down in the ring as in the hospital.

But it seems that Pigsfoot is just out from under the ether when I get to the hospital and he is very weak and what is more he is very fretful because he is in a public ward and he says if I do not get him a private room and a special nurse he will send for a scribe from one of the blats and tell him all about how he was brought to Philadelphia, Pa., by me for the purpose of defrauding the public by going in the tank for Chester Nubbs.

Naturally I am somewhat horrified at this ingratitude on Pigsfoot's part but I can see where a beef from him just at this time may disarrange the plans for the show and perhaps damage my professional reputation, so I order a room and a nurse for him without ever bothering to request him to appear against Chester Nubbs even for a few minutes.

They have Pigsfoot removed to the private room and get in the special nurse for him before I depart and I wish to say I never see a prettier little cupcake than this nurse and in fact she is so cute that I have half a notion to tell Pigsfoot to move over and let me in the kip beside him. She is maybe twenty years old and has black hair and black eyes and is as lively as a pup and the minute Pigsfoot sees her he starts to improve rapidly.

I leave the nurse smoothing Pigsfoot's pillow and go out and stand in front of the hospital a while and give a little earnest thought to this situation and I am very much depressed about it, indeed, because the way I size it up after I pay Pigsfoot's hospital bill and then pay another guy to take his place with Chester Nubbs, I am going to finish away in the red.

In fact, nobody can blame me much if I abandon everything and go on back home but it is well known to one and all that I am all times a loyal character and I cannot bear to leave Pigsfoot in hock to a hospital in spite of his ingratitude, especially as I have many orders on hand for his services in the future.

Well, while I am standing there I notice a young guy leaning against a tree across the street from the hospital and what makes me notice him more than anything else is his size. He is maybe twenty-one or -two years old and stands at least six-three and weighs up around two hundred pounds and naturally I am always bound to notice a young guy this size no matter how many troubles I may have, because any young six-three and weighing two hundred may be the next heavyweight champion of the whole world.

I cross the street and take a closer swivel at the young guy and I can see that he is by no means a city character as he is wearing a checkered cap and a pinch-back coat and has a trusting expression in his eyes. He is watching the door of the hospital and after I case him a while and observe that he looks even bigger and better close up than he does from a distance, I speak to him:

"Son," I say, "what might you be doing here?"

"Why," the young guy says, "I am waiting for my sugar plum, Miss Babs Koogle, to get off work. She is a nurse in this hospital," he says.

"She has a nice name," I say.

"She is nice in every respect," he says. "She is beautiful and good. She comes from my home town of Pottsville, Pa., and we are sweethearts since childhood and," he says, "we are going to be married as soon as I can save up two hundred dollars."

"Son," I say, "that is a wonderful idea. When two parties, male and female, are in love, marriage is the only thing. Son," I say, "what is your name and what is your occupation?"

"My name is Caswell Fish," he says. "I am a lunch-counter waiter by trade when I am employed, but," he says, "I aim to have a diner car of my own in Pottsville, Pa., someday. I will call it Caswell's Eats. I am very ambitious," he says.

"Son," I say, "you are no longer a waiter. You are now a prize fighter and," I say, "your name is the Louisiana Leopard. You are so called because of the animal in you."

Well, at this Caswell becomes greatly alarmed and starts off up the street but I keep right at his hip and explain that all he has to do to make the two hundred clams for himself that will enable him to get married is to let Chester Nubbs wave at him a couple of times and to then remain quite still for ten seconds, although of course I do not explain that Chester may bop him on the button to make sure he remains still.

At first Caswell is greatly opposed to the idea because he says he not only never has a fight but that he considers prize fighting brutal and degrading but finally I tell him that maybe he can get two-fifty for his bit and then he becomes more interested. He says that such a sum will undoubtedly be most convenient to him in every manner but next he gets to worrying that maybe his sweet pea may not like the idea.

However, I explain very carefully to him that there is really no law that requires him to tell her of the matter and that in fact it may be a nice thing to surprise her with the money afterward and Caswell says he can see that I am a very smart fellow to be sure and the upshot of it all is he agrees to become the Louisiana Leopard.

Then I telephone Jack Keegan and explain I have the right party as a substitute for Pigsfoot and that it will be necessary for me to hide him out for a while to coach him in his duties and that I will also require a couple of C's over and above the contract price to pay all this unexpected expense and Jack Keegan says this is fair enough and that he will take care of the matter out of Chester Nubbs' end.

So Caswell calls up the hospital and tells Miss Babs Koogle that he suddenly lands himself a temporary waiter job with a swell hunting party that is leaving for the Pocono Mountains right away and that she may not hear from him for a while and he gives her so many kisses over the phone that the operator charges him an extra dime for overtime and I can see that this is indeed love and that Caswell also has a little natural cunning in being able to think up such a story.

Then I take him to a little country hotel a few miles out of Philadelphia, Pa., and begin schooling him on how to act in the dressing room and in the ring and what to say if any scribes get hold of him and ask him questions and on how to fall properly and I wish to say that Caswell turns out to be a very apt pupil in every respect, particularly in learning how to fall properly.

What is more, he turns out to be a right nice young character and I can see that he will make an excellent husband for Miss Babs Koogle or anybody else for that matter and I am pleased to be able to give him this start in life, especially when he agrees to accept two-twenty-five for his bit instead of two-fifty. He says that with such a sum he can not only get married at once but can make the first down payment on a diner car in Pottsville and he is very happy, indeed, over his prospects.

About the sixth day we are there, Jack Keegan comes out and says he wishes to take a peek at the Louisiana Leopard and when I show him Caswell he looks him over very carefully and nods his head and says that Caswell seems all right.

"Why, Jack," I say, "you are not worrying about someone I personally guarantee, are you?"

"Well, Spide," Jack Keegan says, "I am not worrying, but you know yourself that in this game you cannot afford to take any chances. This one has to be all right because I am unable to get Chester to train a minute for it. He is in love and wishes to get married, and," Jack says, "it is all your fault."

"What do you mean it is my fault?" I say.

"Why," Jack says, "it is your fault for bringing Pigsfoot here with an appendix. Chester goes to the hospital every day and sits with him by the hour and he meets a pancake by the name of Miss Babs Koogle who is nursing Pigsfoot and this is the party he is in love with and wishes to marry."

"Koogle?" I say to Jack Keegan. "Sh-h-h," I say, "not so loud. Why, she is undoubtedly the Louisiana Leopard's nasturtium. Sh-h-h," I say. "If the Leopard finds out about this we will have no Leopard. Does Miss Koogle love Chester?" I say.

"Why, I suppose so," Jack says. "What dame can resist a big swell-looking guy like him and the next heavyweight champion of the whole world to boot? Well, I hope Chester does not find out he is fighting a rival in love or he will try to kill the Leopard and," Jack says, "I do not care to be a party to the murder of a harmless guy like him. This is indeed a situation," he says.

In fact, it is such a situation that I go in to Philadelphia, Pa., and over to the hospital to see Pigsfoot Groody and find out what is going on and by this time he is able to be up and sitting out in the hospital yard and I discover him talking to a nurse who is by no means Miss Babs Koogle but almost as pretty.

"This is Miss Kitty Kronin," Pigsfoot says. "She is a friend of Miss Koogle's and very nice."

Naturally I can see this for myself without Pigsfoot telling me but I request Miss Kronin to move away a few paces while I talk to Pigsfoot and then I ask him what about this business of Chester Nubbs and Miss Babs Koogle.

"Well, Spide," Pigsfoot says, "you cannot blame Chester. Miss Koogle is nice. She is not my type but she is nice. By the way, Spide," he says, "who is this Louisiana Leopard the blats say you get to take my place with Chester? Is he someone I know?"

"Does Miss Babs Koogle love Chester?" I ask, paying no attention to his question.

"Well," Pigsfoot says, "who can tell about such things? Chester has glamor, especially when he lets that left hook go. Miss Babs Koogle is going to the fight as his guest, and," Pigsfoot says, "I guess any broad is bound to admire his left hook. Personally I am only glad I am not the Louisiana Leopard because," he says, "Chester will be putting everything he has got on that left hook to impress Miss Babs Koogle. By the way Spide," he says, "have you noticed how nice Miss Kronin really is?"

Well, to tell the truth I noticed it so much that when a guy in white clothes comes out and says Pigsfoot has got to go in and take a rest I make a date for dinner with Miss Kronin and I find her so nice that I almost forget to return to Caswell.

Naturally, it is most disquieting news to me that Miss Babs Koogle is going to be a spectator at the fight as I can see where it may lead to complications, but I figure the best way to do is to meet complications as they arise, so I continue working with Caswell.

What worries me about him more than anything else is the way he looks when he gets his clothes off. He looks like an athlete with them on but when he strips his skin is as soft as a baby's and whiter than a tombstone and right away you say to yourself that if this guy is a fighter I am a plumber. In fact, he has the softest, whitest skin I ever see in my life, male or female, and when Ike Clonsky the promoter comes out to see what the Louisiana Leopard looks like, he lets out a terrible squawk about Caswell being so white.

Ike says we will all be arrested for putting an invalid in the ring with the leading contender for the heavyweight championship of the whole world and he tells me to get one of those sun lamps and tan Caswell up and make him look athletic so the customers will not think he is a fugitive from a graveyard.

Well, I inquire around and find that sun lamps cost money and I feel that my nut is already big enough as it is for this occasion, so finally I get a bottle of iodine and a brush and paint two coats of it on Caswell's body and he comes out looking just like a bronzed statue and very beautiful.

But it seems that I put too much of the iodine on in spots and after a while Caswell begins to suffer from the sting no little and quite some and in fact he suffers so that he is screaming at the top of his voice and calling me names that I never suspect they even know in Pottsville, Pa., and nothing will do but I must get some soap and water and try to scrub some of the iodine off.

But no matter how much I scrub I cannot erase all the iodine and in fact the scrubbing only leaves Caswell with brown splotches all over him. However, the scrubbing eases the pain no little and Caswell says that is all he is interested in and that he does not care a whoop if he looks athletic or not.

Well, the next night is the night of the fight and by the time Caswell and I arrive at the arena the place is jammed to the doors and thousands of customers are being turned away, for Chester Nubbs is without doubt a wonderful drawing card. Of course all the customers know very well that Chester is only fighting some parasol, for in Philadelphia, Pa., the customers are smartened up to the prize-fight game and they know they are not going to get to see a world war for three dollars tops. In fact, all they care about is seeing Chester Nubbs with his clothes off.

As soon as I plant Caswell in a dressing room in charge of a friend of mine by the name of Kid Slussman who is going to assist me in the corner, I go out into the arena looking for Miss Babs Koogle and sure enough there she is in an aisle seat in the third row and prettier than ever, which makes her very pretty, indeed. I squat down on my haunches beside her and ask her if she remembers me and after gazing at me a while, Miss Babs Koogle says:

"Oh, yes, I remember you," she says. "You are the hardhearted skinflint manager of that poor fellow Mr. Groody that I am attending in the hospital. He tells me all about you," she says. "He tells me you are a terrible person, to be sure."

"Oh," I say, "he does, does he? Well, I will take that up later with him. I have more important business right now. Listen, little miss," I say, "kindly do not be surprised when you see who Chester Nubbs' opponent is and do not create any scenes because he is nobody but a friend of yours by the name of Caswell Fish."

"Caswell Fish is up in the Pocono Mountains," Miss Babs Koogle says.

"Caswell Fish is back here in a dressing room," I say. "You will presently see him in the ring as the Louisiana Leopard, but," I say, "do not be alarmed at his appearance. He has slight discolorations on his person where the iodine fails to come off, but he is all right and in good health and no harm will befall him."

"What iodine?" Miss Babs Koogle asks.

Then I quickly explain to her how I try to tan Caswell up to make him look athletic and how he is to get two-twenty-five cash money for a brief appearance in the ring with Chester Nubbs and how she and Caswell can then get married and embark in business in a diner car in Pottsville, Pa., and what is more I add my blessing, but all the time

I am explaining Miss Babs Koogle seems greatly agitated and finally she says to me like this:

"But Chester will kill Caswell," she says. "Chester tells me only this afternoon that he is going to murder his opponent tonight just to show me how good he is, but of course I have no idea Caswell is the opponent. I do not want Caswell murdered," she says. "I will find Chester and tell him not to commit this crime."

"Look, little miss," I say, "that is the surest way I know to get Caswell really murdered. When Chester says he is going to murder somebody it is just a way of saying and does not mean that he is really going to commit homicide, but," I say, "if Chester thinks you have a kindly interest in Caswell he will most certainly become felonious, because I hear he loves you and Chester is not such a guy as will brook a rival in the land of the living."

Well, by this time Miss Babs Koogle is crying bitterly, so I pat her on the back and say to her in a kindly tone of voice like this:

"Little miss," I say, "if you just let nature take its course Caswell will not get a scratch, unless," I say, "Chester can punch faster than Caswell can fall and the best anybody has ever been able to do on a guy schooled by Spider McCoy is just a glancing blow. Anyway," I say, "promise me no embarrassing scenes."

She looks at me through her tears and nods her head and I return to the dressing room saying to myself that Miss Babs Koogle displays a fine character in not wishing Chester Nubbs to be a murderer and then I escort Caswell into the ring with a bathrobe around him and sit down on a stool in a corner and I am really quite surprised at the way he sits there very composed, looking around at the crowd.

I am wondering what he will say when he sees Miss Babs Koogle there at the ringside but he does not seem to notice her and I am trying to decide if it will be a good idea to call his attention to her when Chester Nubbs comes down the aisle on which she is sitting and the cheering and the confusion generally makes me forget all about her.

"Now, son," I say to Caswell, as I am putting the gloves on his dukes there in the corner, "in a couple of minutes you will be on your own. Just walk out there with your hands up like I show you, and," I say, "when you see or smell something coming your way the thing to do is to fall down and lie perfectly still until you feel me picking you up."

"Mr. McCoy," Caswell says, "I am determined to endeavor to give Chester Nubbs a terrific thrashing. I may go down," he says, "but it will be only after a spirited defense. I refuse to show the white feather in front of a little two-timer like Miss Babs Koogle in the manner you suggest."

"Oh," I say, "you see her, do you?"

"Mr. McCoy," Caswell says, "I first commence to wonder slightly about Miss Babs Koogle the night I overhear Mr. Keegan telling you Chester Nubbs loves her and wishes to marry her. Well," Caswell says, "I figure that even if this is true it is entirely one-sided. I figure that Miss Babs Koogle's love for me will never die but I can scarcely blame another man for loving her, too.

"But," Caswell says, "I just observe something that proves to me that Miss Babs Koogle reciprocates his love. I just observe my former honeysuckle hand him a note as he passes her coming down the aisle," Caswell says. "It must be a love note, because," he says, "you do not notice her handing me any notes, do you? He has it in his glove at this moment. I will endeavor to knock it down his throat. I mean the glove," Caswell says.

"Look, Caswell," I say, "when you get to be as old as I am you will learn that all broads are two-timers. In fact," I say, "some are three-timers, but none of them are worth getting killed for."

But Caswell only shakes his head and looks determined. But I do not have any more time to argue because the referee is calling Chester and Caswell together in the center of the ring for instructions, so I lead Caswell out there.

Well, when I remove Caswell's robe and he stands out under the lights the spots on his body are plain to be seen and in fact he looks as if he has on a brown polka-dot dressing gown and the crowd probably figures that these spots are why he is called the Louisiana Leopard and there is some laughter here and there.

However, I wish to state that I cannot help feeling proud of Caswell, he conducts himself so nobly while listening to instructions and, in fact, you will think he is an old-timer at the business. Then I notice that Chester does not come near the group in the center of the ring but hangs on the outskirts and while I figure this is because Chester is not much interested in these preliminaries I feel that it will make things look better if he does not appear so nonchalant.

But when the bell rings and Caswell walks out of his corner as bold as a lion, I am greatly astonished to see Chester Nubbs go sliding along the ropes away from Caswell instead of stepping forward and hitting Caswell on the pimple per expectations of one and all. The next thing I know there is Caswell running after Chester and Chester is circling the ring like a scared wolf and once when they pass my corner Caswell stops and says to me like this:

"Mr. McCoy," he says, "head him off the next time he comes your way, will you?"

Well, Chester never lets Caswell get near enough to him in the first round to hand him a ripe peach and personally I consider it a most surprising spectacle but the crowd thinks Chester is giving it a run for its money by displaying his skill in keeping away from an opponent and applauds him heartily.

I am wondering myself if this is the idea and then I notice Jack Keegan in Chester's corner and Jack is making signals at me when nobody is looking and I figure he is trying to remind me in sign language of what Caswell is supposed to do and I try to tell him back in sign language that I remember all right but what is the idea of Chester Nubbs running all over town?

But I can see that Jack Keegan is trying to figure this out himself when Chester keeps running away from Caswell all through the second round, too. In fact, six rounds go by before anybody has time to think and Caswell is getting pretty well tuckered out from running and swinging and missing, for not a punch is landed by either Chester or Caswell in these rounds.

By now I can see that there is something radically wrong with Chester and I am wondering if he breaks both hands before coming into the ring or what, and Jack Keegan is being threatened with the air by the boxing inspectors for the language he is using to Chester Nubbs, though afterward I hear Chester never answers a word back and Caswell is unable to say more than yes or no to me because he is puffing so hard from his running.

Well, all of a sudden I realize that there I am with a guy on the verge of going the limit with the leading contender for the heavyweight championship of the whole world and maybe winning the decision, so naturally I begin giving Caswell a little judicious advice, hoping all the time there is really something the matter with Chester Nubbs and that he is not just laying back to the last round to kiss Caswell with his left hook.

I notice Jack Keegan trying to show me a big-bladed pocket knife but by this time I am too excited to pay any attention to sign language and in fact everybody else is somewhat excited although many spectators are speaking most unkindly of Chester Nubbs. As the final bell rings, Chester runs right out of the ring and up the aisle to his dressing room without waiting to hear the decision and the crowd makes such a racket that I scarcely hear it myself but I know it goes to Caswell.

Well, I have a terrible struggle getting Caswell through the throng and back to our dressing room and the first one in there is nobody but Miss Babs Koogle and she throws her arms around Caswell's neck and says to him like this:

"Oh, Caswell," she says, "you are wonderful, and I love you so."

"Miss Koogle," I say, "you are too late. Caswell's eyes are opened at last to your two-timing of him with Chester Nubbs when you pass that love note to Chester tonight."

Well, at this Miss Babs Koogle starts to laugh and she says:

"So it is a love note, is it?" she says. "Mr. McCoy," she says, "don't you know Chester Nubbs is a confirmed hypochondriac?"

"Is that so?" I say. "Well, fighters go up against anything. They get all kinds of habits if you don't watch them," I say.

"It is not a habit," Miss Babs Koogle says. "Chester Nubbs is always worrying about his health and always worrying about catching some disease. The note I hand him tonight," she says, "warns him to observe his opponent's body closely and he will note copper-colored spots all over him. The note suggests that spots of this nature are sometimes characteristic of leprosy and that it may be a good idea for Chester to avoid personal contact with his opponent, and," she says, "you see what happens."

"I see," I say. "But," I say, "I hear that Chester Nubbs wishes to marry you."

"Chester wishes to marry me," Miss Babs Koogle says, "but he does not love me. At least not the way Caswell does. Chester figures it will be mighty convenient for him if he has a trained nurse around all the time to look after him when he does not feel well, and," Miss Babs Koogle says, "Chester never feels well. Anyway, I will never marry a prize fighter."

"Sweetheart," Caswell says, "that is one thing you know I will never be."

At this moment there is some confusion outside the room and in comes Jack Keegan and Chester Nubbs and Jack says to me like this:

"Oh, there you are, you double-crossing old pelican," he says, "take this."

"And this," Chester Nubbs says.

Then they biff me one after the other and although I am somewhat dazed by the force of their blows I always remember that Keegan punches harder than Chester and that when Chester starts his left hook he drops it low and if ever I get a guy with a good right I will show him how to lick this bum with a right-hand shot inside the hook.

But of course the guy will not be Caswell Fish because the last I see of him and Miss Babs Koogle after I pay him off they are headed for Pottsville, Pa., and they never even invite me to come to their wedding. So that is all there is to the story (Spider McCoy says).

"Well, Spider," I say, "I can see it is all a most unhappy experience for you and you have my sympathy, especially," I say, "because of those injuries that leave you so wan and pale."

"Oh," Spider says, "that is something else again. It seems that Miss Kitty Kronin works in the contagious ward of that hospital and Pigs-foot and I are both laid up with the measles for three weeks from associating with her."

Blonde Mink

Now of course there are many different ways of cooking tripe but personally I prefer it stewed with tomatoes and mushrooms and a bit of garlic and in fact I am partaking of a portion in this form in Mindy's restaurant on Broadway one evening in January when a personality by the name of Julie the Starker sits down at my table and leans over and sniffs my dish and says to me like this:

"Tripe," he says. "With garlic," he says. "Why, this is according to the recipe of the late Slats Slavin who obtains it from his old Aunt Margaret in Troy. Waiter," he says, "bring me an order of this delicious concoction only with more garlic. It is getting colder outside and a guy needs garlic in his system to thicken his blood. Well," he says, "this is indeed a coincidence because I just come from visiting the late Slats and having a small chat with him."

Naturally I am somewhat surprised by this statement as I know the late Slats is resting in Woodlawn Cemetery and to tell the truth I remember I am present as a pallbearer when he is placed there to rest but I am also pleased to hear these tidings as Slats is always a good friend of mine and no nicer guy ever steps in shoeleather.

"Well," I say to Julie, "and how is Slats these days?"

"He is cold," Julie says. "He states that it is very crimpy around the edges up there in Woodlawn especially at night. You know the late Slats always hates cold weather. He is usually in Florida by this time of year to duck the chill.

"Furthermore," Julie says, "he is greatly embarrassed up there without a stone over him such as Beatrice promises to get him. He says it makes him feel like a bum with nothing to show who he is when all around him are many fine markers including one of black marble to the memory of the late Cockeyed Corrigan who as you know is of no consequence compared to the late Slats who is really somebody."

Well, of course this is very true because the late Slats is formerly known and esteemed by one and all on Broadway as one of the smartest operators in horse racing that ever draws breath. He is a handicapper by trade and his figures on the horses that are apt to win are so highly prized that one night he is stuck up by a couple of guys when he has six thou in cash money on him but all they want is his figures on the next day's races.

He is a player and a layer. He will bet on the horses himself when he sees spots he fancies or he will let you bet him on them and he has clients all over the United States who call him up at his office on Broadway and transact business with him one way or the other. He is a tall guy in his late forties who is not much thicker than a lath which is why he is called Slats though his first name is really Terence.

He is by no means Mr. America for looks but he dresses well and he is very rapid with a dollar. He is the softest touch in town for busted guys and he will get up in the middle of the night to do somebody a favor, consequently no one gets more or larger hellos along the main drag than the late Slats.

He comes from a little burg upstate by the name of Cohoes and I hear that he and Julie the Starker are friends from their short-pants days there although Julie is about the last one in the world you will expect to see a guy of class like Slats associating with as Julie is strictly in the muggola department.

He is about Slats' age and is short and thick and has a kisser that is surely a pain to even his own mamma. He is called Julie the Starker because starker means a strong rough guy and there is no doubt that Julie answers this description in every manner, shape and form.

He is at one time in his life a prize fighter but strictly a catcher which is a way of saying he catches everything the other guy throws at him and at other times he is a bouncer; I do not know what all else except that he has some Sing Sing background.

At all times he is a most undesirable personality but he is very fond of the late Slats Slavin and vice versa, and they get along together in a way that is most astonishing to behold.

He is not only a handy guy for Slats but he is also a social companion and for some years wherever you see Slats you are apt to see Julie the Starker except when Slats is with his fiancée Miss Beatrice Gee and even then you may see Julie though as a rule Miss Beatrice Gee does not approve of him any more than she does of leprosy. In fact, she makes no bones about considering the very sight of Julie revolting to her.

In addition to being the late Slats' fiancée, Miss Beatrice Gee is at this time a prominent show girl in one of Mike Todd's musical shows and she is conceded by one and all to be the most beautiful object on Manhattan Island or anyway no worse than a photo finish for the most beautiful.

She is an original brunette and is quite tall and carries herself in a way that the late Slats says is dignity, though it really comes of Mike Todd's director putting a big copy of the Bible on her head and saying she will either learn to walk balancing it or else, though he never does tell her or else what.

Other dolls call Miss Beatrice Gee a clothes horse because it seems she wears clothes with great skill and furthermore she is crazy about them although her best hold is not wearing them, which she also does with great skill but of course only on the stage. When she is not on the stage she is always groomed like a stake horse going to the post for a big race, and no one takes greater pride in her appearance than the late Slats Slavin, except Miss Beatrice Gee herself.

While I do not believe the story that once when she has a headache and Doc Kelton puts his thermometer in her mouth, to see if she is running a temperature, the mercury freezes tight, there is no doubt that Beatrice is not the emotional type and to be very frank about the matter many think she is downright frosty. But of course no one ever mentions this to the late Slats because he is greatly in love and the chances are he maybe thinks Beatrice is hotter than a stove and personally I am in no position to deny it.

Well, in much less time than it takes me to tell you all this, Julie the Starker has his tripe and is eating it with more sound than is altogether necessary for tripe no matter how it is cooked and to tell the truth I have to wait until he pauses before I can make him hear my voice above his eating. Then I say to him like this:

"Why, Julie," I say, "I cannot understand why Slats is in the plight you describe with reference to the stone. I am under the impression that he leaves Beatrice well loaded as far as the do-re-mi is concerned and I take it for granted that she handles the stone situation. By the way, Julie," I say, "does Slats say anything to you about any horses anywhere for tomorrow?"

"No," Julie says. "But if you have a minute to spare I will tell you the story of Beatrice and her failure to take care of the matter of the stone for the late Slats. It is really a great scandal."

Then without waiting to hear if I have a minute to spare or not, he starts telling me, and it seems it all goes back to a night in late September when Beatrice informs Slats that she just comes upon a great bargain in a blonde mink coat for twenty-three thousand dollars and that she desires same at once to keep herself warm during the impending winter although she already had enough fur coats in her closet to keep not only herself warm but half of Syracuse, too.

"Pardon me, Julie," I say at this point, "but what is a blonde mink?"

"Why," Julie says, "that is the very question Slats asks and he learns from Beatrice that it is a new light-colored mink fur that is sometimes called blue mink and sometimes platinum mink and sometimes blonde mink and he also learns that no matter what it is called, it is very, very expensive, and after Slats gets all this info he speaks to Beatrice as follows:

" 'Baby,' he says, 'you cut right to the crimp when you mention twenty-three thou because that is exactly the size of the bank roll at this moment. But I just come off a tough season and I will need all my ready for navigating purposes the next few months and besides it looks like a mild winter and you can wear your old last season's leopard or caracul or ermine or Persian lamb or beaver until I get going again.' "

Now at this (Julie the Starker says) Beatrice flies into a terrible rage and tells Slats that he is a tightwad and a skinflint and a miser, and that he has no heart and no pride or he will not suggest that she go around in such shabby old floogers and that she will never humiliate herself in this manner. She says if she waits even a few minutes, someone else is sure to snap up the blonde mink and that she may never again meet with a similar opportunity.

"Well, they have a large quarrel," Julie says, "and when Slats and I get back to his hotel apartment that night he complains of not feeling any too well and in fact he finally keels over on the bed with his tongue hanging out and I send for Doc Kelton who says it is a heart attack and very bad.

"He says to tell the truth it is 100 to 1 Slats will not beat it, and then Doc takes his departure stating that he has so many shorter-priced patients he cannot afford to waste time on long shots and he leaves it to me to notify Slats that his number is up.

"On receiving this information, Slats requests me to find Miss Beatrice Gee and bring her to his bedside, which I do, although at first she is much opposed to leaving her table in the Stork Club where she is the center of a gay throng until I whisper to her that I will be compelled to flatten her and carry her unless she does.

"But on arriving at Slats' apartment and realizing that he is indeed an invalid, Beatrice seems to be quite downcast and starts to shed tears all over the joint, and I have no doubt that some of them are on the level because surely she must remember how kind Slats is to her.

"Then Slats says he wishes to talk to Beatrice alone and requests me to go into the next room, but of course I have a crack in the door so I can hear what goes on between them and what I hear is Slats saying to Beatrice like this:

" 'Baby,' he says, 'reach in under my pillow and get the package of currency there. It is the twenty-three I tell you about and it is all the dough I have in the world. It is all yours except twenty-six hundred which you are to pay Clancy Brothers the tombstone makers in Yonkers for a stone I pick out for myself some time ago and forget to pay for although my plot in Woodlawn is free and clear.

" 'It is a long stone of white Carrara marble in excellent taste,' Slats says. 'It is to lie flat over my last resting place, not to stand upright, and it is cut to exactly cover same from end to end and side to side. I order it in this form,' Slats says, 'because I am always a restless soul and long have a fear I may not lie quietly in my last resting place but may wish to roam around unless there is a sort of lid over me such as this stone. And besides,' he says, 'it will keep the snow off me. I loathe and despise the snow. I will leave the engraving to you, Baby, but promise you will take care of the stone at once.'

"Well, I hear Beatrice promise between sobs, and also no doubt as she is reaching under the pillow for Slats' plant, and when I step back into the room a little later, Slats is a goner and Beatrice is now really letting the salt water flow freely, although her best effort is in Woodlawn two days later when it looks as if we will have to send for a siphon to unflood the premises.

"But to show you what a smart strudel Beatrice is, she is around the day after we place the late Slats to rest saying that he does not leave her a thin dime. You see, she is figuring against the chance that relatives of Slats may show up and claim his estate and she even lets Slats' lodge pay the funeral expenses although of course this is no more than is coming to any departed brother.

"I do not dispute her statement because I think she is entitled to the dough as long as Slats gives it to her and of course I take it for granted that she will split herself out from enough of the swag to buy the stone according to her promise and in fact I am so sure of this that one afternoon last week I go out to Woodlawn not only to pay my respects to the memory of the late Slats but to see how his last resting place looks with the stone over it.

"Well, what do I see but Slats himself walking around and around a mound of dried earth with some withered flowers scattered over it and among these flowers I recognize my own wreath which says 'So long, pal' on it and which costs me a double-saw, but there is no stone whatsoever over the mound, not even as much as a weentsy little pebble."

"Just a minute, Julie," I say. "You state that you see the late Slats walking around and about. Do you see him all pale and vapory?"

"Well," Julie says, "now you mention it, I do seem to recall that Slats is a little on the pale side of what he used to be. But he is otherwise unchanged except that he is not wearing his derby hat as usual. We do not give him his derby hat when we place him to rest, as the undertaker guy says it is not neccessary. Anyway, when he spies me, Slats stops walking and sits down on the edge of the late Cockeyed Corrigan's black marble marker, which is practically next door to him and says to me like this:

" 'Hello, Julie,' he says. 'I am commencing to wonder what becomes of you. I am walking around here for weeks trying to keep warm and I am all tuckered out. What do you suppose is the idea of not providing people with overcoats when they are placed to rest? Only I do not rest, Julie. Do you see Beatrice lately and what does she say about my stone?'

" 'Slats,' I say, 'I must confess I do not see Beatrice lately, but I never dream she does not provide the stone long before this as per her promise which I can tell you now I overhear her make to you. A solemn deathbed promise.'

" 'Never mind what kind of bed it is,' Slats says. 'It is a morbid topic. And I think you have plenty of gall to be on the Erie when I am saying my last goodby to my baby. You owe us both an apology. Look her up right away and give her a good one and ask her what about my stone. The chances are there is a hitch somewhere. Maybe the engraving is causing the delay. I am sure Beatrice will wish something sentimental on it like Sleep well my beloved, and engraving takes time.'

"Well, I am about to mention that she already takes time enough to have George Washington's farewell address engraved on it but all of a sudden the late Slats disappears from sight and I take this as a hint for me to blow, too, and that very night I hunt up Beatrice to give her Slats' message.

"I find her standing at the bar of a gaff called the Palmetto with a couple of guys and I notice she is wearing a fur coat the color of mist that I do not remember ever seeing on her before and I turn to a dame who is sitting at a table and say to her like this:

" 'Pardon me, little miss,' I say, 'but just to satisfy my curiosity, can you tell me the name of the fur that party over yonder is wearing?'

" 'Blonde mink,' she says. 'It is perfectly beautiful too.'

" 'And what does such a garment cost?' I ask.

" 'Why,' she says, 'that one seems to be first-class merchandise. It costs twenty-five thousand dollars. Maybe more, but not much less. It is the very newest fur out.'

"Then I walk over to Beatrice and tap her on the shoulder, and when she turns I motion her out of hearing distance of the guys she is with and speak to her as follows:

" 'Well, Bea,' I say, 'your new coat must hang a little heavy on you considering that it represents the weight of a nice tombstone. I never mention it to you before but I hear your last chat with the late Slats Slavin including your promise but until I find you in this lovely benny no one will ever make me believe you mean to welch on your word.'

" 'All right, all right,' she says. 'So I do not buy the stone. But it costs twenty-six hundred and all I have is twenty-three thousand and an odd tenner and this coat is a steal at twenty-three. If I wait another minute longer someone else is sure to snap it up and the dealer wants his all cash. Besides Slats will never know he does not get the stone.'

" 'Bea,' I says, 'I have a talk with Slats today at Woodlawn. He knows he has no stone and he is upset about it. But he is making excuses for you, Bea. He figures you are unexpectedly delayed a bit in getting it there. You have the guy fooled even yet.'

"At this Beatrice gazes at me for some time without saying a word and I notice that looking into her eyes is just the same as looking into a couple of ice cubes. Then she gives her coat a hitch and brings it closer around her and finally she says:

" 'Julie,' she says, 'I want to tell you something. If ever again you speak to me or about me I will start remembering out loud that Slats has a large bundle of cash on him that last night and I will also start wondering out loud what becomes of it and a guy with your biography cannot stand much wonderment such as that. And if you see Slats again tell him how I look in my new coat.'

" 'Bea,' I say, 'you will never have any luck with your new coat because it means leaving poor Slats up there in Woodlawn restless and cold.'

" 'No luck?' she says. 'Listen,' she says, 'do you see the dopey-looking little punk in the uniform leaning against the bar? His name is Freddy Voogan and his papa is a squillionaire out in Denver and I am going to marry the kid any minute and what do you think gets him for me? My blonde mink. He notices how nice I look in it and insists on meeting me. No luck?' Beatrice says. 'Is kicking up a gold mine no luck?'

" 'Bea,' I say, 'it is bad enough to rob the grave as you already do but it is even worse to rob the cradle.'

" 'Goodby, Julie,' Bea says. 'Do not forget to tell Slats how I looked in my new coat.'

"Well, I will say she looks wonderful in it even though I am greatly disappointed in her because it is plain to be seen that Beatrice has no sentiment about the past. So now I am compelled to report back to the late Slats Slavin that he is on a bust as far as the stone is concerned and I hope and trust that my revelation will not cause him too much anguish."

And with this, Julie the Starker dunks up the last of the tripe gravy
on his plate with a piece of rye bread and gets up to take his departure
and I say to him like this:

"Julie," I say, "if you happen to think of it, kindly ask the late Slats
to look over the entries at Hialeah for the next few days and if he
can send me a winner now and then I can get parties to bet a little
for me."

"Well," Julie says, "Slats has other things on his mind besides horses
right now, but," he says, "I will try to remember your request although
of course you will carry me for a small piece of your end."

Then he leaves me and I am still sitting there when a plain-clothes
copper by the name of Johnny Brannigan comes in and sits down in
the chair Julie just vacates and orders some Danish pastry and a cup
of Java, and then almost as if he hears the conversation between
Julie and me he says:

"Oh, hello," he says. "How well do you know Miss Beatrice Gee
who is formerly the fiancée of the late Slats Slavin? I mean how well
do you know her history and most especially do you know any knocks
against her?"

"Why?" I say.

"Well," Johnny says, "it is strictly an unofficial question. There is
hell up Ninth Street over her. A family out in Denver that must have
more weight than Pike's Peak gets the Denver police department to ask
our department very quietly about her, and our department requests
me to make a few inquiries.

"Of course it is not an official police matter. It is an exchange of
courtesies.

"It seems," Johnny says, "that Miss Beatrice Gee is going to marry
a member of this family who is under twenty-one years of age and his
papa and mamma are doing handstands about it, though personally,"
Johnny says, "I believe in letting love take its course. But," he says, "my
theory has nothing to do with the fact that I promise to make a return
of some kind on this blintz."

"Well, Johnny," I say, "I do not know anything whatever about her
but you just miss a guy who can probably give you a complete run-
down on her. You just miss Julie the Starker. However," I say, "I am
pretty sure to run into him tomorrow and will tell him to contact
you."

But I do not see Julie the next day or for several days after that and
I am greatly disappointed as I not only wish to tell him to get in touch
with Johnny but I am anxious to learn if Slats sends me any info on
the horses. For that matter I do not see Johnny Brannigan either until

late one afternoon I run into him on Broadway and he says to me like this:

"Say," he says, "you are just the guy I am looking for. Do you see the late editions of the blats?"

"No," I say, "why?"

"Well," Johnny says, "they are carrying big stories about the finding of Miss Beatrice Gee in her apartment in East 57th Street as dead as a doornail. It looks as if the young guy from Denver she is going to marry bounces a big bronze lamp off her coco in what the scribes will undoubtedly call a fit of jealous rage because he has a big row with her early in the evening in the Canary Club when he finds a Marine captain from the Pacific teaching her how the island natives in those parts rub noses when they greet each other, although the young guy claims he walks away from her then and does not see her again because he is too busy loading himself up with champagne.

"But," Johnny says, "he is found unconscious from the champagne in his hotel room today and admits he does not remember when or where or what or why. My goodness," Johnny says, "the champagne they sell nowadays is worse than an anesthetic."

Naturally this news about Miss Beatrice Gee is quite distressing to me if only because of her former association with the Slats Slavin and I am sorry to hear of the young guy's plight, too, even though I do not know him. I am always sorry to hear of young guys in trouble and especially rich young guys but of course if they wish to mix bronze lamps with champagne they must take the consequences and I so state to Johnny Brannigan.

"Well," Johnny says, "he does not seem to be the bronze-lamp type, and yet who else has a motive to commit this deed? You must always consider the question of motive in crimes of this nature."

"What about robbery?" I say.

"No," Johnny says. "All her jewelry and other belongings are found in the apartment. The only thing missing as far as her maid and acquaintances can tell seems to be a new fur coat which she probably leaves some place in her wanderings during the evening. But now I remember why I am looking for you. I am still collecting data on Miss Beatrice Gee's background though this time officially and I recall you tell me that maybe Julie the Starker can give me some information and I wish to know where I am apt to find Julie."

"A new fur coat, Johnny?" I say. "Well," I say, "as a rule I am not in favor of aiding and abetting coppers but this matter seems different and if you will take a ride with me I think I may be able to lead you to Julie."

So I call a taxicab and as we get in, I tell the jockey to drive us to Woodlawn Cemetery and if Johnny Brannigan is surprised by our destination he does not crack but whiles away the time on the journey by relating many of his experiences as a copper, some of which are very interesting.

It is coming on dusk when we reach Woodlawn and while I have an idea of the general direction of the late Slats Slavin's last resting place, I have to keep the taxi guy driving around inside the gates for some time before I spot the exact location through recognizing the late Cockeyed Corrigan's black marble marker.

It is a short distance off the auto roadway so I have the hackie stop and Johnny Brannigan and I get out of the cab to walk a few yards to the mound and as we approach same who steps out from the shadow of the late Cockeyed Corrigan's marker but Julie the Starker who speaks to me as follows:

"Hello, hello," he says. "I am glad you see and I know you will be pleased to learn that the late Slats gives me a tip for you on a horse that goes at Hialeah tomorrow but the name escapes me at the moment. He says his figures make it an absolute kick in the pants. Well," Julie says, "stick around a while and maybe I will remember it."

Then he seems to notice the presence of Johnny Brannigan for the first time and to recognize him, too, because all of a sudden he outs with Captain Barker and says:

"Oh, a copper, eh?" he says. "Well, copper, here is a little kiss for you."

And with this he lets go a slug that misses Johnny Brannigan and knocks an arm off a pink stone cherub in the background and he is about to encore when Johnny blasts ahead of him, and Julie the Starker drops his pizzolover and his legs begin bending under him like Leon Errol's when Leon is playing a drunk.

He finally staggers up to the last resting place of the late Slats Slavin and falls there with the blood pumping from the hole that Johnny Brannigan drills in his chest and as I notice his lips moving I hasten to his side figuring that he may be about to utter the name of the horse Slats gives him for me.

Then I observe that there is something soft and fuzzy spread out on the mound under him that Julie the Starker pats weakly with one hand as he whispers to me like this:

"Well," he says, "the late Slats is not only resting in peace now with the same as his stone over him but he is as warm as toast and in fact warmer."

"The horse, Julie," I say. "What is the name of the horse?"

But Julie only closes his eyes and as it is plain to be seen that he now joins out permanently with the population of Woodlawn, Johnny Brannigan steps forward and rolls him off the mound with his foot and picks up the object that is under Julie and examines it in the dim light.

"I always think Julie is a little stir-crazy," Johnny says, "but I wonder why he takes a pop at me when all I want of him is to ask him some questions and I wonder, too, where this nice red fox fur coat comes from?"

Well, of course I know that Johnny will soon realize that Julie probably thinks Johnny wishes to chat with him about the job he does on Miss Beatrice Gee but at the moment I am too provoked about Julie holding out the tip the late Slats Slavin gives him for me to discuss the matter or even to explain that the red is only Julie's blood and that the coat is really blonde mink.

Big Boy Blues

IT IS ALONG toward 2 o'clock one pleasant A.M., and things are unusually quiet in Mindy's restaurant on Broadway and in fact only two customers besides myself are present when who comes in like a rush of air, hot or cold, but a large soldier crying out in a huge voice as follows:

"Hello, hello, hello, hello, hello."

Well, when I take a good glaum at him I can see that he is nobody but a personality by the name of West Side Willie who is formerly a ticket speculator on Broadway and when he comes over to me still going hello, hello, hello, hello, hello, I say to him quite severely like this:

"Willie," I say, "you are three hellos over what anybody is entitled to in Mindy's even if there is anybody here which as you can see for yourself is by no means the situation."

"Oh," Willie says, "I happen to have a few hellos to spare and besides I am so glad to get back on the big street again that I feel liberal. We are here for a run."

"Do you mean the war?" I say.

"I mean *Gee Eyes*, the soldier show I am with," Willie says. "We are a riot on the Coast. We lay them in the aisles in Denver. We kill people in Cleveland. We will do a wonderful trade here."

Then Willie sits down and explains to me that one day when he is in a camp in the desert out in California and practically dying by inches of the heat and the drilling and the victuals and the other hardships of soldier life and especially the victuals, his commanding officer sends for him and says:

"Klump," he says, for such is West Side Willie's family monicker, "they are organizing an all-soldier musical show at Santa Ana and there is a request out for the names of all enlisted men in this area who are formerly connected with show business.

"I understand," the commanding officer says, "that you are familiar with matters of this nature and you will therefore report at once to Santa Ana to participate although personally," he says, "I consider it all just so much fol-de-rol and how the hell we can win the war behind the footlights I do not know."

Well, naturally Willie does not inform the commanding officer that his connections with show business is slightly informal but he gets on a train at once and goes to Santa Ana and there he discovers that the guy who is putting on the show is nobody but a playwright by the name of Hathaway Go who is once befriended by Willie to the extent of a meal in a one-arm gaff in West Forty-ninth and who is grateful ever since.

He is slightly surprised to see Willie appear in answer to a call for show people as he is aware that Willie does not sing or dance or play an instrument but after hearing Willie's description of soldier life in the desert his heart is touched and he says he guesses he can use a sure-footed guy to take tickets although when Willie asks what about selling them Hathaway Go gives him such a long slow look that Willie never renews the subject.

However, he is greatly downcast when he thinks of the opportunities in connection with these pasteboards because he feels that everyone will want them and when Willie is in action on Broadway he is known far and wide for his skill in manipulating with tickets to theaters and prize fights and hockey games and one thing and another that everyone wants but are unable to get unless they see Willie and pay his ice, which is a way of saying his premiums.

I often hear complaint that sometimes Willie asks more ice than the face value of the tickets but this is probably only for tickets that are very hard indeed to get and naturally Willie is entitled to some compensation for saving the customers the trouble of standing in line at the box offices to buy the tickets and then finding the tickets are all gone anyway. Besides Willie frequently has to take acre of others out of his end to get the tickets in the first place so life is really not all ice with him.

"Well," Willie says, "I make the best of the position to which I am appointed although I must say the spectacle of throngs of customers being permitted to buy our tickets at face value at the box office when they will be delighted to pay two, three, four, five or six slugs premium if they cannot get them any other way is most disheartening to me.

"But," Willie says, "I become a terrific ticket taker. In fact," he says, "I am known as the Eisenhower of the front door. Furthermore, this assignment come to me in nick of time because my original outfit is sent to Europe where I understand the victuals are even worse than they are in camp and there is practically no hotel life for an enlisted man."

"Willie," I say, "I am glad to see you again and I congratulate you on your military career and hope and trust you do not sustain any wounds such as tearing off a hangnail by mistake for the stub of a ticket some night. I am sure that your engagement on Broadway will be most auspicious."

"Thanks," Willie says, "but we are all nervous and worried over a situation that develops here. Do you remember Johnny Blues? The one they call Big Boy Blues?"

"Why, certainly," I say. "I remember him as well as if he is my brother only I am thankful such is not the case."

"Do you know Big Boy Blues has a son?" Willie says.

"Yes," I say, "I know it. They call him Little Boy Blues."

"Well," Willie says, "Little Boy Blues is the star of our show. He is the greatest thing in it. He slays the customers. He is wonderful."

"Why, Willie," I say, "I am glad to hear this news. I not only remember Big Boy Blues but come to think of it I remember his ever-loving sheriff who is the mamma of Little Boy Blues, I hope. If he has any talent it must come from her because the only talent Big Boy Blues ever has that I recall is that he can crush a human skull with one blow of his fist even though the skull belongs to a copper.

"In fact," I say, "I recall the night he performs this feat on a copper by the name of Caswell. I seem to remember that Caswell is in Polyclinic hospital for eight weeks but he finally recovers and is now a captain."

"Listen," Willie says. "Little Boy Blues appears in our show as a female ballet dancer. He dresses as a dame in a short skirt and one thing and another."

Well, at this I am slightly horrified as I can see what West Side Willie has in mind. I can see that it is going to be a great shock to Big Boy Blues if he learns of the matter because it is only about a year back that he is along Broadway bragging about his son being in the Army and stating that Little Boy will undoubtedly destroy a large number of the enemy singlehanded.

Naturally, everybody agrees with him as Big Boy Blues strongly disapproves of anyone not agreeing with him and it is plain to be seen that after putting his son away as a destroyer he is apt to be displeased when he finds Little Boy is not only a ballet dancer but one in the attire of a doll and I so state to West Side Willie.

"Yes," Willie says, "that is exactly what we fear. We fear Big Boy will be so vexed he will tear the theater down stone by stone and maybe peg the stones at us. However, it is our information from Little Boy's mamma that Big Boy thinks his son is somewhere overseas and has no idea he is in our show and it is our hope that he does not hear of it until after opening night anyway.

"Then," Willie says, "we expect to be rolling so good that we can replace Little Boy if necessary, but," he says, "we positively need him for the first night because he is the best thing in the show by seven or eight lengths and it is a great pity we dast not give him some advance publicity. Well, I will bid you good night as I must catch myself a few snores. Our company gets into Grand Central at noon and I wish to be there to meet it."

Then Willie takes his departure and I remain sitting there awhile thinking of what a great surprise it is to Broadway years ago when Big Boy Blues hauls off and marries a small canape by the name of Miss Rosie Flynn who is singing in the old Golden Slipper Club in West Forty-eighth Street and how Bookie Bon goes around offering to lay plenty of 9 to 5 that Big Boy gives her at least two broken arms inside of two weeks and finding no takers as Big Boy is known to one and all as a crude character.

He is at least six feet three inches high and he weighs anyway 220 pounds and he has a loud voice that causes parties four blocks away to tremble when he lets it out and he has a record at police headquarters that consists mainly of mayhem. He is a doorman and a bouncer at the Golden Slipper when I first know him but one day he climbs on the seat of a stray truck and drives it off and the next thing anybody knows he has one of the largest trucking businesses in the city.

Now Miss Rosie Flynn does not weigh ninety pounds with her girdle on and she has red hair and freckles and is by no means a spectacular singer but she is practically famous on Broadway because it is generally conceded that she is pure. The chances are she can marry into much more genteel circles than those in which Big Boy Blues moves just on the strength of being pure and it is the popular belief that Big Boy frightens her into marrying him as no one can think of any other reason for this union.

Well, after they are married and before the stray truck comes along to provide the keystone for Big Boy's success they live in a small apartment as far over on West Forty-ninth Street as anyone can live unless they live in a canoe in the North River and it is by no means a fashionable neighborhood but it is the best they can do on their income in those days and it is there a son is born to them who is so small that Big Boy is greatly mortified and slightly perturbed.

In fact, he brings the child over on Broadway and goes around peering into the faces of various Broadway personalities who infest the Golden Slipper and then gazing closely at the child as if he is making comparisons. I never see this child again and to tell the truth I seldom see Big Boy Blues afterwards and then only when I do not learn in advance that he is coming my way but I read now and then in the blats about him slugging his truck drivers or somebody else's truck drivers or just somebody else, so I judge he is the same old Big Boy.

But as the years go on I occasionally run into Rosie Flynn who seems to be fatting up somewhat in spots and she tells me that Big Boy by no means admires the child that she now speaks of as Little Boy Blues because he remains puny and scary but I can see that Rosie thinks very well of him, indeed. In fact, Little Boy Blues is all she talks about and as he gets older I learn from her that she has him away at school as much as possible as he is a great eyesore to Big Boy who keeps him frightened half to death by yelling at him and sometimes giving him a few clops.

From what Rosie tells me, I judge Little Boy Blues is quite a weakling and far from being a credit to a virile personality such as Big Boy but when the war comes on and Little Boy is drafted, Big Boy becomes very proud of him and wishes to be real fatherly toward him.

In fact, one day at Dix where Little Boy Blues is stationed for awhile, Big Boy approaches him with his hand extended to shake hands and Little Boy is so alarmed that he turns and runs away and keeps running until he is so far from camp that he is two days finding his way back and is put down as AWOL.

Well, I become so interested in what West Side Willie tells me about the show that I go to the Grand Central at noon myself the next day to see the soldier company arrive and it is quite an impressive scene as the members are in full marching gear with rifles and all this and that and march from the station through the streets to the theater in West Forty-eight where the show is going to open.

West Side Willie does not march with them but joins me in following them only we stick to the sidewalk and people stop and applaud the company and the members bow right and left and smile and when I say to Willie that I consider this somewhat unmilitary, he says:

"Well," he says, "you see most of these guys are professional actors even if they are soldiers and they are bound to take bows when they hear applause even if they are sitting in the electric chair waiting for the guy to pull the switch."

He points out Little Boy Blues to me and I can see that he is small and frail-looking and seems to be buckling slightly at the knees from the weight of his pack and rifle and that he has red hair like his mamma. I also see Rosie Flynn on the sidewalk ahead of me following the march so I quit West Side Willie and overtake her and say to her like this:

"Well, Rosie," I say, "I notice your offspring has your top piece but the way he does not resemble Big Boy in any manner, shape or form is really remarkable. By the way," I say, "how is Big Boy? Not that I care, Rosie, but I wish to be polite."

"Sh-h-h-h!" she says and looks around as if she is afraid Big Boy may be in earshot. "He is all right except his temper is shorter than ever. He chucks one of his own truck drivers into the river yesterday truck and all. I am so afraid of what will happen if he learns Little Boy is in this show. You see," she says, "I tell him the last time I hear from Little Boy he is with Coogan's Cobras in the Pacific."

"Well," I say, "you do not pick a soft spot for him, anyway. Coogan's Cobras are supposed to be the fightingest outfit in our Army."

"It is because I see the name in the newspapers so much," Rosie says. "It pleases Big Boy to think Little Boy is in such company. I pray he does not learn the truth before the show opens. Poor Big Boy has no appreciation of the fine and delicate and artistic. I often wake up at night in trembling at the thought of his anger if he learns of the large fees I pay for Little Boy's dancing instruction."

I commence trembling myself right then and there thinking of such a situation and at this point I unload Rosie Flynn and go on my way because I realize that if Big Boy learns of the fees she mentions he may not only wipe out Rosie but anyone who ever even knows her. To tell the truth, I am a little disappointed in Rosie as I always figure her to have some sense and while I do not say it is wrong for anybody's son to dance I consider it sinful to pay fees to encourage him to do it.

Well, the day of the opening I am surprised more than no little when West Side Willie hunts me up and gives me a skull, which is a way of saying a free ticket for the show and I figure it must be because business is not up to expectations but when I mention this idea to Willie he becomes quite provoked.

"Why," he says, "we are sold out in advance for half the entire engagement already. This show is the biggest thing since nylons. If you examine your ducket you will observe that no seat is specified. That means you have standing room only."

But standing room is by no means undesirable in a New York theater especially at openings because where you stand is in back of the last row which places you in a position to leave quickly and quietly in case the show is bad and this is where I am located for the opening of *Gee Eyes*.

I am a little late getting to the theater and the audience is pretty well seated when I arrive and as I am going in West Side Willie who is taking tickets with great skill holds back a Broadway columnist and his wife a minute and says to me:

"Who do you think we have with us tonight?" he says. "Why, nobody but Colonel Billy Coogan, the commander of Coogan's Cobras. He is a tall slim guy with a lot of ribbons on his chest and he is in the third row center."

"Yes," the columnist says. "He flies in from the Pacific only today to get a new decoration tomorrow from the President in Washington."

Naturally on taking my place in the rear of the house I spot Colonel Coogan at once by his uniform away down front and I am somewhat astonished to observe next to him a head and a pair of shoulders that even at long distance and from behind I identify as belonging to Big Boy Blues, and what is more he seems to be chatting with Colonel Coogan.

I am standing there wondering about this spectacle but just then the curtain opens and I dismiss the matter from my mind as I can see at once that this is a pretty good show although personally I like a little more sex appeal than it is possible to get into shows in which all the performers are hairy-legged guys with no bims whatever around.

The one thing I am looking for which is Little Boy Blues does not come on until the finale and this is a very large number, indeed, with the entire cast on stage when out comes a slim and graceful young ballet dancer in a flaring short skirt and all who can easily pass for a doll if you do not know it has to be a guy in this company unless somebody makes a serious mistake.

I can see that the dancer is undoubtedly Little Boy Blues even without looking at the program to make sure and while I am by no means a judge of ballet dancing and in fact can do without same entirely in a pinch, I realize that he gives a great performance. In fact, I realize that he is no doubt a genius at ballet dancing and as the curtain closes on him the audience lets out a roar of applause that I afterwards hear shakes the glasses off the back bar in the gin mill next door to the theater.

Then the curtain opens again as is always the case when there is great applause and Little Boy Blues stands there on the stage panting as if he just finishes a fast hundred yards and taking bows with one hand on his stomach and also perspiring no little and the audience applauds with even greater vigor than before and at this moment I observe Big Boy Blues jump up from his seat down front.

I notice his mouth is wide open so I judge he is yelling something and thinks I to myself well, here it comes, although there is too much noise for me to hear what he is yelling about, and besides at almost the same instant he jumps up a guy in the seat directly behind him jumps up too and practically simultaneously with Big Boy's mouth opening a blackjack drops on his sconce and Big Boy sinks back quietly in his seat. Then I recognize the guy behind him as Captain Caswell in civilian clothes.

Well, the uproar from the audience continues but of course it is all over Little Boy Blues' dancing and no one notices what happens to Big Boy although a couple of coppers come down the aisle and lift him out of his seat and drag him away still unconscious. Furthermore, no one pays any attention to Colonel Coogan who is up on his feet and saying to everyone around him that the slugging of Big Boy is the worst outrage since Pearl Harbor though no one seems to listen to him.

By this time Little Boy Blues is panting and perspiring more from taking bows than from his dancing so the curtain closes in on him and the first act for good and nearly everyone in the audience moves out into the lobby for the intermission to smoke and gas and all they are gassing about is Little Boy's dancing. Then I see Captain Caswell talking to Rosie Flynn in a corner of the lobby and I get close enough to hear the captain say:

"Well, Rose," he says, "you certainly do the community a service by requesting police protection here tonight. If it is not for your warning and my skill with a jack we will have serious trouble although to tell you the truth we have enough already with the guy we commandeer the seat from behind Big Boy. I only hope and trust that he does not have as much influence as he claims and anyway he can have the seat now."

Then Colonel Coogan comes into the lobby still stating in a loud voice that the jacking of Big Boy is a scandalous matter and that somebody will hear from the War Department and maybe the OPI, too, when Captain Caswell steps up to him and informs him that Big Boy is jacked because he is about to start wrecking the joint in discovering that his son is a dancer in the show.

"No, no," Colonel Coogan says. "There is a terrible error somewhere. He knows his son is in the show all right because someone calls him up this evening and gives him the information. Mr. Blues introduces himself to me and tells me about it while we are sitting there side by side waiting for the curtain. He does not seem to know just what to think about his son being in the show at first but he asks me as a special favor not to mention it to Mrs. Blues if ever I happen to meet her because she thinks her son is with my command and Mr. Blues fears it will break her heart if she learns the truth."

"Colonel," Captain Caswell says, "I distinctly hear Big Boy yell when he gets up from his seat and our experience with him in the past is that he always prefaces his acts of violence by yelling."

"Yes," Colonel Coogan says, "he yells all right, but so do I and what we are both yelling is bravo."

At this point I hear a slight gasp behind me and on looking around I observe that Rosie Flynn slumps to the floor in a dead faint consequently there is more excitement during which I take my departure without even waiting for the second act as my legs are very tired from the standing room only.

I am again sitting in Mindy's restaurant along about 3 o'clock in the A.M. still resting my legs when who comes in but West Side Willie and I am most distressed to note that he has two black eyes and swollen lips and that he seems greatly disheveled in every respect.

"Why, my good gracious, Willie," I say. "Do you get run over by a tank division or what?"

"No," Willie says, "Big Boy Blues belts me. By the way," he says, "everybody is all wrong about him crushing the human skull with a single blow of his fist. He hits me on top of the head twice with his right and only raises a contusion and I think he damages his duke at that. However," Willie says, "it is only fair to say Big Boy comes to the theater to find me fresh from the hospital after he is treated for the jacking he receives from Captain Caswell and perhaps he does not have all his strength. He inflicts most of my injuries with a left hook."

"Well, Willie," I say, "it shows you how Colonel Coogan is deceived by Big Boy and Captain Caswell is right all the time. I suppose Big Boy's fury over Little Boy being in *Gee Eyes* flares up anew when he has time to think about it and no doubt he assaults you as a representative of the show."

"Oh, no," Willie says. "Big Boy is still all pleasured up over Little Boy's performance, and what is more he and Little Boy and Rosie Flynn are enjoying a happy and very loving family reunion but Big Boy gets to brooding about the ticket speculator who calls him up and tells him of Little Boy's presence in the show and hustles him into buying a ticket for a hundred dollars which is about a ninety-five dollar premium."

"I see," I say. "You are the speculator, of course."

"Well," Willie says, "I am stuck with a ticket that I pay six dollars for myself and I happen to need a hundred and I know Big Boy Blues will pay anything to get in the theater if he hears Little Boy is in the show although naturally I figure it will be only to tear the place apart. But I also know Rosie Flynn arranges for police protection so I do not see how he can do any harm even if he is there.

"So," Willie says, "I call him up and promote him. It is more than human nature can stand to let such an opportunity pass. But besides getting belted I also undergo another slight misfortune tonight. I am relieved of my job with the show and ordered to Colonel Coogan's combat unit in the Pacific."

TAKE IT EASY

All Horse Players Die Broke

IT IS DURING the last race meeting at Saratoga, and one evening I am standing out under the elms in front of the Grand Union Hotel thinking what a beautiful world it is, to be sure, for what do I do in the afternoon at the track but grab myself a piece of a 10-to-1 shot. I am thinking what a beautiful moon it is, indeed, that is shining down over the park where Mr. Dick Canfield once deals them higher than a cat's back, and how pure and balmy the air is, and also what nice-looking Judys are wandering around and about, although it is only the night before that I am standing in the same spot wondering where I can borrow a Betsy with which to shoot myself smack-dab through the pimple.

In fact, I go around to see a character I know by the name of Solly something, who owns a Betsy, but it seems he has only one cartridge to his name for this Betsy and he is thinking some of either using the cartridge to shoot his own self smack-dab through the pimple, or of going out to the race course and shooting an old catfish by the name of Pair of Jacks that plays him false in the fifth race, and therefore Solly is not in a mood to lend his Betsy to anybody else. So we try to figure out a way we can make one cartridge do for two pimples, and in the meantime Solly outs with a bottle of applejack, and after a couple of belts at this bottle we decide that the sensible thing to do is to take the Betsy out and peddle it for whatever we can, and maybe get a taw for the next day.

Well, it happens that we run into an Italian party from Passaic, N. J., by the name of Guiseppe Palladino, who is called Joe for short, and this Joe is in the money very good at the moment, and he is glad to lend us a pound note on the Betsy, because Joe is such a character as never knows when he may need an extra Betsy, and anyway it is the first time in his experience around the race tracks that anybody ever offers him collateral for a loan. So there Solly and I are with a deuce apiece after we spend the odd dollar for breakfast the next day, and I run my deuce up to a total of twenty-two slugs on the 10-to-1 shot in the last heat of the day, and everything is certainly all right with me in every respect.

Well, while I am standing there under the elms, who comes along but a raggedy old Dutchman by the name of Unser Fritz, who is maybe seventy-five years old, come next grass, and who is following the giddyaps since the battle of Gettysburg, as near as anybody can figure out. In fact, Unser Fritz is quite an institution around the race tracks, and is often written up by the newspaper scribes as a terrible example of what a horse player comes to, although personally I always say that what Unser Fritz comes to is not so tough when you figure that he does not do a tap of work in all these years. In his day, Unser Fritz is a most successful handicapper, a handicapper being a character who can dope out from the form what horses ought to win the races, and as long as his figures turn out all right, a handicapper is spoken of most respectfully by one and all, although of course when he begins missing out for any length of time as handicappers are bound to do, he is no longer spoken of respectfully, or even as a handicapper. He is spoken of as a bum.

It is a strange thing how a handicapper can go along for years doing everything right, and then all of a sudden he finds himself doing everything wrong, and this is the way it is with Unser Fritz. For a long time his figures on the horse races are considered most remarkable, indeed, and as he will bet till the cows come home on his own figures, he generally has plenty of money, and a fiancée by the name of Emerald Em. She is called Emerald Em because she has a habit of wearing a raft of emeralds in rings, and pins, and bracelets, and one thing and another, which are purchased for her by Unser Fritz to express his love, an emerald being a green stone that is considered most expressive of love, if it is big enough. It seems that Emerald Em is very fond of emeralds, especially when they are surrounded by large, coarse diamonds. I hear the old-timers around the race tracks say that when Emerald Em is young, she is a tall, goodlooking Judy with yellow hair that is by no means a phony yellow, at that, and with a shape that does not require a bustle such as most Judys always wear in those days.

But then nobody ever hears an old-timer mention any Judy that he remembers from back down the years who is not good-looking, and in fact beautiful. To hear the old-timers tell it, every pancake they ever see when they are young is a double Myrna Loy, though the chances are, figuring in the law of averages, that some of them are bound to be rutabagas, the same as now. Anyway, for years this Emerald Em is known on every race track from coast to coast as Unser Fritz's fiancée, and is considered quite a remarkable scene, what with her emeralds, and not requiring any bustle, and everything else.

Then one day Unser Fritz's figures run plumb out on him, and so does his dough, and so does Emerald Em, and now Unser Fritz is an old pappy guy, and it is years since he is regarded as anything but a crumbo around the race tracks, and nobody remembers much of his story, or cares a cuss about it, for if there is anything that is a drug on the market around the tracks it is the story of a broker. How he gets from place to place, and how he lives after he gets there, is a very great mystery to one and all, although I hear he often rides in the horsecars with the horses, when some owner or trainer happens to be feeling tenderhearted, or he hitchhikes in automobiles, and sometimes he even walks, for Unser Fritz is still fairly nimble, no matter how old he is.

He always has under his arm a bundle of newspapers that somebody throws away, and every night he sits down and handicaps the horses running the next day according to his own system, but he seldom picks any winners, and even if he does pick any winners, he seldom has anything to bet on them. Sometimes he promotes a stranger, who does not know he is bad luck to a good hunting dog, to put down a few dibs on one of his picks, and once in a while the pick wins, and Unser Fritz gets a small stake, and sometimes an old-timer who feels sorry for him will slip him something. But whatever Unser Fritz gets hold of, he bets off right away on the next race that comes up, so naturally he never is holding anything very long.

Well, Unser Fritz stands under the elms with me a while, speaking of this and that, and especially of the races, and I am wondering to myself if I will become as disheveled as Unser Fritz if I keep on following the races, when he gazes at the Grand Union Hotel, and says to me like this: "It looks nice," he says. "It looks cheery-like, with the lights, and all this and that. It brings back memories to me. Emma always lives in this hotel whenever we make Saratoga for the races back in the days when I am in the money. She always has a suite of two or three rooms on this side of the hotel. Once she has four. I often stand here under these trees," Unser Fritz says, "watching her windows to see what time she puts out her lights, because, while I trust Emma implicitly, I know she has a restless nature, and sometimes she cannot resist returning to scenes of gaiety after I bid her good night, especially," he says, "with a party by the name of Pete Shovelin, who runs the restaurant where she once deals them off the arm."

"You mean she is a biscuit shooter?" I say.

"A waitress," Unser Fritz says. "A good waitress. She comes of a family of farm folks in this very section, although I never know much about them," he says. "Shovelin's is a little hole-in-the-wall up the street here somewhere which long since disappears. I go there for my morning java in the old days. I will say one thing for Shovelin," Unser

Fritz says, "he always has good java. Three days after I first clap eyes on Emma, she is wearing her first emerald, and is my fiancée. Then she moves into a suite in the Grand Union. I only wish you can know Emma in those days," he says. "She is beautiful, She is a fine character. She is always on the level, and I love her dearly."

"What do you mean—always on the level?" I say. "What about this Shovelin party you just mention?"

"Ah," Unser Fritz says, "I suppose I am dull company for a squab, what with having to stay in at night to work on my figures, and Emma likes to go around and about. She is a highly nervous type, and extremely restless, and she cannot bear to hold still very long at a time. But," he says, "in those days it is not considered proper for a young Judy to go around and about without a chaperon, so she goes with Shovelin for her chaperon. Emma never goes anywhere without a chaperon," he says.

Well, it seems that early in their courtship, Unser Fritz learns that he can generally quiet her restlessness with emeralds, if they have diamonds on the side. It seems that these stones have a very soothing effect on her, and this is why he purchases them for her by the bucket. "Yes," Unser Fritz says, "I always think of Emma whenever I am in New York City, and look down Broadway at night with the go lights on."

But it seems from what Unser Fritz tells me that even with the emeralds her restless spells come on her very bad, and especially when he finds himself running short of ready, and is unable to purchase more emeralds for her at the moment, although Unser Fritz claims this is nothing unusual. In fact, he says anybody with any experience with nervous female characters knows that it becomes very monotonous for them to be around people who are short of ready. "But," he says, "not all of them require soothing with emeralds. Some require pearls," he says.

Well, it seems that Emma generally takes a trip without Unser Fritz to break the monotony of his running short of ready, but she never takes one of these trips without a chaperon, because she is very careful about her good name, and Unser Fritz's, too. It seems that in those days Judys have to be more careful about such matters than they do now.

He remembers that once when they are in San Francisco she takes a trip through the Yellowstone with Jockey Gus Kloobus as her chaperon, and is gone three weeks and returns much refreshed, especially as she gets back just as Unser Fritz makes a nice score and has a seidel of emeralds waiting for her. He remembers another time she goes to England with a trainer by the name of Blootz as her chaperon and comes home with an English accent that sounds right cute, to find Unser Fritz going like a house afire at Belmont. "She takes a lot of other trips without me during the time we are engaged," Unser Fritz says, "but," he says, "I always know Emma will return to me as soon as she hears I am back in the money and can purchase more emeralds for her. In fact," he says, "this knowledge is all that keeps me struggling now."

"Look, Fritz," I say, "what do you mean, keeps you going? Do you mean you think Emma may return to you again?"

"Why, sure," Unser Fritz says. "Why, certainly, if I get my rushes again. Why not?" he says. "She knows there will be a pail of emeralds waiting for her. She knows I love her and always will," he says.

Well, I ask him when he sees Emerald Em last, and he says it is 1908 in the old Waldorf-Astoria the night he blows a hundred and sixty thousand betting on a hide called Sir Martin to win the Futurity, and it is all the dough Unser Fritz has at the moment. In fact, he is cleaner than a jay bird, and he is feeling somewhat discouraged. It seems he is waiting on his floor for the elevator, and when it comes down Emerald Em is one of the several passengers, and when the door opens, and Unser Fritz starts to get in, she raises her foot and plants it in his stomach, and gives him a big push back out the door and the elevator goes on down without him.

"But, of course," Unser Fritz says, "Emma never likes to ride in the same elevator with me, because I am not always tidy enough to suit her in those days, what with having so much work to do on my figures, and she claims it is a knock to her socially. Anyway," he says, "this is the last I see of Emma."

"Why, Fritz," I say, "nineteen-eight is nearly thirty years back, and if she ever thinks of returning to you, she will return long before this."

"No," Unser Fritz says. "You see, I never make a scratch since then. I am never since in the money, so there is no reason for Emma to return to me. But," he says, "wait until I get going good again and you will see."

Well, I always figure Unser Fritz must be more or less of an old screwball for going on thinking there is still a chance for him around the tracks, and now I am sure of it, and I am about to bid him good evening, when he mentions that he can use about two dollars if I happen to have a deuce on me that is not working, and I will say one thing for Unser Fritz, he seldom comes right out and asks anybody for anything unless things are very desperate with him, indeed. "I need it to pay something on account of my landlady," he says. "I room with old Mrs. Crob around the corner for over twenty years, and," he says, "she only charges me a finnif a week, so I try to keep from getting too far to the rear with her. I will return it to you the first score I make."

Well, of course I know this means practically never, but I am feeling so good about my success at the track that I slip him a deucer, and it is half an hour later before I fully realize what I do, and go looking for Fritz to get anyway half of it back. But by this time he disappears, and I think no more of the matter until the next day out at the course when I hear Unser Fritz bets two dollars on a thing by the name of Speed Cart, and it bows down at 50 to 1, so I know Mrs. Crob is still waiting for hers.

Now there is Unser Fritz with one hundred slugs, and this is undoubtedly more money than he enjoys since Hickory Slim is a two-year-old. And from here on the story becomes very interesting, and in fact remarkable, because up to the moment Speed Cart hits the wire, Unser Fritz is still nothing but a crumbo, and you can say it again, while from now on he is somebody to point out and say can you imagine such a thing happening? He bets a hundred on a centipede called Marchesa, and down pops Marchesa like a trained pig at 20 to 1. Then old Unser Fritz bets two hundred on a caterpillar by the name of Merry Soul, at 4 to 1, and Merry Soul just laughs his way home. Unser Fritz winds up the day betting two thousand more on something called Sharp Practice, and when Sharp Practice wins by so far it looks as if he is a shoo-in, Fritz finds himself with over twelve thousand slugs, and the way the bookmakers in the betting ring are sobbing is really most distressing to hear.

Well, in a week Unser Fritz is a hundred thousand dollars in front, because the way he sends it in is quite astonishing to behold, although the old-timers tell me it is just the way he sends it when he is younger. He is betting only on horses that he personally figures out, and what happens is that Unser Fritz's figures suddenly come to life again, and he cannot do anything wrong. He wins so much dough that he even pays off a few old touches, including my two, and he goes so far as to lend Joe Palladino three dollars on the Betsy that Solly and I hock with Joe for the pound note, as it seems that by this time Joe himself is practically on his way to the poorhouse, and while Unser Fritz has no use whatsoever for a Betsy he cannot bear to see a character such as Joe go to the poorhouse.

But with all the dough Unser Fritz carries in his pockets, and plants in a safe-deposit box in the jug downtown, he looks just the same as ever, because he claims he cannot find time from working on his figures to buy new clothes and dust himself off, and if you tell anybody who does not know who he is that this old crutch is stone rich, the chances are they will call you a liar.

In fact, on a Monday around noon, the clerk in the branch office that a big Fifth Avenue jewelry firm keeps in the lobby of the States Hotel is all ready to yell for the constables when Unser Fritz leans up against the counter and asks to see some jewelry on display in a show-case, as Unser Fritz is by no means the clerk's idea of a customer for jewelry. I am standing in the lobby of the hotel on the off chance that some fresh money may arrive in the city on the late trains that I may be able to connect up with before the races, when I notice Unser Fritz and observe the agitation of the clerk, and presently I see Unser Fritz wav-ing a fistful of bank notes under the clerk's beak, and the clerk starts setting out the jewelry with surprising speed.

I go over to see what is coming off, and I can see that the jewelry Unser Fritz is looking at consists of a necklace of emeralds and dia-monds, with a centerpiece the size of the home plate, and some ear-drops, and bracelets, and clips of same, and as I approach the scene I hear Unser Fritz ask how much for the lot as if he is dickering for a basket of fish.

"One hundred and one thousand dollars, sir," the clerk says. "You see, sir, it is a set, and one of the finest things of the kind in the country. We just got it in from our New York store to show a party here, and," he says, "she is absolutely crazy about it, but she states she cannot give us a final decision until five o'clock this afternoon. Confidentially, sir," the clerk says, "I think the real trouble is financial, and doubt that we will hear from her again. In fact," he says, "I am so strongly of this opinion that I am prepared to sell the goods without waiting on her. It is really a bargain at the price," he says.

"Dear me," Unser Fritz says to me, "this is most unfortunate as the sum mentioned is just one thousand dollars more than I possess in all this world. I have twenty thousand on my person, and eighty thousand over in the box in the jug, and not another dime. But," he says, "I will be back before five o'clock and take the lot. In fact," he says, "I will run in right after the third race, and pick it up." Well, at this, the clerk starts putting the jewelry back in the case, and anybody can see that he figures he is on a lob and that he is sorry he wastes so much time, but Unser Fritz says to me like this: "Emma is returning to me," he says.

"Emma who?" I say.

"Why," Unser Fritz says, "my Emma. The one I tell you about not long ago. She must hear I am in the money again, and she is returning just as I always say she will."

"How do you know?" I say. "Do you hear from her, or what?"

"No," Unser Fritz says, "I do not hear from her direct, but Mrs. Crob knows some female relative of Emma's that lives at Ballston Spa a few miles from here, and this relative is in Saratoga this morning to do some shopping, and she tells Mrs. Crob and Mrs. Crob tells me. Emma will be here tonight. I will have these emeralds waiting for her." Well, what I always say is that every guy knows his own business best, and if Unser Fritz wishes to toss his dough off on jewelry, it is none of my put-in, so all I remark is that I have no doubt Emma will be very much surprised, indeed. "No," Unser Fritz says. "She will be expecting them. She always expects emeralds when she returns to me. I love her," he says. "You have no idea how I love her. But let us hasten to the course," he says. "Cara Mia is a right good thing in the third, and I will make just one bet today to win the thousand I need to buy these emeralds."

"But, Fritz," I say, "you will have nothing left for operating expenses after you invest in the emeralds."

"I am not worrying about operating expenses now," Unser Fritz says. "The way my figures are standing up, I can run a spool of thread into a pair of pants in no time. But I can scarcely wait to see the expression on Emma's face when she sees her emeralds. I will have to make a fast trip into town after the third to get my dough out of the box in the jug and pick them up," he says. "Who knows but what this other party that is interested in the emeralds may make her mind up before five o'clock and pop in there and nail them?"

Well, after we get to the race track, all Unser Fritz does is stand around waiting for the third race. He has his figures on the first two races, and ordinarily he will be betting himself a gob on them, but he says he does not wish to take the slightest chance on cutting down his capital at this time, and winding up short of enough dough to buy the emeralds. It turns out that both of the horses Unser Fritz's figures make on top in the first and second races bow down, and Unser Fritz will have his thousand if he only bets a couple of hundred on either of them, but Unser Fritz says he is not sorry he does not bet. He says the finishes in both races are very close, and prove that there is an element of risk in these races. And Unser Fritz says he cannot afford to tamper with the element of risk at this time.

He states that there is no element of risk whatever in the third race, and what he states is very true, as everybody realizes that this mare Cara Mia is a stick-out. In fact, she is such a stick-out that it scarcely figures to be a contest. There are three other horses in the race, but it is the opinion of one and all that if the owners of these horses have any sense they will leave them in the barn and save them a lot of unnecessary lather.

The opening price offered by the bookmakers on Cara Mia is 2 to 5, which means that if you wish to wager on Cara Mia to win you will have to put up five dollars to a bookmaker's two dollars, and everybody agrees that this is a reasonable thing to do in this case unless you wish to rob the poor bookmaker. In fact, this is considered so reasonable that everybody starts running at the bookmakers all at once, and the bookmakers can see if this keeps up they may get knocked off their stools in the betting ring and maybe seriously injured, so they make Cara Mia 1 to 6, and out, as quickly as possible to halt the rush and give them a chance to breathe.

This 1 to 6 means that if you wish to wager on Cara Mia to win, you must wager six of your own dollars to one of the bookmaker's dollars, and means that the bookies are not offering any prices whatsoever on Cara Mia running second, or third. You can get almost any price you can think of right quick against any of the other horses winning the race, and place and show prices, too, but asking the bookmakers to lay against Cara Mia running second or third will be something like asking them to bet that Mr. Roosevelt is not President of the United States. Well, I am expecting Unser Fritz to step in and partake of the 2 to 5 on Cara Mia for all the dough he has on his person the moment it is offered, because he is very high indeed on this mare, and in fact I never see anybody any higher on any horse, and it is a price Unser Fritz will not back off from when he is high on anything.

Moreover, I am pleased to think he will make such a wager, because it will give him plenty over and above the price of the emeralds, and as long as he is bound to purchase the emeralds, I wish to see him have a little surplus, because when anybody has a surplus there is always a chance for me. It is when everybody runs out of surpluses that I am handicapped no little. But instead of stepping in and partaking, Unser Fritz keeps hesitating until the opening price gets away from him, and finally he says to me like this: "Of course," he says, "my figures show Cara Mia cannot possibly lose this race, but," he says, "to guard against any possibility whatever of her losing, I will make an absolute cinch of it. I will bet her third."

"Why, Fritz," I say, "I do not think there is anybody in this world outside of an insane asylum who will give you a price on the peek. Furthermore," I say, "I am greatly surprised at this sign of weakening on your part on your figures."

"Well," Unser Fritz says, "I cannot afford to take a chance on not having the emeralds for Emma when she arrives. Let us go through the betting ring, and see what we can see," he says. So we walk through the betting ring, and by this time it seems that many of the books are so loaded with wagers on Cara Mia to win that they will not accept any more under any circumstances, and I figure that Unser Fritz blows the biggest opportunity of his life in not grabbing the opening. The bookmakers who are loaded are now looking even sadder than somewhat, and this makes them a pitiful spectacle, indeed.

Well, one of the saddest-looking is a character by the name of Slow McCool, but he is a character who will usually give you a gamble and he is still taking Cara Mia at 1 to 6, and Unser Fritz walks up to him and whispers in his ear, and what he whispers is he wishes to know if Slow McCool cares to lay him a price on Cara Mia third. But all that happens is that Slow McCool stops looking sad a minute and looks slightly perplexed, and then he shakes his head and goes on looking sad again. Now Unser Fritz steps up to another sad-looking bookmaker by the name of Pete Phozzler and whispers in his ear, and Pete also shakes his head and after we leave him I look back and see that Pete is standing up on his stool watching Unser Fritz, and still shaking his head. Well, Unser Fritz approaches maybe a dozen other sad-looking bookmakers, and whispers to them, and all he gets is the old head shake, but none of them seem to become angry with Unser Fritz, and I always say that this proves that bookmakers are better than some people think, because, personally, I claim they have a right to get angry with Unser Fritz for insulting their intelligence, and trying to defraud them, too, by asking a price on Cara Mia third.

Finally we come to a character by the name of Willie the Worrier, who is called by this name because he is always worrying about something, and what he is generally worrying about is a short bank roll, or his ever-loving wife, and sometimes both, though mostly it is his wife. Personally, I always figure she is something to worry about, at that, though I do not consider details necessary. She is a red-headed Judy about half as old as Willie the Worrier, and this alone is enough to start any guy worrying, and what is more she is easily vexed, especially by Willie. In fact, I remember Solly telling me that she is vexed with Willie no longer ago than about 11 A.M. this very day, and gives him a public reprimanding about something or other in the telegraph office downtown when Solly happens to be in there hoping maybe he will receive an answer from a mark in Pittsfield, Mass., that he sends a tip on a horse. Solly says the last he hears Willie the Worrier's wife say is that she will leave him for good this time, but I just see her over on the clubhouse lawn wearing some right classy-looking garments, so I judge she does not leave him as yet, as the clubhouse lawn is not a place to be waiting for a train.

Well, when Unser Fritz sees that he is in front of Willie's stand, he starts to move on, and I nudge him and motion at Willie, and ask him if he does not notice that Willie is another bookmaker, and Unser Fritz says he notices him all right, but that he does not care to offer him any business, because Willie insults him ten years ago. He says Willie calls him a dirty old Dutch bum, and while I am thinking what a wonderful memory Unser Fritz has to remember insults from bookmakers for ten years, Willie the Worrier, sitting there on his stool looking out over the crowd, spots Unser Fritz and yells at him as follows: "Hellow, Dirty Dutch," he says. "How is the soap market? What are you looking for around here, Dirty Dutch? Santa Claus?"

Well, at this, Unser Fritz pushes his way through the crowd around Willie the Worrier's stand, and gets close to Willie, and says: "Yes," he says, "I am looking for Santa Claus. I am looking for a show price on Number Two horse, but," he says, "I do not expect to get it from the shoemakers who are booking nowadays."

Now the chances are Willie the Worrier figures Unser Fritz is just trying to get sarcastic with him for the benefit of the crowd around his stand in asking for such a thing as a price on Cara Mia third, and in fact the idea of anybody asking a price third on a horse that some bookmakers will not accept any more wages on first, or even second, is so humorous that many characters laugh right out loud. "All right," Willie the Worrier says. "No one can ever say he comes to my store looking for a market on anything and is turned down. I will quote you a show price, Dirty Dutch," he says. "You can have 1 to 100." This means that Willie the Worrier is asking Unser Fritz for one hundred dollars to the book's one dollar, if Unser Fritz wishes to bet on Cara Mia dropping in there no worse than third, and of course Willie has no idea Unser Fritz or anybody else will ever take such a price, and the chances are if Willie is not sizzling a little at Unser Fritz, he will not offer such a price, because it sounds foolish.

Furthermore, the chances are if Unser Fritz offers Willie a comparatively small bet at this price, such as may enable him to chisel just a couple of hundred out of Willie's book, Willie will find some excuse to wiggle off, but Unser Fritz leans over and says in a low voice to Willie the Worrier: "A hundred thousand."

Willie nods his head and turns to a clerk alongside him, and his voice is as low as Unser Fritz's as he says to the clerk: "A thousand to a hundred thousand, Cara Mia third."

The clerk's eyes pop open and so does his mouth, but he does not say a word. He just writes something on a pad of paper in his hand, and Unser Fritz offers Willie the Worrier a package of thousand-dollar bills, and says: "Here is twenty," he says. "The rest is in the jug."

"All right, Dutch," Willie says. "I know you have it, although," he says, "this is the first crack you give me at it. You are on, Dutch," he says. "P. S.," Willie says, "the Dirty does not go any more."

Well, you understand Unser Fritz is betting one hundred thousand dollars against a thousand dollars that Cara Mia will run in the money, and personally I consider this wager a very sound business proposition, indeed, and so does everybody else, for all it amounts to is finding a thousand dollars in the street. There is really nothing that can make Cara Mia run out of the money, the way I look at it, except what happens to her, and what happens is she steps in a hole fifty yards from the finish when she is on top by ten, and breezing, and down she goes all spread out, and of course the other three horses run on past her to the wire, and all this is quite a disaster to many members of the public, including Unser Fritz.

I am standing with him on the rise of the grandstand lawn watching the race, and it is plain to be seen that he is slightly surprised at what happens, and personally, I am practically dumfounded because, to tell the truth, I take a nibble at the opening price of 2 to 5 on Cara Mia with a total of thirty slugs, which represents all my capital, and I am thinking what a great injustice it is for them to leave holes in the track for horses to step in, when Unser Fritz says like this: "Well," he says, "it is horse racing."

And this is all he ever says about the matter, and then he walks down to Willie the Worrier, and tells Willie if he will send a clerk with him, he will go to the jug and get the balance of the money that is now due Willie. "Dutch," Willie says, "it will be a pleasure to accompany you to the jug in person." As Willie is getting down off his stool, somebody in the crowd who hears of the wager gazes at Unser Fritz, and remarks that he is really a game guy, and Willie says: "Yes," he says, "he is a game guy at that. But," he says, "what about me?" And he takes Unser Fritz by the arm, and they walk away together, and anybody can see that Unser Fritz picks up anyway twenty years or more, and a slight stringhalt, in the last few minutes.

Then it comes on night again in Saratoga, and I am standing out under the elms in front of the Grand Union, thinking that this world is by no means as beautiful as formerly, when I notice a big, fat old Judy with snow-white hair and spectacles standing near me, looking up and down the street. She will weigh a good two hundred pounds, and much of it is around her ankles, but she has a pleasant face, at that, and when she observes me looking at her, she comes over to me, and says: "I am trying to fix the location of a restaurant where I work many years ago," she says. "It is a place called Shovelin's. The last thing my husband tells me is to see if the old building is still here, but," she says, "it is so long since I am in Saratoga I cannot get my bearings."

"Ma'am," I say, "is your name Emma by any chance, and do they ever call you Emerald Em?"

Well, at this the old Judy laughs, and says: "Why, yes," she says. "That is what they call me when I am young and foolish. But how do you know?" she says. "I do not remember ever seeing you before in my life."

"Well," I say, "I know a party who once knows you. A party by the name of Unser Fritz."

"Unser Fritz?" she says. "Unser Fritz? Oh," she says, "I wonder if you mean a crazy Dutchman I run around with many years ago? My gracious," she says, "I just barely remember him. He is a great hand for giving me little presents, such as emeralds. When I am young, I think emeralds are right pretty, but," she says, "otherwise I cannot stand him."

"Then you do not come here to see him?" I say.

"Are you crazy, too?" she says. "I am on my way to Ballston Spa to see my grandchildren. I live in Macon, Georgia. If ever you are in Macon, Georgia, drop in at Shovelin's restaurant and get some real Southern fried chicken. I am Mrs. Joe Shovelin," she says. "By the way," she says, "I remember more about that crazy Dutchman. He is a horse player. I always figure he must die long ago and that the chances are he dies broke, too. I remember I hear people say all horse players die broke."

"Yes," I say, "he dies all right, and he dies as you suggest, too," for it is only an hour before that they find old Unser Fritz in a vacant lot over near the railroad station with the Betsy he gets off Joe Palladino in his hand and a bullet hole smack-dab through his pimple.

Nobody blames him much for taking this out, and in fact I am standing there thinking long after Emerald Em goes on about her business that it will be a good idea if I follow his example, only I cannot think where I can find another Betsy, when Solly comes along and stands there with me. I ask Solly if he knows anything new. "No," Solly says, "I do not know anything new, except," he says, "I hear Willie the Worrier and his ever-loving make up again, and she is not going to leave him after all. I hear Willie takes home a squarer in the shape of a batch of emeralds and diamonds that she orders sent up here when Willie is not looking, and that they are fighting about all day. Well," Solly says, "maybe this is love."

Lonely Heart

IT SEEMS that one spring day, a character by the name of Nicely-Nicely Jones arrives in a ward in a hospital in the City of Newark, N. J., with such a severe case of pneumonia that the attending physician, who is a horse player at heart, and very absentminded, writes 100, 40 and 10 on the chart over Nicely-Nicely's bed. It comes out afterward that what the physician means is that it is 100-to-1 in his line that Nicely-Nicely does not recover at all, 40-to-1 that he will not last a week, and 10-to-1 that if he does get well he will never be the same again. Well, Nicely-Nicely is greatly discouraged when he sees this price against him, because he is personally a chalk eater when it comes to price, a chalk eater being a character who always plays the short-priced favorites, and he can see that such a long shot as he is has very little chance to win. In fact, he is so discouraged that he does not even feel like taking a little of the price against him to show.

Afterward there is some criticism of Nicely-Nicely among the citizens around Mindy's restaurant on Broadway, because he does not advise them of this market, as these citizens are always willing to bet that what Nicely-Nicely dies of will be overfeeding and never anything small like pneumonia, for Nicely-Nicely is known far and wide as a character who dearly loves to commit eating. But Nicely-Nicely is so discouraged that he does not as much as send them word that he is sick, let alone anything about the price. He just pulls the covers up over his head and lies there waiting for the finish and thinking to himself what a tough thing it is to pass away of pneumonia, and especially in Newark, N. J., and nobody along Broadway knows of his predicament until Nicely-Nicely appears in person some months later and relates this story to me.

So now I will tell you about Nicely-Nicely Jones, who is called Nicely-Nicely because any time anybody asks him how he is feeling, or how things are going with him, he always says nicely, nicely, in a very pleasant tone of voice, although generally this is by no means the gospel truth, especially about how he is going. He is a character of maybe forty-odd, and he is short, and fat, and very good-natured, and what he does for a livelihood is the best he can, which is an occupation that is greatly overcrowded at all times along Broadway.

Mostly, Nicely-Nicely follows the races, playing them whenever he has anything to play them with, but anyway following them, and the reason he finds himself in Newark, N. J., in the first place is because of a business proposition in connection with the races. He hears of a barber in Newark, N. J., who likes to make a wager on a sure thing, now and then, and Nicely-Nicely goes over there to tell him about a sure thing that is coming up at Pimlico the very next Tuesday. Nicely-Nicely figures that the barber will make a wager on this sure thing and cut him in on the profits, but it seems that somebody else gets to the barber the week before with a sure thing that is coming up a Monday, and the barber bets on this sure thing, and the sure thing blows, and now the barber will have to shave half of Newark, N. J., to catch even.

Nicely-Nicely always claims that the frost he meets when he approaches the barber with his sure thing gives him a cold that results in the pneumonia I am speaking of, and furthermore that his nervous system is so disorganized by the barber chasing him nine blocks with a razor in his hand that he has no vitality left to resist the germs. But at that it seems that he has enough vitality left to beat the pneumonia by so far the attending physician is somewhat embarrassed, although afterwards he claims that he makes a mistake in chalking up the 100, 40 and 10 on Nicely-Nicely's chart. The attending physician claims he really means the character in the bed next to Nicely-Nicely, who passes away of lockjaw the second day after Nicely-Nicely arrives.

Well, while he is convalescing in the hospital of this pneumonia, Nicely-Nicely has a chance to do plenty of thinking, and what he thinks about most is the uselessness of the life he leads all these years, and how he has nothing to show for same except some high-class knowledge of race horses, which at this time is practically a drug on the market.

There are many other patients in the same ward with Nicely-Nicely, and he sees their ever-loving wives, and daughters, and maybe their sweet peas visiting them, and hears their cheerful chatter, and he gets to thinking that here he is without chick or child, and no home to go to, and it just about breaks his heart. He gets to thinking of how he will relish a soft, gentle, loving hand on his brow at this time, and finally he makes a pass at one of the nurses, figuring she may comfort his lonely hours, but what she lays on his brow is a beautiful straight right cross, and furthermore she hollers watch, murder, police, and Nicely-Nicely has to pretend he has a relapse and is in a delirium to avoid being mistreated by the internes.

As Nicely-Nicely begins getting some of his strength back, he takes to thinking, too, of such matters as food, and when Nicely-Nicely thinks of food it is generally very nourishing food, such as a nice double sirloin, smothered with chops, and thinking of these matters, and of hamburgers, and wiener schnitzel and goulash with noodles, and lamb stew, adds to his depression, especially when they bring him the light diet provided for invalids by the hospital. He takes to reading to keep himself from thinking of his favorite dishes, and of his solitary life, and one day in a bundle of old magazines and newspapers that they give him to read, he comes upon a bladder that is called the Matrimonial Tribune, which seems to be all about marriage, and in this Matrimonial Tribune Nicely-Nicely observes an advertisement that reads as follows:

Widow of middle age, no children, cheerful companion, neat, excellent cook, owner of nice farm in Central New Jersey, wishes to meet home-loving gentleman of not more than fifty who need not necessarily be possessed of means but who will appreciate warm, tender companionship and pleasant home. Object, matrimony. Address Lonely Heart, this paper.

Well, Nicely-Nicely feels romance stirring in his bosom as he reads these lines, because he is never married, and has no idea that marriage is as described in this advertisement. So what does he do but write a letter to Lonely Heart in care of the Matrimonial Tribune stating that he is looking for a warm, tender companionship, and a pleasant home, and an excellent cook, especially an excellent cook, all his life, and the next thing he knows he is gazing into what at first seems to be an old-fashioned round cheese, but which he finally makes out as the face of a large Judy seated at his bedside. She is anywhere between forty and fifty-five years of age, and she is as big and rawboned as a first baseman, but she is by no means a crow. In fact, she is rather nice-looking, except that she has a pair of eyes as pale as hens' eggs, and these eyes never change expression.

She asks Nicely-Nicely as many questions as an assistant district attorney, and especially if he has any money, and does he have any relatives, and Nicely-Nicely is able to state truthfully that he is all out of both, although she does not seem to mind. She wishes to know about his personal habits, and Nicely-Nicely says they are all good, but of course he does not mention his habit of tapping out any time a 4-to-5 shot comes along, which is as bad a habit as anybody can have, and finally she says she is well satisfied with him and will be pleased to marry him when he is able to walk. She has a short, sharp voice that reminds Nicely-Nicely of a tough starter talking to the jockeys at the post, and she never seems to smile, and, take her all around, the chances are she is not such a character as Nicely-Nicely will choose as his ever-loving wife if he has the pick of a herd, but he figures that she is not bad for an offhand draw.

So Nicely-Nicely and the Widow Crumb are married, and they go to live on her farm in Central New Jersey, and it is a very nice little farm, to be sure, if you care for farms, but it is ten miles from the nearest town, and in a very lonesome country, and furthermore there are no neighbors handy, and the Widow Crumb does not have a telephone or even a radio in her house. In fact, about all she has on this farm are a couple of cows, and a horse, and a very old joskin with a chin whisker and rheumatism and a mean look, whose name seems to be Harley something, and who also seems to be the Widow Crumb's hired hand. Nicely-Nicely can see at once that Harley has no use for him, but afterward he learns that Harley has no use for anybody much, not even himself.

Well, it comes on suppertime the first night. Nicely-Nicely is there and he is delighted to observe that the Widow Crumb is making quite an uproar in the kitchen with the pots and pans, and this uproar is music to Nicely-Nicely's ears as by now he is in the mood to put on the hot meat very good, and he is wondering if the Widow Crumb is as excellent a cook as she lets on in her advertisement. It turns out that she is even better. It turns out that she is as fine a cook as ever straddles a skillet, and the supper she spreads for Nicely-Nicely is too good for a king. There is round steak hammered flat and fried in a pan, with thick cream gravy, and hot biscuits, and corn on the cob, and turnip greens, and cottage fried potatoes, and lettuce with hot bacon grease poured over it, and apple pie, and coffee, and I do not know what all else, and Nicely-Nicely almost founders himself, because it is the first time since he leaves the hospital that he gets a chance to move into real food.

Harley, the old joskin, eats with them, and Nicely-Nicely notices that there is a fourth place set at the table, and he figures that maybe another hired hand is going to show up, but nobody appears to fill the vacant chair, and at first Nicely-Nicely is glad of it, as it gives him more room in which to eat. But then Nicely-Nicely notices that the Widow Crumb loads the plate at the vacant place with even more food than she does any of the others, and all through the meal Nicely-Nicely keeps expecting someone to come in and knock off these victuals. Nobody ever appears, however, and when they are through eating, the Widow Crumb clears up the extra place the same as the others, and scrapes the food off the plate into a garbage pail. Well, of course, Nicely-Nicely is somewhat perplexed by this proceeding, but he does not ask any questions, because where he comes from only suckers go around asking questions. The next morning at breakfast, and again at dinner, and in fact at every meal put on the table the extra place is fixed, and the Widow Crumb goes through the same performance of serving the food to this place, and afterward throwing it away, and while Nicely-Nicely commences thinking it is a great waste of excellent food, he keeps his trap closed.

Now being the Widow Crumb's husband is by no means a bad dodge, as she is anything but a gabby Judy, and will go all day long without saying more than a few words, and as Nicely-Nicely is a character who likes to chat this gives him a chance to do all the talking, although she never seems to be listening to him much. She seldom asks him to do any work, except now and then to help the old joskin around the barn, so Nicely-Nicely commences to figure this is about as soft a drop-in as anybody can wish. The only drawback is that sometimes the Widow Crumb likes to sit on Nicely-Nicely's lap of an evening, and as he does not have much lap to begin with, and it is getting less every day under her feeding, this is quite a handicap, but he can see that it comes of her affectionate nature, and he bears up the best he can.

One evening after they are married several months, the Widow Crumb is sitting on what is left of Nicely-Nicely's lap, and she puts her arms around his neck, and speaks to him as follows: "Nicely," she says, "do you love me?"

"Love you?" Nicely-Nicely says. "Why, I love you like anything. Maybe more. You are a wonderful cook. How can I help loving you?" he says.

"Well," the Widow Crumb says, "do you ever stop to consider that if anything happens to you, I will be left here lone and lorn, because you do not have any means with which to provide for me after you are gone?"

"What do you mean after I am gone?" Nicely-Nicely says. "I am not going anywhere."

"Life is always a very uncertain proposition," the Widow Crumb says. "Who can say when something is apt to happen to you and take you away from me, leaving me without a cent of life insurance?"

Naturally, Nicely-Nicely has to admit to himself that what she says is very true, and of course he never gives the matter a thought before, because he figures from the way the Widow Crumb feeds him that she must have some scratch of her own stashed away somewhere, although this is the first time the subject of money is ever mentioned between them since they are married. "Why," Nicely-Nicely says, "you are quite right, and I will get my life insured as soon as I get enough strength to go out and raise a few dibs. Yes, indeed," Nicely-Nicely says, "I will take care of this situation promptly."

Well, the Widow Crumb says there is no sense in waiting on a matter as important as this, and that she will provide the money for the payment of the premiums herself, and for Nicely-Nicely to forget about going out to raise anything, as she cannot bear to have him out of her sight for any length of time, and then she gets to telling Nicely-Nicely what she is going to give him for breakfast, and he forgets about the insurance business. But the next thing Nicely-Nicely knows, a thin character with a nose like a herring comes out from town, and there is another character with him who has whiskers that smell of corn whisky, but who seems to be a doctor, and in practically no time at all Nicely-Nicely's life is insured for five thousand dollars, with double indemnity if he gets used up by accident, and Nicely-Nicely is greatly pleased by this arrangement because he sees that he is now worth something for the first time in his career, although everybody on Broadway claims it is a terrible overlay by the insurance company when they hear the story.

Well, several months more go by, and Nicely-Nicely finds life on the farm very pleasant and peaceful as there is nothing much for him to do but eat and sleep, and he often finds himself wondering how he ever endures his old life, following the races and associating with the low characters of the turf. He gets along first class with the Widow Crumb and never has a cross word with her, and he even makes friends with the old joskin, Harley, by helping him with his work, although Nicely-Nicely is really not fitted by nature for much work, and what he likes best at the farm is the eating and sleeping, especially the eating. For a while he finds it difficult to get as much sleep as he requires, because the Widow Crumb is a great hand for staying up late reading books in their bedroom by kerosene lamp, and at the same time eating molasses candy which she personally manufactures, and sometimes she does both in bed, and the molasses candy bothers Nicely-Nicely no little until he becomes accustomed to it.

Once he tries reading one of her books to put himself to sleep after she dozes off ahead of him, but he discovers that it is all about nothing but spiritualism, and about parties in this life getting in touch with characters in the next world, and Nicely-Nicely has no interest whatever in matters of this nature, although he personally knows a character by the name of Spooks McGurk who claims to be a spiritualist, and who makes a nice thing of it in connection with tips on the races, until a race-track fuzz catches up with him. Nicely-Nicely never discusses the books with the Widow Crumb, because in the first place he figures it is none of his business, and in the second place, the more she reads the better chance he has of getting to sleep before she starts snoring, because it seems that as a snorer the Widow Crumb is really all-America material, although of course Nicely-Nicely is too much of a gentleman to make an issue of this.

She gives him three meals every day, and every meal is better than the last, and finally Nicely-Nicely is as fat as a goose, and can scarcely wobble. But he notices that the Widow Crumb never once fails to set the fourth place that nobody ever fills, and furthermore he suddenly commences to notice that she always puts the best cuts of meat, and the best of everything else on the plate at this place, even though she throws it all away afterward. Well, this situation preys on Nicely-Nicely's mind, as he cannot bear to see all this good fodder going to waste, so one morning he gets hold of old Harley and puts the siphon on him, because by this time Harley talks freely with Nicely-Nicely, although Nicely-Nicely can see that Harley is somewhat simple in spots and his conversation seldom makes much sense.

Anyway, he asks Harley what the Widow Crumb's idea is about the extra place at the table, and Harley says like this: "Why," he says, "the place is for Jake."

"Jake who?" Nicely-Nicely says.

"I do not recall his other name," Harley says. "He is her third or fourth husband, I do not remember which. Jake is the only one the Widow Crumb ever loves, although she does not discover this until after Jake departs. So," Harley says, "in memory of Jake she always sets his place at the table, and gives him the best she has. She misses Jake and wishes to feel that he is still with her."

"What happens to Jake?" Nicely-Nicely says.

"Arsenic," Harley says. "Jake departs ten years ago."

Well, of course all this is news to Nicely-Nicely, and he becomes very thoughtful to be sure, because in all the time he is married to her the Widow Crumb does not crack to him about her other husbands, and in fact Nicely-Nicely has no idea there is ever more than one. "What happens to the others?" he says. "Do they depart the same as Jake?"

"Yes," Harley says, "they all depart. One by one. I remember No. 2 well. In fact, you remind me of him. Carbon monoxide," Harley says. "A charcoal stove in his room. It is most ingenious. The coroner says No. 3 commits suicide by hanging himself with a rope in the barn loft. No. 3 is small and weak, and it is no trouble whatever to handle him. Then comes Jake," Harley says, "unless Jake is No. 3 and the hanging item is No. 4. I do not remember exactly. But the Widow Crumb never employs arsenic or other matters of this nature again. It is too slow. Jake lingers for hours. Besides," Harley says, "she realizes it may leave traces if anybody happens to get nosey. Jake is a fine-looking character," Harley says. "But a ne'er-do-well. He is a plumber from Salt Lake City, Utah, and has a hearty laugh. He is always telling funny stories. He is a great eater, even better than you, and he loves beans the way the Widow Crumb cooks them, with bacon and tomatoes. He suffers no little from the arsenic. He gets it in his beans. No. 5 comes upon a black widow spider in his bed. He is no good. I mean No. 5."

Well, by this time, Nicely-Nicely is very thoughtful to be sure, because what Harley says is commencing to sound somewhat disquieting.

"No. 6 steps on a plank in the doorway of the house that drops a 200-pound keystone on his head," Harley says. "The Widow Crumb personally figures this out herself. She is very bright. It is like a figure-4 trap, and has to be very accurate. An inch one way or the other, and the stone misses No. 6. I remember he has a big wen on the back of his neck. He is a carpenter from Keokuk, Iowa," Harley says.

"Why," Nicely-Nicely says, "do you mean to say that the Widow Crumb purposely arranges to use up husbands in the manner you describe?"

"Oh, sure," Harley says. "Why do you suppose she marries them? It is a good living to her because of the insurance," he says, "although," he says, "to show you how bright she is, she does not insure No. 5 for a dime, so people can never say she is making a business of the matter. He is a total loss to her, but it quiets talk. I am wondering," Harley says, "what she will think up for you."

Well, Nicely-Nicely now commences to wonder about this, too, and he hopes and trusts that whatever she thinks up it will not be a black widow spider, because if there is one thing Nicely-Nicely despises, it is insects. Furthermore, he does not approve of hanging, or of dropping weights on people. After giving the matter much thought, he steps into the house and mentions to the Widow Crumb that he will like to pay a little visit to town, figuring that if he can get to town, she will never see him again for heel dust. But he finds that the Widow Crumb is by no means in favor of the idea of him visiting the town. In fact, she says it will bring great sorrow to her if he absents himself from her side more than two minutes, and moreover, she points out that it is coming on winter, and that the roads are bad, and she cannot spare the horse for such a trip just now.

Well, Nicely-Nicely says he is a fair sort of walker and, in fact, he mentions that he once walks from Saratoga Springs to Albany to avoid a bookmaker who claims there is a slight difference between them, but the Widow Crumb says she will not hear of him trying to walk to town because it may develop varicose veins in his legs. In fact, Nicely-

Nicely can see that the subject of his leaving the farm is very distasteful to her in every respect, and the chances are he will feel quite flattered by her concern for him if he does not happen to go into the house again a little later this same afternoon, and find her cleaning a double-barreled shotgun.

She says she is thinking of going rabbit hunting, and wishes him to keep her company, saying it may take his mind off the idea of a visit to town; but she goes out of the room for a minute, and Nicely-Nicely picks up one of the shotgun shells she lays out on a table, and notices that it is loaded with buckshot. So he tells her he guesses he will not go, as he is not feeling so good, and in fact he is not feeling so good, at that, because it seems that Nicely-Nicely is a rabbit hunter from infancy, and he never before hears of anyone hunting these creatures with buckshot. Then the Widow Crumb says all right, she will postpone her hunting until he feels better, but Nicely-Nicely cannot help noticing that she loads the shotgun and stands it in a corner where it is good and handy.

Well, Nicely-Nicely now sits down and gives this general situation some serious consideration, because he is now convinced that the Widow Crumb is unworthy of his companionship as a husband. In fact, Nicely-Nicely makes up his mind to take steps at his earliest convenience to sue her for divorce on the grounds of incompatibility, but in the meantime he has to think up a means of getting away from her, and while he is thinking of this phase of the problem, she calls him to supper. It is now coming on dark, and she has the lamps lit and the table set when Nicely-Nicely goes into the dining room, and a fire is going in the base burner, and usually this is a pleasant and comforting scene to Nicely-Nicely, but tonight he does not seem to find it as attractive as usual.

As he sits down at the table he notices that Harley is not present at the moment, though his place at the table is laid, and as a rule Harley is Johnny-at-the-rat-hole when it comes time to scoff, and moreover he is a pretty good doer, at that. The fourth place that nobody ever occupies is also laid as usual, and now that he knows who this place is for, Nicely-Nicely notes that it is more neatly laid than his own, and that none of the china at this place is chipped, and that the bread and butter, and the salt and pepper, and the vinegar cruet and the bottle of Worcestershire sauce are handier to it than to any other place, and naturally his feelings are deeply wounded.

Then the Widow Crumb comes out of the kitchen with two plates loaded with spareribs and sauerkraut, and she puts one plate in front of Nicely-Nicely, and the other at Jake's place, and she says to Nicely-

Nicely like this: "Nicely," she says, "Harley is working late down at the barn, and when you get through with your supper, you go down and call him. But," she says, "go ahead and eat first."

Then she returns to the kitchen, which is right next to the dining room with a swinging door in between, and Nicely-Nicely now observes that the very choicest spareribs are on Jake's plate, and also the most kraut, and this is really more than Nicely-Nicely can bear, for if there is one thing he adores it is spareribs, so he gets to feeling very moody to be sure about this discrimination, and he turns to Jake's place, and in a very sarcastic tone of voice he speaks out loud as follows: "Well," he says, "it is pretty soft for you, you big lob, living on the fat of the land around here."

Now, of course what Nicely-Nicely is speaking is what he is thinking, and he does not realize that he is speaking out loud until the Widow Crumb pops into the dining room carrying a bowl of salad, and looking all around and about. "Nicely," she says, "do I hear you talking to someone?"

Well, at first Nicely-Nicely is about to deny it, but then he takes another look at the choice spareribs on Jake's plate, and he figures that he may as well let her know that he is on to her playing Jake for a favorite over him, and maybe cure her of it, for by this time Nicely-Nicely is so vexed about the spareribs that he almost forgets about leaving the farm, and is thinking of his future meals, so he says to the Widow Crumb like this: "Why, sure," he says. "I am talking to Jake."

"Jake?" she says. "What Jake?" And with this she starts looking all around and about again, and Nicely-Nicely can see that she is very pale, and that her hands are shaking so that she can scarcely hold the bowl of salad, and there is no doubt but what she is agitated no little, and quite some. "What Jake?" the Widow Crumb says again.

Nicely-Nicely points to the empty chair, and says: "Why, Jake here," he says. "You know Jake. Nice fellow, Jake." Then Nicely-Nicely goes on talking to the empty chair as follows: "I notice you are not eating much tonight, Jake," Nicely-Nicely says. "What is the matter, Jake? The food cannot disagree with you, because it is all picked out and cooked to suit you, Jake. The best is none too good for you around here, Jake," he says. Then he lets on that he is listening to something Jake is saying in reply, and Nicely-Nicely says is that so, and I am surprised, and what do you think of that, and tut-tut, and my-my, just as if Jake is talking a blue streak to him, although of course, Jake is by no means present.

Now Nicely-Nicely is really only being sarcastic in this conversation for the Widow Crumb's benefit, and naturally he does not figure that she will take it seriously, because he knows she can see Jake is not there, but Nicely-Nicely happens to look at her while he is talking, and he observes that she is still standing with the bowl of salad in her hands, and looking at the empty chair with a most unusual expression on her face, and in fact, it is such an unusual expression that it makes Nicely-Nicely feel somewhat uneasy, and he readies himself up to dodge the salad bowl at any minute.

He commences to remember the loaded shotgun in the corner, and what Harley gives him to understand about the Widow Crumb's attitude toward Jake, and Nicely-Nicely is sorry he ever brings Jake's name up, but it seems that Nicely-Nicely now finds that he cannot stop talking to save his life with the Widow Crumb standing there with the unusual expression on her face, and then he remembers the books she reads in bed at night, and he goes on as follows: "Maybe the pains in your stomach are just indigestion, Jake," he says. "I have stomach trouble in my youth myself. You are suffering terribly, eh, Jake? Well, maybe a little of the old bicarb will help you, Jake. Oh," Nicely-Nicely says, "there he goes."

And with this he jumps up and runs to Jake's chair and lets on that he is helping a character up from the floor, and as he stoops over and pretends to be lifting this character, Nicely-Nicely grunts no little, as if the character is very heavy, and the grunts are really on the level with Nicely-Nicely as he is now full of spareribs, because he never really stops eating while he is talking, and stooping is not easy for him. At these actions the Widow Crumb lets out a scream and drops the bowl of salad on the floor.

"I will help you to bed, Jake," he says. "Poor Jake. I know your stomach hurts, Jake. There now, Jake," he says, "take it easy. I know you are suffering horribly, but I will get something for you to ease the pain. Maybe it is the sauerkraut," Nicely-Nicely says. Then when he seems to get Jake up on his legs, Nicely-Nicely pretends to be assisting him across the floor toward the bedroom and all the time he is talking in a comforting tone to Jake, although you must always remember that there really is no Jake.

Now, all of a sudden, Nicely-Nicely hears the Widow Crumb's voice, and it is nothing but a hoarse whisper that sounds very strange in the room, as she says like this: "Yes," she says. "It is Jake. I see him. I see him as plain as day." Well, at this Nicely-Nicely is personally somewhat startled, and he starts looking around and about himself, and it is a good thing for Jake that Nicely-Nicely is not really assisting Jake or Jake will find himself dropped on the floor, as the Widow Crumb says: "Oh, Jake," she says, "I am so sorry. I am sorry for you in your suffering. I am sorry you ever leave me. I am sorry for everything. Please forgive me, Jake," she says. "I love you."

Then the Widow Crumb screams again and runs through the swinging door into the kitchen and out the kitchen door and down the path that leads to the barn about 200 yards away, and it is plain to be seen that she is very nervous. In fact, the last Nicely-Nicely sees of her before she disappears in the darkness down the path, she is throwing her hands up in the air, and letting out little screams, as follows: eee-eee-eee, and calling out old Harley's name.

Then Nicely-Nicely hears one extra loud scream, and after this there is much silence, and he figures that now is the time for him to take his departure, and he starts down the same path toward the barn, but figuring to cut off across the fields to the road that leads to the town when he observes a spark of light bobbing up and down on the path ahead of him, and presently he comes upon old Harley with a lantern in his hand. Harley is down on his knees at what seems to be a big, round hole in the ground, and this hole is so wide it extends clear across the path, and Harley is poking his lantern down the hole, and when he sees Nicely-Nicely, he says: "Oh," he says. "There you are. I guess there is some mistake here," he says. "The Widow Crumb tells me to wait in the barn until after supper and she will send you out after me, and," Harley says, "she also tells me to be sure and remove the cover of this old well as soon as it comes on dark. And," Harley says, "of course, I am expecting to find you in the well at this time, but who is in there but the Widow Crumb. I hear her screech as she drops in. I judge she must be hastening along the path and forgets about telling me to remove the cover of the well," Harley says. "It is most confusing," he says.

Then he pokes his lantern down the well again, and leans over and shouts as follows: "Hello, down there," Harley shouts. "Hello, hello, hello." But all that happens is an echo comes out of the well like this: Hello. And Nicely-Nicely observes that there is nothing to be seen down the well but a great blackness. "It is very deep, and dark, and cold down there," Harley says. "Deep, and dark, and cold and half full of water. Oh, my poor baby," he says. Then Harley busts out crying as if his heart will break, and in fact he is so shaken by his sobs that he almost drops the lantern down the well.

Naturally Nicely-Nicely is somewhat surprised to observe these tears because personally he is by no means greatly distressed by the Widow Crumb being down the well, especially when he thinks of how she tries to put him down the well first, and finally he asks Harley why he is so downcast, and Harley speaks as follows: "I love her," Harley says.

"I love her very, very very much. I am her No. 1 husband, and while she divorces me thirty years ago when it comes out that I have a weak heart, and the insurance companies refuse to give me a policy, I love her just the same. And now," Harley says, "here she is down a well." And with this he begins hollering into the hole some more, but the Widow Crumb never personally answers a human voice in this life again and when the story comes out, many citizens claim this is a right good thing, to be sure.

So Nicely-Nicely returns to Broadway, and he brings with him the sum of eleven hundred dollars, which is what he has left of the estate of his late ever-loving wife from the sale of the farm, and one thing and another, after generously declaring old Harley in for fifty per cent of his bit when Harley states that the only ambition he has left in life is to rear a tombstone to the memory of the Widow Crumb, and Nicely-Nicely announces that he is through with betting on horses and other frivolity, and will devote his money to providing himself with food and shelter, and maybe a few clothes. Well, the chances are Nicely-Nicely will keep his vow, too, but what happens the second day of his return, but he observes in the entries for the third race at Jamaica a horse by the name of Apparition, at 10-to-1 in the morning line, and Nicely-Nicely considers this entry practically a message to him, so he goes for his entire bundle on Apparition.

And it is agreed by one and all along Broadway who knows Nicely-Nicely's story, that nobody in his right mind can possibly ignore such a powerful hunch as this, even though it loses, and Nicely-Nicely is again around doing the best he can.

A Piece of Pie

ON BOYLSTON STREET, in the city of Boston, Mass., there is a joint where you can get as nice a broiled lobster as anybody ever slaps a lip over, and who is in there one evening partaking of this tidbit but a character by the name of Horse Thief and me. This Horse Thief is called Horsey for short, and he is not called by this name because he ever steals a horse but because it is the consensus of public opinion from coast to coast that he may steal one if the opportunity presents. Personally, I consider Horsey a very fine character, because any time he is holding anything he is willing to share his good fortune with one and all, and at this time in Boston he is holding plenty. It is the time we make the race meeting at Suffolk Down, and Horsey gets to going very good, indeed, and in fact he is now a character of means, and is my host against the broiled lobster.

Well, at a table next to us are four or five characters who all seem to be well-dressed, and stout-set, and red-faced, and prosperous-looking, and who all speak with the true Boston accent, which consists of many ah's and very few r's. Characters such as these are familiar to anybody who is ever in Boston very much, and they are bound to be politicians, retired cops, or contractors, because Boston is really quite infested with characters of this nature.

I am paying no attention to them, because they are drinking local ale, and talking loud, and long ago I learn that when a Boston character is engaged in aleing himself up, it is a good idea to let him alone, because the best you can get out of him is maybe a boff on the beezer. But Horsey is in there on the old Ear-ie, and very much interested in their conversation, and finally I listen myself just to hear what is attracting his attention, when one of the characters speaks as follows: "Well," he says, "I am willing to bet ten thousand dollars that he can outeat anybody in the United States any time."

Now at this, Horsey gets right up and steps over to the table and bows and smiles in a friendly way on one and all, and says: "Gentlemen," he says, "pardon the intrusion, and excuse me for billing in, but," he says, "do I understand you are speaking of a great eater who resides in your fair city?"

Well, these Boston characters all gaze at Horsey in such a hostile manner that I am expecting any one of them to get up and request him to let them miss him, but he keeps on bowing and smiling, and they can see that he is a gentleman, and finally one of them says: "Yes," he says, "we are speaking of a character by the name of Joel Duffle. He is without doubt the greatest eater alive. He just wins a unique wager. He bets a character from Bangor, Me., that he can eat a whole window display of oysters in this very restaurant, and he not only eats all the oysters but he then wishes to wager that he can also eat the shells, but," he says, "it seems that the character from Bangor, Me., unfortunately taps out on the first proposition and has nothing with which to bet on the second."

"Very interesting," Horsey says. "Very interesting, if true, but," he says, "unless my ears deceive me, I hear one of you state that he is willing to wager ten thousand dollars on this eater of yours against anybody in the United States."

"Your ears are perfect," another of the Boston characters says. "I state it, although," he says, "I admit it is a sort of figure of speech. But I state it all right," he says, "and never let it be said that a Conway ever pigs it on a betting proposition."

"Well," Horsey says, "I do not have a tenner on me at the moment, but," he says, "I have here a thousand dollars to put up as a forfeit that I can produce a character who will outeat your party for ten thousand, and as much more as you care to put up."

And with this, Horsey outs with a bundle of coarse notes and tosses it on the table, and right away one of the Boston characters, whose name turns out to be Carroll, slaps his hand on the money and says: "Bet."

Well, now this is prompt action to be sure, and if there is one thing I admire more than anything else, it is action, and I can see that these are characters of true sporting instincts and I commence wondering where I can raise a few dibs to take a piece of Horsey's proposition, because of course I know that he has nobody in mind to do the eating for his side but Nicely-Nicely Jones. And knowing Nicely-Nicely Jones, I am prepared to wager all the money I can possibly raise that he can outeat anything that walks on two legs. In fact, I will take a chance on Nicely-Nicely against anything on four legs, except maybe an elephant, and at that he may give the elephant a photo finish.

I do not say that Nicely-Nicely is the greatest eater in all history, but what I do say is he belongs up there as a contender. In fact, Professor D., who is a professor in a college out West before he turns to playing the horses for a livelihood, and who makes a study of history in his time, says he will not be surprised but what Nicely-Nicely figures one-two. Professor D. says we must always remember that Nicely-Nicely eats under the handicaps of modern civilization, which require that an eater use a knife and fork, or anyway a knife, while in the old days eating with the hands was a popular custom and much faster. Professor D. says he has no doubt that under the old rules Nicely-Nicely will hang up a record that will endure through the ages, but of course maybe Professor D. overlays Nicely-Nicely somewhat.

Well, now that the match is agreed upon, naturally Horsey and the Boston characters begin discussing where it is to take place, and one of the Boston characters suggests a neutral ground, such as New London, Conn., or Providence, R. I., but Horsey holds out for New York, and it seems that Boston characters are always ready to visit New York, so he does not meet with any great opposition on this point. They all agree on a date four weeks later so as to give the principals plenty of time to get ready, although Horsey and I know that this is really unnecessary as far as Nicely-Nicely is concerned, because one thing about him is he is always in condition to eat.

This Nicely-Nicely Jones is a character who is maybe five feet eight inches tall, and about five feet nine inches wide, and when he is in good shape he will weigh upward of 283 pounds. He is a horse player by trade, and eating is really just a hobby, but he is undoubtedly a wonderful eater even when he is not hungry. Well, as soon as Horsey and I return to New York, we hasten to Mindy's restaurant on Broadway and relate the bet Horsey makes in Boston, and right away so many citizens, including Mindy himself, wish to take a piece of the proposition that it is oversubscribed by a large sum in no time.

Then Mindy remarks that he does not see Nicely-Nicely Jones for a month of Sundays, and then everybody present remembers that they do not see Nicely-Nicely around lately, either, and this leads to a discussion of where Nicely-Nicely can be, although up to this moment if nobody sees Nicely-Nicely but once in the next ten years it will be considered sufficient. Well, Willie the Worrier, who is a bookmaker by trade, is among those present, and he remembers that the last time he looks for Nicely-Nicely hoping to collect a marker of some years standing, Nicely-Nicely is living at the Rest Hotel in West 49th Street, and nothing will do Horsey but I must go with him over to the Rest to make inquiry for Nicely-Nicely, and there we learn that he leaves a forwarding address away up on Morningside Heights in care of somebody by the name of Slocum.

So Horsey calls a short, and away we go to this address, which turns out to be a five-story walk-up apartment, and a card downstairs shows that Slocum lives on the top floor. It takes Horsey and me ten minutes to walk up the five flights as we are by no means accustomed to exercise of this nature, and when we finally reach a door marked Slocum, we are plumb tuckered out, and have to sit down on the top step and rest awhile. Then I ring the bell at this door marked Slocum, and who appears but a tall young Judy with black hair who is without doubt beautiful, but who is so skinny we have to look twice to see her, and when I ask her if she can give me any information about a party named Nicely-Nicely Jones, she says to me like this: "I guess you mean Quentin," she says. "Yes," she says, "Quentin is here. Come in, gentlemen."

So we step into an apartment, and as we do so a thin, sickly-looking character gets up out of a chair by the window, and in a weak voice says good evening. It is a good evening, at that, so Horsey and I say good evening right back at him, very polite, and then we stand there waiting for Nicely-Nicely to appear, when the beautiful skinny young Judy says: "Well," she says, "this is Mr. Quentin Jones."

Then Horsey and I take another swivel at the thin character, and we can see that it is nobody but Nicely-Nicely, at that, but the way he changes since we last observe him is practically shocking to us both, because he is undoubtedly all shrunk up. In fact, he looks as if he is about half what he is in his prime, and his face is pale and thin, and his eyes are away back in his head, and while we both shake hands with him it is some time before either of us is able to speak. Then Horsey finally says: "Nicely," he says, "can we have a few words with you in private on a very important proposition?"

Well, at this, and before Nicely-Nicely can answer aye, yes or no, the beautiful skinny young Judy goes out of the room and slams a door behind her, and Nicely-Nicely says: "My fiancée, Miss Hilda Slocum," he says. "She is a wonderful character. We are to be married as soon as I lose twenty pounds more. It will take a couple of weeks longer," he says.

"My goodness gracious, Nicely," Horsey says. "What do you mean lose twenty pounds more? You are practically emaciated now. Are you just out of a sick bed, or what?"

"Why," Nicely-Nicely says, "certainly I am not out of a sick bed. I am never healthier in my life. I am on a diet. I lose eighty-three pounds in two months, and am now down to 200. I feel great," he says. "It is all because of my fiancée, Miss Hilda Slocum. She rescues me from gluttony and obesity, or anyway," Nicely-Nicely says, "this is what Miss Hilda Slocum calls it. My, I feel good. I love Miss Hilda Slocum very much," Nicely-Nicely says. "It is a case of love at first sight on both sides the day we meet in the subway. I am wedged in one of the turnstile gates, and she kindly pushes on me from behind until I wiggle through. I can see she has a kind heart, so I date her up for a movie that night and propose to her while the newsreel is on. But," Nicely-Nicely says, "Hilda tells me at once that she will never marry a fat slob. She says I must put myself in her hands and she will reduce me by scientific methods and then she will become my ever-loving wife, but not before. So," Nicely-Nicely says, "I come to live here with Miss Hilda Slocum and her mother, so she can supervise my diet. Her mother is thinner than Hilda. And I surely feel great," Nicely-Nicely says. "Look," he says. And with this, he pulls out the waistband of his pants, and shows enough spare space to hide War Admiral in, but the effort seems to be a strain on him, and he has to sit down in his chair again.

"My goodness gracious," Horsey says. "What do you eat, Nicely?"

"Well," Nicely-Nicely says, "I eat anything that does not contain starch, but," he says, "of course everything worth eating contains starch, so I really do not eat much of anything whatever. My fiancée, Miss Hilda Slocum, arranges my diet. She is an expert dietitian and runs a widely known department in a diet magazine by the name of Let's Keep House."

Then Horsey tells Nicely-Nicely of how he is matched to eat against this Joel Duffle, of Boston, for a nice side bet, and how he has a forfeit of a thousand dollars already posted for appearance, and how many of Nicely-Nicely's admirers along Broadway are looking to win themselves out of all their troubles by betting on him, and at first Nicely-Nicely listens with great interest, and his eyes are shining like six bits, but then he becomes very sad, and says: "It is no use, gentlemen," he says. "My fiancée, Miss Hilda Slocum, will never hear of me going off my diet even for a little while. Only yesterday I try to talk her into letting me have a little pumpernickel instead of toasted whole wheat bread, and she says if I even think of such a thing again, she will break our engagement. Horsey," he says, "do you ever eat toasted whole wheat bread for a month hand running? Toasted?" he says.

"No," Horsey says. "What I eat is nice, white French bread, and corn muffins, and hot biscuits with gravy on them."

"Stop," Nicely-Nicely says. "You are eating yourself into an early grave, and, furthermore," he says, "you are breaking my heart. But," he says, "the more I think of my following depending on me in this emergency, the sadder it makes me feel to think I am unable to oblige them. However," he says, "let us call Miss Hilda Slocum in on an outside chance and see what her reactions to your proposition are." So we call Miss Hilda Slocum in, and Horsey explains our predicament in putting so much faith in Nicely-Nicely only to find him dieting, and

Miss Hilda Slocum's reactions are to order Horsey and me out of the joint with instructions never to darken her door again, and when we are a block away we can still hear her voice speaking very firmly to Nicely-Nicely.

Well, personally, I figure this ends the matter, for I can see that Miss Hilda Slocum is a most determined character, indeed, and the chances are it does end it, at that, if Horsey does not happen to get a wonderful break. He is at Belmont Park one afternoon, and he has a real good thing in a jump race, and when a brisk young character in a hard straw hat and eyeglasses comes along and asks him what he likes, Horsey mentions this good thing, figuring he will move himself in for a few dibs if the good thing connects. Well, it connects all right, and the brisk young character is very grateful to Horsey for his information, and is giving him plenty of much-obliges, and nothing else, and Horsey is about to mention that they do not accept much-obliges at his hotel, when the brisk young character mentions that he is nobody but Mr. McBurgle and that he is the editor of the Let's Keep House magazine, and for Horsey to drop in and see him any time he is around his way.

Naturally, Horsey remembers what Nicely-Nicely says about Miss Hilda Slocum working for this Let's Keep House magazine, and he relates the story of the eating contest to Mr. McBurgle and asks him if he will kindly use his influence with Miss Hilda Slocum to get her to release Nicely-Nicely from his diet long enough for the contest. Then Horsey gives Mr. McBurgle a tip on another winner, and Mr. McBurgle must use plenty of influence on Miss Hilda Slocum at once, as the next day she calls Horsey up at his hotel before he is out of bed, and speaks to him as follows: "Of course," Miss Hilda Slocum says, "I will never change my attitude about Quentin, but," she says, "I can appreciate that he feels very bad about you gentlemen relying on him and having to disappoint you. He feels that he lets you down, which is by no means true, but it weighs upon his mind. It is interfering with his diet.

"Now," Miss Hilda Slocum says, "I do not approve of your contest, because," she says, "it is placing a premium on gluttony, but I have a friend by the name of Miss Violette Shumberger who may answer your purpose. She is my dearest friend from childhood, but it is only because I love her dearly that this friendship endures. She is extremely fond of eating," Miss Hilda Slocum says. "In spite of my pleadings, and my warnings, and my own example, she persists in food. It is disgusting to me but I finally learn that it is no use arguing with her. She remains my dearest friend," Miss Hilda Slocum says, "though she continues her practice of eating, and I am informed that she is phenomenal in this respect. In fact," she says, "Nicely-Nicely tells me to say to you that if Miss Violette Shumberger can perform the eating exploits I relate to him from hearsay she is a lily. Goodby," Miss Hilda Slocum says. "You cannot have Nicely-Nicely."

Well, nobody cares much about this idea of a stand-in for Nicely-Nicely in such a situation, and especially a Judy that no one ever hears of before, and many citizens are in favor of pulling out of the contest altogether. But Horsey has his thousand-dollar forfeit to think of, and as no one can suggest anyone else, he finally arranges a personal meet with the Judy suggested by Miss Hilda Slocum. He comes into Mindy's one evening with a female character who is so fat it is necessary to push three tables together to give her room for her lap, and it seems that this character is Miss Violette Shumberger. She weighs maybe 250 pounds, but she is by no means an old Judy, and by no means bad-looking. She has a face the size of a town clock and enough chins for a fire escape, but she has a nice smile, and pretty teeth, and a laugh that is so hearty it knocks the whipped cream off an order of strawberry shortcake on a table fifty feet away and arouses the indignation of a customer by the name of Goldstein who is about to consume same. Well, Horsey's idea in bringing her into Mindy's is to get some kind of line on her eating form, and she is clocked by many experts when she starts putting on the hot meat, and it is agreed by one and all that she is by no means a selling-plater. In fact, by the time she gets through, even Mindy admits she has plenty of class, and the upshot of it all is Miss Violette Shumberger is chosen to eat against Joel Duffle.

Maybe you hear something of this great eating contest that comes off in New York one night in the early summer of 1937. Of course eating contests are by no means anything new, and in fact they are quite an old-fashioned pastime in some sections of this country, such as the South and East, but this is the first big public contest of the kind in years, and it creates no little comment along Broadway. In fact, there is some mention of it in the blats, and it is not a frivolous proposition in any respect, and more dough is wagered on it than any other eating contest in history, with Joel Duffle a 6 to 5 favorite over Miss Violette Shumberger all the way through.

This Joel Duffle comes to New York several days before the contest with the character by the name of Conway, and requests a meet with Miss Violette Shumberger to agree on the final details and who shows up with Miss Violette Shumberger as her coach and adviser but Nicely-Nicely Jones. He is even thinner and more peaked-looking than when Horsey and I see him last, but he says he feels great, and that he is within six pounds of his marriage to Miss Hilda Slocum. Well, it seems that his presence is really due to Miss Hilda Slocum herself, because she says that after getting her dearest friend Miss Violette Shumberger into this jack pot, it is only fair to do all she can to help her win it, and the only way she can think of is to let Nicely-Nicely give Violette the benefit of his experience and advice.

But afterward we learn that what really happens is that this editor, Mr. McBurgle, gets greatly interested in the contest, and when he discovers that in spite of his influence, Miss Hilda Slocum declines to permit Nicely-Nicely to personally compete, but puts in a pinch eater, he is quite indignant and insists on her letting Nicely-Nicely school Violette. Furthermore we afterward learn that when Nicely-Nicely returns to the apartment on Morningside Heights after giving Violette a lesson, Miss Hilda Slocum always smells his breath to see if he indulges in any food during his absence.

Well, this Joel Duffle is a tall character with stooped shoulders, and a sad expression, and he does not look as if he can eat his way out of a tea shoppe, but as soon as he commences to discuss the details of the contest, anybody can see that he knows what time it is in situations such as this. In fact, Nicely-Nicely says he can tell at once from the way Joel Duffle talks that he is a dangerous opponent, and he says while Miss Violette Shumberger impresses him as an improving eater, he is only sorry she does not have more seasoning. This Joel Duffle suggests that the contest consist of twelve courses of strictly American food, each side to be allowed to pick six dishes, doing the picking in rotation, and specifying the weight and quantity of the course selected to any amount the contestant making the pick desires, and each course is to be divided for eating exactly in half, and after Miss Violette Shumberger and Nicely-Nicely whisper together a while, they say the terms are quite satisfactory.

Then Horsey tosses a coin for the first pick, and Joel Duffle says heads, and it is heads, and he chooses, as the first course, two quarts of ripe olives, twelve bunches of celery, and four pounds of shelled nuts, all this to be split fifty-fifty between them. Miss Violette Shumberger names twelve dozen cherrystone clams as the second course, and Joel Duffle says two gallons of Philadelphia pepperpot soup as the third. Well, Miss Violette Shumberger and Nicely-Nicely whisper together again, and Violette puts in two five-pound striped bass, the heads and tails not to count in the eating, and Joel Duffle names a twenty-two-pound roast turkey. Each vegetable is rated as one course, and Miss Violette Shumberger asks for twelve pounds of mashed potatoes with brown gravy. Joel Duffle says two dozen ears of corn on the cob, and Violette replies with two quarts of lima beans. Joel Duffle calls for twelve bunches of asparagus cooked in butter, and Violette mentions ten pounds of stewed new peas. This gets them down to the salad, and it is Joel Duffle's play, so he says six pounds of mixed green salad with vinegar and oil dressing, and now Miss Violette Shumberger has the final selection, which is the dessert. She says it is a pumpkin pie, two feet across, and not less than three inches deep.

It is agreed that they must eat with knife, fork or spoon, but speed is not to count, and there is to be no time limit, except they cannot pause more than two consecutive minutes at any stage, except in case of hiccoughs. They can drink anything, and as much as they please, but liquids are not to count in the scoring. The decision is to be strictly on the amount of food consumed, and the judges are to take account of anything left on the plates after a course, but not of loose chewings on bosom or vest up to an ounce. The losing side is to pay for the food, and in case of a tie they are to eat it off immediately on ham and eggs only.

Well, the scene of this contest is the second-floor dining room of Mindy's restaurant, which is closed to the general public for the occasion, and only parties immediately concerned in the contest are admitted. The contestants are seated on either side of a big table in the center of the room, and each contestant has three waiters. No talking, and no rooting from the spectators is permitted, but of course in any eating contest the principals may speak to each other if they wish, though smart eaters never wish to do this, as talking only wastes energy, and about all they ever say to each other is please pass the mustard.

About fifty characters from Boston are present to witness the contest, and the same number of citizens of New York are admitted, and among them is this editor, Mr. McBurgle, and he is around asking Horsey if he thinks Miss Violette Shumberger is as good a thing as the jumper at the race track.

Nicely-Nicely arrives on the scene quite early, and his appearance is really most distressing to his old friends and admirers, as by this time he is shy so much weight that he is a pitiful scene, to be sure, but he tells Horsey and me that he thinks Miss Violette Shumberger has a good chance.

"Of course," he says, "she is green. She does not know how to pace herself in competition. But," he says, "she has a wonderful style. I love to watch her eat. She likes the same things I do in the days when I am eating. She is a wonderful character, too. Do you ever notice her smile?" Nicely-Nicely says. "But," he says, "she is the dearest friend of my fiancée, Miss Hilda Slocum, so let us not speak of this. I try to get Hilda to come to see the contest, but she says it is repulsive. Well, anyway," Nicely-Nicely says, "I manage to borrow a few dibs, and am wagering on Miss Violette Shumberger. By the way," he says, "if you happen to think of it, notice her smile."

Well, Nicely-Nicely takes a chair about ten feet behind Miss Violette Shumberger, which is as close as the judges will allow him, and he is warned by them that no coaching from the corners will be permitted, but of course Nicely-Nicely knows this rule as well as they do, and furthermore by this time his exertions seem to have left him without any more energy. There are three judges, and they are all from neutral territory. One of these judges is a party from Baltimore, Md., by the name of Packard, who runs a restaurant, and another is a party from Providence, R. I., by the name of Croppers, who is a sausage manufacturer. The third judge is an old Judy by the name of Mrs. Rhubarb, who comes from Philadelphia, and once keeps an actors' boardinghouse, and is considered an excellent judge of eaters.

Well, Mindy is the official starter, and at 8:30 P.M. sharp, when there is still much betting among the spectators, he outs with his watch, and says like this: "Are you ready, Boston? Are you ready, New York?" Miss Violette Shumberger and Joel Duffle both nod their heads, and Mindy says commence, and the contest is on, with Joel Duffle getting the jump at once on the celery and olives and nuts.

It is apparent that this Joel Duffle is one of these rough-and-tumble eaters that you can hear quite a distance off, especially on clams and soups. He is also an eyebrow eater, an eater whose eyebrows go up as high as the part in his hair as he eats, and this type of eater is undoubtedly very efficient. In fact, the way Joel Duffle goes through the groceries down to the turkey causes the Broadway spectators some uneasiness, and they are whispering to each other that they only wish the old Nicely-Nicely is in there. But personally, I like the way Miss Violette Shumberger eats without undue excitement, and with great zest. She cannot keep close to Joel Duffle in the matter of speed in the early stages of the contest, as she seems to enjoy chewing her food, but I observe that as it goes along she pulls up on him, and I figure this is not because she is stepping up her pace, but because he is slowing down.

When the turkey finally comes on, and is split in two halves right down the middle, Miss Violette Shumberger looks greatly disappointed, and she speaks for the first time as follows: "Why," she says, "where is the stuffing?" Well, it seems that nobody mentions any stuffing for the turkey to the chef, so he does not make any stuffing, and Miss Violette Shumberger's disappointment is so plain to be seen that the confidence of the Boston characters is somewhat shaken. They can see that a Judy who can pack away as much fodder as Miss Violette Shumberger has to date, and then beef for stuffing, is really quite an eater.

In fact, Joel Duffle looks quite startled when he observes Miss Violette Shumberger's disappointment, and he gazes at her with great respect as she disposes of her share of the turkey, and the mashed potatoes, and one thing and another in such a manner that she moves up on the pumpkin pie on dead even terms with him. In fact, there is little to choose between them at this point, although the judge from Baltimore is calling the attention of the other judges to a turkey leg that he claims Miss Violette Shumberger does not clean as neatly as Joel Duffle does his, but the other judges dismiss this as a technicality.

Then the waiters bring on the pumpkin pie, and it is without doubt quite a large pie, and in fact it is about the size of a manhole cover, and I can see that Joel Duffle is observing this pie with a strange expression on his face, although to tell the truth I do not care for the expression on Miss Violette Shumberger's face, either. Well, the pie is cut in two dead center, and one half is placed before Miss Violette Shumberger, and the other half before Joel Duffle, and he does not take more than two bites before I see him loosen his waistband and take a big swig of water, and thinks I to myself, he is now down to a slow walk, and the pie will decide the whole heat, and I am only wishing I am able to wager a little more dough on Miss Violette Shumberger. But about this moment, and before she as much as touches her pie, all of a sudden Violette turns her head and motions to Nicely-Nicely to approach her, and as he approaches, she whispers in his ear.

Now at this, the Boston character by the name of Conway jumps up and claims a foul, and several other Boston characters join him in this claim, and so does Joel Duffle, although afterwards even the Boston characters admit that Joel Duffle is no gentleman to make such a claim against a lady. Well, there is some confusion over this, and the judges hold a conference, and they rule that there is certainly no foul in the actual eating that they can see, because Miss Violette Shumberger does not touch her pie so far. But they say that whether it is a foul otherwise all depends on whether Miss Violette Shumberger is requesting advice on the contest from Nicely-Nicely and the judge from Providence, R. I., wishes to know if Nicely-Nicely will kindly relate what passes between him and Violette so they may make a decision.

"Why," Nicely-Nicely says, "all she asks me is can I get her another piece of pie when she finishes the one in front of her."

Now at this, Joel Duffle throws down his knife, and pushes back his plate with all but two bites of his pie left on it, and says to the Boston characters like this: "Gentlemen," he says, "I am licked. I cannot eat another mouthful. You must admit I put up a game battle, but," he says, "it is useless for me to go on against this Judy who is asking for more pie before she even starts on what is before her. I am almost dying as it is, and I do not wish to destroy myself in a hopeless effort. Gentlemen," he says, "she is not human."

Well, of course this amounts to throwing in the old napkin and Nicely-Nicely stands up on his chair, and says: "Three cheers for Miss Violette Shumberger!" Then Nicely-Nicely gives the first cheer in person, but the effort overtaxes his strength, and he falls off the chair in a faint just as Joel Duffle collapses under the table, and the doctors at the Clinic Hospital are greatly baffled to receive, from the same address at the same time, one patient who is suffering from undernourishment, and another patient who is unconscious from overeating.

Well, in the meantime, after the excitement subsides, and wagers are settled, we take Miss Violette Shumberger to the main floor in Mindy's for a midnight snack, and when she speaks of her wonderful triumph, she is disposed to give much credit to Nicely-Nicely Jones. "You see," Violette says, "what I really whisper to him is that I am a goner. I whisper to him that I cannot possibly take one bite of the pie if my life depends on it, and if he has any bets down to try and hedge them off as quickly as possible. I fear," she says, "that Nicely-Nicely will be greatly disappointed in my showing, but I have a confession to make to him when he gets out of the hospital. I forget about the contest," Violette says, "and eat my regular dinner of pig's knuckles and sauerkraut an hour before the contest starts, and," she says, "I have no doubt this tends to affect my form somewhat. So," she says, "I owe everything to Nicely-Nicely's quick thinking."

It is several weeks after the great eating contest that I run into Miss Hilda Slocum on Broadway, and it seems to me that she looks much better nourished than the last time I see her, and when I mention this she says: "Yes," she says, "I cease dieting. I learn my lesson," she says. "I learn that male characters do not appreciate anybody who tries to ward off surplus tissue. What male characters wish is substance. Why," she says, "only a week ago my editor, Mr. McBurgle, tells me he will love to take me dancing if only I get something on me for him to take hold of. I am very fond of dancing," she says.

"But," I say, "what of Nicely-Nicely Jones? I do not see him around lately."

"Why," Miss Hilda Slocum says, "do you not hear what this cad does? Why, as soon as he is strong enough to leave the hospital, he elopes with my dearest friend, Miss Violette Shumberger, leaving me a note saying something about two souls with but a single thought. They are down in Florida running a barbecue stand, and," she says, "the chances are, eating like seven mules."

"Miss Slocum," I says, "can I interest you in a portion of Mindy's chicken fricassee?"

"With dumplings?" Miss Hilda Slocum says. "Yes," she says, "you can. Afterwards I have a date to go dancing with Mr. McBurgle. I am crazy about dancing," she says.

Tight Shoes

ALL THIS begins the day a young character by the name of Rupert Salsinger sells Hymie Minsk, the horse player, a pair of shoes that are too tight. This Rupert Salsinger works in Bilby's shoe store on Broadway, near Mindy's restaurant, and Hymie stops in there on his way to the Belmont race track early one afternoon, and buys the shoes.

Now Hymie is in pretty much of a hurry, as he knows of a right good thing in the first race at Belmont, so he tells Rupert Salsinger to kindly get out a pair of shoes, size 8½ D, and make haste about it. Well, Rupert Salsinger takes one look at Hymie's dogs, and he can see that Hymie can no more wear an 8½ D than he can fly, for Hymie has large, flat Bronx feet that can cover as much ground as there is between second and third when Hymie is just standing still. So Rupert Salsinger gets out a measuring gadget, and puts one of Hymie's feet in it, and tells Hymie that what he really needs is a 10½ EE, but Hymie immediately becomes very indignant, as he is extremely sensitive about the size of his feet, and he says he knows what size shoes he wears, and if Rupert Salsinger does not care to give him what he wants, he will take his custom elsewhere.

Now if old man Bilby is personally present, he will know enough to give Hymie his usual 10½ EE's, and tell him they are 8½ D's, and Hymie will go on about his business, and think nothing more of it, but Rupert Salsinger is new to Bilby's store, and furthermore he is a very honest and conscientious young character, and does not believe in skull-duggery even about a pair of shoes, so he outs with some 8½ D's and shows Hymie the mark in them, and Hymie puts them on, and says they are just the right size, and away he goes to the race track.

Well, the good thing in the first race blows, and right away Hymie commences to notice that his shoes seem full of feet, for there is nothing like a loser in the first race for making a guy notice his feet. Then Hymie gets five more losers in a row, so by the time the races are over his feet are almost killing him. In fact, anybody will tell you that six losers in a row will make a guy's feet hurt, even if he is barefooted, so a pair of tight shoes on such an occasion is practically murder in the first degree. Hymie has to take his shoes off in the train going back to

New York to rest his feet, and one and all are most sympathetic with him, because they realize how keenly he must be suffering between the tight shoes and the six losers, and especially the six losers.

Well, Hymie Minsk goes right up to Bilby's shoe store in the tight shoes, and what does he do but use these shoes to kick Rupert Salsinger in the pants all the way from Bilby's store to Fifty-third Street, three blocks away, and the chances are he will be kicking Rupert Salsinger to this very day, if one foot does not finally connect with a book by Karl Marx, which Rupert is wearing in his hip pocket, and which almost breaks Hymie's big toe, it being a very solid book. But everybody agrees that Hymie does the right thing, especially when Hymie explains that the shoes hurt his feet so at the track that he does not really know what he is doing after the first race, and his pain causes him to bet on horses that he has no right to consider in any manner, shape or form whatever. In fact, everybody agrees that Rupert is a very dangerous character to have on Broadway, as he may take to selling tight shoes to horse players generally, and thus cause untold suffering among them, besides upsetting their figures on the horse races.

Furthermore, when Rupert Salsinger gets back to the shoe store old man Bilby pays him off and fires him, and also personally takes a few kicks at Rupert Salsinger's pants himself as Rupert is going out the door, and old man Bilby's aim is much better than Hymie's, and he does not hit the volume of Karl Marx even once.

So there Rupert Salsinger is without a position, and with only half a week's wages consisting of about seven slugs in his pocket, and as it is the first position Rupert has since the depression sets in, he is downcast no little, especially as he is hoping to save enough money in this position to justify him in asking Miss Minnie Schultz, who lives over on Tenth Avenue, to be his bride. He is in love with Miss Minnie Schultz for several years, and expects to one day ask her to marry him, but Rupert Salsinger is such a conscientious young character that he will never think of making such a request until he becomes a provider, and anyway, Miss Minnie Schultz's papa, who keeps a delicatessen store, by no means approves of Rupert Salsinger, because Rupert is always so thoughtful and studious, and also always so much out of a position.

In fact, Miss Minnie Schultz's papa considers Rupert nothing but a bum, and he wishes his daughter to marry an entirely different character by the name of Gus Schmelk, who runs a delicatessen store right across the street from the Schultz store, and is giving Miss Minnie Schultz's papa such tough competition that her papa figures it will be a nice business deal for her to marry Gus Schmelk and combine the stores. But Miss Minnie Schultz is rather fond of Rupert Salsinger, as he is tall and thin, and has thick black hair, and a very serious expression, and wears spectacles, and is really much better than a raw hand when it comes to making love, even though he is so conservative about speaking of marriage.

Well, anyway, Rupert Salsinger goes up Broadway feeling very sad and blue, and finally he stops in the Bridle Grill, and steps up to the bar and calls for a glass of beer, and while he is drinking this beer, he gets to thinking what a cruel world it is to be sure, so he calls for another beer, with a little rye whisky on the side, for while Rupert Salsinger is by no means a rum-dum, he feels that this is an occasion that calls for a few drams, anyway.

It is now along about eight bells in the evening, and not many cash customers are in the Bridle Grill, when all of a sudden in comes a tall, good-looking young fellow in evening clothes, including a high hat, and an opera cape, lined with white silk, and who is this young fellow but Calvin Colby, who is known far and wide as a great pain in the neck to his loving parents. He is also known as a character who likes to get around and, in fact, Calvin Colby's only occupation is getting around. His people are as rich as mud, and to tell the truth, richer, and what is more they are in the Social Register and, in fact, Calvin Colby is in the Social Register himself until the publishers come upon his name one day and see that it is a typographical error. He is often in the newspapers, because it is really remarkable how Calvin Colby's automobiles can spill dolls up against telegraph poles along the Boston Post Road, when he happens to strike these obstacles, and the dolls are always suing Calvin Colby for breaking their legs, or spoiling their complexions. It finally gets so there is talk of taking Calvin's driving license away from him before he shatters all the telegraph poles along the Boston Post Road. He is without doubt strictly a Hoorah Henry, and he is generally figured as nothing but a lob as far as ever doing anything useful in this world is concerned, although everybody admits that he has a nice disposition, and is as good a right guard as ever comes out of Yale.

Calvin Colby is undoubtedly slightly mulled when he enters the Bridle Grill, and he steps up to the bar alongside Rupert Salsinger, and calls for an old-fashioned cocktail, and after he inhales this, he calls for three more of the same, one right after the other, and about this time, Rupert Salsinger, who is standing there thinking of the wrongs he suffers at the feet of Hymie Minsk and old man Bilby, lets out a terrible sigh, as follows: "Hah-ah-ah-hah."

Well, at this, Calvin Colby gazes at Rupert Salsinger in surprise, as Rupert's sigh sounds very much like wind escaping from a punctured tire, and Calvin speaks to Rupert like this: "What is eating you?" Calvin says. "Have a drink," he says.

Naturally, Rupert has a drink, because it is very seldom in his life that he gets a drink for nothing, and this time he calls for an old-fashioned, too, as he is tired of beer and rye whisky, and moreover he figures it will be polite to drink the same as his host, and then he says to Calvin Colby: "Comrade," he says, "this is an awful world. There is no justice."

"Well," Calvin Colby says, "I never give the matter much thought, because personally I never have any occasion for justice. But," he says, "you may be right. Have a drink." So they have this second drink, and also quite a few other drinks, and presently they are as friendly as a new bride and groom, and Rupert Salsinger tells Calvin Colby about the shoes, and Hymie Minsk, and old man Bilby, and also about Miss Minnie Schultz, and when he gets to Miss Minnie Schultz, he sheds tears all over Calvin Colby's white pique vest.

Well, Calvin Colby is practically petrified with horror to think of what Rupert Salsinger suffers, although he does not consider Rupert's tears over Miss Minnie Schultz quite manly, as Calvin Colby personally never experiences love, and regards dolls as only plaintiffs, but he admits that his soul seethes with indignation at the idea of Miss Minnie Schultz's papa wishing to force her into a marriage with Gus Schmelk. In fact, Calvin Colby says that while he does not know this Gus Schmelk he is willing to make a little wager that he is nothing but a bounder and a cad.

Now it seems that Calvin Colby is all dressed up to go somewhere, but by this time he cannot remember where, and he suggests to Rupert Salsinger that they take a little stroll and see if the old-fashioneds are up to standard in other parts of the city. So they leave the Bridle Grill, and the bartender is not sorry to see them depart, at that, as they are making him work too hard, and they walk north on Broadway, arm-in-arm, stopping here and there to have a few drinks, and all the time Calvin Colby is talking about the great injustice that has been done Rupert Salsinger. By and by they come to Columbus Circle, and in Columbus Circle there are many little groups of citizens, and each group is gathered around a guy standing on a box making a speech, so there are maybe ten different groups, and ten different guys making speeches, although each guy is only talking to his own group, but they are all talking at once, so they make quite a racket.

Now of course all this is a very familiar scene to anybody that ever goes through Columbus Circle in the evening, but it seems that Calvin Colby never before witnesses such a thing, as he does not visit Columbus

Circle since infancy, and he is greatly astonished at what he beholds, and asks Rupert Salsinger what is the meaning of this. Well, it seems that Rupert Salsinger knows all about the matter, and in fact it seems that Rupert Salsinger often takes part in these meetings personally when he has nothing else to do, and he explains to Calvin Colby that each of the speakers has a message of some kind to deliver to the people about one thing and another, and they are delivering them in Columbus Circle because it is a sort of public forum, and the coppers are not permitted to bother anybody with a message here, although they may run them bowlegged if they try to deliver any message anywhere else.

Now Calvin Colby becomes greatly interested in this proposition and he listens in here and there on different groups, but he is unable to make heads or tails of what the speakers are talking about, except that most of them are weighing in the sacks on the rich, and on the government, and on this and that, and finally Calvin Colby says to Rupert Salsinger like this: "Why," Calvin Colby says, "the trouble with these parties is they are all over the layout. They are scattering their play too much. What we need here is a little centralization of ideas. Get me a box," Calvin says.

Well, all the boxes around and about are occupied, but by this time, what with the beer, and the old-fashioneds, and all, Rupert Salsinger is a character of great determination, and he goes up to one speaker and yanks the box right from under him without saying aye, yes, or no, and this action leaves the speaker flat in Columbus Circle, but it seems that the speaker is about all out of ideas, anyway, and cannot think of anything more to say, so he does not mind losing his box as much as you might expect. Then Rupert takes the box and plants it right in the center of all the groups, and Calvin Colby gets up on the box and begins letting out loud yells to attract attention. Naturally Calvin Colby can out-yell any of the speakers in Columbus Circle, because he is fresh, and furthermore he is full of old-fashioneds, and it is well known that there is nothing like old-fashioneds to help anybody yell.

Well, everyone in the Circle turns at once to see what the yelling is about and when they see a party in evening clothes, with a high hat and a white-lined opera cape on, naturally they are somewhat impressed, and they leave all the other speakers and gather around Calvin Colby. Some think at first that maybe he is selling a patent medicine, or ballyhooing a dance hall with forty hostesses, and they expect to see his shirt bosom light up with an ad on it, as they cannot figure any other reason for anybody in such a make-up to be in Columbus Circle, but when Calvin Colby finally gets a big crowd around him, including not only the citizens who are listening to the other speakers, but many characters, male and female, who happen to be passing along the sidewalks and hear his yells, he speaks to them as follows, and to wit: "Comrades," Calvin Colby says, "when I think of all the injustice in this world it almost makes me bust right out crying. My heart bleeds. I am very sad. All humanity cries out 'Justice, justice,' but what is the answer. Nothing, Comrades," he says.

Now at this point somebody back in the crowd pegs an egg at Calvin Colby's high hat, and cries out in a loud, coarse voice: "Look at the daffydill." The egg just misses Calvin Colby's hat and continues on and strikes a member of the Communist party on the chin, and the member of the Communist party is slightly irritated, as he says he can use the egg for breakfast if it does not break when it meets his chin.

Well, naturally this interruption annoys Calvin Colby no little, and he stops a moment and tries to see who it is that is guilty of such uncouth conduct, and then he says: "Comrades," he says, "if the jerk who just hurls the aforesaid remark and egg at me will kindly hold still until I reach him, I will guarantee to yank one of his arms off and beat his brains out with it." At this the crowd cheers Calvin Colby quite some, and there are cries for him to continue his address, although Calvin Colby has half a notion to stop right there and go to work on the party who pegs the egg, because such a course promises more fun for Calvin Colby than making a speech, but finally he resumes as follows: "No, Comrades," he says, "there is no justice, and to prove it I wish to present to you my friend, my pal, my comrade, Mr. Rupert Salsinger, who will now address you."

So he makes room for Rupert Salsinger on the box, and Rupert puts on a really wonderful speech, because it seems that Rupert is not only a natural-born speaker, but he knows extracts from great speeches by such characters as Father Coughlin, Patrick Henry, F. D. Roosevelt, Abraham Lincoln and Robert Ingersoll, and he drops in these extracts here and there as he goes along, and they are very effective. He tells of his own personal experiences with representatives of the capitalistic system, and while he does not mention them by name, he undoubtedly means Hymie Minsk and old man Bilby, and Rupert's remarks about his own suffering touch every heart, and there are cries of pity and rage from all parts of the crowd, although Rupert himself afterwards admits that maybe he does give Hymie and old man Bilby a shade the worst of it in his statements.

By the time Rupert finishes, his audience is greatly excited, and Calvin Colby is sitting on the edge of the box half asleep, so Rupert wakes him up to make some more remarks, but now Calvin Colby is slightly bored by his surroundings and wishes to get away from this spot, and all he can think of to say is as follows: "Comrades," he says, "let us stop talking, and go into action. The cry," he says, "is forward!" And with this, Calvin Colby starts off down Broadway, walking in the middle of the street, and all he is thinking of at the moment is to remove himself from Columbus Circle, and Rupert starts off with him, but all the other citizens present fall in behind them, so there they are leading a big march.

There are only a few hundred citizens behind them when they start, but before they go two blocks this number increases to several thousand, because naturally the spectacle of a character in a high hat and a white-lined opera cape leading a procession down Broadway is most intriguing to one and all who behold same, and everybody wishes to find out what it means. Of course Calvin and Rupert Salsinger have no idea where they are going when they start off, and when they arrive at Fiftieth and Broadway, Calvin Colby is getting sick and tired of walking, and wishes one of his cars will come along and pick him up, and furthermore he is yearning for a few old-fashioned cocktails.

In fact, Calvin Colby is getting ready to cop a sneak on his followers, when Rupert Salsinger points out old man Bilby's shoe store, which of course is closed at this hour, as the seat of much of the injustice to him, and the member of the Communist party, who is in the procession, still thinking about the loss of the egg, hears what Rupert says, and steps over on the sidewalk and kicks in old man Bilby's door. Well, in five minutes old man Bilby's shoe store is a total wreck, and everybody has a pair of shoes, including many characters who are never in the procession at all, and are by no means entitled to same. There is great confusion, and some of the shoes get all mixed up in this confusion, and in fact for weeks afterwards parties are around Broadway with odd shoes trying to match them up.

Naturally the commotion brings out a number of officers of the law, who go around inquiring what is coming off here, and when they are unable to learn what is coming off, they start slapping citizens right and left with their nightsticks, and the result is a great deal of new business for the near-by hospitals. But this part of it no longer interests Calvin Colby and Rupert Salsinger, who retire from the scene and go else-where, but not before Rupert Salsinger gets into the store and picks out a pair of shoes for himself and carries them off under his arm.

Well, by and by the reporters from the newspapers arrive on the scene and start getting interviews here and there about the goings-on, and it seems from the stories in the papers the next morning that the reporters learn that it is all the upshot of a great new movement for social justice organized by Rupert Salsinger, a famous young student of such matters, and supported by Calvin Colby, the well-known young multimillionaire thinker, although of course it is a big surprise to Rupert Salsinger to learn that he is famous, and a much bigger surprise to Calvin Colby to hear that he is a thinker, and in fact this sounds like libel to Calvin Colby, when he gets around to reading it. But it seems that what the newspapers see in this movement for social justice led by such young characters as Rupert Salsinger and Calvin Colby, more than anything else, is a revolution of youth against the old order, and in fact the papers make it a matter of great importance and by eight A.M. the next morning the reporters and photographers from the afternoon bladders are almost breaking down the doors of Calvin Colby's apartment on Park Avenue to interview him and take his picture.

Naturally, Calvin Colby is still in the hay at such an hour, and he does not wake up until one-thirty P.M. and by this time he does not remember about the movement for social justice, and in fact he will be greatly nonplussed to find himself sleeping with such a character as Rupert Salsinger if it is not for the fact that Calvin Colby is accustomed to finding himself sleeping with all kinds of characters. He wakes Rupert Salsinger up and asks him what about a little of the hair of the dog that bites them, but Rupert is very ill, and all he can bear is a little straight Scotch, and then Rupert commences to recall vaguely some of the events of the night before, when Calvin Colby's butler brings in the morning papers, and tells them that fifty reporters and photographers are still waiting outside to see Calvin Colby, and that they are getting fretful, and that moreover Calvin Colby's loving parents are calling up every few minutes, wishing to know what he means by becoming a thinker. Then Calvin Colby commences remembering a few things himself, and he worries no little about how he is going to explain to his loving parents. Naturally he cannot face reporters and photographers while he is in such a state of mind, so he gives Rupert Salsinger a little more straight Scotch, and lends Rupert a dressing-gown, and sends him out to see the reporters and photographers.

Well, Rupert Salsinger gives them quite an interview, and in fact he repeats as much of the speech he makes in Columbus Circle as he can remember, including the extracts from the speeches of F. D. Roosevelt and Abraham Lincoln, and he tells them that he and Calvin Colby will continue this movement for social justice until the bad place freezes over, if necessary, because by now the straight Scotch is working very good in Rupert Salsinger, and he is by no means at any loss for words.

Now Rupert Salsinger is a very serious-minded young character and by no means a chump, and he sees that all this publicity may lead somewhere, so what does he do in the next few days but organize the American Amalgamation for Social Justice, with himself as president, and Calvin Colby as treasurer, and Calvin Colby's loving parents are so proud of their son becoming prominent at something else besides spilling dolls out of his automobiles that they donate five thousand slugs to the cause. Furthermore, they settle with old man Bilby for the wrecking of his shoe store, and the loss of his shoes, including the pair taken away by Rupert Salsinger, although of course nobody but Rupert knows about these shoes, and he does not mention the matter publicly.

But Calvin Colby is getting sick and tired of all this business, because the reporters are always after him for interviews, and it is commencing to interfere with his occupation of getting around, especially as Rupert Salsinger is always after him, too, telling him to do this and that, and one thing and another, and Calvin Colby is delighted when Rupert announces himself as a candidate for Congress on the Social Justice ticket, because Calvin figures that with Rupert in Congress he will not bother him any more, and he can resume getting around just where he leaves off. Well, it seems that about the time Rupert Salsinger makes his announcement, Tammany Hall is greatly dissatisfied with the character who already represents it in Congress from Rupert's district, because he often votes in a manner that is by no means to the interest of this splendid organization, so somebody from the Hall has a talk with Rupert Salsinger, and reports that he is an honest, clean, upright young character, who is by no means sore at Tammany, or at least not so sore that he can never get over it.

Then it seems that Tammany quietly passes the word around Rupert Salsinger's district to vote for this honest, clean, upright young character, and such a word means that Rupert is 1 to 20 in the betting to be elected, even on a platform for social justice, and about this time Rupert begins thinking more than somewhat of Miss Minnie Schultz, and of how much he loves her. Rupert is so busy that it is quite a spell since he finds leisure to get over to Tenth Avenue to see Miss Minnie Schultz, and he requests Calvin Colby, as a personal favor, to step over and explain to Miss Minnie Schultz why he cannot appear before her in person.

So Calvin Colby goes over to Tenth Avenue and locates Miss Minnie Schultz at her papa's delicatessen store, and explains to her about Rupert, and Calvin Colby is greatly surprised to notice that Miss Minnie Schultz is very beautiful. He notices that she has taffy-colored hair, and big blue eyes, and a lovely speaking voice, and hands like the ears of little tiny white rabbits, and feet like little tiny mice, and a complexion like Grade-A milk, and a shape that is wonderful to behold, and great intelligence, and charm, and in fact Miss Minnie Schultz is the first doll Calvin Colby ever beholds that he does not figure a plaintiff. He also notices a character skulking in the background of Miss Minnie Schultz whose name seems to be Gus Schmelk, and whose features seem to be very familiar to Calvin Colby, and also very distasteful, especially as this Gus Schmelk seems to be on very friendly terms with Miss Minnie Schultz, and in fact in the presence of Calvin Colby he gives her a pat on the pistol pocket, causing Calvin Colby's blood to boil out of loyalty to Rupert Salsinger.

However, Miss Minnie Schultz seems quite interested in hearing about Rupert, and says she hopes and trusts he is enjoying the best of health, and that he will come to see her soon, though she realizes from what she reads in the papers how busy he is, and she also says that she is personally as well and as happy as can be expected, and that business in her papa's delicatessen store is picking up.

Well, Calvin Colby reports much of the above situation to Rupert Salsinger, especially about Gus Schmelk, and tells Rupert that Gus impresses him as a low, degraded character, who will steal another's doll without any compunction of conscience whatever, and in fact Calvin Colby says to Rupert like this: "If I am you," he says, "I will dispense with this social justice for a while and look after my interests with Miss Minnie Schultz. It is seldom in my career," Calvin says, "that I see such a shape as Miss Minnie Schultz possesses."

Well, Rupert Salsinger sighs, and says he realizes that Calvin Colby's statements are only too true, especially about Gus Schmelk, and also about Miss Minnie Schultz's shape, but Rupert says he feels that social justice must come first with him above all else, even Miss Minnie Schultz's shape. Then Rupert says to Calvin Colby: "Comrade," he says, "I realize that you loathe and despise all characters of a female nature, but," he says, "I am going to ask you to make a great sacrifice for me. I will deem it an act of fealty to our cause, and of personal friendship," Rupert says, "if you will occasionally go over to Tenth Avenue and do anything you can to protect me in that direction from vipers in my bosom, and snakes in the grass." There are tears in Rupert's eyes as he makes this request, and naturally Calvin Colby promises to assist him in this emergency, and presently between looking after Rupert's interests with Miss Minnie Schultz and signing checks as treasurer of the American Amalgamation for Social Justice for Rupert's campaign, Calvin Colby finds little time for his occupation of getting around.

Now in the meantime, in spite of being so busy, Rupert Salsinger finds himself brooding no little over Miss Minnie Schultz and Gus Schmelk, and finally one day he decides that he can spare a couple of hours to go over to Tenth Avenue and see Miss Minnie Schultz and present his proposal of marriage to her in person, so he calls her up and requests an interview with her, and it seems she can tell by the tone of his voice what is on his chest, and she says all right but to be sure and get over in an hour.

So Rupert Salsinger puts everything else aside, and dresses himself up in a new suit of clothes which he purchases from the treasury of the Amalgamated Association for Social Justice as part of his campaign expenses, and puts on the new shoes that he secures at old man Bilby's shoe store, and starts out from Calvin Colby's residence on Park Avenue, where Rupert is living ever since the first night he lands there. Well, Rupert is passing the corner of Fiftieth Street and Broadway, when who does he see standing in front of Mindy's restaurant but Hymie Minsk, the horse player, and then Rupert suddenly remembers that while social justice is going forward very nicely in most quarters that he never really gets justice from Hymie Minsk.

So Rupert Salsinger steps up behind Hymie, and takes him by the nape of the neck, and kicks Hymie's pants up the street to Fifty-third, using his new shoes for this purpose, and, what is more, doing a much better job on Hymie than Hymie does on him, as Hymie has no books whatsoever in his hip pocket to slow up Rupert's kicking. When he finally lets Hymie go with a final kick in the pants, Rupert starts across Fifty-third Street toward Tenth Avenue, but after he goes a couple of blocks he notices that his feet are giving him great pain, and he realizes that his new shoes must be too tight for him, and what with his walking, and the extra exertion of kicking Hymie Minsk's pants, these shoes are commencing to pinch his puppies quite some.

The pain finally becomes so great that Rupert sits down on the steps of a school house and takes off his shoes to let his feet stop aching, and he sits there for anyway fifteen minutes, when it occurs to him that the hour Miss Minnie Schultz mentions is up, so he tries to put the shoes back on his feet again, but it seems his feet swell up to such an extent that the shoes will not go on again, so Rupert resumes his journey in his stocking feet, but carrying the shoes in his hand. When he arrives in sight of the delicatessen store conducted by Miss Minnie Schultz's papa, he sees Miss Minnie Schultz standing on the sidewalk out in front, and he also sees Gus Schmelk walking across the street, and disappearing inside his own store, which is a scene that is most odious to Rupert Salsinger, although he does not see a large automobile with Calvin Colby in it just going around the corner.

Well, Rupert Salsinger hastens forward with a glad smile, and he tips his hat with the hand which is not carrying the shoes, and he says to Miss Minnie Schultz, like this: "Minnie," Rupert says, "I love you with all my heart and soul, and now that my future is open before me, bright and shining, I wish you to be my wife, and never mind what your papa says to the contrary about Gus Schmelk. He is strictly a wrong gee. I mean Gus Schmelk," Rupert says. "Let us be married at once, and my friend, my pal, my comrade, Mr. Calvin Colby, will stand up with us as my best man."

"Rupert," Miss Minnie Schultz says, "if you are here fifteen minutes ago, I will undoubtedly accept you. When you call me on the telephone and make an appointment for an interview with me, I say to myself, I wait all these years for Rupert to speak, and now I will give him just one more hour of my life, and not one minute more, for another is requesting my hand. On the expiration of the hour to the dot," Miss Minnie Schultz says, "I pledge myself to him. Rupert," she says, "as far as I am personally concerned you are a goner."

Naturally, Rupert Salsinger is greatly vexed to hear this news, and in fact he is so vexed that he takes the tight shoes that are the cause of his tardiness, and throws them as far as he can, and as straight as he can, which is plumb across the street and through the plate-glass window of Gus Schmelk's delicatessen store. The next thing anybody knows, Rupert Salsinger is hastening up Tenth Avenue in his stocking feet, and Gus Schmelk is right behind him calling him names of such a crude nature that Miss Minnie Schultz retires to her papa's delicatessen store, although this does not prevent her from seeing a character leave Gus Schmelk's store with Rupert's tight shoes under his arm, and it does not prevent her from recognizing this character as the member of the Communist party.

Well, I see in the papers that Congressman Rupert Salsinger is going to marry some society doll in Washington, who is a widow with plenty of money left to her by her late husband, but I do not believe Rupert will be any happier than Calvin Colby, who is very busy at this time opening the twenty-second branch of the Schultz-Colby Delicatessen Stores, Inc., and who is greatly pleased over being married to Miss Minnie Schultz.

But although Gus Schmelk's store is in the new combination, and Gus himself is a member of the Board of Directors of same, Calvin Colby never really forgets that Gus Schmelk is the party who almost ruins his high hat with an egg in Columbus Circle the night Calvin makes the public address.

Situation Wanted

ONE EVENING in the summer of 1936, I am passing in front of Mindy's restaurant on Broadway, when the night manager suddenly opens the door and throws a character in a brown suit at me. Fortunately, the character just misses me, and hits a yellow short that is standing at the curb, and dents a mud guard, because he is a little character, and the night manager of Mindy's can throw that kind with an incurve. Naturally, I am greatly vexed, and I am thinking of stepping into Mindy's and asking the night manager how dare he hurl missiles of this nature at me, when I remember that the night manager does not care for me, either, and in fact he hates me from head to foot, and does not permit me in Mindy's except on Fridays, because of course he does not have the heart to keep me from enjoying my chicken soup with matzoth dumplings once a week.

So I let the incident pass, and watch the jockey of the yellow short nail the character in the brown suit with a left hook that knocks him right under my feet, and then, as he gets up and dusts himself off with his hands and starts up the street, I see that he is nobody but a character by the name of Asleep, who is called by this name because he always goes around with his eyes half closed, and looking as if he is dozing off. Well, here is a spectacle that really brings tears to my eyes, as I can remember when just a few years back the name of Asleep strikes terror to the hearts of one and all on Broadway, and everywhere else in this town for that matter, because in those days he is accounted one of the greatest characters in his line in the world, and in fact he is generally regarded as a genius.

Asleep's line is taking care of anybody that somebody wishes taken care of, and at one time he is the highest-priced character in the business. For several years along in the late 'twenties, he handles all of the late Dave the Dude's private business when Dave the Dude is at war with the late Big Moey, and when somebody finally takes care of Dave the Dude himself, Asleep is with Moey for quite a while. In six or seven years, the chances are Asleep takes care of scores of characters of one kind and another, and he never looks for any publicity or glory. In fact, he is always a most retiring character, who goes about very quietly, minding his own affairs, and those who know him think very well of him indeed.

The bladders print many unkind stories about Asleep when he is finally lumbered in 1931 and sent to college, and some of them call him a torpedo, and a trigger, and I do not know what all else, and these names hurt Asleep's feelings, especially as they seem to make him out no better than a ruffian. In fact, one bladder speaks of him as a killer, and this title causes Asleep to wince more than anything else. He is in college at Dannemora from 1931 until the late spring of 1936, and although I hear he is back, this is the first time I see him in person, and I hasten to overtake him to express my sympathy with him on his treatment by the night manager of Mindy's and also by the jockey of the yellow short, and to deplore the lack of respect now shown on Broadway for a character such as Asleep.

He seems glad to see me, and he accepts my expressions gratefully, and we go into the Bridle Grill and have a couple of drinks and then Asleep says to me like this: "I only go into Mindy's seeking a situation," he says. "I hear Benny Barker, the bookie, is in there, and I understand that he has a disagreement with another bookie by the name of Jersey Cy down at Aqueduct, and that Jersey Cy punches Benny's beezer for him. So," Asleep says, "I figure Benny will wish to have Cy taken care of immediately and that it will be a nice quick pickup for me, because in the old days when Benny is a bookie, he is one of my best customers.

"It is the first time I see Benny since I get back," Asleep says, "but instead of being glad to see me, he seems very distant to me, and the minute I begin canvassing him for the business, he turns as white as one of Mindy's napkins, and in fact whiter, and says for me to get out of there, or he will call the law. Benny says he will never even dream of such a thing as having anybody taken care of, and," Asleep says, "when I start to remind him of a couple of incidents back down the years, he carries on in a way you will never believe. I even offer to cut my fee for him," Asleep says, "but Benny only gets more excited, and keeps yelling no, no, no, until the night manager appears, and you see for yourself what happens to me. I am publicly embarrassed," he says.

"Well, Sleeps," I say, "to tell the truth, I am somewhat amazed that you do not out with that thing and resent these familiarities."

But Asleep seems somewhat horrified at this suggestion, and he sets his glass down, and gazes at me awhile in pained silence, and finally he says: "Why," he says, "I hope and trust that you do not think I will ever use that thing except for professional purposes, and when I am paid for same. Why," he says, "in all my practice, covering a matter of nearly ten years, I never lift a finger against as much as a flea unless it is a business proposition, and I am not going to begin now."

Well, I remember that this is indeed Asleep's reputation in the old days, and that a midget can walk up to him and tweak his ear without running any risk, and of course I am bound to respect his ethics, although I am sorry he cannot see his way clear to making an exception in the case of the night manager of Mindy's.

"I do not understand the way times change since I am in college," Asleep says. "Nobody around here wishes anybody taken care of any more. I call on quite a number of old customers of mine before I visit Benny Barker, but they have nothing for me, and none of them suggests that I call again. I fear I am *passé*," Asleep says. "Yet I am the one who first brings the idea to Brooklyn of putting them in the sack. I originate picking them off in barber chairs. I am always first and foremost with innovations in my business, and now there is no business. It is a tough break for me," Asleep says, "just when I happen to need a situation more than at any other time in my life. I simply must make good," he says, "because I am in love and wish to be married. I am in love with Miss Anna Lark, who dances behind bubbles over in the Starlight Restaurant. Yes," he says, "Miss Anna Lark is my sweet pea, and she loves me as dearly as I love her, or anyway," he says, "she so states no longer ago than two hours."

"Well," I say, "Miss Anna Lark has a shape that is a lulu. Even behind bubbles," I say, and this is a fact that is well known to one and all on Broadway, but I do not consider it necessary to mention to Asleep that it is also pretty well known along Broadway that Benny Barker, the bookie, is deeply interested in Miss Anna Lark, and, to tell the truth, is practically off his onion about her, because I am by no means a chirper.

"I often notice her shape myself," Asleep says. "In fact, it is one of the things that starts our romance before I go away to college. It seems to me it is better then than it is now, but," he says, "a shape is not everything in this life, although I admit it is never any knock. Miss Anna Lark waits patiently for me all the time I am away, and once she writes me a screeve, so you can see that this is undoubtedly true love. But," Asleep says, "Miss Anna Lark now wishes to abandon the bubble dodge, and return to her old home in Miami, Florida, where her papa is in the real-estate business. Miss Anna Lark feels that there is no future behind bubbles, especially," he says, "since she recently contracts arthritis in both knees from working in drafty night clubs. And she wishes me to go to Miami, Florida, too, and perhaps engage in the real-estate business like her papa, and acquire some scratch so we can be married, and raise up children, and all this and that, and be happy ever after. But," Asleep says, "it is very necessary for me to get hold of a taw to make a start, and at this time I do not have as much as two white quarters to rub together in my pants pocket, and neither has Miss Anna Lark, and from what I hear, the same thing goes for Miss Anna Lark's papa, and with conditions in my line what they are, I am greatly depressed, and scarcely know which way to turn."

Well, naturally, I feel very sorry for Asleep, but I can offer no suggestions of any value at the moment, and in fact the best I can do is to stake him to a few dibs for walk-about money, and then I leave him in the Bridle Grill looking quite sad and forlorn, to be sure. I do not see Asleep for several months after this, and am wondering what becomes of him, and I watch the bladders for news of happenings that may indicate he finally gets a break, but nothing of interest appears, and then one day I run into him at Broadway and Forty-sixth Street.

He is all sharpened up in new clothes, and a fresh shave, and he is carrying a suitcase, and looks very prosperous, indeed, and he seems happy to see me, and leads me around into Dinty Moore's, and sits me down at a table, and orders up some drinks, and then he says to me like this: "Now," he says, "I will tell you what happens. After you leave me in the Bridle Grill, I sit down and take to reading one of the evening bladders, and what I read about is a war in a place by the name of Spain, and from what I read, I can see that it is a war between two different mobs living in this Spain, each of which wishes to control the situation. It reminds me of Chicago the time Big Moey sends me out to Al. Thinks I to myself," Asleep says, "where there is a war of this nature, there may be employment for a character of my experience, and I am sitting there pondering this matter when who comes in looking for me but Benny Barker, the bookie. Well," Asleep says, "Benny states that he gets to thinking of me after I leave Mindy's, and he says he remembers that he really has a soft place in his heart for me, and that while he has no business for me any more, he will be glad to stake me to go wherever I think I may find something, and I remember what I am just reading in the evening bladder, and I says all right, Spain.

" 'Where is this Spain?' Benny Barker asks.

"Well," Alseep says, "of course I do not know where it is myself, so we inquire of Professor D, the educated horse player, and he says it is to hell and gone from here. He says it is across the sea, and Benny Barker says he will arrange my passage there at once, and furthermore that he will give me a thousand slugs in ready, and I can pay him back at my convenience. Afterwards," Asleep says, "I recall that Benny Barker seems greatly pleased that I am going far away, but I figure his conscience hurts him for the manner in which he rebuffs me in Mindy's, and he wishes to round himself up with me. So I go to this Spain," Asleep says, "and now," he says, "if you wish to hear any more, I will be glad to oblige."

Well, I tell Asleep that if he will keep calling the waiter at regular intervals, he may proceed, and Asleep proceeds as follows:

I go to this Spain seeking employment, and you will scarcely believe the trouble and inconvenience I am put to in getting there. I go by way of a ship that takes me to France, which is a place I remember somewhat, because I visit there in my early youth, in 1918, with the 77th Division, and which is a nice place, at that, especially the *Folies-Bergères,* and I go across France and down to a little jerkwater town just over the border from this Spain, and who do I run into sitting in front of a small gin-mill in the town but a Spanish character by the name of Manuel something. He is once well known along Broadway as a heavyweight fighter, and he is by no means a bad fighter in his day, and he now has a pair of scrambled ears to prove it. Furthermore, he is bobbing slightly, and seems to have a few marbles in his mouth, but he is greatly pleased to see me.

Manuel speaks English very good, considering the marbles, and he tells me he is personally in the fighting in this Spain for several weeks, but he is unable to find out what he is fighting about, so finally he gets tired, and is over in France taking a recess, and when I tell him I am going to this Spain, and what for, he says he has no doubt I will do very nice for myself, because of course Manuel knows my reputation in the old days in New York. Furthermore, he says he will go with me, and act as my manager, and maybe take a piece of my earnings, just as his American managers do with him when he is active in the ring, and when I ask him what he calls a piece, he says 65 per cent is the way his American managers always slice him, but naturally I do not agree to any such terms. Still, I can see that Manuel is such a character as may come in handy to me, what with knowing how to speak Spanish, as well as English, so I say I will look out for him very nicely when the time comes for a settlement, and this satisfies him.

We go across the border into this Spain by night, and Manuel says he will lead me to a spot where the fighting is very good, and by and by we come to a fair-sized town, with houses, and steeples, and all this and that, and which has a name I do not remember, and which I cannot pronounce, even if I do remember it. Manuel says we are now in the war, and in fact I can hear shooting going on although it does not seem to be interfering with public business in the town, as many characters, male and female, are walking around and about, and up

and down, and back and forth, and none of them seem to be disturbed
by anything much.

But Manuel and I follow the sound of the shooting, and finally we
come upon a large number of characters behind a breastworks made
out of sandbags, and they all have rifles in their hands, and are shooting
now and then at a big stone building on a high hill about three blocks
away, and from this building also comes a lot of firing, and there are
occasional bur-ur-ur-ups on both sides that I recognize as machine
guns, and bullets are zinging about the sandbags quite some. Well,
Manuel says this is some of the war, but all the characters behind the
sandbags seem to be taking things easy, and in fact some are sitting in
chairs and firing their rifles from a rest over the bags while so seated,
and thinks I to myself, this is a very leisurely war, to be sure. But about
two blocks from the breastworks, and on a rise of ground almost as high
as the hill the building is on, there is a field gun, and this is also firing
on the building about every fifteen minutes, and I can see that it seems
to be doing some real damage, at that, what with knocking off pieces
of the architecture, and punching holes in the roof, although now and
then it lets go a shell that misses the mark in a way that will never be
tolerated by the character who commands the battery I serve with in
France.

Many of the characters behind the sandbags seem to know Manuel,
who appears to be a famous character in this Spain, and they stop
shooting, and gather about him, and there is much conversation among
them, which of course I do not understand, so after a while I request
Manuel to pay more attention to me and to kindly explain the situation
I find here. Well, Manuel says the building on the hill is an old castle
and that it is being held by a lot of Spanish characters, male and female, who are as mad at the characters behind the sandbags as the
Republicans are mad at the Democrats in my country, and maybe
madder. Manuel says the characters in the castle represent one side of
the war in this Spain, and the characters behind the sandbags represent
the other side, although Manuel does not seem to know which is which,
and naturally I do not care.

"Well," I says to Manuel, "this is a good place to start business. Tell
them who I am," I say, "and ask them how much they will give me for
taking care of these parties in the castle."

So Manuel makes quite a speech, and while I do not understand
what he is saying, I can see that he is putting me away with them very
good, because they are gazing at me with great interest and respect.
When he concludes his speech they give me a big cheer and crowd
around me shaking hands, and I see Manuel talking with some char-

acters who seem to be the mains in this situation, and they are listening eagerly to his remarks, and nodding their heads, and Manuel says to me like this: "Well," Manuel says, "I tell them you are the greatest American gangster that ever lives, and that they undoubtedly see you often in the movies, and they are in favor of your proposition 100 per cent. They are anxious to see how you operate," Manuel says, "because they wish to install similar methods in this country when things get settled down."

"Kindly omit referring to me as a gangster," I say. "It is a most uncouth word, and besides I never operate with a gang in my life."

"Well, all right," Manuel says, "but it is a word they understand. However," he says, "the trouble here is they do not have much *dinero,* which is money. In fact, they say the best they can offer you to take care of the parties in the castle is two pesetas per head."

"How much is two pesetas?" I ask.

"The last time I am here, it is about forty cents in your language," Manuel says.

Naturally, I am very indignant at this offer, because in my time I get as high as twenty thousand dollars for taking care of a case, and never less than five hundred, except once when I do a favor for one-fifty, but Manuel claims it is not such a bad offer as it sounds, as he says that at the moment two pesetas is by no means alfalfa in this Spain, especially as there are maybe four hundred heads in the castle, counting everything. Manuel says it really is an exceptional offer as the characters behind the sandbags are anxious to conclude the siege because certain friends of the parties in the castle are arriving in a near-by town, and anyway, sitting behind these sandbags is getting most monotonous to one and all. Furthermore, Manuel says, when they are not sitting behind the sandbags, these characters are required to work every day digging a tunnel into the hill under the castle, and they regard this work as most enervating. Manuel says the idea of the tunnel is to plant dynamite under the castle and blow it up.

"But you see," Manuel says, "digging is no work for proud souls such as Spaniards, so if you can think of some other way of taking care of these parties in the castle, it will be a great relief to my friends here."

"To the dickens with these skinflints," I say. "Let us go to the castle and see what the parties there will give us for taking care of these cheap skates behind the sandbags. Never," I say, "will I accept such a reduction."

Well, Manuel tells the mains behind the sandbags that I will take their offer under consideration, but that I am so favorably disposed toward it that I am going into the castle and examine the surroundings, and this pleases them no little, so Manuel ties his handkerchief on a stick and says this is a flag of truce and will get us into the castle safe and sound, and we set out. Presently characters appear at the windows, and at holes in the walls of the castle, and Manuel holds a conversation with them in the Spanish language, and by and by they admit us to the castle yard, and one character with whiskers leads us into the building and down stone steps until we arrive in what seems to be a big basement far underground. And in this basement I behold a very unusual scene to be sure. There are many characters present, male and female, also numerous small children, and they seem to be living in great confusion, but they are greatly interested in us when we appear, especially a tall, thin elderly character with white hair, and a white tash, and a white goatee, who seems to be a character of some authority.

In fact, Manuel says he is nobody but a character by the name of General Pedro Vega, and that this castle is his old family home, and that he is leader of these other characters in the basement.

I can see at once that Manuel and the general are old friends, because they make quite a fuss over meeting up in this manner, and then Manuel introduces me, and delivers another speech about me, explaining what a wonderful character I am. When he gets through, the general turns to me, and in very good English he speaks as follows: "I am very glad to meet you, Señor Asleep," he says. "I once live in your country a couple of years," he says. "I live in your Miami, Florida."

Well, I am glad to find somebody who can talk English, so I can do my own negotiating, and in a few words I state my proposition to the general to take care of the characters behind the sandbags and call for his bid on same.

"Alas," the general says, "money is something we do not have. If you are offering to take care of the enemy at one centavo each," he says, "we still cannot pay. I am most regretful. It will be a big convenience to have you take care of the enemy, because we can then escape from this place and join our friends in a near-by city. Our food runs low," he says. "So does our ammunition. Some of our females and children are ill. The longer we remain here the worse it gets. If I do not know the caliber of the enemy," he says, "I will gladly surrender. But," he says, "we will then all be backed up against a wall and executed. It is better that we die here."

Well, being backed up against a wall strikes me as a most undesirable fate, to be sure, but of course it is nothing to me, and all I am thinking of is that this is a very peculiar country where nobody has any scratch, and it is commencing to remind me of home. And I am also thinking that the only thing I can do is to accept the two pesetas per head offered by the characters behind the sandbags, when a very beautiful young Judy, with long black hair hanging down her back, approaches, and speaks to me at some length in the Spanish language. Manuel says: "She says," he says, " 'Oh, sir, if you can help us escape from this place you will earn my undying gratitude.' She says," Manuel says, " 'I am in love with a splendid young character by the name of Señor José Valdez, who is waiting for me with our friends in the near-by town. We are to be married as soon as the cruel war is over,' she says," Manuel says. "It seems to be a most meritorious case," Manuel says.

Now naturally this statement touches my heart no little, because I am in love myself, and besides the young Judy begins weeping, and if there is one thing I cannot stand it is female tears, and in fact my sweet pea, Miss Anna Lark, can always make me do almost anything she wishes by breaking out crying. But of course business is business in this case, and I cannot let sentiment interfere, so I am about to bid one and all farewell when General Pedro Vega says: "Wait!"

And with this he disappears into another part of the basement, but is back pretty soon with a small black tin box, and out of this box he takes a batch of papers, and hands them to me, and says: "Here are the deeds to some property in your Miami, Florida," he says. "I pay much money for it in 1925. They tell me at the time I am lucky to get the property at the price, but," he says, "I will be honest with you. It is unimproved property, and all I ever get out of it so far is notices that taxes are due, which I always pay promptly. But now I fear I will never get back to your Miami, Florida, again, and if you will take care of enough of the enemy for us to escape, the deeds are yours. This is all I have to offer."

Well, I say I will take the deeds and study them over and let him know my answer as soon as possible, and then I retire with Manuel, but what I really study more than anything else is the matter of the beautiful young Judy who yearns for her sweet pea, and there is no doubt but what my studying of her is a point in favor of General Vega's proposition in my book, although I also do some strong studying of the fact that taking care of these characters in the castle is a task that will be very tough.

So after we leave the castle, I ask Manuel if he supposes there is a telegraph office in operation in town, and he says of course there is, or how can the newspaper scribes get their thrilling stories of the war out, so I get him to take me there, and I send a cablegram addressed to Mr. Lark, real estate, Miami, Florida, U. S. A., which reads as follows: IS FIFTY ACRES LANDSCRABBLE SECTION ANY ACCOUNT. Then there is nothing for me to do but wait around until I get an answer, and this takes several days, and I devote this period to seeing the sights with Manuel, and I wish to say that some of the sights are very interesting. Finally, I drop around to the telegraph office, and sure enough there is a message there for me, collect, which says like this: LANDSCRABBLE SECTION GREAT POSSIBILITIES STOP WHY . . . LARK . . . Now I do not know Mr. Lark personally, and he does not know me, and the chances are he never even hears of me before, but I figure that if he is half as smart as his daughter, Miss Anna Lark, his judgment is worth following, so I tell Manuel it looks as if the deal with General Vega is on, and I begin giving my undivided attention to the case.

I can see at once that the key to the whole situation as far as I am concerned is the field piece on the hill, because there are really too many characters behind the sandbags for me to take care of by myself, or even with the assistance of Manuel, and of course I do not care to get Manuel involved in my personal business affairs any more than I can help. However, at my request, he makes a few innocent inquiries among the characters behind the sandbags, and he learns that there are always seven characters on the hill with the gun, and that they sleep in little homemade shelters made of boards, and canvas, and tin, and one thing and another, and that these shelters are scattered over the top of the hill, and the top of the hill is maybe the width of a baseball diamond. But I can observe for myself that they do no firing from the hilltop after sundown, and they seldom show any lights, which is maybe because they do not wish to have any airplanes come along and drop a few hot apples on them.

Manuel says that the characters behind the sandbags are asking about me, and he says they are so anxious to secure my services that he will not be surprised if I cannot get three pesetas per head, and I can see that Manuel thinks I am making a mistake not to dicker with them further. But I tell him I am now committed to General Vega, and I have Manuel obtain a twelve-inch file for me in the city, and also some corks out of wine bottles, and I take the file and hammer it down, and smooth it out, and sharpen it up nicely, and I make a handle for it out of wood, according to my own original ideas, and I take the corks, and burn them good, and I find a big piece of black cloth and make myself a sort of poncho out of this by cutting a hole in the center for my head to go through.

Then I wait until it comes on a night to suit me, and it is a dark night, and rainy, and blowy, and I black up my face and hands with the burnt cork, and slip the black cloth over my clothes, and put my file down the back of my neck where I can reach it quickly, and make my way very quietly to the foot of the hill on which the field gun is located. Now in the darkness, I begin crawling on my hands and knees, and wiggling along on my stomach up the hill, and I wish to state that it is a monotonous task because I can move only a few feet at a clip, and there are many sharp rocks in my path, and once an insect of some nature crawls up my pant leg and gives me a severe nip. The hill is maybe as high as a two-story building, and very steep, and it takes me over an hour to wiggle my way to the top, and sometimes I pause en route and wonder if it is worth it. And then I think of the beautiful young Judy in the castle, and of the property in Miami, Florida, and of Miss Anna Lark, and I keep on wiggling.

Well, just as Manuel reports, there is a sentry on duty on top of the hill, and I can make out his shape in the darkness leaning on his rifle, and this sentry is a very large character, and at first I figure that he may present difficulties, but when I wiggle up close to him I observe that he seems to be dozing, and it is quiet as can be on the hilltop. The sentry is really no trouble at all, and then I wiggle my way slowly along in and out of the little shelters, and in some shelters there is but one character, and in others two, and in one, three, and it is these three that confuse me somewhat, as they are three more than the seven Manuel mentions in his census of the scene, and I will overlook them entirely if one of them does not snore more than somewhat. Personally, I will always say that taking care of these ten characters one after the other, and doing it so quietly that not one of them ever wakes up, is the high spot of my entire career, especially when you consider that I am somewhat rusty from lack of experience, and that my equipment is very crude.

Well, when morning dawns, there I am in charge of the hilltop, and with a field gun at my disposal, and I discover that it is nothing but a French 75, with which I am quite familiar, and by and by Manuel joins me, and while the characters behind the sandbags are enjoying their breakfast, and the chances are, not thinking of much, I plant four shells among them so fast I ruin their morning meal, because, if I do say it myself, I am better than a raw hand with a French 75. Then I remember that the characters who are boring under the castle are perhaps inside the tunnel at this time, so I peg away at the hole in the hill until the front of it caves in and blocks up the hole very neatly, and Manuel afterward claims that I wedged in the entire night shift.

Well, of course these proceedings are visible to the occupants of the castle, and it is not long before I see General Pedro Vega come marching out of the castle with the whole kit and caboodle of characters, male and female, and small children behind him, and they are laughing and shouting, and crying and carrying on no little. And the last I see of them as they go hurrying off in the direction of the near-by town where their friends are located, the beautiful young Judy is bringing up the rear and throwing kisses at me and waving a flag, and I ask Manuel to kindly identify this flag for me so I will always remember which side of the war in this Spain it is that I assist. But Manuel says his eyesight is bad ever since the night Jim Sharkey sticks a thumb in his eye in the fifth round in Madison Square Garden, and from this distance he cannot tell whose flag it is, and in fact, Manuel says, he does not give a Spanish cussword.

"And there you are," Asleep says to me in Dinty Moore's.

"So," I say, "you are now back in New York looking for business again?"

"Oh, no," Asleep says. "I now reside in Miami, Florida, and I am going to marry Miss Anna Lark next month. I am doing very well for myself, too," he says. "You see, we turn the property that I get from General Vega into a cemetery, and I am now selling lots in same for our firm which is headed by Miss Anna Lark's papa. Manuel is our head gravedigger, and we are all very happy," Asleep says.

Well, afterwards I hear that the first lot Asleep sells is to the family of the late Benny Barker, the bookie, who passes away during the race meeting in Miami, Florida, of pneumonia, superinduced by lying out all night in a ditch full of water near the home of Miss Anna Lark, although I also understand that the fact that Benny is tied up in a sack in the ditch is considered a slight contributing cause of his last illness.

Cemetery Bait

ONE PLEASANT morning in early April, a character by the name of Gentleman George wakes up to find himself in a most embarrassing predicament. He wakes up to find himself in a cell in the state penitentiary at Trenton, N. J., and while a cell in a state penitentiary is by no means a novelty to George, and ordinarily will cause him no confusion whatever, the trouble is this particular cell is in what is known as the death house. Naturally, George is very self-conscious about this, as it is only the second time in his life he ever finds himself in such a house, and the first time is so far back in his youth that it leaves scarcely any impression on him, especially as he is commuted out of it in less than sixty days. Well, George sits there on the side of the cot in his cell this pleasant April morning, thinking what a humiliating circumstance this is to a proud nature such as his, when all of a sudden he remembers that on the morrow he is to be placed in Mister Edison's rocking chair in the room adjoining his cell, and given a very severe shock in the seat of his breeches.

On remembering this, George becomes very thoughtful to be sure, and sighs to himself as follows: Heigh-ho, heigh-ho, heigh-ho. And then he sends for me to come and see him, although George is well aware that I have no use for penitentiaries, or their environs, and consider them a most revolting spectacle. In fact, I have such a repugnance for penitentiaries that I never even glance at them in passing, because I am afraid that peepings may be catchings, but of course in a situation such as this I can scarcely deny the call of an old friend. They let me talk to George through the bars of his cell, and naturally I am somewhat perturbed to observe him in this plight, although I can see that his surroundings are clean and sanitary, and that the hacks seem kindly disposed toward him, except one big doorknob who is inclined to be somewhat churlish because George just beats him in a game of two-handed pinochle.

Furthermore, I can see that George is in pretty fair physical condition, although a little stouter than somewhat, and that he looks as if he is getting some rest. He is at this time about forty-five years of age, and is still as good-looking as in the days when he is known far and wide as the handsomest and most genteel character on Broadway. His brown hair now has some gray in it along the edges, and there are lines of care in his face, and, of course, George is not dressed as fashionably as usual. In fact, his clothes need pressing, and he can stand a haircut, and a shave, and when I mention this to George he says he understands they are going to give him all the haircutting he requires before morning, and maybe a close shave, too.

In the old days, Gentleman George is very prominent in the jewelry trade with Tommy Entrata, and his associates, and anybody will tell you that Tommy and his crowd are the best in the country, because they pursue strictly business methods, and are very high-principled. They generally work with a character by the name of Lou Adolia, who is a private fuzz often employed by big insurance companies that make a specialty of insuring jewelry for wealthy female parties, a fuzz being a way of saying a detective, although the chances are Lou Adolia cannot really find his hip pocket with both hands.

But when Tommy Entrata and his associates come into possession of jewelry belonging to these wealthy female parties, they notify Lou Adolia, and he arranges with the insurance companies to pay a certain sum for the return of the merchandise, and no beefs, and everybody is satisfied, especially the insurance companies, because, of course, if they do not get the goods back, the companies will have to pay the full amount of the insurance. As Tommy Entrata is generally very reasonable in his fees on jewelry that comes into his possession, it really is a most economical arrangement for the insurance companies, and for everybody else concerned, and it is also very nice for Lou Adolia, as he always gets a reward from the companies, and sometimes a piece of what Tommy Entrata collects. Then a piece always goes to the stout fellow in the city in which Tommy Entrata and his associates are operating, the stout fellow being the local fix, because, of course, you understand that in a business as large as this carried on by Tommy Entrata it is necessary to take care of all angles. So the stout fellow looks after the local law to see that it does not interfere with Tommy Entrata any more than is absolutely necessary.

To tell the truth, when Tommy Entrata and his associates go into a town, it is generally as well-organized from top to bottom as Standard Oil, and Tommy not only has a complete roster of all the local jewelry owners, and what they are insured for, from Lou Adolia, but also a few diagrams as to where this jewelry is located, and Tommy never fails to make ample provision for one and all in the town who may be concerned before he turns a wheel. In fact, I hear that in a spot up in the Northwest Tommy once even declares the mayor and the commissioner of public safety in on one of his transactions, just out of the goodness of his heart, and this unselfishness in his business operations makes Tommy highly respected far and wide.

Anyway, Gentleman George is one of Tommy Entrata's experts in the matter of coming into possession of jewelry, and Tommy appreciates George no little, as George is strictly a lone hand at his work, and he never carries that thing on him, and considers all forms of violence most revolting, so he never gets into trouble, or at least not much. I am telling you all this so you will understand that Tommy Entrata conducts his business in a high-class, conservative manner, and personally I consider him a great boon to a community, because he teaches people the value of insurance, and now I will return to Gentleman George in his cell in the death house in Trenton, N. J.

"Well," George says, "there you are, and here I am, and you are the only friend that comes to see me since the judge mentions the date that now becomes of some importance in my life, and which is in fact tomorrow. And now I wish to tell you a story, which will be the truth, the whole truth, and nothing but the truth, and the object of this story is to show that I once perform a great service to the public." At this, I become uneasy, because I am afraid it may be a tedious story, and I do not care to remain in such surroundings listening to reminiscence, so I request George to epitomize as much as possible, and to omit all reference to low characters and sordid situations, and then George states as follows, and to wit, viz.:

In the winter of 1935, I am going southward by train on business bent, and the reason I do not reveal my destination at this time is because I do not wish to be recalled as ever hollering copper, even on a city, but I will say that it is a certain winter resort spot about as far below the Mason and Dixon's line as you can get before you start swimming, and a very pleasant spot it is, at that. The first night out on the train, I go into the diner and partake of a fish that is on the menu, because the steward of the diner weighs in with a strong shill for this fish, and the next thing I know I am back in my compartment as sick as anything, and maybe a little bit sicker. To tell the truth, I am so sick that I think I am going to pass away, and this thought disturbs me no little, as Tommy Entrata is looking forward to my arrival with keen interest, and I know that he is apt to take my passing away as a personal affront.

Well, while I am lying in my berth as sick as stated, all of a sudden the door of my compartment opens, and a pair of specs and a short, scrubby, gray tash appear, and behind the specs and the tash is a stern-looking character of maybe fifty-odd, who speaks to me in a gruff voice, as follows: "See here, now," he says, "what is all this runting and grunting about? Are you sick?"

"Well," I say, "if I am not sick, I will do until an invalid comes along." And then I start retching again, and in between retches, I mention the dining-car fish, and I tell the stern-looking character that if he will kindly get the dining-car steward to step into my compartment for just one minute I will die happy.

"You speak great nonsense," the stern-looking character says. "You are not going to die, although," he says, "who knows but what you may be better off if you do? Not enough people know when to die. What ails you is ptomaine poisoning, and I will take charge of this situation myself because I will be unable to sleep in this car with you scrooning and mooning all night. I once get the same thing myself in Gloucester, Mass.," he says. "You will expect the fish to be all right in Gloucester, Mass. If I remember," he says, "it is mackerel in my case."

Then he rings for the porter, and pretty soon he has the train secretary, and the Pullman conductor, and even a couple of other passengers running in and out of my compartment getting him this, and that, and one thing and another, and dosing me with I do not know what, and sick as I am, I can see that this stern-looking character is accustomed to having people step around when he speaks. Well, for a while I am thinking that the best break I can get is to pass away without any further lingering; then, by and by, I commence feeling better, and finally I doze off to sleep. But I seem to remember the stern-looking character mentioning that he is going to the same place that I am, and that he is just returning from a hunting trip in Canada, and I also seem to recall him telling me what a wonderful shot he is with any kind of firearms.

Afterward, however, I figure I must dream all this because the next morning the stern-looking character just glances in on me once and asks how I feel in a tone of voice that indicates he does not care much one way or the other, and after this I do not see hide or hair of him, and I can see that he does not mean to make a friendship of the matter. In fact, when I am getting off the train at my destination, I suddenly remember that I do not even know the stern-looking character's name, and I am sorry about this, as so few people in the world are ever good to me that I wish to cherish the names of those who are. But, of course, I now have no time for sentiment, as duty calls me, and I do not bother to inquire around and about with reference to the stern-looking character.

I telephone Tommy Entrata, and make a meet with him for dinner in a night club that is called by the name of the Bath and Sail Club, although there is no bathing connected with it whatever, and no sailing either, for that matter, and while I am waiting there for Tommy, I observe at another table the most beautiful Judy I see in many a day, and you know very well that few better judges of beauty ever live than yours sincerely, G. George. She is young, and has hair the color of straw, and she is dressed in a gorgeous white evening gown, and she has plenty of junk on her in the way of diamonds, and she seems to be waiting for someone and I find myself regretting that it is not me. I am so impressed by her that I call Emil, the headwaiter, and question him, because Emil is an old friend of mine, and I know he always has a fund of information on matters such as this. "Emil," I say, "who is the lovely pancake over there by the window?"

"Cemetery bait," Emil says, so I know he means she is married, and has a husband who is selfish about her, and naturally I cast no sheep's eyes in her direction, especially as Tommy Entrata comes in about now and takes me to a private room where we have a nice dinner, and discuss my business in this city.

It is in pursuit of this business, at the hour of 1 A.M. on a warm Sunday morning, that I am making a call at the residence of a character by the name of Colonel Samuel B. Venus, and am in the boudoir of his ever-loving wife, and a beautiful room it is, at that, with the windows on one side looking out over the sea waves, and the windows on the other side overlooking a patio of whispering palm trees. The moon is shining down on this scene, and it is so lovely that I stand at the front windows a few moments looking out over the water before I start seeking the small can, or safe, that I know is concealed in a clothes closet in the room unless the butler in the Venus house is telling a terrible falsehood and accepting money from us under false pretenses for this information and for admitting me to the premises. Of course, Colonel Samuel B. Venus' ever-loving wife is not present in her boudoir at this hour, and neither is Colonel Samuel B. Venus, and in fact I afterward learn that the only way Colonel Samuel B. Venus can get in there is on a writ of habeas corpus, but this has nothing to do with my story.

My information is that Colonel Samuel B. Venus is a very wealthy character of maybe sixty years of age, come next grass, and that his ever-loving wife is less than half of that, and has some of the finest jewelry in this country, including pearls, diamonds, star rubies, emeralds, and I do not know what all else, and I am given to understand that Colonel Samuel B. Venus leaves the night before on a fishing trip, and that Mrs. Colonel Samuel B. Venus is out somewhere wearing only a couple of pounds of her jewels, so the rest of her stuff is bound to be in the little can in her boudoir. Well, the little can is in the closet just

where the butler reports, and I observe that it is such a can as I will
be able to open with a toothpick if necessary, although, of course, I
bring along my regular can opener, which is a tool for cutting open
safes that I personally invent, as you perhaps remember, although I
never think to get a patent on it from the government, and I am about
to start operations when I hear voices, and two characters, male and
female, enter the boudoir.

So there I am in the closet among a lot of dresses and coats, and all
this and that, and, what is more, I leave the closet door open a little
when I go in, as I figure I may require a little air, and I am now afraid
to close the door for fear of making a noise, and the best I can make of
this situation is that I am a gone gosling. To tell the truth, it is one of
the few times in my life that I regret I do not have that thing on me,
just for self-defense. I can see right away from the way she talks that the
female character must be Mrs. Colonel Samuel B. Venus, but the character with her is by no means her husband, and naturally I am greatly
scandalized to think that a married broad will bring a party not her
husband into her boudoir with her at such an hour, and I am wondering what on earth the world is coming to. But although I listen keenly,
there seems to be no goings-on, and in fact all they are doing is talking,
so I figure the character with Mrs. Colonel Samuel B. Venus must be
a character without any imagination whatever.

Finally, when I judge from their conversation that they are looking
at the view of the sad sea waves, I cop a quick peek, and I see that Mrs.
Colonel Samuel B. Venus is nobody but the blonde I admire at the
Bath and Sail Club, and while this surprises me no little, it does not
surprise me half as much as the fact that the character with her is
a party by the name of Count Tomaso, who is known far and wide as
a most unworthy character. In fact, Count Tomaso is regarded in some
circles as a 22-carat fink, a fink being a character who is lower than a
mudcat's vest pocket. He is a small, slim-built character, with dark hair
greased down on his head, and he wears a monocle, and seems very
foreign in every respect. In fact, Count Tomaso claims to belong to the
Italian nobility, but he is no more a count than I am, and to tell the
truth, he is nothing but a ginzo out of Sacramento, and his right name
is Carfarelli.

For a matter of twenty years or more, this Count Tomaso is on the
socket, which is a way of saying his dodge is blackmail, and of course
there is little or no class to such a dodge as this. He generally pitches
to foolish old married Judys, and gets them wedged in with letters,
and one thing and another, and then puts the shake on them. Personally, I rarely criticize anybody else's methods of earning a liveli-

hood, but I can never approve of the shake, although I must admit that from what I hear of Count Tomaso, he really is an artist in his line, and can nine those old phlugs in first-class style when he is knuckling.

I only hope and trust that his presence in Mrs. Colonel Samuel B. Venus' boudoir does not mean that Count Tomaso is trespassing in any way upon my affairs, as I can see where this will produce complications, and it is always my policy to avoid complications, so I remain very quiet, with a firm grip on my can opener in case Mrs. Colonel Samuel B. Venus or Count Tomaso happens to come to the closet. But it seems to be nothing but a social visit, as I can hear her getting out some liquor, and after a couple of drinks they begin speaking of nothing much in particular, including the weather. Presently the conversation becomes quite dull, for it is all about love, and conversation about love always bores me no little unless I am making the conversation myself, although I can see that Mrs. Colonel Samuel B. Venus is better than a raw hand in conversation of this nature.

I am so bored that I put down my can opener and am about to doze off among the dresses, when all of a sudden the conversation takes a very unusual turn, to be sure, for Mrs. Colonel Samuel B. Venus says to Count Tomaso like this: "I know you love me," she says, "and I love you madly in return, but what good will it do us? I am married to a character old enough to be my father, and although he does not know it, I hate and despise him. But even if I tell him this, I know he will never give me a divorce, and, besides, if I do get a divorce, he is sure to put me off with a mere pittance. I am bound to him as long as he lives," she says. "As long as he lives, Tomaso."

Well, Count Tomaso says this is certainly a sad state of affairs, and seems to be taking another drink, and she goes on as follows: "Of course," she says, "if he passes away, Tomaso, I will marry you the next day, or anyway," she says, "as soon as my mourning goes out of style. Then we can go all over the world and enjoy our love, because I know his will leaves me all his vast fortune. I am afraid it is wicked," she says, "but sometimes I wish an accident will befall him."

Now I can see that what is coming off here is that Mrs. Colonel Samuel B. Venus is giving Count Tomaso a hint in a roundabout way to cause an accident to befall Colonel Samuel B. Venus, and thinks I to myself there in the closet, it is a pretty how-do-you-do if such goings-on are tolerated in society circles, and I am glad I am not in society. To tell the truth, I consider Mrs. Colonel Samuel B. Venus' attitude most unbecoming.

Well, they converse at some length about various forms of accidents that they hear of, but they seem unable to arrive at any definite conclusion, and I am almost sorry I am unable to join in the discussion and offer a few original ideas of my own, when Mrs. Colonel Samuel B. Venus says: "Well," she says, "we are sailing next week on the Castilla for New York, and you can come on the same ship. New York is a better place for accidents than down here, because they are not apt to attract so much attention there. But, Tomaso," she says, "be very careful the colonel does not see you on the trip, as he has been hearing things here, and he is terribly jealous, and has a violent temper, and, furthermore, he always has deadly weapons around, and he claims he is a wonderful marksman. Oh, Tomaso," she says, "is it not awful to be yoked to an old character who thinks of nothing but hunting, and fishing, and business, when I love you so much?"

Well, Tomaso says it is, indeed, and does she have a few dibs on her to tide him over the week end, and it seems she has, and then there is a little offhand billing and cooing that I consider very bad taste in her under her own roof, and finally they go out of the boudoir. As soon as they depart, I turn to my own business of opening the little can and removing the jewelry, which I deliver to Tommy Entrata, who gives it to Lou Adolia, and this is the time that Lou Adolia gets eighty thousand dollars from the insurance companies for the return of the goods, and then disappears with all the sugar, and without as much as saying aye, yes or no to anybody.

But I am getting ahead of my story.

A couple of days later, I am reclining on the beach with Tommy Entrata, taking a little sun for my complexion, when who comes along in a bathing suit which displays a really remarkable shape but Mrs. Colonel Samuel B. Venus, and who is with her but the stern-looking character who doctors me up on the train, and at first I have half a notion to jump up and say hello to him and thank him for his kindness to me about the fish, but he looks right through me as if he never sees me before in his life, and I can see that he does not remember me, or if he does, he does not care to make anything of it.

So I do not give him a blow, because the way I look at it, the fewer people you know in this world, the better you are off. But I ask Tommy Entrata who the stern-looking character is, and I am somewhat surprised when Tommy says: "Why," he says, "he is Colonel Samuel B. Venus, the party you knock off the other night, but," Tommy says, "let us not speak of that now. Colonel Samuel B. Venus is a most irascible character, and he is making quite a chirp about matters, and it is very fortunate for us that he and his wife are sailing for New York, because the stout fellow is getting nervous about the outcry. By the way," Tommy says, "I do not wish to seem inhospitable in suggesting your departure from these pleasant scenes, but it may be a good idea for you to take it on the Jesse Owens until the beef is chilled. There are many nightingales in these parts," he says, "and they will sing to the law on very slight provocation, for instance such a character as Count Tomaso. I notice him around here nuzzling up to Mrs. Colonel Samuel B. Venus, and while the chances are he is on a business mission of his own, Count Tomaso knows you, and it is always my opinion that he is a singer, at heart."

Well, I do not mention the incident in Mrs. Colonel Samuel B. Venus' boudoir to Tommy Entrata, because in the first place I do not consider it any of his business, and in the second place I know Tommy is not apt to be interested in such a matter, but I get to thinking about the conversation between Mrs. Colonel Samuel B. Venus and Count Tomaso, and I also get to thinking about Colonel Samuel B. Venus being so nice to me in connection with the bad fish. And thinks I, as long as I must take my departure anyway, a little sea voyage may be beneficial to my health, and I will go on the Castilla myself, and will look up Count Tomaso and admonish him that I will hold him personally responsible if any accident happens to Colonel Samuel B. Venus, as I feel that it is only fair to do what I can to discharge my debt of gratitude to Colonel Samuel B. Venus concerning the fish.

So when the Castilla sails a few days later, I am a passenger, and, furthermore, I have a nice cabin on the same deck as Colonel Samuel B. Venus and his ever-loving wife, because I always believe in traveling with the best people, no matter what. I see Colonel Samuel B. Venus, and I also see Mrs. Colonel Samuel B. Venus on the first day out, and I observe that Colonel Samuel B. Venus is looking sterner than ever, and also that Mrs. Colonel Samuel B. Venus is growing lovelier by the hour, but never do I see Count Tomaso, although I am pretty sure he does not miss the boat. I figure that he is taking Mrs. Colonel Samuel B. Venus' advice about keeping out of sight of Colonel Samuel B. Venus.

I do not bother to go looking for Count Tomaso on the Castilla to admonish him about Colonel Samuel B. Venus, because I figure I am bound to catch up with him getting off the boat in New York, and that in the meantime Colonel Samuel B. Venus is safe from accident, especially as it comes up stormy at sea after we are a few hours out, and Colonel Samuel B. Venus and his ever-loving wife seem to be keeping close to their cabin, and in fact so is everybody else.

Well, the storm keeps getting worse, and it is sleety and cold all around and about, and the sea is running higher than somewhat, and now one night off the Jersey coast when I am sleeping as peacefully as anything, I am awakened by a great to-do and it seems that the Castilla is on fire. Naturally, I do not care to be toasted in my cabin, so I don my clothes, and pop out into the passageway and start for the nearest exit, when I remember that in moments of confusion many characters, male and female, are apt to forget articles of one kind and another that may come in handy to somebody such as me later on, for instance bits of jewelry, and other portable merchandise. So I try various doors as I go along the passageway, and all of them are open and unoccupied, as the Castilla is an old-time vessel with cabin doors that lock with keys, and not with snap locks, and, just as I suspect, I find numerous odds and ends in the way of finger rings, and bracelets and clips and pins and necklaces, and watches, and gold cigarette cases, and even a few loose bundles of ready scratch, so I am very glad, indeed, that I am gifted with foresight.

Finally I come to one door that seems to be locked, and I remember that this is the cabin occupied by Colonel Samuel B. Venus and his ever-loving wife, and after first knocking at the door and receiving no reply, I figure they hastily depart and carelessly lock the door after them, and I also figure that I am bound to garner something of more than ordinary value there. So I kick the door in, and who is in the cabin on a bed, all trussed up like a goose, with a towel tied across his mouth to keep him from hollering out loud, but Colonel Samuel B. Venus, in person. Naturally, I am somewhat surprised at this spectacle, and also somewhat embarrassed to have Colonel Samuel B. Venus find me kicking in his door, but of course this is no time for apologies, so I take a quick swivel about the cabin to see if there are any articles lying around that I may be able to use. I am slightly disappointed to note that there appears to be nothing, and I am about to take my departure, when all of a sudden I remember my debt of gratitude to Colonel Samuel B. Venus, and I realize that it will be most unkind to leave him in this predicament to be barbecued like a steer without being able to move hand or foot.

So I out with my pocket shiv, and cut him loose, and I also remove the towel, and as soon as he can talk, Colonel Samuel B. Venus issues a statement to me in a most severe tone of voice, as follows: "They try to murder me," he says. "My own wife, Cora, and a character in a white polo coat with a little cap to match. When the alarm of fire is sounded," Colonel Samuel B. Venus says, "she starts screaming, and he comes banging up against our door, and she unlocks it and lets him in before I have time to think, and then he knocks me down with something, I do not know what."

"The chances are," I say, "it is a blunt instrument."

"You may be right," Colonel Samuel B. Venus says. "Anyway, after he knocks me down, my own wife, Cora, picks up one of my shoes and starts belting me over the head with the heel, and then she helps the character in the polo coat and the little cap to match tie me up as you find me."

"It is a scurvy trick," I say.

"I am half unconscious," Colonel Samuel B. Venus says, "but I remember hearing my own wife, Cora, remark that the fire is a wonderful break for them, and will save them a lot of bother in New York. And then before they leave, she hits me another belt on the head with the shoe. I fear," Colonel Samuel B. Venus says, "that my own wife, Cora, is by no means the ever-loving helpmeet I think. In fact," he says, "I am now wondering about the overdose of sleeping powders she gives me in London, England, in 1931, and about the bomb in my automobile in Los Angeles, Cal., in 1933."

"Well, well, well," I say, "let us let bygones be bygones, and get off this tub, as it seems to be getting hotter than a ninth-inning finish around here."

But Colonel Samuel B. Venus remains very testy about the incident he just describes, and he fumbles around under a pillow on the bed on which I find him, and outs with that thing, and opens the cylinder as if to make sure it is loaded, and says to me like this: "I will shoot him down like a dog," he says. "I mean the character in the white polo coat and the little cap to match. He undoubtedly leads my poor little wife, Cora, astray in this, although," he says, "I do not seem to recall him anywhere in the background of the overdose and the bomb matters. But she is scarcely more than a child and does not know right from wrong. He is the one who must die," Colonel Samuel B. Venus says. "I wonder who he is?" he says.

Well, of course I know Colonel Samuel B. Venus must be talking about Count Tomaso, but I can see that Count Tomaso is a total stranger to him, and while I am by no means opposed to Colonel Samuel B. Venus' sentiments with reference to Count Tomaso, I do not approve of his spirit of forgiveness toward Mrs. Colonel Samuel B. Venus, because I figure that as long as she is around and about, Colonel Samuel B. Venus will always be in danger of accidents. But I do not feel that this is a time for argument, so I finally get him to go up on the deck with me, and as soon as we are on deck, Colonel Samuel B. Venus leaves me and starts running every which way as if he is looking for somebody.

There seems to be some little agitation on deck, what with smoke and flame coming out of the Castilla amidships, and many characters, male and female, running up and down, and around and about, and small children crying. Some of the crew are launching lifeboats, and then getting into these boats themselves, and pulling away from the burning ship without waiting for any passengers, which strikes me as most discourteous on the part of the sailors and which alarms many passengers so they start chucking themselves over the rail into the sea trying to catch up with the boats.

Well, this scene is most distasteful to me, so I retire from the general melee, and go looking elsewhere about the ship, figuring I may find an opportunity to ease myself quietly into a boat before all the seats are taken by sailors, and finally I come upon a group trying to launch a big life raft over the rail, and about this time I observe Colonel Samuel B. Venus standing against the rail with that thing in his hand, and peering this way and that. And then I notice a boat pulling away from the ship, and in the stern of the boat I see a character in a white polo coat, and a little cap to match, and I call the attention of Colonel Samuel B. Venus to same.

The boat is so overcrowded that it is far down in the water, but the waves, which are running very high, are carrying it away in long lunges, and it is fully 100 yards off, and is really visible to the naked eye by the light of the flames from the Castilla only when it rises a moment to the top of a wave, and Colonel Samuel B. Venus looks for some time before he sees what I wish him to see. "I spot him now," he says. "I recognize the white polo coat and the little cap to match." And with this, he ups with that thing and goes rooty-toot-toot out across the water three times, and the last I see of the white polo coat and the little cap to match they are folding up together very gently just as a big wave washes the boat off into the darkness beyond the light of the burning ship.

By this time the raft is in the water, and I take Colonel Samuel B. Venus and chuck him down onto the raft, and then I jump after him, and as the raft is soon overcrowded, I give the foot to a female character who is on the raft before anybody else and ease her off into the water. As this female character disappears in the raging sea, I am not surprised to observe that she is really nobody but Count Tomaso, as I seem to remember seeing Count Tomaso making Mrs. Colonel Samuel B. Venus change clothes with him at the point of a knife.

Well, some of the boats get ashore, and some do not, and in one that does arrive, they find the late Mrs. Colonel Samuel B. Venus, and everybody is somewhat surprised to note that she is in male garments with a white polo coat and a little cap to match. I wish to call attention to the public service I render in easing Count Tomaso off the raft, because here is a character who is undoubtedly a menace to the sanctity of the American home.

And I take pride in the fact that I discharge my debt of gratitude to Colonel Samuel B. Venus, and it is not my fault that he permits himself to be so overcome by his experience on the ship and on the raft that he turns out to be a raving nut, and never has the pleasure of learning that his aim is still so good that he can put three slugs in a moving target within the span of a baby's hand.

"Why, George," I say to Gentleman George, "then you are the victim of a great wrong, and I will see the governor, or somebody, in your behalf at once. They cannot do this to you, when, according to your own story, you are not directly connected with the matter of Mrs. Colonel Samuel B. Venus, and it is only a case of mistaken identity, at best."

"Oh, pshaw!" Gentleman George says. "They are not taking the severe measures they contemplate with me because of anything that happens to Mrs. Colonel Samuel B. Venus.

"They are vexed with me," George says, "because one night I take Lou Adolia's automobile out on the salt meadows near Secaucus, N. J., and burn it to a crisp, and it seems that I forget to remove Lou Adolia first from same."

"Well, George," I say, "bon voyage."

"The same to you," George says, "and many of them."

Baseball Hattie

IT COMES on springtime, and the little birdies are singing in the trees in Central Park, and the grass is green all around and about, and I am at the Polo Grounds on the opening day of the baseball season, when who do I behold but Baseball Hattie. I am somewhat surprised at this spectacle, as it is years since I see Baseball Hattie, and for all I know she long ago passes to a better and happier world. But there she is, as large as life, and in fact twenty pounds larger, and when I call the attention of Armand Fibleman, the gambler, to her, he gets up and tears right out of the joint as if he sees a ghost, for if there is one thing Armand Fibleman loathes and despises, it is a ghost. I can see that Baseball Hattie is greatly changed, and to tell the truth, I can see that she is getting to be nothing but an old bag. Her hair that is once as black as a yard up a stovepipe is gray, and she is wearing gold-rimmed cheaters, although she seems to be pretty well dressed and looks as if she may be in the money a little bit, at that.

But the greatest change in her is the way she sits there very quiet all afternoon, never once opening her yap, even when many of the customers around her are claiming that Umpire William Klem is Public Enemy No. 1 to 16 inclusive, because they think he calls a close one against the Giants. I am wondering if maybe Baseball Hattie is stricken dumb somewhere back down the years, because I can remember when she is usually making speeches in the grandstand in favor of hanging such characters as Umpire William Klem when they call close ones against the Giants. But Hattie just sits there as if she is in a church while the public clamor goes on about her, and she does not as much as cry out robber, or even you big bum at Umpire William Klem. I see many a baseball bug in my time, male and female, but without doubt the worst bug of them all is Baseball Hattie, and you can say it again. She is most particularly a bug about the Giants, and she never misses a game they play at the Polo Grounds, and in fact she sometimes bobs up watching them play in other cities, which is always very embarrassing to the Giants, as they fear the customers in these cities may get the wrong impression of New York Womanhood after listening to Baseball Hattie awhile.

The first time I ever see Baseball Hattie to pay any attention to her is in Philadelphia, a matter of twenty-odd years back, when the Giants are playing a series there, and many citizens of New York, including Armand Fibleman and myself, are present, because the Philadelphia customers are great hands for betting on baseball games in those days, and Armand Fibleman figures he may knock a few of them in the creek. Armand Fibleman is a character who will bet on baseball games from who-laid-the-chunk, and in fact he will bet on anything whatever, because Armand Fibleman is a gambler by trade and has been such since infancy. Personally, I will not bet you four dollars on a baseball game, because in the first place I am not apt to have four dollars, and in the second place I consider horse races a much sounder investment, but I often go around and about with Armand Fibleman, as he is a friend of mine, and sometimes he gives me a little piece of one of his bets for nothing.

Well, what happens in Philadelphia but the umpire forfeits the game in the seventh inning to the Giants by a score of nine to nothing when the Phillies are really leading by five runs, and the reason the umpire takes this action is because he orders several of the Philadelphia players to leave the field for calling him a scoundrel and a rat and a snake in the grass, and also a baboon, and they refuse to take their departure, as they still have more names to call him. Right away the Philadelphia customers become infuriated in a manner you will scarcely believe, for ordinarily a Philadelphia baseball customer is as quiet as a lamb, no matter what you do to him, and in fact in those days a Philadelphia baseball customer is only considered as somebody to do something to.

But these Philadelphia customers are so infuriated that they not only chase the umpire under the stand, but they wait in the street outside the baseball orchard until the Giants change into their street clothes and come out of the clubhouse. Then the Philadelphia customers begin pegging rocks, and one thing and another, at the Giants, and it is a most exciting and disgraceful scene that is spoken of for years afterwards. Well, the Giants march along toward the North Philly station to catch a train for home, dodging the rocks and one thing and another the best they can, and wondering why the Philadelphia gendarmes do not come to the rescue, until somebody notices several gendarmes among the customers doing some of the throwing themselves, so the Giants realize that this is a most inhospitable community, to be sure.

Finally all of them get inside the North Philly station and are safe, except a big, tall, left-handed pitcher by the name of Haystack Duggeler, who just reports to the club the day before and who finds him-

self surrounded by quite a posse of these infuriated Philadelphia customers, and who is unable to make them understand that he is nothing
but a rookie, because he has a Missouri accent, and besides, he is half
paralyzed with fear. One of the infuriated Philadelphia customers is
armed with a brickbat and is just moving forward to maim Haystack
Duggeler with this instrument, when who steps into the situation but
Baseball Hattie, who is also on her way to the station to catch a train,
and who is greatly horrified by the assault on the Giants.

She seizes the brickbat from the infuriated Philadelphia customer's
grasp, and then tags the customer smack-dab between the eyes with his
own weapon, knocking him so unconscious that I afterwards hear he
does not recover for two weeks, and that he remains practically an
imbecile the rest of his days. Then Baseball Hattie cuts loose on the
other infuriated Philadelphia customers with language that they never
before hear in those parts, causing them to disperse without further
ado, and after the last customer is beyond the sound of her voice, she
takes Haystack Duggeler by the pitching arm and personally escorts
him to the station.

Now out of this incident is born a wonderful romance between Baseball Hattie and Haystack Duggeler, and in fact it is no doubt love at
first sight, and about this period Haystack Duggeler begins burning
up the league with his pitching, and at the same time giving Manager
Mac plenty of headaches, including the romance with Baseball Hattie,
because anybody will tell you that a left-hander is tough enough on a
manager without a romance, and especially a romance with Baseball
Hattie. It seems that the trouble with Hattie is she is in business up in
Harlem, and this business consists of a boarding and rooming house
where ladies and gentlemen board and room, and personally I never
see anything out of line in the matter, but the rumor somehow gets
around, as rumors will do, that in the first place, it is not a boarding
and rooming house, and in the second place that the ladies and gentlemen who room and board there are by no means ladies and gentlemen,
and especially ladies.

Well, this rumor becomes a terrible knock to Baseball Hattie's social
reputation. Furthermore, I hear Manager Mac sends for her and
requests her to kindly lay off his ballplayers, and especially off a character who can make a baseball sing high *C* like Haystack Duggeler. In
fact, I hear Manager Mac gives her such a lecture on her civic duty
to New York and to the Giants that Baseball Hattie sheds tears, and
promises she will never give Haystack another tumble the rest of the
season. "You know me, Mac," Baseball Hattie says. "You know I will
cut off my nose rather than do anything to hurt your club. I sometimes

figure I am in love with this big bloke, but," she says, "maybe it is only gas pushing up around my heart. I will take something for it. To hell with him, Mac!" she says.

So she does not see Haystack Duggeler again, except at a distance, for a long time, and he goes on to win fourteen games in a row, pitching a no-hitter and four two-hitters among them, and hanging up a reputation as a great pitcher, and also as a hundred-percent heel.

Haystack Duggeler is maybe twenty-five at this time, and he comes to the big league with more bad habits than anybody in the history of the world is able to acquire in such a short time. He is especially a great rumpot, and after he gets going good in the league, he is just as apt to appear for a game all mulled up as not. He is fond of all forms of gambling, such as playing cards and shooting craps, but after they catch him with a deck of readers in a poker game and a pair of tops in a crap game, none of the Giants will play with him any more, except of course when there is nobody else to play with. He is ignorant about many little things, such as reading and writing and geography and mathematics, as Haystack Duggeler himself admits he never goes to school any more than he can help, but he is so wise when it comes to larceny that I always figure they must have great tutors back in Haystack's old home town of Booneville, Mo.

And no smarter jobbie ever breathes than Haystack when he is out there pitching. He has so much speed that he just naturally throws the ball past a batter before he can get the old musket off his shoulder, and along with his hard one, Haystack has a curve like the letter Q. With two ounces of brains, Haystack Duggeler will be the greatest pitcher that ever lives. Well, as far as Baseball Hattie is concerned, she keeps her word about not seeing Haystack, although sometimes when he is mulled up he goes around to her boarding and rooming house, and tries to break down the door.

On days when Haystack Duggeler is pitching, she is always in her favorite seat back of third, and while she roots hard for the Giants no matter who is pitching, she puts on extra steam when Haystack is bending them over, and it is quite an experience to hear her crying lay them in there, Haystack, old boy, and strike this big tramp out, Haystack, and other exclamations of a similar nature, which please Haystack quite some but annoy Baseball Hattie's neighbors back of third base, such as Armand Fibleman, if he happens to be betting on the other club.

A month before the close of his first season in the big league, Hay-

stack Duggeler gets so ornery that Manager Mac suspends him, hoping
maybe it will cause Haystack to do a little thinking, but naturally Haystack is unable to do this, because he has nothing to think with. About
a week later, Manager Mac gets to noticing how he can use a few ball
games, so he starts looking for Haystack Duggeler, and he finds him
tending bar on Eighth Avenue with his uniform hung up back of the
bar as an advertisement. The baseball writers speak of Haystack as
eccentric, which is a polite way of saying he is a screwball, but they
consider him a most unique character and are always writing humorous
stories about him, though any one of them will lay you plenty of nine
to five that Haystack winds up an umbay. The chances are they will
raise their price a little, as the season closes and Haystack is again under
suspension with cold weather coming on and not a dime in his pants
pockets.

It is sometime along in the winter that Baseball Hattie hauls off and
marries Haystack Duggeler, which is a great surprise to one and all,
but not nearly as much of a surprise as when Hattie closes her boarding
and rooming house and goes to live in a little apartment with Haystack
Duggeler up on Washington Heights.

It seems that she finds Haystack one frosty night sleeping in a hallway, after being around slightly mulled up for several weeks, and she
takes him to her home and gets him a bath and a shave and a clean
shirt and two boiled eggs and some toast and coffee and a shot or two
of rye whisky, all of which is greatly appreciated by Haystack, especially
the rye whisky. Then Haystack proposes marriage to her and takes a
paralyzed oath that if she becomes his wife he will reform, so what
with loving Haystack anyway, and with the fix commencing to request
more dough off the boarding-and-rooming-house business than the
business will stand, Hattie takes him at his word, and there you are.
The baseball writers are wondering what Manager Mac will say when
he hears these tidings, but all Mac says is that Haystack cannot possibly
be any worse married than he is single-o, and then Mac has the club
office send the happy couple a little paper money to carry them over
the winter. Well, what happens but a great change comes over Haystack
Duggeler. He stops bending his elbow and helps Hattie cook and wash
the dishes, and holds her hand when they are in the movies, and speaks
of his love for her several times a week, and Hattie is as happy as nine
dollars' worth of lettuce. Manager Mac is so delighted at the change
in Haystack that he has the club office send over more paper money,
because Mac knows that with Haystack in shape he is sure of twenty-
five games, and maybe the pennant.

In late February, Haystack reports to the training camp down South still as sober as some judges, and the other ballplayers are so impressed by the change in him that they admit him to their poker game again. But of course it is too much to expect a man to alter his entire course of living all at once, and it is not long before Haystack discovers four nines in his hand on his own deal and breaks up the game.

He brings Baseball Hattie with him to the camp, and this is undoubtedly a slight mistake, as it seems the old rumor about her boarding-and-rooming-house business gets around among the ever-loving wives of the other players, and they put on a large chill for her. In fact, you will think Hattie has the smallpox. Naturally, Baseball Hattie feels the frost, but she never lets on, as it seems she runs into many bigger and better frosts than this in her time. Then Haystack Duggeler notices it, and it seems that it makes him a little peevish toward Baseball Hattie, and in fact it is said that he gives her a slight pasting one night in their room, partly because she has no better social standing and partly because he is commencing to cop a few sneaks on the local corn now and then, and Hattie chides him for same.

Well, about this time it appears that Baseball Hattie discovers that she is going to have a baby, and as soon as she recovers from her astonishment, she decides that it is to be a boy who will be a great baseball player, maybe a pitcher, although Hattie admits she is willing to compromise on a good second baseman. She also decides that his name is to be Derrill Duggeler, after his paw, as it seems Derrill is Haystack's real name, and he is only called Haystack because he claims he once makes a living stacking hay, although the general opinion is that all he ever stacks is cards. It is really quite remarkable what a belt Hattie gets out of the idea of having this baby, though Haystack is not excited about the matter. He is not paying much attention to Baseball Hattie by now, except to give her a slight pasting now and then, but Hattie is so happy about the baby that she does not mind these pastings.

Haystack Duggeler meets up with Armand Fibleman along in midsummer. By this time, Haystack discovers horse racing and is always making bets on the horses, and naturally he is generally broke, and then I commence running into him in different spots with Armand Fibleman, who is now betting higher than a cat's back on baseball games.

It is late August, and the Giants are fighting for the front end of the league, and an important series with Brooklyn is coming up, and everybody knows that Haystack Duggeler will work in anyway two games of the series, as Haystack can generally beat Brooklyn just by throwing his glove on the mound. There is no doubt but what he has the old Indian sign on Brooklyn, and the night before the first game, which he is sure to work, the gamblers along Broadway are making the Giants two-to-one favorites to win the game.

This same night before the game, Baseball Hattie is home in her little apartment on Washington Heights waiting for Haystack to come in and eat a delicious dinner of pigs' knuckles and sauerkraut, which she personally prepares for him. In fact, she hurries home right after the ball game to get this delicacy ready, because Haystack tells her he will surely come home this particular night, although Hattie knows he is never better than even money to keep his word about anything. But sure enough, in he comes while the pigs' knuckles and sauerkraut are still piping hot, and Baseball Hattie is surprised to see Armand Fibleman with him, as she knows Armand backwards and forwards and does not care much for him, at that. However, she can say the same thing about four million other characters in this town, so she makes Armand welcome, and they sit down and put on the pigs' knuckles and sauerkraut together, and a pleasant time is enjoyed by one and all. In fact, Baseball Hattie puts herself out to entertain Armand Fibleman, because he is the first guest Haystack ever brings home.

Well, Armand Fibleman can be very pleasant when he wishes, and he speaks very nicely to Hattie. Naturally, he sees that Hattie is expecting, and in fact he will have to be blind not to see it, and he seems greatly interested in this matter and asks Hattie many questions, and Hattie is delighted to find somebody to talk to about what is coming off with her, as Haystack will never listen to any of her remarks on the subject. So Armand Fibleman gets to hear all about Baseball Hattie's son, and how he is to be a great baseball player, and Armand says is that so, and how nice, and all this and that, until Haystack Duggeler speaks up as follows, and to wit: "Oh, dag-gone her son!" Haystack says. "It is going to be a girl, anyway, so let us dismiss this topic and get down to business. Hat," he says, "you fan yourself into the kitchen and wash the dishes, while Armand and me talk."

So Hattie goes into the kitchen, leaving Haystack and Armand sitting there talking, and what are they talking about but a proposition for Haystack to let the Brooklyn club beat him the next day so Armand Fibleman can take the odds and clean up a nice little gob of money, which he is to split with Haystack. Hattie can hear every word they say, as the kitchen is next door to the dining room where they are sitting, and at first she thinks they are joking, because at this time nobody ever even as much as thinks of skulduggery in baseball, or anyway, not much. It seems that at first Haystack is not in favor of the idea, but Armand Fibleman keeps mentioning money that Haystack owes him for bets on the horses races, and he asks Haystack how he expects to continue betting on the races without fresh money, and Armand also speaks of the great injustice that is being done Haystack by the Giants in not paying him twice the salary he is getting, and how the loss of one or two games is by no means such a great calamity.

Well, finally Baseball Hattie hears Haystack say all right, but he wishes a thousand dollars then and there as a guarantee, and Armand Fibleman says this is fine, and they will go downtown and he will get the money at once, and now Hattie realizes that maybe they are in earnest, and she pops out of the kitchen and speaks as follows: "Gentlemen," Hattie says, "you seem to be sober, but I guess you are drunk. If you are not drunk, you must both be daffy to think of such a thing as phenagling around with a baseball game."

"Hattie," Haystack says, "kindly close your trap and go back in the kitchen, or I will give you a bust in the nose."

And with this he gets up and reaches for his hat, and Armand Fibleman gets up, too, and Hattie says like this: "Why, Haystack," she says, "you are not really serious in this matter, are you?"

"Of course I am serious," Haystack says. "I am sick and tired of pitching for starvation wages, and besides, I will win a lot of games later on to make up for the one I lose tomorrow. Say," he says, "these Brooklyn bums may get lucky tomorrow and knock me loose from my pants, anyway, no matter what I do, so what difference does it make?"

"Haystack," Baseball Hattie says, "I know you are a liar and a drunkard and a cheat and no account generally, but nobody can tell me you will sink so low as to purposely toss off a ball game. Why, Haystack, baseball is always on the level. It is the most honest game in all this world. I guess you are just ribbing me, because you know how much I love it."

"Dry up!" Haystack says to Hattie. "Furthermore, do not expect me home again tonight. But anyway, dry up."

"Look, Haystack," Hattie says, "I am going to have a son. He is your son and my son, and he is going to be a great ballplayer when he grows up, maybe a greater pitcher than you are, though I hope and trust he is not left-handed. He will have your name. If they find out you toss off a game for money, they will throw you out of baseball and you will be disgraced. My son will be known as the son of a crook, and what chance will he have in baseball? Do you think I am going to allow you to do this to him, and to the game that keeps me from going nutty for marrying you?"

Naturally, Haystack Duggeler is greatly offended by Hattie's crack about her son being maybe a greater pitcher than he is, and he is about to take steps, when Armand Fibleman stops him. Armand Fibleman is commencing to be somewhat alarmed at Baseball Hattie's attitude, and he gets to thinking that he hears that people in her delicate condition are often irresponsible, and he fears that she may blow a whistle on this enterprise without realizing what she is doing. So he undertakes a few soothing remarks to her. "Why, Hattie," Armand Fibleman says, "nobody can possibly find out about this little matter, and Haystack will have enough money to send your son to college, if his markers at the race track do not take it all. Maybe you better lie down and rest awhile," Armand says.

But Baseball Hattie does not as much as look at Armand, though she goes on talking to Haystack. "They always find out thievery, Haystack," she says, "especially when you are dealing with a fink like Fibleman. If you deal with him once, you will have to deal with him again and again, and he will be the first to holler copper on you, because he is a stool pigeon in his heart."

"Haystack," Armand Fibleman says, "I think we better be going."

"Haystack," Hattie says, "you can go out of here and stick up somebody or commit a robbery or a murder, and I will still welcome you back and stand by you. But if you are going out to steal my son's future, I advise you not to go."

"Dry up!" Haystack says. "I am going."

"All right, Haystack," Hattie says, very calm. "But just step into the kitchen with me and let me say one little word to you by yourself, and then I will say no more." Well, Haystack Duggeler does not care for even just one little word more, but Armand Fibleman wishes to get this disagreeable scene over with, so he tells Haystack to let her have her word, and Haystack goes into the kitchen with Hattie, and Armand cannot hear what is said, as she speaks very low, but he hears Haystack laugh heartily and then Haystack comes out of the kitchen, still laughing, and tells Armand he is ready to go.

As they start for the door, Baseball Hattie outs with a long-nosed .38-caliber Colt's revolver, and goes root-a-toot-toot with it, and the next thing anybody knows, Haystack is on the floor yelling bloody murder, and Armand Fibleman is leaving the premises without bothering to open the door. In fact, the landlord afterwards talks some of suing Haystack Duggeler because of the damage Armand Fibleman does to the door. Armand himself afterwards admits that when he slows down for a breather a couple of miles down Broadway he finds splinters stuck all over him.

Well, the doctors come, and the gendarmes come, and there is great confusion, especially as Baseball Hattie is sobbing so she can scarcely make a statement, and Haystack Duggeler is so sure he is going to die that he cannot think of anything to say except oh-oh-oh, but finally the landlord remembers seeing Armand leave with his door, and everybody starts questioning Hattie about this until she confesses that Armand is there all right, and that he tries to bribe Haystack to toss off a ball game, and that she then suddenly finds herself with a revolver in her hand, and everything goes black before her eyes, and she can remember no more until somebody is sticking a bottle of smelling salts under her nose. Naturally, the newspaper reporters put two and two together, and what they make of it is that Hattie tries to plug Armand Fibleman for his rascally offer, and that she misses Armand and gets Haystack, and right away Baseball Hattie is a great heroine, and Haystack is a great hero, though nobody thinks to ask Haystack how he stands on the bribe proposition, and he never brings it up himself.

And nobody will ever offer Haystack any more bribes, for after the doctors get through with him he is shy a left arm from the shoulder down, and he will never pitch a baseball again, unless he learns to pitch right-handed. The newspapers make quite a lot of Baseball Hattie protecting the fair name of baseball. The National League plays a benefit game for Haystack Duggeler and presents him with a watch and a purse of twenty-five thousand dollars, which Baseball Hattie grabs away from him, saying it is for her son, while Armand Fibleman is in bad with one and all.

Baseball Hattie and Haystack Duggeler move to the Pacific Coast, and this is all there is to the story, except that one day some years ago, and not long before he passes away in Los Angeles, a respectable grocer, I run into Haystack when he is in New York on a business trip, and I say to him like this: "Haystack," I say, "it is certainly a sin and a shame that Hattie misses Armand Fibleman that night and puts you on the shelf. The chances are that but for this little accident you will hang up one of the greatest pitching records in the history of baseball. Personally," I say, "I never see a better left-handed pitcher."

"Look," Haystack says. "Hattie does not miss Fibleman. It is a great newspaper story and saves my name, but the truth is she hits just where she aims. When she calls me into the kitchen before I start out with Fibleman, she shows me a revolver I never before know she has, and says to me, 'Haystack,' she says, 'if you leave with this weasel on the errand you mention, I am going to fix you so you will never make another wrong move with your pitching arm. I am going to shoot it off for you.'

"I laugh heartily," Haystack says. "I think she is kidding me, but I find out different. By the way," Haystack says, "I afterwards learn that long before I meet her, Hattie works for three years in a shooting gallery at Coney Island. She is really a remarkable broad," Haystack says.

I guess I forget to state that the day Baseball Hattie is at the Polo Grounds she is watching the new kid sensation of the big leagues, Derrill Duggeler, shut out Brooklyn with three hits.

He is a wonderful young left-hander.

Big Shoulders

ONE NIGHT I am sitting in Mindy's restaurant on Broadway partaking of some delicious gefüllte fish, when a very beautiful young Judy comes in and sits down at my table and starts in sobbing as if her little heart will break. I am about to call a waiter and have her chucked out of the place as her sobbing interferes with my enjoyment of the gefüllte fish, when I observe that she is nobody but Zelma Bodinski, the daughter of Blooch Bodinski, a character who is well known to one and all along Broadway as a small operator in betting matters.

Well, every time I see Zelma Bodinski, she always makes me think I am looking at a ghost, because she is a dead ringer for her mama, Zelma O'Dare, who once does a hot wiggle in the old Garden Café on Seventh Avenue a matter of some twenty-odd years back, and who confirms a general suspicion that she is none too bright by marrying Blooch Bodinski and going to live in the Bronx. However, as near as anybody can figure out, they get along together pretty well down through the years, because all Zelma O'Dare ever says is yes and no, and this is enough for Blooch, who does not understand many longer words, anyway, and when Zelma finally dies of influenza, she leaves him this daughter, who looks so much like her the chances are Blooch never misses the original.

This Blooch Bodinski is a short, fat, scary-looking little character who wears a derby hat and loud clothes when he marries Zelma O'Dare, and who always has a sad expression, and he does not change much in appearance as he grows older, except maybe to look sadder. He comes up out of Essex Street to Broadway, and he does this and that, and one thing and another, to make a living, until finally he gets to taking bets on prize fights and baseball games, and scalping the bets. That is, if somebody gives Blooch a bet on a proposition, right away he hustles around and gets somebody else to take it off his hands, generally at a shade better price than Blooch gives in the first place. Besides, he knocks off five percent on a winning bet as his commission for his trouble, so he really is nothing but a sort of middleman, or broker, though what he calls himself is a betting commissioner. He never risks anything on his own account, no matter what, because

Blooch is a very careful character by nature, and about as loose as concrete with his money. So it gets around that you can always place a bet on almost any proposition through Blooch Bodinski, and that he is an honest character and always pays off, and by and by Blooch opens an office and goes grinding and chiseling along in a modest way for quite a spell, making a few dibs here and there, and having Zelma O'Dare stash them away in a jug uptown against a rainy day.

I hear Blooch has quite a package planted when the jug fails and he is knocked out and has to start all over again, and there is a rumor around and about that things are none too good for Blooch at the time I am speaking of. He still has his office, and his credit remains A-1 with the trade all over the country, and anybody will accept a commission from Blooch because they know he never offers any bets he cannot guarantee, but the trouble is most of his old customers are also pretty well out of money, and new customers are scarce.

Anyway, here is Blooch Bodinski's daughter sobbing in Mindy's Restaurant, so naturally I ask her what ails her, and Zelma looks at me out of her big, black, wet eyes that are blacker than ever, what with the tears making the mascara run, and she says to me like this: "It is Poppa," she says. "Poppa wishes me to marry Jake Applebaum, the druggist, and I hate druggists, especially when they are Jake Applebaum. Poppa wishes me to marry Jake because he owes Jake ten thousand dollars borrowed money, and Jake is getting tough about it."

"Jake Applebaum already has ten thousand dollars," I say. "Twice," I say. "Maybe five or ten times. Jake Applebaum is fatter than a goose when it comes to money. Besides," I say, "Jake Applebaum is not hard to take. He is by no means bad-looking. He has a kind heart, unless you are asking him for dough. In fact, somebody tells me that you and Jake are almost an entry."

"Yes," she says, "I promised to marry him six months back. This is why he lends Poppa the ten thousand, which Poppa needs for the overhead. Up to yesterday, I practically love Jake Applebaum. Then I meet Charley." Well, I do not ask her Charley who, as I figure it may be one of those knock-knock things, and anyway, I can see that if I just let her talk I will get the whole story. I am thinking of the difference between her and her mama, Zelma O'Dare, who never makes a longer speech than to say she will have another rye high, but who foals a chatterbox. "Charley is a Yale," Zelma says. "He is very handsome and full of fun and not like Jake Applebaum, who only thinks of betting on something when he is not thinking of his drugstore."

"Jake makes a nice bet, at that," I say. "But where do you meet this Charley and what happens?"

"He comes into Poppa's office yesterday," Zelma says. "You know I am working in Poppa's office since last summer because Poppa cannot afford a regular office girl just now. I wish you could see his eyes. They are blue-gray. I am glad the baseball season is over because I get sick and tired of sitting there all day long telephoning bets on the Giants and the Yankees and the Cubs and Joe Louis, to Brad Cross in Fort Worth, and Dutch Ambrose in Omaha, and Izzy Harter in Indianapolis. They get awfully fresh with you. I mean the people in Izzy Harter's office."

"You are speaking of Charley's eyes," I say.

"Oh, yes," Zelma says. "He wishes to make a small bet on the Yales to beat the Princetons tomorrow. Somebody sends him to Poppa's office thinking we take football bets. Poppa is not there, so he talks to me. I tell him we not only do not take football bets but that it makes Poppa mad to even mention them, because he thinks football is silly. Poppa says football is nothing but a lot of big shoulders, and zing-boom-bah, and that anybody who bets on such a matter is a sucker. Well," Zelma says, "Charley says Poppa is wrong, and that he is making a big mistake not to take football bets. He says football is the coming big-betting proposition of this country. He talks to me four hours. He is a poor boy and works his way through college. This is his last year. He says I look like Mona Lisa, and he likes my shape."

"Well," I say, "the bloke is no chump about some things, anyway, although I cannot say much for his idea of betting on the Yales to beat the Princetons. The Princetons are one-to-four favorites in the betting."

"Yes," Zelma says, "Charley says it is a wonderful opportunity for everybody to get rich betting on the Yales. He says he is only sorry he does not have more than ten dollars to bet on them. He says they cannot possibly lose. He says he personally dopes the game for the Yales to win. I ask him if he is certain, and he crosses his heart and hopes to die if it is not the truth. I am going to tell Poppa about it as soon as I get back to the office. Just think," Zelma says. "Poppa can win enough money on this game to pay Jack Applebaum back and then give me some so Charley and I can get married and go into business."

"Just a minute," I say. "Does Charley ask you to marry him already?"

"Why, sure," Zelma says. "Do I not tell you we talk four hours? What else is there to talk about so long? He goes on to Princeton to the game, and he is coming back here as soon as he can and take me to dinner. He plays substitute in the game, and he simply has to be there. But now I must go back to the office and tell Poppa what a wonderful opportunity this is for him."

Well, I figure that listening to Blooch Bodinski when he is propositioned to bet his own money on something, and especially a football game, will make Broadway history, so I tell Zelma I wish to see her papa about a little business matter, and I go with her to Blooch's office, which at this time is a rat hole in an old building in West Forty-ninth Street, with just a desk and a couple of chairs and only one telephone in it, and as we come in, Blooch is slamming the receiver back on the hook and talking out loud to himself. "Big shoulders!" Blooch is saying to himself. "Zing-boom-bah, eight to five." Then he sees me, and he says to me like this: "Baseball, yes," Blooch says. "Prize fights, yes. Hockey, yes. Elections, yes. Big shoulders, no. Fifty times a day they call asking for prices on Mr. Minnesota, or Mr. Wisconsin, or somebody. I am about crazy. What do I know about prices on the big shoulders?"

"Why, Poppa," Zelma says, "Charley says it is your duty to hire college parties who can handicap the games for you, and get out your own prices and make your own book. Charley says most of the betting figures on the football games are a joke, and that if he is in the business he can get rich taking bets at his own prices and then catching the other fellows out of line and laying the bets off to them at their odds." Well, Blooch Bodinski looks at her for a minute without saying a word, and Zelma goes right ahead as follows: "Charley says football betting is in its infancy," she says. "But the big thing is about the Yales tomorrow," she says. "Charley says they cannot possibly lose to the Princetons, and you can make yourself well off for life by betting on them."

"Charley?" Blooch says. "Charley what?"

At this Zelma pauses to think, but she is never much of a hand at thinking, just like her mama, Zelma O'Dare, so she soon gives it up and says like this: "I forgot what," she says. "Maybe he never tells me. Anyway, you are to bet on the Yales. Charley says they are like wheat in the bin."

Well, Blooch finally shakes his head and looks at me and says: "Yes, I am crazy. The big shoulders get me at last. What are the Yales?" he says.

"They are four to one," I say.

Well, at this, Blooch drops his head on the desk and groans, and I can see that he is overcome at the idea that anybody in this whole world thinks he will bet on a four-to-one shot, but Zelma pays no attention to him and goes right on gabbing. "Charley says college football and Presidential elections are the only things it is safe to bet on," she says. "Charley says they are the only propositions that give you a dead-square rattle. Charley says nobody can cheat you in college football or Presidential elections."

Blooch raises his head and sits there looking at her as if he never sees her before in his life, and moreover he acts as if he does not hear a word she says for a while. But finally, when Zelma has to stop for breath, he holds up one hand to keep her from starting off again and says like this: "My own daughter," he says, "she wishes me to bet my own dough on something. The whole world is crazy. Listen," Blooch says. "For nearly thirty years I grind along in this town and never do I risk a single dib of my own on a bet. I take it off the top, or I take it off the bottom. Always something for nothing is my motto. And if ever I do bet it will not be on the big shoulders, and what is more, Jake Applebaum is in here a little while ago about you standing him up last night, so," Blooch says, "never you mind about somebody called Charley."

"He loves me," Zelma says.

"So he tells me," Blooch says.

"I mean Charley loves me," Zelma says. Then all of a sudden Zelma begins sobbing again, and I wish to say that when it comes to a job of sobbing she is much better than a raw hand, and between sobs she says she works hard all summer in this dirty old office, taking the insults of people over the telephone, and she never gets to go anywhere or see anything, and she wishes she is dead, and if her poppa loves her as he claims he does, he will take her to see the Yales and the Princetons play, even if he refuses a chance to bet on an absolutely sure thing like the Yales.

Well, I can see that these tears make Blooch Bodinski very uneasy, and he says there, there, and now, now, and my, my, to Zelma, but she only sobs all the harder, and says for two cents she will pitch herself off the new Triboro bridge, and finally Blooch is almost crying himself, and he pats Zelma on the head with his hand and says to her like this: "Why," Blooch says, "I remember hearing Jake Applebaum say he is going to this very game, and I know he will be glad to take you. I will call Jake up at once if you will just stop crying."

Now I claim Zelma is sobbing right up there around the record from the beginning, but when Blooch says this she turns on a notch higher and says it shows her that her poppa does not love her at all, to wish to shove her off on Jake Applebaum when she has only one desire in the world and this is to be with her only parent, so finally Blooch says all right, he will go around to Jack's ticket office and see if he can buy some tickets to the game, on condition that I go along.

Well, naturally, Zelma has no reason to bar me, so there we are the next morning taking a special train to Princeton, and I remember seeing Jake Applebaum at a distance in the Pennsylvania Station before we start, but he does not see us, and I also remember that Zelma seems to maneuver us around so we do not make the same train that Jake does, or connect with him when we hit Princeton.

Blooch dozes most of the way, because it seems he is awake most of the night worrying about the way Zelma is acting toward Jake Apple-baum, and I sit in a seat with Zelma and listen to her talk about Charley. I also listen to what some of the other characters in our Pull-man are saying, and although most of them seem to be Yales, I judge that they figure this game is just a breeze for the Princetons, and I say as much to Zelma. "No," she says, "they are wrong. Charley says the Yales are a cinch. Charley says the handicapping of football teams so you can determine the winner of a game is an exact science and not mere guesswork as many people may think, and," Zelma says, "Charley says he applies scientific methods to handicapping this game, and he makes it close but certain for the Yales."

She places so much faith in what Charley says that I am wondering if maybe I am making a mistake in not taking advantage of the price, for if there is anything I dearly love it is a long shot, and in football four to one is a very long shot indeed, and they do not often get down there in front. Then I remember that some handicappers who are maybe about as smart as Charley make this price, so I decide I am just as well off keeping my dough in my kick, although I do not speak of this to Zelma.

Blooch wakes up when our special pulls into Princeton, and we get off and start walking to the football yard with the rest of the crowd, and I am thinking that these scenes must be quite a novelty to him, when we pass a bunch of characters who are offering to buy or sell tickets to the game, and who are what is known as ticket hustlers, and a couple of old characters among them give Blooch a blow, and he stops to talk to them. When he joins us again, Blooch is smiling, and he says to me like this: "I hustle duckets with those parties among these same crowds over twenty years ago," he says. "They remember old Blooch. I am a champion in those days, too." He livens up quite some after this and begins taking an interest in his surroundings and talking about the good old days, but as near as I can make out, Blooch's good old days are about the same as everybody else's good old days, and most of the time he is half starving.

Well, by this time Zelma is paying no attention whatever to us, but is looking all around and about, and I can see that she is hoping she may get a swivel at Charley, but naturally he is not to be seen, so she does the next best thing and takes to looking at other young characters who are quite numerous all over the place, and they look right back at her, if anybody asks you, and personally I do not blame them. She is the prettiest thing that ever steps in shoe leather this particular day, what with her eyes shining, and her cheeks red with excitement, and all this and that.

Our seats in the football stadium are not so good because they are right behind the goal posts at one end of the field, and close to the ground, and we are not able to see a whole lot of the game, especially when the ball is in the middle of the field or down toward the other end, and Zelma is disappointed no little and Blooch is saying he will see Jack when he gets home about this, but personally I do not care where we are as long as we are at a football game, because football is one of my favorite dishes. Even Blooch partakes of the general excitement when we get settled down, and the bands play, and the young characters in the stands begin letting out cheers. Zelma keeps watching the Yales' bench trying to locate Charley, but we are too far away for her to see good, and anyway, the game gets going and takes her attention, especially as right away the Princetons start running all over the Yales in a most disquieting manner. I can see in about two plays why the Princetons are one-to-four favorites, and I say to Zelma like this: "I am afraid Charley is wrong," I say. "This looks as if it may be murder."

"Never fear," Zelma says, "Charley gives me his word the Yales will win."

"Where are the big shoulders?" Blooch says. "These parties are a lot of midgets."

Well, all of a sudden the Yales commence playing better football, and instead of running over them, the Princetons now have a tough time keeping from getting run over themselves, and the game goes this way and that way, and nothing happens in the way of a score, and the Yales in the stands are in quite a hubbub, and are singing Boola-boola and I do not know what all else, and Zelma is jumping up and down and shrieking, "Charley is right!" All the time she is trying to locate Charley on the field or on the side lines, but there seems to be no Charley, and I am commencing to wonder if some character does not play a joke on her. She is somewhat downhearted when the second half starts and Charley remains invisible, although she is still confident that the Yales will win. Personally, I figure a tie is about the answer.

Well, it is getting on toward the end of the game, and the goal in front of us belongs at this time to the Princetons, and the Yales start a march that winds up with them losing the ball on downs on the Princetons' one-inch line, and everybody is half insane, especially Zelma, and even Blooch Bodinski is saying out loud to the Yales: "Come on, big shoulders!" But it is no go, and it is coming on dark when the Yales lose the ball, and one of the Yales gets hurt on the last play, and there is a substitution, and when they line up again one of the Princetons goes back behind his own goal to kick out of danger, and he is standing just a short distance from where we are sitting waiting for the pass. Then, just as the ball is flipped to the Princeton back of the line, Zelma Bodinski lets out a shriek like a steam whistle, because it seems that she just spots the last Yale substitute, and she screams as follows: "Char-lee!"

Well, afterwards I read what the reporters say about the darkness and the slippery ball and all this and that, but it seems to me that I see the Princeton character back of the line jump at the scream and half turn his head, and the next thing anybody knows he drops the football out of his hands, and then as all the Yales are coming at him, he falls on it behind his own goal for what is called a safety, and this means two points against the Princetons.

And a few seconds later the whistle blows, and there the Princetons are, licked by the Yales by a score of two to nothing, which is very discouraging to the Princetons, to be sure. Naturally, there are some great goings-on over this business among the Yales, and nobody is more delighted than Zelma Bodinski, and I hear her saying to Blooch like this: "Well," Zelma says, "now everything is all right. Jake Applebaum is paid off, and we have all the money we need. I am glad, because it proves Charley is right."

"What do you mean Jake Applebaum is paid off?" Blooch says. "And what do you mean we have all the money we need? If you do not marry Jake, we will be on relief in a month."

"Oh," Zelma says, "I forget to tell you. This morning before we leave New York, I go to the office and call up Dutch Ambrose and Brad Cross and Izzy Harter and bet them two thousand dollars each in your name on Yale at four to one. Then I happen to have a date with Jake Applebaum the night before, and I tell him you have a commission of two thousand dollars from out of town to place on the Yales at the best price you can get, and Jake says he will lay five to one, because it is just the same as finding the two thousand in the street. So," Zelma says, "we pay off Jake and win twenty-four thousand in cash. Even if we lose," she says, "the most we can lose is eight thousand dollars, but I know that Charley says there is no chance of our losing. I will always believe Charley all my life, no matter what."

Well, Blooch stands there as if he is thinking this over, and there is a very strange expression on his face, and about this time who comes up but Jake Applebaum, and it is plain to be seen that Jake is very angry, and he shakes his finger in Zelma Bodinski's beautiful face and says to her like this: "See here," Jake says. "I hear all about you this morning when I am at breakfast in Mindy's. I hear all about you being in love with a Yale by the name of Charley, and now I know why you are jerking me around. But do not forget your old man owes me plenty, and I will make him hard to catch."

Naturally, Jake's statement is most uncouth, and Zelma is starting to turn on the sobs, when a large young character in football clothes approaches, and I can see that he is nobody but the Princeton who fumbles the ball, and I can also see that he seems to be slightly perturbed as he says to us like this: "Where is the pancake who sings out Charley over here? My name is Charley."

Well, personally, I do not care for his attitude, and I do not think it shows proper college training for him to be speaking of pancakes, but before I can decide what to do about the situation, Jake Applebaum steps forward and says: "Oh, so you are Charley, are you, you snake in the grass? Well, my lady friend here that you try to steal from me is the one who sings out. Why?" Jake says. "What do you wish to make of it?"

"Only this!" the football character says, and then he lets go as neat a left hook as ever I could wish to behold and stretches Jake as flat as a pancake, and immediately disappears in the dusk.

We leave Jake there and start walking back to the railroad, and all this time Blooch never says a word but seems to be thinking of something, and finally he turns to Zelma and speaks as follows: "You mean to say I stand to lose eight thousand of my own money on a four-to-one shot in this game?" Blooch says.

"Yes, Poppa," Zelma says, "you can figure it in such a way. But Charley says—"

Then without finishing she lets out a scream, because Blooch falls in a dead faint and starts rolling down a little hill, and the chances are he will be rolling yet if a big blond young character does not come leaping out of the dusk to grab him and set him on his pins again and shake him out of his faint. At the sight of this young character Zelma lets out another scream and says like this: "Char-lee!"

So now Blooch Bodinski has a big suite of offices, and fifty telephones, and he calls himself the Flannagan Brokerage Company and makes the biggest football book in this country, and everybody along Broadway is pretty jealous about this, although Mindy, the restaurant man, says: "Well, you must give Blooch credit for digging up Charley Flannagan, the best football handicapper in the world, for a son-in-law." And every time Blooch looks at Charley, he nods his head to show he approves him, and sometimes Blooch says out loud: "Big shoulders!"

Too Much Pep

IT IS REALLY surprising how many wicked people there are in this world, and especially along East 114th Street up in Harlem. Of course I do not say that all the wicked people in the world are along East 114th Street, because some of them are on East 115th Street, and maybe on East 116th Street, too, but the wicked people on East 114th Street are wickeder than somewhat, especially Ignazio Vardarelli and his mob.

This Ignazio Vardarelli is called Ignaz the Wolf, and he is an Italian party from Calabria, with a noggin shaped like the little end of an ice cream cone, and a lot of scars on his face which make him look very fierce. All his mob are also Italians, and most of them have noggins shaped like Ignaz', and some of them have even more scars on their kissers, and therefore look even fiercer than he does, which is very, very fierce, indeed. Now Ignaz the Wolf is a guy who never works, and neither does anybody else in his mob, and what they do for a living is very simple, and I do not mind saying I am sorry I never have the nerve to invent something as easy, because after all work is a great bother.

In Harlem there are a great many Italians, and among them are quite a lot of Mustache Petes, who are old-time Italians with large black mustaches, and who have little stores in cellars and such places and sell spaghetti, and macaroni, and cheeses, and other articles of which Italian persons are very fond. I like spaghetti myself now and then, and also pasta fagiole, and broccoli, cooked with garlic, which is very good for the old stomach. In fact, it is because I like such things that I come to hear about Ignazio Vardarelli, because I often go to a spot in Harlem where a guy can get good Italian food, especially devilfish fixed a certain way, and maybe a little red wine which the guy who owns the joint makes right in his own cellar by walking up and down in his bare feet in a tub of grapes. In fact, one time when the guy has very painful corns on his feet, and cannot walk up and down in the tub of grapes, I take off my shoes and walk for him, but whoever sells him the grapes leaves a big rock among them, and I get a bad stone bruise from it on my heel. There are always some very nice Italian people sitting around and about this joint, and I love to listen to them eat spaghetti, and talk, though I do not understand much of what they are saying because Italian is one language I never learn. In fact, I never learn any other language except English, and a very little bit of Yiddish, because a guy who lives in New York can get around most anywhere on these two languages, with a few signs mixed up with them.

Anyway, I have a lot of very good friends among the Italians, and I never speak of them as wops, or guineas, or dagoes, or grease balls, because I consider this most disrespectful, like calling Jewish people mockies, or Heebs, or geese. The way I look at it, if a guy is respectful to one and all, why, one and all will be respectful to him, and anyway there are many Italians, and Jewish people too, who are apt to haul off and knock you bow-legged if you call them such names.

Well, these Mustache Petes I am talking about are very industrious, and very saving, and most of them have a few bobs laid away for a rainy day, so when Ignaz the Wolf feels that he needs a little money to take care of his overhead, he picks out some Mustache Pete that he figures is able to contribute and writes him a nice letter about as follows: "Dear Joe" (or maybe Tony, for most Italians are called Joe or Tony), "please call and see me with five hundred dollars. Yours sincerely, Ignazio."

Then Ignazio waits two or three days, and if Joe or Tony does not show up with the five yards, or whatever it is that Ignazio asks for, Ignazio writes him another letter, which is a sort of follow-up letter, the same as any business concern sends out to a customer, and this follow-up letter is about as follows: "Dear Joe" (or Tony), "I am sorry to hear you have a headache. I figure you must have a headache, because you do not call to see me with the five hundred dollars. I hope and trust you get over this headache very soon, as I am waiting for the five hundred. With kindest regards, I am yours truly, Ignazio."

He puts a black mark on this letter, and shoves it under Joe or Tony's door, and then he waits a couple of days more. By this time Ignaz the Wolf is naturally getting a little bit impatient, because he is a good business man, and business men like to see their letters receive prompt attention. If he gets no answer from Joe or Tony, there is nothing else for Ignaz the Wolf to do but put a little bomb under the joint where the Mustache Pete lives to remind him of the letter, and very few of Ignaz' customers wait any longer to settle after the first bomb. So Ignaz the Wolf and his mob do very well for themselves and are able to wear good clothes, and jewelry, and sit around eating spaghetti and drinking dago red and having a nice time generally, and everybody that sees them says hello, very pleasant, even including the Mustache Petes, although of course the chances are they are not on the level with their hellos and secretly hope that Ignaz falls over dead.

Personally, I never hear much of Ignaz the Wolf until I run into a young Italian guy in the Harlem eating joint by the name of Marco Sciarra, or some such, who is a very legitimate guy up in Harlem, being in the artichoke business with his old man. It seems that the artichoke business is a first-class business in Harlem, though personally I will not give you ten cents for all the artichokes you can pack in the Hudson tubes, as I consider them a very foolish fruit any way you look at them. But Marco and his old man do very good with artichokes, and in fact they do so well that Marco is able to play plenty of horses, which is how I come to get acquainted with him, because it is well known to one and all that I am one of the greatest horse players in New York, and will be a very rich guy if it is not for crooked jockeys riding the horses different from the way I dope them.

Anyway, one night Marco somehow starts beefing about Ignaz the Wolf and his mob, and finally he lets it out that Ignaz is trying to put the arm on him and his old man for five G's, for no reason except that Ignaz seems to need it. Now Marco is born and raised right here in this man's town, and he is quite an all-around guy in many respects, and he is certainly not the kind of guy anybody with any sense will figure a chump. He is not the kind of a guy a smart guy will figure to hold still for five G's for no reason, and the chances are Ignaz the Wolf is not thinking of Marco in the first place. The chances are he is thinking more of Marco's old man, who is a Mustache Pete in every way. Furthermore, if it is left to the old man, he will kick in the five G's to Ignaz without a yip, just to avoid trouble, but Marco can see where he can use any stray five G's himself to pay off a few bookmakers. Anyway, Marco tells me he will see Ignaz in the place where Ignaz is a sure thing to go some day before he will give up five G's, or any part of five G's, and I say I do not blame him, for five G's is plenty of sugar, even if you do not have it.

This is the last I see of Marco for a couple of weeks. Then one day I happen to be in Harlem, so I go over to his place of business on East 114th Street. The Marcos have an office on the ground floor of a two-story building, and live upstairs, and when I get there I notice that the glass in all the windows seems to be out, and that things are generally upset. Well, when I find Marco he explains to me that somebody puts a fifteen-dollar bomb in the joint the night before, and while Marco does not say right out that Ignaz the Wolf does this, he says he is willing to lay 8 to 5 and take Ignaz against the field, because it seems he sends word to Ignaz that he need not expect the five G's he is looking for.

Then Marco explains to me that the fifteen-dollar bomb is only meant as a sort of convincer, and that according to the rules Ignaz will next put a thirty-two-dollar bomb in the joint, which will be a little more powerful than the fifteen-dollar bomb. In fact, Marco says, the thirty-two-dollar bomb will be powerful enough to lift them out of their beds upstairs a foot to a foot and a half. But finally, if the five G's is not paid to Ignaz the Wolf in the meantime, he will put a fifty-four-dollar bomb under them, and this bomb will practically ruin everything in the neighborhood, including the neighbors. Well, naturally I am very indignant about the whole proposition, but Marco says it is only fair to Ignaz the Wolf to say he writes them a couple of very polite letters before he makes a move, and does nothing whatever underhand before sending the bomb.

"But my old man is now very much displeased with Ignaz," Marco says. "He is even more displeased than I am. It takes quite a little to displease my old man, but when he is displeased, he is certainly greatly displeased, indeed. In fact," Marco says, "my old man and other Italian citizens of Harlem hold a meeting today, and they come to the conclusion that it is for the best interests of the community to have Ignaz put in his place before he cleans everybody out. So they are going to put Ignaz in his place."

"Well," I say, "what is Ignaz' place?"

"Ignaz' place is six feet underground," Marco says, "and this is where the citizens are going to put him."

"Why, Marco," I say, "this is most horrifying, indeed, although personally I am in favor of it. But," I say, "I do not think Ignaz will care to be put in his place, and as he is well mobbed I do not see how it can be brought about without somebody getting in trouble. I hope and trust, Marco," I say, "that neither you or your old man are going to get tangled up in this proposition."

"No," Marco says, "we will not get tangled up. In fact, nobody in Harlem will get tangled up, because they are sending to Sicily for a certain party to put Ignaz in his place. They are sending for Don Pep'."

Well, I finally make out from what Marco tells me that at this meeting many of the old-fashioned Italians of Harlem are present, with their mustaches sticking right out straight with indignation, and it is the opinion of one and all that Ignaz shall be put in his place as quickly as possible. But Marco says there is quite a difference of opinion as to who shall put Ignaz in his place, and the meeting lasts a long time, and there is plenty of argument. It seems that all of these old-timers know of some party back in Italy that they figure is just the one to put Ignaz in his place, and they get up and make speeches about their guys as if they are delegates to a convention boosting candidates for a nice nomination.

Marco says an old Mustache Pete by the name of Bianchini, who is a shoemaker, almost carries the meeting in favor of a guy by the name of Corri, who, it seems, makes a great showing putting parties in their places around Napoli, and who is favorably remembered by many of the citizens present. Marco says old Bianchini is a good speaker and he talks for almost an hour telling about how his guy puts parties in their places by slipping a little short rope around their necks and guzzling them before they have time to say Jack Robinson, and it is commencing to look as if Corri is the guy, when Marco's old man steps forward and raises his hand to stop all of this cheering for Corri. "I will not take up much of your time in presenting the name of my choice," Marco says his old man says. "It is a name that is well known to many of you older delegates. It is the name of one who has made history at putting parties in their places, the name of a celebrated citizen of Sicily, experienced and skilful in his calling—a name that is above reproach. I give you, fellow citizens, the name of Don Pep', of Siracusa."

Well, at this everybody becomes very enthusiastic, Marco says, and also their blood runs cold, because it seems that Don Pep' is for many years the outstanding man in all Italy at putting parties in their places. All the old-timers know of him by reputation, and some of them even see him when they are young guys back in the old country, while Marco's old man knows him personally. It seems that Don Pep' has a record like a prize fighter, and Marco's old man reads this record to the meeting, as follows:

Milan, 1899, 2 men.
Venice, 1904, 1 man.
Naples, 1909, 3 men.
Rome, 1913, 1 man.
Genoa, 1921, 2 men, 4 horses.
Nice, 1928, 1 man.

Well, when the thing comes to a vote, Don Pep' gets all the votes but one, old Bianchini sticking to Corri, and the meeting adjourns with everybody satisfied that Ignaz the Wolf is to be put in his place in first-class style. Now getting Don Pep' over to this country to put Ignaz in his place is going to cost something, so Marco, seeing a chance to turn a few honest bobs, propositions his old man to get Ignaz put in his place for about half of what Don Pep' will cost, Marco figuring that he can find a couple of guys downtown who are willing to work cheap, but his old man refuses to listen to him. His old man says this business must be transacted in a dignified way, and under the old-fashioned rules, though Marco says he does not see what difference it makes if a guy is to be put in his place whether it is under the old-fashioned rules or the new no-foul system, especially as nobody explains the old-fashioned rules, or seems to know what they are.

Personally, if I am planning to get a guy put in his place I will not go around telling people about it. In fact, I will keep it a very great secret for fear the guy may hear of it and take steps, but these Mustache Petes make no bones whatever about sending for Don Pep', and everybody in the neighborhood knows it, including Ignaz the Wolf and his mob. I figure that maybe the Mustache Petes want Ignaz to know it, thinking he may decide to haul ashes out of Harlem before anything happens to him, but Ignaz is a pretty bold guy one way and another, and he only laughs about Don Pep'. Ignaz says Don Pep' is old stuff, and may go in Italy years ago, but not in the U. S. A. in these times.

Naturally, I am greatly interested in Don Pep', and I make Marco promise to tell me when he arrives. I love to look at a top-notcher in any line, and I judge from Don Pep's record that he is a champion of the world. So some weeks later when I get a telephone call from Marco that Don Pep' is here, I hurry up to Harlem and meet Marco, and he promises to show me Don Pep' after it gets dark, because it seems Don Pep' moves around only at night. He is living in the basement of a tenement house in East 114th Street with an old Sicilian by the name of Sutari, who is a real Mustache Pete and who has a shoe-shining joint downtown. He is a nice old man, and a good friend of mine, though afterwards I hear he is a tough guy back in his old home town in Sicily.

Well, when I get a peek at Don Pep', I almost bust out laughing, for what is he but a little old man wearing a long black coat that trails the ground, and a funny flat black hat with a low crown and a stiff brim. He looks to me like somebody out of a play, especially as he has long white hair, and bushy white whiskers all over his face like a poodle dog. But when I get close to him, I do not feel so much like laughing, because he raises his head and stares at me through the whiskers and I see a pair of black eyes like a snake's eyes, with a look in them such as gives me the shivers all over. Personally, I never see such a look in anybody's eyes before in my life, and I am very glad indeed to walk briskly away from Don Pep'.

I peek back over my shoulder, and Don Pep' is standing there with his head bowed on his chest, as harmless-looking as a rabbit, and I feel

like laughing again at the idea of such an old guy being brought all
the way from Sicily to put Ignaz the Wolf in his place. Then I think
of those eyes, and start shivering harder than ever, and Marco shivers
with me and explains to me what happens when Don Pep' first arrives,
and since. It seems that Marco's old man and a lot of other Mustache
Petes meet Don Pep' at the boat that brings him from Sicily, and they
are wishing to entertain him, but Don Pep' says he is not here for
pleasure, and all they can do for him is to show him the guy he is to
put in his place. Well, naturally, nobody wishes to put the finger on
Ignaz the Wolf in public, because Ignaz may remember same, and feel
hurt about it, so they give Don Pep' a description of Ignaz, and his
address, which is a cigar store on East 114th Street, where Ignaz and his
mob always hang out.

A few hours later when Ignaz is sitting in the cigar store playing
klob with some of his mob, in comes Don Pep', all bundled up in his
black cloak, though it is a warm night, at that. He has a way of walking
along very slow, and he is always tap-tapping on the sidewalk ahead
of him with a big cane, like a blind man, but his feet never make a
sound. Well, naturally Ignaz the Wolf jumps up when such a strange-
looking party bobs in on him, for Ignaz can see that this must be Don
Pep', the guy who is coming to put him in his place, and knowing
where his place is, Ignaz is probably on the lookout for Don Pep', anyway. So Ignaz stands there with his cards in his hand staring at Don
Pep', and Don Pep' walks right up to him, and shoots his head up out
of his cloak collar like a turtle and looks Ignaz in the eye.

He never says one word to Ignaz, and while Ignaz tries to think of
something smart to say to Don Pep', he cannot make his tongue move
a lick. He is like a guy who is hypnotized. The other guys at the table
sit there looking at Ignaz and Don Pep', and never making a wrong
move, though on form any one of them figures to out with the old
equalizer and plug Don Pep'. Finally, after maybe three minutes hand
running of looking at Ignaz, Don Pep' suddenly makes a noise with his
mouth like a snake hissing, and then he turns and walks out of the
joint, tap-tapping with his cane ahead of him. After he is gone, Ignaz
comes up for air, and starts explaining why he does not do something
about Don Pep', but even Ignaz' own mobsters figure the old guy runs
something of a sandy on Ignaz. What puzzles them no little is that Don
Pep' makes no move to put Ignaz in his place then and there, as long
as he comes all the way from Sicily to do it.

But two nights later, when Ignaz the Wolf is again playing klob in
the cigar store, who pops in but old Don Pep', and once more he stands
looking Ignaz in the eye and never saying as much as howdy. This time

Ignaz manages to get a few words out but Don Pep' never answers him, and winds up his looking at Ignaz with that same hissing sound, like a snake. After this Ignaz does not keep his old hours around the cigar store, but he starts in getting very tough with the Mustache Petes, and writing them very stiff business notes about sending in their contributions.

Well, it seems that the citizens around and about get very independent after Don Pep' arrives, and commence paying no attention to Ignaz' notes, and even take to giving Ignaz' collectors the old ha-ha, in Italian, which burns Ignaz up quite some. He complains that Don Pep' is hurting his business, and lets it out here and there that after he takes care of Don Pep' he is going to make his old customers very sorry that they ignore him. But somehow Ignaz does not put any more bombs around, except a few fifteen-dollar ones on guys who do not count much. In the meantime, old Don Pep' goes walking up and down the streets, his whiskers down in his cloak collar, no matter how warm it gets, and the citizens lift their hats to him as he passes by. In fact, I lift my own lid one evening when he passes me, because I feel that a guy with his record is entitled to much respect. But knowing Ignaz the Wolf, I figure it is only a question of time when we will be walking slow behind the old guy, especially as he does not seem to be making any kind of move to put Ignaz in his place, per agreement.

Always late at night Don Pep' stands in front of an areaway between the tenement house where he lives and the house next door, leaning up against a sort of iron grating that walls off the areaway from the street. It happens that no light shines on the areaway, so all you see as you pass by is a sort of outline of Don Pep' against the grating, and now and then a little glow as he puffs at a cigarette through his whiskers. He is certainly a strange-looking old crocodile, and I often wonder what he is thinking about as he stands there.

I can see now how smart the Mustache Petes are in making no secret of what Don Pep' is here for, because the publicity he gets keeps Ignaz the Wolf from doing anything to him. Naturally if anything drastic happens to Don Pep', the coppers will figure Ignaz responsible, and the coppers in this town are waiting for several years to find something drastic that Ignaz is responsible for.

But there is no doubt Ignaz the Wolf is getting sick and tired of Don Pep', especially since business is so bad, so one night the thing that is a sure thing to happen comes off: An automobile tears past the spot where Don Pep' is standing, as usual, in front of the areaway, and out of this automobile comes a big blooey-blooey, with four guys letting go with sawed-off shotguns at once. As the automobile cuts in close to the curb, this puts the gunners only the distance across the sidewalk from Don Pep', so there is little chance that four guys using shotguns are going to miss, especially as the shotguns are loaded with buckshot, which scatters nice and wide.

Well, there are very few citizens around the spot at this hour, and they start running away lickity-split as soon as they hear the first blooey, because the citizens of this part of Harlem know that a blooey is never going to do anybody much good. But before they start running, some of the citizens see old Don Pep' fold up in a little black pile in front of the areaway as the automobile tears on down the street, with Ignaz the Wolf sitting back in it laughing very heartily. I will say one thing for Ignaz, that when it comes down to cases, he is always ready to go out on his own jobs himself, although this is mainly because he wishes to see that the jobs are well done.

Then minutes later, Ignaz is walking into the cigar store so as to be playing klob and looking very innocent when the coppers come around to speak to him about the matter of Don Pep'. And he is no sooner inside the joint than right at his heels steps nobody in all this world but Don Pep', who has a license to be laying up against the areaway grating as dead as a doornail. Well, old Don Pep' is huddled up in his cape and whiskers as usual, but he seems to be stepping spryer than somewhat, and as Ignaz the Wolf turns around and sees him and lets out a yell, thinking he is seeing a ghost, Don Pep' closes in on him and grabs Ignaz as if he is giving him a nice hearty hug. Ignaz the Wolf screams once very loud, and the next thing anybody knows he is stretched out on the floor as stiff as a board and Don Pep' is stepping out of the cigar store.

Nobody ever sees Don Pep' again as far as I know, although the coppers still have the straw-stuffed black suit, and the black hat and cape, as well as the false whiskers with which Sutari, the shoe shiner, fixes up a phony Don Pep' to lean against the areaway grating for Ignaz the Wolf and his gunners to waste their buckshot on, because it seems from what Sutari says that Don Pep' carries two outfits of clothes for just such a purpose. Personally, I consider this very deceitful of Don Pep', but nobody else seems to see anything wrong in it.

Well, when the croakers examine Ignaz' body they do not find a mark of any kind on him, and they are greatly puzzled indeed, because naturally they expect to find a knife or maybe a darning needle sticking in him. But there is nothing whatever to show what makes Ignaz the Wolf die, and Marco tells me afterwards that his old man and all the other Mustache Petes are laughing very heartily at the idea that Don Pep' uses any such articles. Marco tells me his old man says if the croakers have any sense they will see at once that Ignaz the Wolf dies of heart disease, and Marco says his old man claims anybody ought to know this heart disease is caused by fright because Don Pep' is putting guys in their places in such a way for many years. Furthermore, Marco says his old man states that this is according to the old-fashioned rules, and very dignified, though if you ask me I think it is a dirty trick to scare a guy to death.

A Job for The Macarone

WHEN THE last race meeting of the winter season closes in Miami and it is time for one and all to move on to Maryland, I take a swivel at the weather reports one day and I observe that it is still down around freezing in those parts. So thinks I to myself, I will remain in the sunny southland awhile longer and continue enjoying the balmy breezes, and the ocean bathing, and all this and that, until the weather settles up yonder, and also until I acquire a blow stake, for at this time my bank roll is worn down to a nubbin and, in fact, I do not have enough ready to get myself as far as Jax, even by walking.

Well, while waiting around Miami, trying to think of some way of making a scratch, I spend my evenings in the Shark Fin Grill, which is a little scatter on Biscayne Boulevard near the docks that is conducted by a friend of mine by the name of Chesty Charles. He is called by this name because he has a chest like a tub and he walks with it stuck out in front of him, and the reason Charles keeps his chest out is because if he pulls it in, his stomach will take its place, only farther down, and Charles does not wish his stomach to show in this manner, as he likes to think he has a nice shape.

At the time I am speaking of, Chesty Charles is not as young as he used to be, and he wishes to go along very quiet and avoiding undue excitement, but anybody can see that he is such a character as observes a few things in his time. In fact, anybody can see that he is such a character as is around and about no little and quite some before he settles down to conducting the Shark Fin Grill. The reason Charles calls his place the Shark Fin Grill is because it sounds nice, although, of course, Charles does not really grill anything there, and, personally, I think the name is somewhat confusing to strangers.

In fact, one night a character with a beard, from Rumson, New Jersey, comes in and orders a grilled porterhouse; and when he learns he cannot get same, he lets out a chirp that Charles has no right to call his place a grill when he does not grill anything and claims that Charles is obtaining money under false pretenses. It finally becomes necessary for Charles to tap him on the pimple with a beer mallet, and afterwards the constables come around, saying what is going on here, and what do you mean by tapping people with beer mallets, and the only way Charles can wiggle out of it is by stating that the character with the beard claims that Mae West has no sex appeal. So the constables go away saying Charles does quite right and one of them has half a mind to tap the character himself with something.

Well, anyway, one night I am in the Shark Fin Grill playing rummy with Charles and there is nobody else whatever in the joint, because by this time the quiet season is on in Miami and Charles' business thins out more than somewhat; and just as I beat Charles a pretty good score, who comes in but two characters in sport shirts, and one of them has that thing in his hand and he says to us like this: "Reach," he says. "This is a stick-up. No beefs, now," he says.

Well, Chesty Charles and me raise our hands as high as possible, and, in fact, I am only sorry I cannot raise mine higher than possible, and Chesty Charles says: "No beefs," he says. "But," he says, "boys, you are on an awful bust. All you are liable to get around this drum is fleas. If there is any dough here I will be using it myself," Chesty says.

"Well," one of the characters says, "we will have a look at your damper, anyway. Maybe you overlook a few coarse notes here and there."

So one character keeps that thing pointed at Chesty Charles and me, and the other goes through the cash register, but, just as Charles says, there is nothing in it. Then the character comes over and gives Charles and me a fanning, but all he finds is eighty cents on Charles, and he seems inclined to be a little vexed at the scarcity of ready between us and he acts as if he is thinking of clouting us around some for our shortage, as these git-'em-up characters will sometimes do if they are vexed, when all of a sudden Charles looks at one of the characters and speaks as follows: "Why," Chesty Charles says, "do my eyes deceive me, or do I behold The Macarone, out of Kansas City?"

"Why, yes," the character says. "Why, hello, Chesty," he says. "Meet my friend Willie," he says. "He is out of Kansas City too. Why, I never expect to find you in such a joint as this, Chesty," he says. "Especially a joint where there is so little dough."

"Well," Chesty Charles says, "you ought to drop around when the season is on. Things are livelier then. But," he says, "sit down and let's have a talk. I am glad to see you, Mac," he says. So they sit down and Chesty Charles puts out a bottle of Scotch and some glasses and we become quite sociable, to be sure, and presently The Macarone is explaining that Willie and him have been over in Havana all winter, working with a pay-off mob out of Indianapolis, Indiana, that has a store there, but that business is rotten, and they are now en route north and just stop over in Miami to pick up a few dibs, if possible, for walk-about money.

The Macarone seems to be quite an interesting character in many respects and I can see that he and Charles know each other from several places. The Macarone is maybe around forty and he is tall and black-looking, but the character he calls Willie is younger and by no means gabby, and, in fact, he scarcely has a word to say. We sit there quite awhile drinking Scotches and speaking of this and that, and finally Chesty Charles says to The Macarone: "Mac," he says, "come to think of it, I may be able to drop something in your lap, at that. Only last night a character is in here with a right nice proposition, but," Chesty says, "it is not in my line, so it does not interest me."

"Chesty," The Macarone says, "any proposition that is not in your line must be a very unusual proposition indeed. Let me hear this one," he says.

"Well," Chesty says, "it is a trifle unusual, but," he says, "it seems quite sound, and I only regret that I cannot handle it in person. I am froze in here with this business and I do not feel free to engage in any outside enterprises. The character I refer to," he says, "is Mr. Cleeburn T. Box, who lives on a big estate over here on the bay front with his nephew. Mr. Cleeburn T. Box wishes to quit these earthly scenes," Chesty says. "He is sick and tired of living. His nerves are shot to pieces. He cannot eat. He is in tough shape. But," Chesty says, "he finds he does not have the nerve to push himself off. So he wishes to find some good reliable party to push him off, for which service he will pay five thousand dollars cash money. He will deposit the dough with me," Chesty says. "He realizes that I am quite truthworthy. It is a soft touch, Mac," he says. "Of course," he says, "I am entitled to the usual twenty-five per cent commission for finding the plant."

"Well," The Macarone says, "this Mr. Box must be quite an eccentric character. But," he says, "I can understand his reluctance about pushing himself off. Personally, I will not care to push myself off. However," he says, "the proposition seems to have complications. I hear it is against the law in Florida to push people off, even if they wish to be pushed."

"Well," Chesty says, "Mr. Box thinks of this too. His idea is that the party who is to do this service for him will slip into his house over on the bay front some night and push him off while he is asleep, so he will never know what happens to him. You understand, he wishes this matter to be as unexpected and painless as possible. Then," Chesty says, "the party can leave that thing with which he does the pushing on the premises and it will look as if Mr. Box does the pushing in person."

"What about a club?" The Macarone says. "Or maybe a shiv? That thing makes a lot of racket."

"Why," Chesty says, "how can you make a club or shiv look like anything but something illegal if you use them to push anybody? You need not be afraid of making a racket, because," he says, "no one lives within hearing distance of the joint, and Mr. Box will see that all his servants and everybody else are away from the place every night, once I give him the word the deal is on. He will place the dough at my disposal when he gets this word. Of course he does not wish to know what night it is to happen, but it must be some night soon after the transaction is agreed to."

"Well," The Macarone says, "this is one of the most interesting and unusual propositions ever presented to me. Personally," he says, "I do not see why Mr. Box does not get somebody to put something in his tea. Anybody will be glad to do him such a favor."

"He is afraid of suffering," Chesty Charles says. "He is one of the most nervous characters I ever encounter in my life. Look, Mac," he says, "this is a job that scarcely requires human intelligence. I have here a diagram that shows the layout of the joint." And with this, Chesty Charles outs with a sheet of paper and spreads it out on the table, and begins explaining it to The Macarone with his finger. "Now," he says, "this shows every door and window on the ground floor. Here is a wing of the house. Here is Mr. Cleeburn T. Box's room on the ground floor overlooking the bay. Here is a French window that is never locked," he says. "Here is his bed against the wall, not two steps from the window. Why," Chesty says, "it is as simple as WPA."

"Well," The Macarone says, "you are dead sure Mr. Box will not mind being pushed? Because, after all, I do not have any reason to push him on my own account, and I am doing my best at this time to lead a clean life and keep out of unpleasant situations."

"He will love it," Chesty says.

So The Macarone finally says he will give the matter his earnest consideration and will let Chesty Charles have his answer in a couple of days. Then we all have some more Scotches, and it is now past closing time, and The Macarone and Willie take their departure, and I say to Chesty like this: "Chesty," I say, "all this sounds to me like a very strange proposition, and I do not believe anybody in this world is dumb enough to accept same."

"Well," Chesty says, "I always hear The Macarone is the dumbest character in the Middle West. Maybe he will wind up taking in the

South too," he says, and then Chesty laughs and we have another Scotch by ourselves before we leave.

Now, the next afternoon I am over on South Beach, taking a little dip in the ocean, and who do I run into engaged in the same pastime but The Macarone and Willie. There are also numerous other parties along the beach, splashing about in the water in their bathing suits or stretched out on the sand, and The Macarone speaks of Chesty Charles' proposition like this: "It sounds all right," The Macarone says. "In fact," he says, "it sounds so all right that the only thing that bothers me is I cannot figure out why Chesty does not take it over one hundred per cent. But," he says, "I can see Chesty is getting old, and maybe he loses his nerve. Well," The Macarone says, "that is the way it always is with old folks. They lose their nerve." Then The Macarone starts swimming toward a float pretty well out in the water, and what happens when he is about halfway to the float but he starts flapping around in the water no little, and it is plain to be seen that he is in some difficulty and seems about to drown. In fact, The Macarone issues loud cries for help, but, personally, I do not see where it is any of my put-in to help him, as he is just a chance acquaintance of mine and, furthermore, I cannot swim.

Well, it seems that Willie cannot swim either, and he is saying it is too bad that The Macarone has to go in such a fashion, and he is also saying he better go and get The Macarone's clothes before some one else thinks of it. But about this time a little Judy with about as much bathing suit on as will make a boxing glove for a mosquito jumps off the float and swims to The Macarone and seizes him by one ear and holds his head above the water until a lifeguard with hair on his chest gets out there and takes The Macarone off her hands.

Well, the lifeguard tows The Macarone ashore and rolls him over a barrel and gets enough water out of him to float the Queen Mary, and by and by The Macarone is as good as new, and he starts looking around for the little Judy who holds him up in the water. "She almost pulls my ear out by the roots," The Macarone says. "But," he says, "I will forgive this torture because she saves my life. Who is she, and where is she?"

Well, the lifeguard, who turns out to be a character by the name of Dorgan, says she is Miss Mary Peering and that she works in the evening in a barbecue stand over on Fifth Street, and what is more, she is a right nifty little swimmer, but, of course, The Macarone already knows this. But now nothing will do but we must go to the barbecue stand and find Miss Mary Peering, and there she is in a blue linen uniform and with a Southern accent, dealing hot dogs and hamburger sandwiches and one thing and another, to the customers. She is a pretty iittle Judy who is maybe nineteen years of age, and when The Macarone steps forward and thanks her for saving his life, she laughs and says it is nothing whatever, and at first The Macarone figures that this crack is by no means complimentary, and is disposed to chide her for same, especially when he gets to thinking about his ear. But he can see that the little Judy has no idea of getting out of line with him, and he becomes very friendly toward her.

We sit there quite awhile with The Macarone talking to her between customers, and finally he asks her if she has a sweet pea anywhere in the background of her career, and at this she bursts into tears and almost drops an order of pork and beans. "Yes," she says, "I am in love with a wonderful young character by the name of Lionel Box. He is a nephew of Mr. Cleeburn T. Box, and Mr. Cleeburn T. Box is greatly opposed to our friendship. Lionel wishes to marry me, but," she says, "Mr. Cleeburn T. Box is his guardian and says he will not hear of Lionel marrying beneath his station. Lionel will be very rich when he is of age, a year from now, and then he can do as he pleases, but just at present his Uncle Cleeburn keeps him from even seeing me. Oh," she says, "I am heartbroken."

"Where is this Lionel now?" The Macarone says.

"That is just it," Miss Mary Peering says. "He is home, sick with the grippe or some such, and his Uncle Cleeburn will not as much as let him answer the telephone. His Uncle Cleeburn acts awful crazy, if you ask me. But," she says, "just wait until Lionel is of age and we can be married. Then we will go so far away from his Uncle Cleeburn he can never catch up with us again." Well, at this news The Macarone seems to become very thoughtful, and at first I think it is because he is disappointed to find Miss Mary Peering has a sweet pea in the background, but after a little more talk, he thanks her again for saving his life and pats her hand and tells her not to worry about anything, not even about what she does to his ear.

Then we go to the Shark Fin Grill and find Chesty Charles sitting out in front with his chair tilted up against the wall, and The Macarone says to him like this: "Chesty," he says, "have the dough on call for me from now on. I will take care of this matter for Mr. Cleeburn T. Box. I study it over carefully," The Macarone says, "and I can see how I will render Mr. Box a service and at the same time do a new friend of mine a favor. In the meantime," The Macarone says, "you keep Willie here amused. It is a one-handed job, and I do not care to use him on it in any manner, shape or form. He is a nice character, but," The Macarone says, "he sometimes makes wrong moves. He is too handy with that thing to suit me. By the way, Chesty," he says, "what does Mr. Cleeburn T. Box look like?"

"Well," Chesty says, "he will be the only one you find in the room indicated on the diagram, so his looks do not make any difference, but," he says, "he is smooth-shaved and has thick black hair."

Now, several nights pass away, and every night I drop into the Shark Fin Grill to visit with Chesty Charles, but The Macarone does not show up but once, and this is to personally view the five thousand dollars that Charles now has in his safe, although Willie comes in now and then and sits around awhile. But Willie is a most restless character, and he does not seem to be able to hold still more than a few minutes at a time, and he is always wandering around and about the city. Finally, along toward four bells one morning, when Chesty Charles is getting ready to close the Shark Fin Grill, in walks The Macarone, and it is plain to be seen that he has something on his mind.

A couple of customers are still in the joint and The Macarone waits until they depart, and then he steps over to the bar, where Chesty Charles is working, and gazes at Chesty for quite a spell without saying as much as aye, yes, or no. "Well?" Chesty says.

"Well, Chesty," The Macarone says, "I go to the home of your Mr. Cleeburn T. Box a little while ago. It is a nice place. A little more shrubbery than we like in Kansas City, but still a nice place. It must stand somebody maybe half a million. I follow your diagram, Chesty," he says. "I find the wing marked X and I make my way through plenty of cactus and Spanish bayonets, and I do not know what all else, and enter the house by way of an open French window. I find myself in a room in which there are no lights, but," The Macarone says, "as soon as my eyes become accustomed to the darkness, I can see that it is all just as the diagram shows. There is a bed within a few steps of the window, and there is a character asleep on the bed. He is snoring pretty good too. In fact," The Macarone says, "he is snoring about as good as anybody I ever hear, and I do not bar Willie, who is a wonderful snorer."

"All right," Chesty Charles says.

"Show me the dough again, Chesty," The Macarone says.

So Chesty goes to his safe and opens it and outs with a nice package of the soft and places it on the back bar where The Macarone can see it, and the sight of the money seems to please The Macarone no little. "All right," Chesty says. "Then what?"

"Well, Chesty," The Macarone says, "there I am with that thing in my hand, and there is this character on the bed asleep, and there is no sound except his snoring and the wind in some palm trees outside.

Chesty," he says, "are you ever in a strange house at night with the
wind working on the palm trees outside?"

"No," Chesty says. "I do not care for palm trees."

"It is a lonesome sound," The Macarone says. "Well," he says, "I
step over to the bed, and I can see by the outline of the character on
the bed that he is sleeping on his back, which is a good thing, as it
saves me the trouble of turning him over and maybe waking him up.
You see, Chesty," he says, "I give this matter some scientific study
beforehand. I figure that the right idea in this case is to push this
character in such a manner that there can be no doubt that he pushes
himself, so it must be done from in front, and from close up. Well,"
The Macarone says, "I wait right over this character on the bed until
my eyes make out the outline of his face in the dark, and I put that
thing down close to his nose, and just as I am about to give it to him,
the moon comes out from behind a cloud over the bay and spills plenty
of light through the open French window and over the character on
the bed.

"And," The Macarone says, "I observe that this character on the
bed is holding some object clasped to his breast, and that he has a
large smile on his face, as if he is dreaming very pleasant dreams, indeed; and when I gently remove the object from his fingers, thinking
it may be something of value to me, and hold it up to the light, what
is it but a framed stand photograph of a young friend of mine by the
name of Miss Mary Peering. But," The Macarone says, "I hope and
trust that no one will ever relate to Miss Mary Peering the story of me
finding this character asleep with her picture, and snoring, because,"
he says, "snoring is without doubt a great knock to romance."

"So?" Chesty Charles says.

"So," The Macarone says, "I come away as quietly as possible without disturbing the character on the bed, and here I am, Chesty, and
there you are, and it comes to my mind that somebody tries to drop me
in on a great piece of skulduggery." And all of a sudden, The Macarone outs with that thing and jams the nozzle of it into Chesty Charles'
chest, and says: "Hand over that dough, Chesty," he says. "A nice thing
you are trying to get a respectable character like me into, because you
know very well it cannot be your Mr. Cleeburn T. Box on the bed
in that room with Miss Mary Peering's photograph clasped to his
breast and smiling so, Chesty," he says, "I fear you almost make a
criminal of me, and for two cents I will give you a pushing for your
own self, right here and now."

"Why, Mac," Chesty says, "you are a trifle hasty. If it is not Mr.
Cleeburn T. Box in that bed, I cannot think who it can be, but," he

says, "maybe some last-minute switch comes up in the occupant of the bed by accident. Maybe it is something Mr. Cleeburn T. Box will easily explain when I see him again. Why," Chesty says, "I cannot believe Mr. Cleeburn T. Box means any fraud in this matter. He seems to me to be a nice, honest character and very sincere in his wish to be pushed."

Then Chesty Charles goes on to state that if there is any fraud in this matter, he is also a victim of same, and he says he will surely speak harshly to Mr. Cleeburn T. Box about it the first time he gets a chance. In fact, Chesty Charles becomes quite indignant when he gets to thinking that maybe Mr. Cleeburn T. Box may be deceiving him, and finally The Macarone says: "Well, all right," he says. "Maybe you are not in on anything, at that, and, in fact, I do not see what it is all about, anyway; but," he says, "it is my opinion that your Mr. Cleeburn T. Box is without doubt nothing but a great scalawag somewhere. Anyway, hand over the dough, Chesty," he says. "I am going to collect on my good intentions."

So Chesty Charles takes the package off the back bar and hands it over to The Macarone, and as The Macarone is disposing of it in his pants pocket, Chesty says to him like this: "But look, Mac," he says, "I am entitled to my twenty-five per cent for finding the plant, just the same." Well, The Macarone seems to be thinking this over, and, personally, I figure there is much justice in what Chesty Charles says, and while The Macarone is thinking, there is a noise at the door of somebody coming in, and The Macarone hides that thing under his coat, though I notice he keeps his hand under there, too, until it turns out that the party coming in is nobody but Willie.

"Well," Willie says, "I have quite an interesting experience just now while I am taking a stroll away out on the Boulevard. It is right pretty out that way, to be sure," he says. "I meet a cop and get to talking to him about this and that, and while we are talking the cop says, 'Good evening, Mr. Box,' to a character who goes walking past. The cop says this character is Mr. Cleeburn T. Box," Willie says, "I say Mr. Box looks worried, and the cop says yes, his nephew is sick, and maybe he is worrying about him. But," Willie says, "the cop says, 'If I am Mr. Box, I will not be worrying about such a thing, because if the nephew dies before he comes of age, Mr. Box is the sole heir to his brother's estate of maybe ten million dollars, and the nephew is not yet of age.'

" 'Well, cop,' I say," Willie says, " 'are you sure this is Mr. Cleeburn T. Box?' and the cop says yes, he knows him for over ten years, and that he meets up with him every night on the Boulevard for the past week, just the same as tonight, because it seems Mr. Cleeburn T. Box takes to strolling that way quite some lately. So," Willie says, "I figure to save everybody a lot of bother, and I follow Mr. Cleeburn T. Box away out the Boulevard after I leave the cop, and when I get to a spot that seems nice and quiet and with nobody around, I step close enough for powder marks to show good and give it to Mr. Cleeburn T. Box between the eyes. Then," Willie says, "I leave that thing in his right hand, and if they do not say it is a clear case of him pushing himself when they find him, I will eat my hat."

"Willie," The Macarone says, "is your Mr. Cleeburn T. Box clean-shaved and does he have thick black hair?"

"Why, no," Willie says. "He has a big mouser on his upper lip and no hair whatsoever on his head. In fact," he says, "he is as bald as a biscuit, and maybe balder."

Now, at this The Macarone turns to Chesty Charles, but by the time he is half turned, Chesty is out the back door of the Shark Fin Grill and is taking it on the Jesse Owens up the street, and The Macarone seems greatly surprised and somewhat disappointed, and he says to me like this: "Well," he says, "Willie and me cannot wait for Chesty to return, but," he says, "you can tell him for me that, under the circumstances, I am compelled to reject his request for twenty-five per cent for finding the plant. And," The Macarone says, "if ever you hear of the nephew of the late Mr. Cleeburn T. Box beefing about a missing photograph of Miss Mary Peering, you can tell him that it is in good hands."

The Big Umbrella

Now NO. 23 is a very high-class trap which is patronized only by the better element of rumpots in New York, and what I am doing in these unusual surroundings with Spider McCoy, the fight manager, is something that requires a job of telling. This No. 23 is a spot where wealthy characters assemble on an afternoon and evening to sit around tables or stand at the bar guzzling old-fashioneds, and Scotches, and other delicacies of this nature, and there are always many swell-looking Judys present, so it is generally a scene of great gaiety, but it is certainly about the last place you will ever expect to find Spider McCoy and me. But there we are, and the reason we are there starts in front of Mindy's restaurant on Broadway, when I observe Spider McCoy walking along the street following close behind a tall young character of most unique appearance in many respects.

This tall young character cannot be more than twenty-one years of age, and he is maybe six feet two inches tall and must weigh around one hundred and ninety pounds. He has shoulders like the back of a truck, and he has blond hair, and pink cheeks, and is without doubt as good-looking as any male character has a right to be without causing comment. He is wearing a pair of striped pants, and a cutaway coat, and a white vest, and a high hat, and in fact he is dressed as if he just comes from a high-toned wedding such as you see in pictures in the Sunday blats, and this is by no means a familiar costume in front of Mindy's, so naturally the tall young character attracts no little attention, and many citizens wonder what he is advertising.

Well, as soon as he sees me, Spider McCoy beckons me to join him, and as I fall into step with him behind the tall young character, Spider McCoy says to me: "Sh-h-h-h!" Spider McCoy says. "Here is without doubt the next heavyweight champion of the whole world. I just see him kiss the jockey of a short down the street with a right-hand shot that is positively a lily. It does not travel more than three inches. The jockey takes a run at this party quite ferocious and bap, down he goes as still as a plank under his own cab. It is the best natural right hand I ever see. He reminds me of Jack Dempsey," Spider McCoy says. "Also Gene Tunney." Well, it is very seldom I see Spider McCoy but what he is speaking of some guy who is the next heavyweight champion of the world, and they nearly always remind him of Jack Dempsey and Gene Tunney, and sometimes of Max Schmeling, so I am about to go about my business when Spider grabs me by the arm and compels me to accompany him.

"Who is the guy, Spider?" I say.

"What difference does it make who a guy is that can punch like he can?" Spider says. "All I know is he is the next heavyweight champion of the world if he gets in the proper hands, such as mine. The broads will go crazy about his looks and the way he dresses. He will be a wonderful card," Spider says. "You can see by the way he carries himself that he is a natural fighter. He is loose and light on his feet," he says. "Chances are there is plenty of animal in him. I like my fighters to have plenty of animal in them, especially," Spider says, "my heavyweights."

"Well, Spider," I say, "from the way your heavyweights I see knock off that hot meat on you, there is plenty of animal in them. But," I say, "how do you know this party wishes to be a fighter, anyway? Maybe he has other plans in life."

"We will find out," Spider McCoy says. "We will tail him until we learn where he hangs out so I can make a connection with him. Look at his chest development," Spider says. "Look at his small waistline," he says. "Look at the shape of his head." So we follow the tall young character until he leads us into No. 23, and I notice that Sammy the doorman gives him a very small hello, and I figure the tall young character cannot be anybody much, because when anybody is anybody much, Sammy the doorman gives them a very large hello, indeed. In fact, Sammy's hello to the tall young character is almost as small as the hello he gives us, and this is practically unnoticeable.

Well, I know Sammy the doorman from back down the years when he is not working in a joint as classy as No. 23, and to tell the truth I know him when he is nothing but a steer for a bust-out joint in West Forty-third, a bust-out joint being a joint where they will cheat your eyeballs out at cards, and dice, and similar devices. So I ask Sammy who the tall young character is, and Sammy says: "Oh," he says, "he is one of these ex-kings. He comes from some nickel country over in Europe. A dictator gives him the foot off the throne and then chases him out of the country and takes personal charge of matters. His name is Jonas. I mean the ex-king," Sammy says. "They are getting to be quite a nuisance around."

"Is this ex-king holding anything?" I say.

"Nothing," Sammy says. "Not a quarter. The hotel where he is stopping catches him out to a society tea the other afternoon and puts a hickey in his keyhole and now he cannot get at his other clothes and has to go around the way you see him. The chances are," Sammy says, "he is in here looking to cadge a drink or a bite to eat."

Well, Spider McCoy is looking the joint over to see if he can find anybody he knows to introduce him to the ex-king, but when I tell him what Sammy says, Spider at once eases himself up alongside the ex-king and begins talking to him, because Spider knows that when guys are not holding anything they are willing to talk to anybody. He is somewhat surprised to find that the ex-king speaks English and seems to be a nice, pleasant young character, and the chances are he is by no means high-toned even when he is holding something, so pretty soon Spider is buying him Scotches, although this is by no means a dram that Spider approves of for fighters unless they buy them themselves, and finally Spider says to him like this: "I see you tag that taxi jockey over on Broadway," Spider says. "I never see a more beautiful right in my born days. It reminds me something of Georges Carpentier's right, only," Spider says, "Georges always pulls his just a little before shooting to get more leverage, and you just barely move yours. Why," Spider says, "the more I think of it, the more I am amazed. What does the guy do to vex you?"

"Why," the ex-king says, "he does not do anything to vex me. I am quite unvexed at the time. It is almost inadvertent. The taxi driver gets off his seat and starts to run after a passenger that fails to settle his account with him, and he is about to collide with me there on the sidewalk, so," he says, "I just put out my right hand to ward him off, and he runs into it with his chin and knocks himself unconscious. I must look him up some day, and express my regrets. But," he says, "I will never think of deliberately striking anybody without serious provocation."

Well, at this, Spider McCoy is somewhat nonplused, because he can now see that what he takes for the ex-king's natural punch is merely an accident that may not happen if it is on purpose, and furthermore, the ex-king's expressions are scarcely the expressions of anybody with much animal in them, and Spider is commencing to regret the purchase of the Scotches for the ex-king. In fact, I can see that Spider is reaching a state of mind that may cause him to take a pop at the ex-king for grossly deceiving him. But Spider McCoy cannot look at six feet two and 190 pounds of anybody under thirty without becoming most avaricious, and so after a couple of more Scotches, he begins feeling the ex-king's muscles, which causes the ex-king to laugh quite heartily, as it seems he is a little ticklish in spots, and finally Spider says: "Well," he says, "there is undoubtedly great natural strength here, and all it needs is to be properly developed. Why," Spider says, "the more I think of you knocking a guy out by just letting him run into your hand, the more impressed I am. In fact," he says, "I can scarcely get over it. How do you feel about becoming a professional?"

"A professional what?" the ex-king says.

"A professional boxer," Spider says. "It is a name we have in this country for prize fighters."

"I never give such a matter a thought," the ex-king says. "What is the idea?"

"The idea is money," Spider McCoy says. "I hear of other ideas for professional boxing, but," he says, "I do not approve of them, your Majesty."

"Call me Jonas," the ex-king says. "Do you mean to tell me I can make money out of boxing? Well, I will feel right kindly toward anything I can make money out of. I find," he says, "that money seems to be somewhat necessary in this country." So then Spider McCoy explains to him how he can make a ton of money by winning the heavyweight championship of the world and that all he requires to do this is to have Spider for his manager. Furthermore, Spider explains that all he will ask for being the manager is thirty-three and a third per cent of the ex-king's earnings, with the expenses off the top, which means before they cut up anything.

Well, the ex-king listens very intently and keeps nodding his head to show that he understands, and finally he says: "In the meantime," he says, "do I eat?"

"The best, your Majesty," Spider says.

"Call me Jonas," the ex-king says again. "All right, then," Jonas says, "I will become heavyweight champion of the world as you say, and make a ton of money, and then I can snap my fingers at Dictator Poltafuss, the dirty rat."

"The big heel," Spider says.

So Spider McCoy takes Jonas to his home, which is in an apartment in West Fiftieth Street, where his orphan niece, Miss Margie Grogan, keeps house for him, and bosses him around no little, and quite some, and I go with them to lend moral support to Spider, because by this time he is slightly Scotched up, and he always likes to have a little moral support when he goes home Scotched. His niece, Miss Margie Grogan, is a Judy of maybe twenty, and if you like them small, and lively, and with huckleberry hair, and blue eyes, and freckles on the nose, and plenty of temper, she is all right. In fact, I hear some say that Margie is extra all right, but those who say this are younger than I am and maybe not such good judges. Personally, I like them with more heft, and less temper.

It is not a large apartment where Spider McCoy lives, but it is a neat and clean little joint, at that, for Margie is without doubt a good all-around housekeeper. Furthermore, she is much better than a raw hand with a skillet, and she comes flying out of the kitchen with her face red, and her hair all tousled up to meet Spider, but when she sees Jonas behind him she stops, and speaks as follows: "Good grief," Margie says, "another big umbrella."

"What do you mean umbrella?" Spider says.

"Why," Margie says, "something that folds up. I never know you to bring home any other kind."

"This is no umbrella," Spider says. "This is the next heavyweight champion of the world."

"No," Margie says, "it cannot be, for two months you tell me that somebody called Ben Robbins is the next heavyweight champion of the world."

"Ben Robbins is nothing but a bum," Spider says.

"So I find out," Margie says. "Well," she says, "come on in, you and your next heavyweight champion of the world. We are about to put on the corned beef and." Then Spider introduces Jonas to her, and right away Jonas grabs her hand and lifts it to his lips, and this astonishes Margie no little, and afterward she tells me that she regrets for a moment that she just recently sticks her hand in a pot of boiled onions, and the chances are Jonas does too.

But Miss Margie Grogan is by no means in favor of prize fighters in any manner, shape or form, because all they ever mean to her is an extra plate, and more cooking, and it is plain to be seen that though he seems to be an expert hand-kisser, Jonas is no more welcome than any of the others that Spider brings home, and he brings them home too often to suit Margie. The ones he brings home are always heavyweight prospects, for while Spider McCoy manages a number of fighters, he never gets excited about anything but a heavyweight, and this is the way all fight managers are. A fight manager may have a lightweight champion of the world, but he will get more heated up about some sausage who scarcely knows how to hold his hands up if he is a heavyweight.

Personally, I consider it most remarkable that Margie is able to spot Jonas as one of Spider's heavyweight prospects in a high hat and a cutaway coat, but Margie says it is a sixth sense with her. She says Spider once brings home a party with a beard halfway down to his waist, but that as soon as she opens the door she pegs him as a heavyweight prospect that Spider does not yet have time to get shaved. But she says she is so fond of Spider that she takes them all in, and feeds them up good, and the only time she ever bars anybody on him is the time Spider brings home a big widow he finds in Mickey Walker's bar and claims he is going to make her the only female contender for the heavyweight title in the world. Miss Margie Grogan says she has to draw the line somewhere on Uncle Spider's prospects.

Well, from now on, Spider has Jonas in the gymnasium for several hours every day, teaching him to box, and anybody will tell you that Spider is as good a teacher as there is in the world, especially of a punch that is called the one-two, although this punch is really two punches. It is a left jab followed through fast with a right cross, and it is considered quite a gravy punch if properly put on. Jonas lives in a spare room in Spider's apartment, and takes his meals there, and Spider tells me everything will be very nice, indeed, for them all, if Margie does not happen to take more of a dislike than somewhat to Jonas, especially when she learns that he is once a king and gets the old hoovus-goovus from a dictator.

Margie tells Spider McCoy that it proves there must be anyway a trace of umbrella in a character who lets anybody run him out of his own country, and Spider says the only reason he does not give her an argument on the matter is that he is not sure but what she is right, though not because Jonas lets himself get run out.

"I do not figure this in at all," Spider says. "I sometimes let myself get run out of places, and I do not think there is umbrella in me, or anyway not much. But," he says, "a young heavyweight prospect is a peculiar proposition. You can find out in the gymnasium if he can box, if he is fast, and if he can punch, but you cannot find out if he can take a punch and if he is dead game until you see him boffed around good in the ring. And," Spider says, "this is what you must find out before you know if you have a heavyweight contender, or just a heavyweight. This Jonas looks great in the gym, but," he says, "sometimes I wonder about him. I do not know why I wonder, but I remember I wonder the same way about Ben Robbins, who is such a gymnasium marvel that I turn down twenty thousand for his contract. Then," Spider says, "I put him with this punching bag, Joe Grosher, in Newark, and my guy geeks it the first good smack he gets. Somehow," Spider says, "Jonas has a certain look in his eyes that reminds me of Ben Robbins."

"Well," I says, "if you are not sure about him, why not chuck him in with somebody the same as you do Ben, and find out if he can fight, or what?"

"Look," Spider McCoy says, "I will never find out anything more about this guy than I know now, if the offers I am getting keep on coming in. I will not have to find out," he says. "We must have a hundred propositions right now, and I am going to commence taking some."

Naturally the blats make quite an uproar when they discover that an ex-king is training to be a fighter, and they are full of stories and pictures about Jonas every day, and of course Spider does not discourage this publicity because it is responsible for the offers of matches for Jonas from all over the country. But the matches Spider finally commences accepting are not the matches the promoters offer, because the promoters offer opponents who may have no respect for royalty, and may try to knock Jonas' brains out. The matches Spider accepts have his own personal supervision. and they are much better for Jonas than what the promoters might think up.

These matches are with sure-footed watermen, who plunge in swiftly and smoothly when Jonas waves at them, and while everybody knows these matches are strictly tank jobs, nobody cares, especially the customers who almost break down the doors of the clubs where Jonas appears, trying to get in. The customers are so greatly pleased to be permitted to observe an ex-king in short pants that they scarcely pause for their change at the box-office windows.

Of course Spider does not tell Jonas that these contests are dipsy-doos and Jonas thinks he really is belting out these porterhouses, and as he is getting pretty nice money for the work, he feels very well, indeed. Anybody will tell you that it helps build up a young fighter's confidence to let him see a few people take naps in front of him as he is coming along, though Jonas is slightly bewildered the night at the Sun Casino when a generally very reliable waterboy by the name of Charley Drunckley misses his cue and falls down before Jonas can hit him. The boxing commission is somewhat bewildered, too, and asks a few questions that nobody tries to answer, and Spider McCoy explains to Jonas that he hits so fast he cannot notice his punches landing himself, but even then Jonas continues to look somewhat bewildered.

He continues living at Spider McCoy's apartment, because Spider is by no means sucker enough to let Jonas get very far away from him, what with so many unscrupulous characters around the boxing game who are always looking to steal somebody's fighter, especially a fighter who is worth his weight in platinum, like Jonas, but from what I hear Miss Margie Grogan continues to play plenty of ice for him.

She goes to see him fight once, because everybody else in town is trying to go, but Margie is pretty cute, and she can spot a tank job as far as anybody, and while she knows very well that it is Spider McCoy and not Jonas who is responsible for these half-Gainors that are going on, she tells Spider that if Jonas is not a big umbrella he will be fighting somebody who can really fight.

"Over my dead body," Spider says. "If I ever hear of anybody that can really fight trying to fight my Jonas, I will cause trouble. And Margie," Spider says, "do not call Jonas an umbrella in my presence. It hurts my feelings."

But Jonas is a great disappointment to Spider in some respects, especially about publicity angles. Spider wishes to get a tin crown made for him to wear going into the ring, but Jonas will not listen to this, and what is more he will not stand for as much as a monocle, because he claims he does not know how to keep one in his eye. Well, the dough is rolling in on Spider and Jonas just with tank acts, but some of the boxing scribes are commencing to say Jonas ought to meet real competition, and I tell Spider myself it may be a good idea to see if Jonas really can fight.

"Yes," Spider says, "I am sometimes tempted myself. He shapes up so good that I get to thinking maybe he is the makings, at that. But I think I will let well enough alone. Anyway," Spider says, "what a sap I will be to throw him in with competition as long as the suckers will pay to see him as he is. I can go on with him indefinitely this way," Spider says, "but one smack on the chops may finish us up for good. Yes," he says, "I think I will let well enough alone."

Now, one day a chunky guy with a big mustache and his hair cut short comes to see Jonas and has a long talk with him, and Jonas tells Spider that this guy is from his home country over in Europe, and that he is sent by the dictator who runs Jonas off, and his cabinet, who wish Jonas to return home to talk to them about certain matters, which may include a proposition for him to be king again, and Jonas says it sounds like a fair sort of proposition, at that. "Why," Spider says, "nobody can talk business with you now. I am your manager, and all propositions must come to me first. Is there any chance of us making any real dough out of your going back to being king?" Well, Jonas says it is by no means definite that he is to be king again, but that there is something in the air, and as he now has plenty of dough, and it is safe for him to return, he wishes to go home awhile if only to pick up a few belongings that he does not have time to collect the last time he departs.

Furthermore, nothing will do but Spider must go with him, and Spider says this means Miss Margie Grogan will have to go, too, because she is practically his right arm in business, and every other way, and Jonas says he thinks this is an excellent idea. He says Margie looks to him as if a sea voyage will do her good, and when Spider mentions this opinion to Margie, she says she wishes the big umbrella will stop looking at her to see how she looks, but that she will go just to spite him, and so they sail away.

Well, it is some months before I see Spider McCoy again, and then I run into him on Broadway one afternoon, and he is all dressed up in striped pants, and white spats, and a cutaway coat, and a high hat, and before I can start asking him questions he says to me like this: "Come with me to No. 23," he says. "I am on a meet there with somebody, and I will tell you all."

So from now on for a while this is Spider McCoy's story:

Well (Spider says), we have a most satisfactory journey in every respect. Going over on the boat, what happens what with the moon, and the stars, and the music, and dancing, and all this and that, but Margie and Jonas get so they are on slightly better terms, and this makes things more pleasant for me, as they are together quite a bit, and this gives me time to catch up on my drinking, which I neglect no little when I am so busy looking after Jonas' interests.

He gets a wonderful reception when we reach his old home country, what with bands, and soldiers, and one thing and another, but I am surprised to find that none of the natives hear of me as his manager. In fact, it seems that his reputation there rests entirely on once being king, and they never hear of his accomplishments in the ring, which consist of eighteen consecutive k. o.'s This really hurts my feelings after all my work with him in the gym and the trouble I go to in picking his opponents. Personally, his country does not strike me as much of a country, and in fact it strikes me as nothing but a sort of double Jersey City, and the natives speak a language of their own, and the scenery is filled with high hills, and take it all around, I do not consider it anything to get excited about, but it is plain to be seen that Jonas is glad to get back there.

Well, we are not there more than a few hours before we get a line on what is doing, and what is doing is that the people wish Jonas to be king again, and they are making life a burden for this Dictator Polta-fuss, and his cabinet, and Poltafuss figures it will be a good scheme to put Jonas back, all right, but first he wishes to discuss certain terms of his own with Jonas.

The very afternoon of the day we arrive, there is a cabinet meeting in the palace, which is a building quite similar to a country courthouse, and Jonas is invited to this meeting. They do not invite me, but naturally as Jonas' manager, I insist on going to protect his interests, and in fact I consider it quite unethical for them to be inviting my fighter to discuss terms of any kind and not including me, and then Jonas requests Margie to also accompany him. The cabinet meeting is in a big room with high windows overlooking a public square and in this square a large number of natives of Jonas' country gather while the meeting is in progress, and talk among themselves in their own language.

There must be thirty characters of one kind and another sitting around a big table when we enter the room, and I figure they are the cabinet, and it does not take me long to pick Dictator Poltafuss. He is sitting at the head of the table and he is wearing a uniform with about four pounds of medals on his chest, and he has short black whiskers, and a fierce eye, and anybody can see that he is built from the ground up. He is as big as a Russian wrestler, and looks to me as if he may be a tough character in every respect. A solid-looking Judy in a black dress is sitting in a chair behind him with some knitting in her hands, and she does not seem to be paying much attention to what is going on.

Well, as we enter the room and Jonas sees Poltafuss, a look comes into Jonas' eyes that is without doubt the same look I sometimes see in the gymnasium and in the ring, and which is the look that makes me wonder about him and keeps me from ever putting him in without knowing his opponent's right name and address, and, thinks I to myself, he is afraid of the guy with the sassafras. Thinks I to myself, Margie is right. He is a big umbrella.

Poltafuss begins talking very fast to Jonas, and in their own language, and after he gets through, Jonas does a lot of talking in the same language, and finally Jonas turns to us, and in our language he tells us what Poltafuss says to him and what he says to Poltafuss, and what Poltafuss says is really somewhat surprising. "He says," Jonas says, "that I will be returned to the throne if I first marry his sister. She is the chromo sitting behind him. I tell him she is older than he is, and has a big nose, and a mustache. He says," Jonas says, "that she is only a year older which puts her shading forty, and that a big horn indicates character, and a mustache is good luck. Then," Jonas says, "I tell him the real reason I will not marry her, which is because I am going to marry someone else."

"Wait a minute, Jonas," I say. "You mustn't never tell a lie, even to be king. You know you are not going to marry anybody. I do not permit my fighters to marry," I say. "It takes their mind off their business."

"Yes," Jonas says, "I am going to marry Miss Margie Grogan. We fix it up on the ship."

Then all of a sudden Poltafuss jumps up and says to Margie in English like this: "Why," he says, "the idea is ridiculous. He cannot marry you. He is of royal blood. You are of common stock," he says.

"Look, Jonas," Margie says, "are you going to stand here and hear me insulted? If you are, I am leaving right now," she says.

Then she starts for the door, and Jonas runs after her and grabs her by the arm and says: "But, Margie," he says, "what can I do?"

"Well," Margie says, "you can boff this big ape for one thing, as any gentleman is bound to do, unless," she says, "there is even more umbrella in you than ever I suspect."

"Why, yes," Jonas says. "To be sure, and certainly," he says. And with this he walks over to Poltafuss, but old Polty hears what Margie says, and as Jonas gets near him, he lets go a big right hand that starts down around China and bangs Jonas on the chin, and Jonas goes down.

Well, I thinks to myself, I am only glad this does not occur at the Garden some night when the joint is packed. Then I hear Margie's voice saying like this: "Get up, Jonas," Margie says. "Get up and steady yourself."

"It is no use, Margie," I say. "You are right, he is an umbrella."

"You are a liar," Margie says.

"Margie," I say, "remember you are speaking to your Uncle Spider." I am still thinking of how disrespectfully Margie addresses me, when I notice that Jonas is up on his feet, and as he gets up he sticks out his left in time to drive it through Poltafuss' whiskers, as Poltafuss rushes at him. This halts Polty for an instant, then he comes on again swinging both hands. He is strictly a wild thrower, but he hits like a steer kicking when he lands, and he has Jonas down three times in as many minutes, and every time I figure Jonas will remain there and doze off, but Margie says get up, and Jonas gets up, and when he gets up he has sense enough to stick his left in Poltafuss' beard.

There seems to be some slight confusion among the members of the cabinet as the contest opens, and I take a good strong grip on a big chair, just in case of fire or flood, but I wish to say I never witness a finer spirit of fair play than is exhibited by the members of the cabinet. They stand back against the wall and give Jonas and Poltafuss plenty of elbow room, and they seem to be enjoying the affair no little. In fact, the only spectator present who does not seem to be enjoying it is Poltafuss' sister, who does not get up out of her chair to get a better view, and furthermore does not stop her knitting, so I can see she is by no means a fight fan.

Pretty soon Jonas' left-hand sticking has Poltafuss' nose bleeding, and then one eye begins to close, and I find myself getting very much interested, because I now see what I am looking for all my life, which is a dead game heavyweight, and I can see that I will no longer have to be worrying about who I put Jonas in with. I see the next heavyweight champion of the world as sure as I am standing there, and I now begin coaching Jonas in person. "Downstairs, Jonas," I say. "In the elly-bay, Jonas," I say. So Jonas hits Poltafuss a left hook in the stomach, and Polty goes oof. "The old one-two, Jonas," I say, and Jonas stabs Poltafuss' nose with a long left, then follows through with a right cross, just as I educate him to do, and this right-hand cross lands on Polty's chin, among the whiskers, and down he goes stiff as a board on his face, and when they fall in this manner, you may proceed at once to the payoff window.

The next thing I know, Margie is in Jonas' arms, dabbing at his bloody face with a little handkerchief, and shedding tears, and a member of the cabinet that I afterward learn is the secretary of war is at one of the windows yelling down to the natives in the square and they are yelling back at him, and later someone tells me that what he yells is that the king just flattens Poltafuss and what they are yelling back is long live the king.

"Spider," Jonas says, "I never have any real confidence in myself before, but I have now. I just lick the party who can lick any six guys in my country all at once and with one hand tied behind him. Spider," he says, "I know now I will be heavyweight champion of the world."

Well, Poltafuss is sitting up on the floor holding his nose with both hands, and looking somewhat disheveled, but at this he puts his hands down long enough to speak as follows: "No," he says, "you will be king, and your sweetheart there will be queen." And this is the way it turns out (Spider says) and Jonas and Poltafuss get along very nicely indeed together afterward, except once at a cabinet meeting when King Jonas has to flatten Poltafuss again to make him agree to some unemployment measure.

"But, Spider," I say, as Spider McCoy finishes his story, "you do not state what becomes of the dictator's sister."

"Well," Spider says, "I will tell you. It seems to me that the dictator's sister gets a rough deal, one way and another, especially," he says, "as her beezer is by no means as big as some people think. So," Spider says, "while I will always regret blowing the next heavyweight champion of the world, I console myself with the thought that I get a wonderful and ever-loving wife, and if you will wait a few minutes longer, I will introduce you to the former Miss Sofia Poltafuss, now Mrs. Spider McCoy."

Neat Strip

———————◆◈◆———————

Now this Rose Viola is twenty years old and is five feet five inches tall in her high-heeled shoes, and weighs one hundred and twenty pounds, net, and has a twenty-six waist, and a thirty-six bust, and wears a four and one-half shoe. Moreover, she has a seven-inch ankle, and an eleven-inch calf, and the reason I know all these intimate details is because a friend of mine by the name of Rube Goldstein has Rose Viola in a burlesque show and advertises her as the American Venus, and he always prints these specifications in his ads.

But of course Rube Goldstein has no way of putting down in figures how beautiful Rose Viola is, because after all any pancake may have the same specifications and still be a rutabaga. All Rube can do is to show photographs of Rose Viola and after you see these photographs and then see Rose Viola herself you have half a mind to look the photographer up and ask him what he means by so grossly under-estimating the situation.

She has big blue eyes, and hair the color of sunup and furthermore this color is as natural as a six and five. Her skin is as white and as smooth as ivory and her teeth are like rows of new corn on the cob and she has a smile that starts slow and easy on her lips and in her eyes and seems to sort of flow over the rest of her face until any male characters observing same are wishing there is a murder handy that they can commit for her.

Well, I suppose by this time you are saying to yourself, what is such a darberoo doing in a burlesque turkey, for burlesque is by no means an intellectual form of entertainment, and the answer to this question is that Rube Goldstein pays Rose Viola four hundred dollars per week, and this is by no means tin. And the reason Rube Goldstein pays her such a sum is not because Rube is any philanthropist but because Rose Viola draws like a flaxseed poultice, for besides her looks she has that certain something that goes out across the footlights and hits every male character present smack-dab in the kisser and makes him hate to go home and gaze upon his ever-loving wife. In fact, I hear that for three weeks after Rose Viola plays a town the percentage of missing husbands appalls the authorities.

It seems that the first time Rube Goldstein sees Rose Viola is in the city of Baltimore, Md., where his show is playing the old Gaiety, and one of Rube's chorus Judys, a sod widow who is with him nearly thirteen years and raises up three sons to manhood under him, runs off and marries a joskin from over on the eastern shore. Naturally, Rube considers this a dirty trick, as he is so accustomed to seeing this Judy in his chorus that he feels his show will never look the same to him again; but the same night the widow is missing, Rose Viola appears before him asking for a situation.

Rube tells me he is greatly surprised at such a looking Judy seeking a place in a burlesque show and he explains to Rose Viola that it is a very tough life, to be sure, and that the pay is small, and that she will probably do better for herself if she gets a job dealing them off her arm in a beanery, or some such, but she requests Rube to kindly omit the alfalfa and give her a job, and Rube can see at once by the way she talks that she has personality. So he hires her at twenty-five slugs per week to start with and raises her to half a C and makes her a principal the second night when he finds eighteen blokes lined up at the stage door after the show looking to date her up. In three weeks she is his star and he is three-sheeting her as if she is Katharine Cornell.

She comes out on the stage all dressed up in a beautiful evening gown and sings a little song, and as soon as she begins singing you wonder, unless you see her before, what she really is, as you can see by her voice that she is scarcely a singer by trade. Her voice is not at all the same as Lily Pons' and in fact it is more like an old-fashioned coffee grinder, and about the time you commence to figure that she must be something like a magician and will soon start pulling rabbits out of a hat, Rose Viola begins to dance. It is not a regular dance, to be sure. It is more of a hop and a skip and a jump back and forth across the stage, and as she is hopping and skipping and jumping, Rose Viola is also feeling around for zippers here and there about her person, and finally the evening gown disappears and she seems to be slightly dishabille but in a genteel manner, and then you can see by her shape that she is indeed a great artist.

Sometimes she will come down off the stage and work along the center aisle, and this is when the audience really enjoys her most, as she will pretend to make a great fuss over him, singing to him, and maybe kissing him on top of the bald head and leaving the print of her lips in rouge there, which sometimes puts bald-headed characters to a lot of bother explaining when they get home. She has a way of laughing and talking back to an audience and keeping it in good humor while she is working, although outside the theater Rose Viola is very serious, and seldom has much to say. In fact, Rose Viola has so little to say that there are rumors in some quarters that she is a trifle dumb, but personally I would not mind being dumb myself at four hundred boffoes per week.

Well, it seems that a character by the name of Newsbaum, who runs a spot called the Pigeon Club, hears of Rose Viola, and he goes to see her one night at the old Mid Theater on Broadway where Rube's show is playing a New York engagement, and this Newsbaum is such a character as is always looking for novelties for his club and he decides that Rose Viola will go good there. So he offers her a chance to double at his club, working there after she gets through with her regular show, and Rube Goldstein advises her to take it, as Rube is very fond of Rose and he says this may be a first step upward in her career because the Pigeon Club is patronized only by very high-class rumpots.

So Rose Viola opens one night at the Pigeon Club, and she is working on the dance floor close to the tables, and doing the same act she does in burlesque, when a large young character who is sitting at one of the front tables with a bunch of other young characters, including several nice-looking Judys, reaches out and touches Rose Viola with the end of a cigarette in a spot which she just unzippers. Now of course this is all in a spirit of fun, but it is something that never happens in a burlesque house, and naturally Rose is startled no little, and quite some, and in addition to this she is greatly pained, as it seems that it is the lighted end of the cigarette that the large young character touches her with. So she begins letting out screams, and these screams attract the attention of Rube Goldstein, who is present to see how she gets along at her opening, and although Rube is nearly seventy years old, and is fat and slow and sleepy-looking, he steps forward and flattens the large young character with a dish of chicken à la king, which he picks up off a near-by table.

Well, it seems that the large young character is nobody but a character by the name of Mr. Choicer, who has great sums of money, and a fine social position, and this incident creates some little confusion, especially as old Rube Goldstein also flattens Newsbaum with another plate, this one containing lobster Newburg, when Newsbaum comes along complaining about Rube ruining his chinaware and also one of his best-paying customers. Then Rube puts his arm around Rose Viola and makes her get dressed and leads her out of the Pigeon Club and up to Mindy's restaurant on Broadway, where I am personally present to observe much of what follows.

They sit down at my table and order up a couple of oyster stews, and Rose Viola is still crying at intervals, especially when she happens to rub the spot where the lighted cigarette hits, and Rube Goldstein is saying that for two cents he will go back to the Pigeon Club and flatten somebody again, when all of a sudden the door opens and in comes a young character in dinner clothes. He is without a hat, and he is looking rumpled up no little, and on observing him, Rose Viola lets out a small cry, and Rube Goldstein picks up his bowl of oyster stew and starts getting to his feet, for it seems that they both recognize the young character as one of the characters at Mr. Choicer's table in the Pigeon Club.

This young character rushes up in great excitement, and grabs Rube's arm before Rube can let fly with the oyster stew, and he holds Rube down in his chair, and looks at Rose Viola and speaks to her as follows: "Oh," he says, "I search everywhere for you after you leave the Pigeon Club. I wish to beg your pardon for what happens there. I am ashamed of my friend Mr. Choicer. I will never speak to him again as long as I live. He is a scoundrel. Furthermore, he is in bad shape from the chicken à la king. Oh," the young character says, "please forgive me for ever knowing him."

Well, all the time he is talking, he is holding Rube Goldstein down and looking at Rose Viola, and she is looking back at him, and in five minutes more they do not know Rube Goldstein and me are in the restaurant, and in fact they are off by themselves at another table so the young character can make his apologies clearer, and Rube Goldstein is saying to me that after nearly seventy years he comes to the conclusion that the Judys never change. So, then, this is the beginning of a wonderful romance, and in fact it is love at first sight on both sides, and very pleasant to behold, at that.

It seems that the name of the young character is Daniel Frame, and that he is twenty-six years of age, and in his last year in law school at Yale, and that he comes to New York for a week-end visit and runs into his old college chum, Mr. Choicer, and now here he is in love. I learn these details afterward from Rose Viola, and I also learn that this Daniel Frame is an only child, and lives with his widowed mother in a two-story white colonial house with ivy on the walls, and a yard around it, just outside the city of Manchester, N. H. I learn that his mother has an old poodle dog by the name of Rags, and three servants, and that she lives very quietly, and never goes anywhere much except maybe to church and that the moonlight is something wonderful up around Manchester, N. H. Furthermore, I learn that Daniel Frame comes of the best people in New England, and that he likes skiing, and Benny Goodman's band, and hates mufflers around his neck, and is very fond of pop-overs for breakfast, and that his eyes are dark brown, and that he is six feet even and weighs one hundred and eighty pounds and that he never goes to a dentist in his life. I also learn that the ring he wears on the little finger of his left hand is his family crest, and that he sings baritone with a glee club, and the chances are I will learn plenty more about Daniel Frame if I care to listen any further to Rose Viola.

"He wishes to marry me," Rose says. "He wishes to take me to the white colonial house outside of Manchester, N. H., where we can raise Sealyham terriers, and maybe children. I love Sealyham terriers," she says. "They are awfully cute. Daniel wishes me to quit burlesque entirely. He sees me work at the Mid the other night and he thinks I am wonderful, but," Rose says, "he says it worries him constantly to think of me out there on that stage running the risk of catching colds. Another thing," Rose Viola says, "Daniel wishes me to meet his mother, but he is afraid she will be greatly horrified if she finds out the way I am exposed to the danger of catching colds. He says," Rose says, "that his mother is very strict about such things."

Personally, I consider Daniel Frame a very wishy-washy sort of character, and by no means suitable to a strong personality such as Rose Viola, but when I ask Rube Goldstein what he thinks about it, Rube says to me like this: "Well," he says, "I think it will be a fine thing for her to marry this young character, although," Rube says, "from what he tells her of his mother, I do not see how they are going to get past her. I know these old New England broads," he says. "They consider burlesque anything but a worthy amusement. Still," he says, "I have no kick coming about the male characters of New England. They are always excellent customers of mine."

"Why," I say, "Rose Viola is a fine artist, and does not need such a thing as marriage."

"Yes," Rube says, "she is the finest artist in her line I ever see but one. Laura Legayo is still tops with me. She retires on me away back yonder before you ever see one of my shows. But," he says, "if Rose marries this young character, she will have a home, and a future. Rose needs a future. This burlesque business is about done around here for a while," Rube says. "I can see the signs. The blats are beefing, and the cops are complaining about this and that, and one thing and another. They have no soul for art, and besides we are the easiest marks around when the reformers start rousing the cops for anything whatever. It is always this way in burlesque," Rube says. "It is up and down. It is on the way down now, and Rose may not still be young enough by the time it goes up again. Yes," he says, "Rose needs a future."

Well, it seems that old Rube is a pretty good guesser, because a couple of nights later he gets an order from the police commissioner that there must be no more of this and that, and one thing and another, in his show, and what is more the police commissioner puts cops in all the burlesque houses to see that his order is obeyed. At first Rube Goldstein figures that he may as well close down his New York run at once, and move to some city that is more hospitable to art, but he is wedged in at the Mid on a contract to pay rent for a few weeks longer, so while he is trying to think what is the best thing to do, he lets the show go on just the same, but omitting this and that, and one thing and another, so as not to offend the police commissioner in case he comes around looking for offense, or the cop the commissioner places on duty in the Mid, who is a character by the name of Halligan.

So there is Rose Viola out on the stage of the Mid doing her number in full costume without ever reaching for as much as a single zipper, and I can see what Rube Goldstein means when he says Rose needs a future, because looking at Rose in full costume really becomes quite monotonous after a while. To tell the truth, the only one who seems to appreciate Rose in full costume is Daniel Frame when he comes down from Yale one week end and finds her in this condition. In fact, Daniel Frame is really quite delighted with her.

"It is wonderful," he say. "It is especially wonderful because I tell my mother all about you, and she is talking of coming down from Manchester, N. H., to see you perform, and I have been worrying myself sick over her beholding you out there in danger of catching colds. I know she will be greatly pleased with you now, because," he says, "you look so sweet and modest and so well dressed."

Naturally, as long as he is pleased, Rose Viola is pleased too, except that she suffers somewhat from the heat, for there is no doubt but what Rose is greatly in love with him and she scarcely ever talks about anything else, and does not seem to care if her art suffers from the change.

Now it comes on another Saturday night and I am backstage at the Mid talking to Rube Goldstein and he is telling me that he is greatly surprised to find business holding up so good. The house is packed to the doors, and I tell Rube that maybe he is wrong all these years and that the public appreciates art even when it has clothes on, but Rube says he thinks not. He says he thinks it is more likely that the customers are just naturally optimists. Rose Viola is on the stage in full costume singing her song when all of a sudden somebody in the back of the audience lets out a yell of fire and this is an alarming cry in any theater, to be sure, and especially in a spot like the Mid as it is an old house, and about as well fixed to stand off a fire as a barrel of grease. Then a city fireman by the name of Rossoffsky, who is always on duty in the Mid when a show is on, comes rushing backstage and says it is a fire all right.

It seems that a cafeteria next door to the Mid is blazing inside and the flames are eating their way through the theater wall at the front of the house by the main entrance, and in fact when the alarm is raised the whole wall is blazing on both sides, and it is a most disturbing situation, to be sure. Well, the audience in the Mid is composed mostly of male characters, because male characters always appreciate burlesque much more than females or children, and these male characters now rise from their seats and start looking for the exits nearest to them, but by now they are shut off from the main entrance by the fire.

So they commence looking for other exits, and there are several of these, but it seems from what Rossoffsky says afterward that these exits are not used for so long that nobody figures it will ever be necessary to use them again, and the doors do not come open so easy, especially with so many trying to open them at once. Then the male characters begin fighting with each other for the privilege of opening the doors, and also of getting out through the doors after they are opened, and this results in some confusion. In fact, it is not long before the male characters are fighting all over the premises, and knocking each other down, and stepping on each other's faces in a most discourteous manner. While it is well known to one and all that a burlesque theater is no place to take an ever-loving wife to begin with, it seems that some of these male characters have their wives with them, and these wives start screaming, but of course they are among the first knocked down and stepped on, so not much is heard of them until afterward. A few of the male characters are smart enough to leap up on the stage and hightail it out of there by the back way, but most of them are so busy fighting on the floor of the theater that they do not think of this means of exit, and it is just as well that they do not think of it all at once, at that, as there is but one narrow stage door, and a rush will soon pile them up like jackrabbits there.

The orchestra quits playing and the musicians are dropping their instruments and getting ready to duck under the stage and Rose Viola is standing still in the center of the stage with her mouth open, looking this way and that in some astonishment and alarm, when all of a sudden a tall, stern-looking old Judy with white hair, and dressed in gray, stands up on a seat in the front row right back of the orchestra leader, and says to Rose Viola like this: "Quick," she says. "Go into your routine."

Well, Rose Viola still stands there as if she cannot figure out what the old Judy is talking about, and the old Judy makes motions at her with her hands, and then slowly unbuttons a little gray jacket she is wearing, and tosses it aside, and Rose gets the idea. Now the stern-looking old Judy leans over to the orchestra leader, who is a character by the name of Butwell, and who is with Rube Goldstein's burlesque show since about the year one, and says to him: "Hit 'er, Buttsy."

Well, old Buttsy takes a look at her, and then he takes another look, and then he raises his hand, and his musicians settle back in their chairs, and as Buttsy lets his hand fall, they start playing Rose Viola's music, and the tall, stern-looking old Judy stands there on the seat in the front row pointing at the stage and hollering so loud her voice is heard above all the confusion of the male characters at their fighting. "Look, boys," she hollers. And there on the stage is Rose Viola doing her hop, skip and a jump back and forth and feeling for the zippers here and there about her person, and finding same.

Now, on hearing the old Judy's voice, and on observing the scene on the stage, the customers gradually stop fighting with each other and begin easing themselves back into the seats, and paying strict attention to Rose Viola's performance, and all this time the wall behind them is blazing, and it is hotter than one hundred and six in the shade, and smoke is pouring into the Mid, and anybody will tell you that Rose Viola's feat of holding an audience against a house afire is really quite unsurpassed in theatrical history. The tall, stern-looking old Judy remains standing on the seat in the front row until there are cries behind her to sit down, because it seems she is obstructing the view of some of those back of her, so finally she takes her seat, and Rose Viola keeps right on working.

By this time the fire department arrives and has the situation in the cafeteria under control, and the fire in the wall extinguished, and a fire captain and a squad of men come into the Mid, because it seems that rumors are abroad that a great catastrophe takes place in the theater. In fact, the captain and his men are greatly alarmed because they cannot see a thing inside the Mid when they first enter on account of the smoke, and the captain sings out as follows: "Is everybody dead in here?" Then he sees through the smoke what is going on there on the stage, and he stops and begins enjoying the scene himself, and his men join him, and a good time is being had by one and all until all of a sudden Rose Viola keels over in a faint from her exertions. Rube orders the curtain down but the audience, including the firemen, remain for some time afterward in the theater, hoping they may get an encore.

While I am standing near the stage door in readiness to take it on the

Jesse Owens out of there in case the fire gets close, who comes running up all out of breath but Daniel Frame. "I just get off the train from New Haven," he says. "I run all the way from the station on hearing a report that the Mid is on fire. Is anybody hurt?" he says. "Is Rose safe?"

Well, I suggest that the best way to find out about this is to go inside and see, so we enter together, and there among the scenery we find Rube Goldstein and a bunch of actors still in their make-ups gathered about Rose Viola, who is just getting to her feet and looking somewhat nonplused. At this same moment, Halligan, the cop stationed in the Mid, comes backstage, and pushes his way through the bunch around Rose Viola and taps her on the shoulder and says to her: "You are under arrest," Halligan says. "I guess I will have to take you, too, Mr. Goldstein," he says.

"My goodness," Daniel Frame says. "What is Miss Viola under arrest for?"

"For putting on that number out there just now," Halligan says. "It's a violation of the police commissioner's order."

"Heavens and earth," Daniel Frame says. "Rose, do not tell me you are out there tonight running the risk of catching cold, as before?"

"Yes," Rose says.

"Oh, my goodness," Daniel Frame says, "and all the time my mother is sitting out there in the audience. I figure this week is a great time for her to see you perform, Rose," he says. "I cannot get down from New Haven in time to go with her, but I send her alone to see you, and I am to meet her after the theater with you and introduce you to her. What will she think?"

"Well," Halligan says, "I have plenty of evidence against this party. In fact, I see her myself. Not bad," he says. "Not bad."

Rose Viola is standing there looking at Daniel Frame in a sad way, and Daniel Frame is looking at Rose Viola in even a sadder way, when Rossoffsky, the fireman, shoves his way into the gathering, and says to Halligan: "Copper," he says, "I overhear your remarks. Kindly take a walk," he says. "If it is not for this party putting on that number out there, the chances are there will be a hundred dead in the aisles from the panic. In fact," he says, "I remember seeing you yourself knock over six guys trying to reach an exit before she starts dancing. She is a heroine," he says. "That is what she is, and I will testify to it in court."

At this point who steps in through the stage door but the tall, stern-looking old Judy in gray, and when he sees her, Daniel Frame runs up to her and says: "Oh, Mother," he says, "I am so mortified. Still," he says, "I love her just the same."

But the old Judy scarcely notices him because by this time Rube Goldstein is shaking both of her hands, and then over Rube's shoulder she sees Rose Viola, and she says to Rose like this: "Well, Miss," she says, "that is a right neat strip you do out there just now, although," she says, "you are mighty slow getting into it. You need polishing in spots, and then you will be okay. Rube," she says, "speaking of neat strips, who is the best you ever see?"

"Well," Rube Goldstein says, "if you are talking of the matter as art, I will say that thirty years ago, if they happen to be holding any competitions anywhere, I will be betting on you against the world, Laura."

Nothing Happens in Brooklyn

MONDAY night my wife Ethel ses to me Joe nothing ever happens in this Godforsaken part of Brooklyn. We might as well be dead and buried for all we ever see over here. I ses look Ethel I have saw all I ever want to see and I am only too glad to get home to where it is peace and quiet after working hard all day. I ses anyway this part of Brooklyn is not Godforsaken. I ses my family the Turps have lived around here all my life and so has yours and none of them ever kicked about it much.

Ethel ses yes, but nothing ever happens here. I get awful tired of setting around where nothing happens. I ses what do you want to happen? She ses well anything except morning noon and night. I would like to see something new and exciting now and then. I ses well Ethel if you want a little excitement why don't you go down the street past the Cassidys' house. I ses I saw Mabel Cassidy going home just now and it is six thirty so she is bound to be late getting Jim's dinner and he will be boiling mad at her. I ses the fight is about due to start right now.

Ethel ses well that is not new or exciting and Jim Cassidy is no gentleman. He is awfully jealous of Mabel and every time she is two minutes late he thinks she stopped to talk to some fellow. I ses maybe she did and Ethel ses well all right suppose she did what harm is there in that? Does somebody's husband have to get jealous every time somebody talks to a fellow?

I ses no I guess not Ethel and she ses would you be jealous of me if I stopped to talk to some fellow? I ses what fellow? She ses any fellow. I ses of course not Ethel baby. I ses I would never be jealous of you and she ses now that's just it. You do not love me like Jim Cassidy loves Mabel or you would be jealous of me. Everybody is jealous of somebody they really love. I ses listen Ethel sugar plum, I ses you know I love you ten times more than Jim Cassidy loves Mabel and to prove it I am going to give you a kiss and take you to the movies to see Joan Crawford. Ethel ses why that will be fine Joe and we can stop at the Cassidys' afterwards and find out what happened.

Tuesday night Clem Chambers who lived next door came knocking at our back door and when I opened it and ses hello Clem he ses Joe this neighborhood is getting terrible. Here I come home to visit my Moms and I find a cop setting out on our front steps with Myrt McGuire. It is enough to make a fellow feel like moving somewheres else.

My wife Ethel heard him and she ses why Clem that is only Petey Angelo setting there with Myrt. Clem ses I know who he is all right but he has got an awful gall setting there on our front steps when I want to see my Moms. Ethel ses why Clem he has been setting somewheres with Myrt for six years and you know it and they are as much her front steps as they are yours. When people live in two-family houses upstairs and down the front steps belong to both. Myrtle McGuire has been living downstairs next door as long as you have been living upstairs and that is since you was kids.

O Clem ses you are always taking somebody else's part and Ethel ses anyway if you want to see your Moms why don't you come around when you know Petey Angelo will be on duty over on Flatbush Avenue? Clem ses well Ethel I would only Petey is on duty in the daytime and you know I cannot come around this neighborhood in the daytime because I never get up early enough. My business keeps me going all night.

Ho Ethel ses that is not the reason. You are afraid people in this neighborhood would recognize you in the daytime and tell the cops. You better not let Petey see you or he will put you in the jail house. I hear every cop in this town is looking for you and so you better lay low. Clem says O let them look. Nobody is afraid of cops. Nobody cares anything about cops. Look at Petey Angelo setting there on my front steps. Would anybody be afraid of him? If Myrt was not out there with him I would go out and throw him into the street but that would make Myrt mad at me. He is the only fellow she ever had and I guess she is afraid of losing him.

I ses well Clem I guess you could throw Petey Angelo into the street all right unless he has got a lot stronger than he was when we was kids and you have got weaker. I ses it has always been a funny thing to me about Petey going on the cops because he was always such a quiet kid. I ses Clem do you remember the time you pulled him out of the water when we was swimming under the bridge at Sand Street and he was about to drown?

Clem ses yes I remember it all right. I grabbed him by the hair and almost pulled it out by the roots and you and Johnny Cronin just stood there and hollered and never made a move to help me. I ses well Clem you know I could not swim so good and Clem ses I never noticed that either of you tried that day. I got a good belting from my old man God rest his soul when I went home for getting my clothes wet. I ses well you saved Petey's life that day Clem and Clem ses so what? Now he is a cop. If I ever thought Petey was going to turn out to be a cop I would have let him drown. I hate cops. Still if I had let him drown Myrt would not have had no fellow now.

I ses you used to keep the big kids from picking on him too and Clem ses well I tell you I did not know he was going to turn out to be a cop. I ses I remember Myrt used to run to you any time anybody was going to do anything to Petey. I ses I guess Myrt liked Petey even when they was little kids and Clem ses you are getting to be a regular mind reader Joe.

Then Clem went to the front window and pulled the curtain to one side a little and peeped out and ses can you imagine the gall of that cop with his arm around Myrt and her red head on his shoulder? It makes me sick to my stomach. They are setting right where he would be bound to see me if I tried to go up our stairs too.

Ethel ses look Clem you must not talk like it was just any cop that had his arm around Myrt and her head on his shoulder. It is Petey Angelo and he has a right to have his arm there and her head there because they are in love. You thought you was in love with somebody once yourself Clem so do not make fun of things like that. Ho ho ho Clem ses. I thought I was in love did I? Well if I was I wound up behind the eight ball and anyway forget it Ethel and give me something to eat. I could plug that cop through the window from here if I wanted to but just think how mad Myrt would be. Ethel ses you better think how mad I would be. It would make me awfully impatient if you did a thing like that in my house.

Then Ethel went into the kitchen and got Clem some ham and eggs and he ate like he was half starved to death and while he was eating I ses listen Clem a nice swell-looking young fellow like you has no business to be around always dodging the cops. I ses you are getting a terrible reputation. I ses think how it worries your Moms not to know where you are or what you are doing. I ses why don't you settle down and get a job?

Clem laughed and ses Joe you are a good skate and so is Ethel but I am not built like you are. I have got to have my excitement. I could never settle down and live by the clock like you do especially in a neighborhood like this. It is too dead for me.

Ethel ses that is exactly what I told Joe last night Clem. Nothing ever happens around here. Look at Joe now. It is hardly ten o'clock and he is ready to go to bed and start snoring and that is the way everybody else is in this neighborhood. It is disgusting. I ses see here Ethel I do not want to bring out any family secrets in front of an outsider but when it comes to snoring I know some other people that do a pretty good job of it. I ses I get sleepy early because I work hard all day to earn a living for you. I ses I do not need excitement like Clem here but what does it get him? I ses he comes around afraid to let the cops see him and hungry enough to eat half a ham and four eggs and I bet on top of that he needs a couple of bucks for his pocket.

Clem laughed again and ses Joe now I know you really are a mind reader so I gave him a couple of bucks and he went out our back door again without trying to go upstairs next door to see his Moms because Petey Angelo was still setting there with Myrt McGuire and he had his arm around her tighter than ever.

I ses Ethel why don't those two people get married and have it over with and set inside out of the night air? I ses are they still trying to make up their minds after six years or what? Ethel ses Joe it took you five years to marry me and my Moms and my Pops was getting ready to ask you to call it off and give somebody else a chance so you let Myrtle and Petey alone. They will get married when they are good and ready. I ses all right Ethel and now I am going to bed and if I snore a little I hope you will not tell it all over town.

Wednesday night my wife Ethel ses look Joe old Missus Chambers is sick. She was taken down with the flu this morning. Doc Curtcher ses he thinks she is going to pass on. All she talks about is Clem and she wants to see him. Where do you suppose that no account Clem is? Why Ethel I ses how in the world would I know where Clem Chambers is? I don't keep track of people like him. I ses wherever he is he will not come to any good end. I ses I read in the paper this morning where they have got him tied in with that big mail-truck robbery. I ses I never thought a fellow from this neighborhood would turn out to be a tough guy like Clem.

O Ethel ses Clem is not a tough guy. He is just full of pep. I remember how he used to like to tie my pig tails to his desk when we was little kids and he sat behind me in school. I ses look Ethel robbing a mail truck is a little different from tying your pig tails to a desk and it is something more than just pep too. I ses that Clem is plenty tough now and Ethel ses well anyway I wish I knew where he is because Doc Curtcher ses old Missus Chambers cries for him all the time. She is the nicest old thing in this neighborhood and I am going to take her some soup in a little while. If you hear anything of Clem you be sure and tell me.

Thursday morning my wife Ethel woke me up and ses hey Joe it just ses on the radio that the cops have got Clem Chambers penned up in a building on Clinton Street and that two hundred cops and the fire department are around the place trying to get him out. They are shooting and throwing tear-gas bombs into the building but Clem just will not come out and he is shooting back at them too.

I ses they ought to try the fire hose on him Ethel. I ses when Clem was here the other night he did not smell to me like he had taken a bath since the time he pulled Petey Angelo out of the river. I ses I guess that two bucks I gave him is a goner all right although I did not expect anything else and Ethel ses well I am going to run over there and tell Clem his Moms is sick before something happens to him.

I ses from what you tell me the radio ses Ethel old Clem may not be seeing callers but Ethel ses Joe you come on now and stop arguing. Missus Chambers was pretty bad when I saw her last night and Doc Curtcher ses he will bet anybody she does not last two days longer and I promised I would bring Clem to her as soon as I could find him.

So my wife Ethel put on her new hat and I got out the old bucket and we drove down to Clinton Street. We found the street all roped off and just like the radio ses there was a lot of cops banging away with pistols and rifles at a building. It was a little flat one-story building that had been a store of some kind but was empty with the windows boarded up in front and sometimes some of the cops hit the building too but that was only the best shots.

My wife Ethel started to duck under a rope half a block away from the building and a cop pushed her back and ses you cannot go through that street. She ses why not? The cop ses because that is my orders. Ethel ses who gave you those orders? The cop ses my captain gave them to me and who wants to know anyway? Ethel ses look cop I must go and speak to the fellow you have got penned up in that building. I must tell him about his Moms. She is sick and wants to see him. Doc Curtcher ses it will be for the last time so I have to hurry.

The cop ses lady you must be crazy. Ethel ses well it is a good thing you are a cop or my husband here would slap you down for calling me crazy. The cop looked at me and ses don't let me being a cop bother you Mack. If you feel like slapping somebody down just start slapping now. I ses look cop I am not after any trouble with anybody and my name is not Mack. It is Joe. I ses I am just here with my wife on an errand. O the cop ses then you are not going to slap me down like your wife ses hey Mack? I ses cop I make my own matches not my wife and he laughed and ses well you are lucky Mack. It is sometimes the other way around with me. Anyway the best thing you two can do is to take a nice walk because this is a bad spot right now.

Ethel ses cop I tell you I must talk to the fellow in that building and tell him about his Moms. If your Moms was so sick she could not get well and she wanted to see you what would you think if a cop tried to keep somebody from telling you? The cop ses lady please go away because here comes my captain and he will be sore if he finds me talking to you. The captain was a fat fellow and had a sour-looking face and Ethel ses to him Captain you are just the man I want to see. This cop here ses I cannot go through this rope to see the fellow you have got penned up in that building and tell him his Moms is sick.

The captain looked sourer than ever and ses you must be crazy and Ethel ses listen Captain do all the cops in Brooklyn go around telling people they are crazy? The captain ses yes when they talk like you. You look like a nice respectable lady but you talk awful crazy. Madam that fellow in that building is one of the most desperate men in the world.

Ethel ses O he is not. He is only Clem Chambers. I know him well. The captain ses O you do hey? Ethel ses yes I do and so does my husband Joe here. We was raised up with him. The captain looked at me and ses maybe I ought to lock you up and I ses what for? He ses I do not know yet but I may think of something later. I ses look Captain you are big people and we are only little people but do not be talking about locking somebody up unless they have done something and what have we done? I ses Captain I am a citizen of the United States of America and I know my rights. He ses O you do hey? I ses yes I do and he ses what else do you know?

I ses I know Sweeney the district leader and he will not stand for you locking me up unless I have done something. The captain ses you know Sweeney do you? I ses yes I do. I ses he ses hello to me any time I see him. Well the captain ses all right then you go on about your business and take your wife with you.

Ethel ses yes but I tell you I have got to see Clem Chambers and give him a message about his Moms and the captain ses Madam that fellow in there would shoot you down like a pigeon if you went near him. He has already winged three of my men and a bystander name of Coolidge and Coolidge is bad off. O Ethel ses you talk foolish. Clem would not shoot me down. If he shot your cops it was just in fun. He did not mean it. I do not know anything about that fellow Coolidge but what was he doing around here anyway? The captain ses O he did not mean it hey? It was just in fun hey? Well do you know he has also got a cop captured in there with him? He has got Officer Angelo and has probably shot him too by now.

Ethel ses that is funny and the captain ses what's funny? Ethel ses why that must be Petey Angelo. The captain ses his name is Pete all right. Do you know him too? Do you know everybody in Brooklyn? Ethel ses Clem Chambers and Petey Angelo are not everybody in

Brooklyn but I know them all right and they are both nice fellows only Clem does not like Petey for going on the cops.

All this time there was shooting at the building going on from cops in doorways along the street inside the ropes and from the tops of other buildings and once in a while a shot came from the building and everybody ducked and the captain ses you see how dangerous it is around here? I ses yes I see only we were on the same side of the street as the building and at an angle where Clem Chambers shots were not liable to hit us unless he could throw curves like Mungo the Dodgers pitcher.

While I was talking to the captain my wife Ethel ducked under the rope and past the cop inside and ran down the sidewalk toward the building where Clem was and everybody yelled hey at her but she paid no attention. The captain ses that woman is a dee fool. I ses Captain you are speaking about my wife and he ses so what? She is still a dee fool and what do you want to make of it? I ses nothing Captain. I ses you have got that uniform on and you are big people and I guess you can talk to little people like me any way you want but I will have to tell Sweeney you called my wife a dee fool. The captain ses all women are dee fools. I am a married man myself.

By this time Ethel was in front of the building pounding with her fist on one of the boarded-up windows and the cops had stopped shooting and were watching her. Ethel told me afterwards that when she had pounded her fist black and blue Clem Chambers ses who is it? Who is out there making all that racket? Ethel ses it is me Clem. It is Ethel Turp and don't you go shooting off those pistols at me because I have got my new hat on. Clem says O hello Ethel. You better go away from here. This is no place for a lady. I will not shoot you but those cops might. They don't shoot very good and might hit you accidental. How is Joe?

Joe is all right Ethel ses. He is up the street now arguing with the cops. But I come to tell you about your Moms Clem. She is awful sick and she wants to see you. Clem I think you better go see her because she is sick in bed. Clem ses she is? Ethel ses yes she is. Another thing Clem what are you doing in there with Petey Angelo?

Clem ses why Ethel I am not doing a thing in this world with him. He climbed on the roof of this joint and was looking around for some way to get in and arrest me and he fell through the skylight right on top of me. He cut a big gash in his side on the glass coming through and if I was not here to bandage him up he would have bled to death.

Ethel ses what is he doing now? Clem ses he is laying here quiet. I have got him tied up with his shirt so he will not go near a window and get shot by those cops. I don't want Myrt blaming me for him getting shot. He does not feel good. Ethel ses tell him hello Clem. Tell him Joe and me are out here. Clem ses all right Ethel but I have got his mouth stuffed up so he cannot say hello back to you. Ethel ses look Clem don't you let Petey Angelo come to no harm like choking to death and Clem ses hey Ethel if I had wanted him to come to harm I would not have bandaged him up or I would have shot him coming through the skylight. I don't want anything to happen to Myrt's only fellow any more than you do.

Ethel ses well I think it is a mean trick to stuff a fellow's mouth up so he cannot say hello to people. You ought to be ashamed of yourself Clem Chambers for doing a trick like that to an old friend. Clem ses he is no friend of mine. He was trying to cop a sneak on me but don't you worry about him and tell Myrt if you see her not to worry either.

Well all right Ethel ses but you come on out of there and go with me and Joe to see your Moms right away. Clem ses why Ethel those cops would pick me off the minute I stepped out of this place. I guess they will get me in the long run anyway but I will get some of them first.

Ethel ses look here Clem Chambers you stop this foolishness. Your Moms is not going to get well and she wants to see you before she goes away. So you come on out of there and bring Petey Angelo with you and take that stuffing out of his mouth.

Clem ses Ethel you mean my Moms is going to die? Ethel said yes Clem that is what I mean and I am awfully sorry. Clem ses well that is different. If she is going to die I guess I ought to see her. I would hate for her to go without me seeing her. She was always a wonderful Moms to me Ethel but how am I going to get out of here without those cops picking me off? Ethel ses why Clem I will ask the cops not to shoot you when you come out if you promise to give yourself up to them and then they can take you to your house and let you see your Moms. Clem ses I do not want any cops going with me when I see her. I do not want my Moms to know I am in trouble like that. Ethel you tell those cops if they will not shoot at me when I come out I will go home with you and see my Moms and then give myself up to them or else I will stay here and get plenty of them before they get me because I am a better shot.

Ethel ses all right Clem but you send Petey Angelo out here at once so I can take that stuffing out of his mouth or Myrt will be good and mad at you and Clem says okay Ethel but you be sure and tell Myrt that no matter how bad Petey looks I had nothing to do with it. He had no business falling through the skylight. Then pretty soon the front door of the building opened a little ways and Petey came out and he must have been pushed from behind by Clem because he almost fell over on Ethel. Petey was pretty white and weak as he leaned up against Ethel when they walked back to where I was still standing with the captain. Ethel ses hello Captain I see you are still here. Well I talked with Clem and he ses if you cops will let him go with me to see his Moms he will give himself up to them afterwards. The captain ses O he does hey? That is very very nice of him. Madam do you know I may put you under arrest for communicating with a criminal? Ethel ses what is that? The captain ses what is what? Ethel ses what is communicating with a criminal?

The captain ses look Madam you ses yourself you talked to that fellow in that building yonder and that is communicating with a criminal. Ethel ses O you mean Clem Chambers. Why all I did was to take a message to him about his Moms and I got Petey Angelo here out of that place when he was laying there with his mouth stuffed up and I have brought a message back to you and I do not think it is very nice of you to talk of putting me under arrest. The captain ses O is that so? Ethel ses yes that is so. If you want to arrest Clem Chambers without no more trouble you let him see his Moms first and then he will give himself up but if you want to try to arrest him anyway and get some more of your cops shot up why you just go ahead.

The captain ses O you are trying to dictate to somebody hey? Ethel ses no I am not but I see a lot of fellows up the street with cards in their hats and I bet they are newspaper reporters and if you get any more of your cops shot up by Clem Chambers when it is unnecessary I will tell them why it happened that way.

Look lady the captain ses will you please stop talking a while and let me think? How do you know this fellow will keep his word about giving himself up after he sees his Moms if we let him go there without any cops? Ethel ses well you let Petey Angelo here follow us if Petey is not too sick only he must not come too close because Clem does not like him since he went on the cops.

Petey ses I am all right except I am a little weak. He ses Captain if Clem Chambers told Missus Turp here he would give himself up he will do it. I will vouch for it myself. The captain ses O you will huh? Well who will vouch for you? I ses I will Captain. I ses you ask Sweeney the district leader about me and he will tell you Joe Turp's word is as good as wheat in the bin. I ses Sweeney will tell you that I always vote the right way.

The captain thought a while and then he ses well maybe it is a good idea not to get any more cops shot up than is necessary. We need all the men we got in Brooklyn just now. Lady you go ahead and tell that fellow okay but keep away from those reporters. I will do all the talking to them that is to be done.

So my wife Ethel went back to the building and pounded on the boarded up window again and ses come on out Clem everything is all right and Clem came out and got in the old bucket with us and I drove him home and Petey Angelo followed on a motorcycle. Thursday night Clem walked out of the front door of his house and Petey Angelo was setting on the door steps waiting for him and Clem ses well cop it is all over. Moms just died. Myrt is up there with her. Say cop I guess you can keep setting on my front door steps from now on.

Monday night six months later my wife Ethel ses to me Joe this is certainly the deadest neighborhood in Brooklyn. I do wish something would happen here once in a while and I ses Ethel they pushed Clem Chambers off at Sing Sing today for shooting that fellow that died the day after he gave himself up. I ses what was that fellow's name?

Ethel ses his name was Coolidge. That's too bad about Clem. He was the only fellow in this neighborhood that ever had much pep but I am glad his Moms did not live to see how he ended up. Well maybe if he had not been unlucky in love he would have turned out different.

I ses Ethel I heard you crack something once before about Clem being in love with somebody. I ses I knew Clem Chambers pretty well all his life and I never knew him to be in love with anybody except himself and Ethel ses no Joe you did not know. In some ways Clem was a gentleman. He never told anybody but me.

I ses O then he loved you did he? I ses it is a fine thing for a man's wife to have a dirty crook like Clem Chambers in love with her and Ethel ses O Joe now I know you love me because you are jealous but Clem was not in love with me. If you must know Joe it was Petey Angelo's wife Myrt.

A Call on the President

WHEN I GOT home from work the other night my wife Ethel ses O Joe, an awful thing has happened. Jim the mailman got fired. I ses who fired him? She ses why, the Government fired him. Somebody told the Government that they saw him take a letter out of his mail sack and burn it. The Government ses Jim, why did you do such a thing, and Jim would not tell so they fired him.

She ses Joe, you go and see some politicians and have them make the Government put Jim the mailman back to work right away because he is too old to do anything else but carry the mail and he would starve to death in no time. It is not justice to fire a man who has carried the mail for over thirty years, she ses. I ses Ethel sweets, I do not know no politicians that have got anything to do with the Government or justice. I ses anyway we are only little people and they are big people and what is the use of talking to them? I ses they would only give me a pushing around because that is what big people always do to little people.

Well, Ethel ses, who runs the Government? I ses the President of the United States runs the Government and she ses I bet anything the President of the United States would give Jim the mailman back his job if we tell him about it. Lets us go see the President of the United States. I ses Ethel sugar plum, the President of the United States lives in Washington and he is a busy fellow and I do not think he would have time to see us even if we went there, and she ses now there you go rooting against yourself like you always do. We will go to Washington and see the President of the United States because it is important that Jim the mailman gets his job back. Why, she ses Jim the mailman would simply lay down and die if he could not keep on carrying the mail.

So the next day I got a days layoff and then we climbed in the old bucket and drove to Washington and my wife Ethel wore her best dress and her new hat, and I put on my gray suit and a necktie and when we arrived in Washington about noon, I ses to a cop, look cop, where do you find the President of the United States? He ses I never find him.

O, I ses, a wise guy, hay? I ses cop, I am a citizen of the United

States of America and this is my wife Ethel and she is a citizen too and I asked you a question like a gentleman and you have a right to answer me like a gentleman. Yes, my wife Ethel ses, we are from Brooklyn and we do not like to have hick cops get fresh with us. O, the cop ses, I am a hick am I, and she ses well you look like one to me. I ses pipe down Ethel honey, and let me do the talking will you, and the cop ses Buddy I have got one of those too, and I sympathize with you.

He ses you have to go to the White House to find the President of the United States. You follow this street a ways he ses, and you cannot miss. Give him my regards when you see him, the cop ses. I ses what name will I tell him. The cop ses George, and I ses George what? My wife Ethel ses drive on Joe, that hick cop is just trying to kid people.

So we followed the street like the cop ses and pretty soon we came to a big building in a yard and I ses well, Ethel, I guess that is the White House all right. Then I parked the old bucket up against the curb and we got out and walked into the yard and up to the door of this building and at the door was another cop. He ses what do you want? I ses who wants to know? He ses I do. I ses all right, we want to see the President of the United States and he ses so does a hundred million other people. He ses what do you want to see him about anyway? My wife Ethel ses Joe, why do you waste your time talking to hick cops? I never saw so many hick cops in my life. She ses in Brooklyn people do not have to go around answering questions from cops.

Well, go back to Brooklyn the cop ses. Anyway, get away from here. I do not like to look at you he ses. Your faces make me tired. I ses cop, you are no rose geranium yourself when it comes to looks. I ses I am a citizen of the United States of America and I know my rights. I do not have to take no lip off of cops. I ses it is a good thing for you that you have got that uniform on, and that I have respect for the law or I would show you something.

He ses you and who else? I ses I do not need nobody else and my wife Ethel ses show him something anyway, Joe, and I might have showed him something all right but just then a fellow with striped pants on came out of the door and ses what is the trouble here? I ses there is no trouble, just a fresh cop. I ses my wife Ethel and me want to see the President of the United States and this jerk here ses we cannot do so. I ses that is always the way it is with cops, when they get that uniform on they want to start pushing people around.

I ses I am a citizen of the United States of America and it is a fine note if a citizen cannot see the President of the United States when he wants to without a lot of cops horning in. I ses it is not justice for cops to treat a citizen that way. I ses what is the President of the United

States for if a citizen cannot see him? My wife Ethel ses yes, we are not going to eat him, and I ses Ethel baby, you better let me handle this situation.

The fellow in the striped pants ses what do you want to see the President of the United States about? I ses look Mister, we came all the way from Brooklyn to see the President of the United States and I have got to be back to work on my job tomorrow and if I stop and tell everybody what I want to see him about I won't have no time left. I ses Mister, what is so tough about seeing the President of the United States? When he was after this job he was glad to see anybody. I ses is he like those politicians in Brooklyn now or what?

Wait a minute, the fellow in the striped pants ses, and he went back into the building and after awhile he came out again and ses the President of the United States will see you at once. What is your name? I ses my name is Joe Turp and this is my wife Ethel. He ses I am pleased to meet you and I ses the same to you. Then he took us into the building and finally into a big office, and there was the President of the United States all right. I could tell him from his pictures.

He smiled at us and the fellow in the striped pants who took us in ses this is Joe Turp of Brooklyn and his wife Ethel, and the President of the United States shook hands with us and ses I am glad to see you, and I ses likewise. He ses how are things in Brooklyn? Rotten, I ses. They always are. The Dodgers are doing better but they need more pitching, I ses. How are things in Washington? He ses not so good. He ses I guess we need more pitching here too. He told us to set down and then he ses, what is on your mind Joe, but there was some other fellows in the office and I ses Your Honor, what my wife Ethel and me want to see you about is strictly on the q t and he laughed and motioned at the other fellows and they went out of the room laughing too and my wife Ethel ses what is so funny around here anyway? I ses nix Ethel. I ses nix now. Kindly let me handle this situation.

Then I ses to the President of the United States, Your Honor, you do not know me and I do not know you so we start even. I know you are a busy fellow and I will not waste your time any more than I have to so I better come to the point right away, I ses. My wife Ethel and me want to talk to you about Jim the mailman. Yes, Ethel ses, he got fired from his job. I ses Ethel sugar plum, please do not butt in on this. I will tell the President of the United States all about it. Your Honor, I ses, when women start to tell something they always go about it the wrong end to, and he ses yes but they mean well. Who is Jim the mailman?

I ses Your Honor, Jim the mailman is a fellow over sixty years old and he has been carrying the mail in our neighborhood for thirty some odd years. My wife Ethel and me were little kids when Jim the mailman started carrying the mail. Your Honor, I ses, you may not believe it but my wife Ethel was a good looking little squab when she was a kid. I can well believe it, the President of the United States ses. Well, Your Honor, I ses, you would think Jim the mailman was a grouchy old guy until you got to know him. He is a tall thin fellow with humped over shoulders from carrying that mail sack around and he has long legs like a pair of scissors and gray hair and wears specs. He is no where near as grouchy as he looks. The reason he looks grouchy is because his feet always hurt him.

Yes, my wife Ethel ses, I gave him some lard to rub on his feet one day and Jim the mailman ses he never had anything help him so much. My mother used to rub my pops feet with lard when he came home with them aching. My pops was a track walker in the subway she ses. I ses look Ethel, the President of the United States is not interested in your pops feet and she ses well that is how I thought of the lard for Jim the mailman.

I ses Your Honor, Jim the mailman was always real nice to kids. I remember one Christmas he brought me a sack of candy and a Noahs ark. Yes, my wife Ethel ses, and once he gave me a doll that ses mama when you punched it in the stomach. I ses Ethel, honey, the President of the United States does not care where you punched it. Well, she ses you punched it in the stomach if you wanted it to say mama.

Your Honor, I ses, old Missus Crusper lived a couple of doors from us and she was about the same age as Jim the mailman. She was a little off her nut. My wife Ethel ses Your Honor, she was not so. She was just peculiar. You should not say such things about Missus Crusper the poor old thing Joe, she ses. You ought to be ashamed of yourself to say such things. All right, Ethel baby, I ses. She was peculiar Your Honor. I mean Missus Crusper. She was a little old white-haired lady with a voice like a canary bird and she had not been out of her house in twenty-five years and most of the time not out of bed. Something happened to her when her son Johnny was born.

I had to stop my story a minute because I noticed Ethel at a window acting very strange and I ses Ethel, what is the idea of looking out that window and screwing up your face the way you are doing and she ses I am making snoots at that hick cop. He is right under this window and I have got him half crazy. I ses Your Honor, kindly excuse my wife Ethel, but she is getting even with a cop who tried to keep us from seeing you and the President of the United States laughed and ses well, what about Missus Crusper?

I ses well, Missus Crusper's name before she got married was Kitten O'Brien, Your Honor, and her old man ran a gin mill in our neighborhood but very respectable. She married Henry Crusper when she was eighteen and the old folks in our neighborhood ses it broke Jim the mailman's heart. He went to school with her and Henry Crusper and Jim the mailman used to follow Kitten O'Brien around like a pup but he never had no chance.

Henry Crusper was a good-looking kid, I ses, and Jim the mailman was as homely as a mule and still is. Besides he was an orphan and Henry Crusper's old man had a nice grocery store. He gave the store to Henry when he married Kitten O'Brien. But Jim the mailman did not get mad about losing Missus Crusper like people do nowadays. He ses he did not blame her and he ses he certainly did not blame Henry Crusper. He stayed good friends with them both and used to be around with them a lot but he never looked at another broad again. The President of the United States ses another what? Another broad I ses. Another woman I ses. O, he ses. I see.

Yes, my wife Ethel ses, I bet you would not be the way Jim the mailman was, Joe Turp. I bet you would have been as sore as a goat if I had married Linky Moses but I bet you would have found somebody else in no time. I ses please, Ethel. Please now. Anyway, I ses, look how Linky Moses turned out. How did Linky Moses turn out, the President of the United States ses, and I ses he turned out a bum.

Your Honor, I ses, Missus Crusper married Henry Crusper when she was about eighteen. Henry was a good steady-going fellow and he made her a fine husband from what everybody ses and in our neighborhood if anybody does not make a fine husband it gets talked around pretty quick. She was crazy about him but she was crazier still about her son Johnny especially after Henry died. That was when Johnny was five or six years old. Henry got down with pneumonia during a tough winter.

Yes, my wife Ethel ses, my mother ses he never would wear an overcoat no matter how cold it was. My mother ses not wearing overcoats is why lots of people get pneumonia and die. I always try to make Joe wear his overcoat and a muffler too, Ethel ses. I ses Ethel, never mind what you make me wear, and she ses well Joe, I only try to keep you healthy.

Missus Crusper must have missed Henry a lot, Your Honor, I ses. Henry used to carry her up and down stairs in his arms. He waited on her hand and foot. Of course much of this was before my time and what I tell you is what the old people in our neighborhood told me. After Henry died it was Jim the mailman who carried Missus Crusper up and down stairs in his arms until she got so she could not leave her bed at all and then Jim the mailman spent all his spare time setting there talking to her and waiting on her like she was a baby.

I ses I did not know Missus Crusper until I was about ten years old and got to running around with Johnny. He was a tough kid, Your Honor, and I had him marked stinko even then and so did all the other kids in the neighborhood. His mother could not look out after him much and he did about as he pleased. He was a natural-born con artist and he could always salve her into believing whatever he wanted her to believe. She thought he was the smartest kid in the world and that he was going to grow up to be a big man. She was proud of Johnny and what he was going to be. Nobody in our neighborhood wanted to tell her that he was no good. I can see her now, Your Honor, a little lady with a lace cap on her head leaning out of the window by her bed and calling Johnny so loud you could hear her four blocks away because she always called him like she was singing.

My wife Ethel had quit making snoots at the cop and was sitting in a chair by the window and she jumped out of the chair and ses yes, Your Honor, Missus Crusper sing-sanged O hi, Johnny, and a hey Johnny, and a ho, Johnny, just like that.

The fellow in the striped pants stuck his head in the door but the President of the United States waggled a finger at him and he closed the door again and I ses look Ethel, when you holler like that you remind me of your mother. She ses what is the matter with my mother, and I ses nothing that being deaf and dumb will not cure. I ses Ethel, it is not dignified to holler like that in the presence of the President of the United States. Why, Ethel ses, I was only showing how Missus Crusper used to call Johnny by sing-sanging O hi Johnny, and a hey Johnny, and a ho, Johnny. I ses Ethel, that will do. I ses do you want to wake the dead?

Your Honor, I ses, Jim the mailman was around Missus Crusper's house a lot and he was around our neighborhood a good deal too and he knew what Johnny was doing. As Johnny got older Jim the mailman tried to talk to him and make him behave but that only made Johnny take to hating Jim the mailman. The old folks ses Jim the mailman wanted to marry Missus Crusper after she got over being so sorry about Henry but one day she told him she could never have anything to do with a man who spoke disrespectfully of her late husband and ordered him out of her house. Afterwards Jim the mailman found out that Johnny had told her Jim had said something bad about Henry Crusper around the neighborhood and nothing would make her believe any different until long later. Your Honor, I ses, Johnny Crusper was one of the best liars in the world even when he was only a little kid.

The fellow in the striped pants came in the room about now and he bent over and said something in a whisper to the President of the United States but the President waved his hand and ses tell him I am busy with some friends from Brooklyn and the fellow went out again.

Your Honor, I ses, this Johnny Crusper got to running with some real tough guys when he was about seventeen and pretty soon he was in plenty of trouble with the cops but Jim the mailman always managed to get him out without letting his mother know. The old folks ses it used to keep Jim the mailman broke getting Johnny out of trouble. Finally one day Johnny got in some real bad trouble that Jim the mailman could not square or nobody else and Johnny had to leave town in a big hurry. He did not stop to say good-by to his mother. The old folks ses Jim the mailman hocked his salary with a loan shark to get Johnny the dough to leave town on and some ses he sent Johnny more dough afterwards to keep going. But Jim the mailman never ses a word himself about it one way or the other so nobody but him and Johnny knew just what happened about that.

Your Honor, I ses, Johnny going away without saying good-by made Missus Crusper very sick and this was when she commenced being peculiar. Old Doc Steele ses she was worrying herself to death because she never heard from Johnny. He ses he would bet if she knew where Johnny was and if he was all right it would save her life and her mind too but nobody knew where Johnny was so there did not seem to be anything anybody could do about that.

Then one day Jim the mailman stopped at Missus Crusper's house and gave her a letter from Johnny. It was not a long letter and it was from some place like Vancouver and it ses Johnny was working and doing well and that he loved her dearly and thought of her all the time. I know it ses that, Your Honor, because Jim the mailman wrote it all out himself and read it to me and ses how does it sound? I ses it sounded great. It looked great too because Jim the mailman had fixed up the envelope at the post office so it looked as if it had come through the mail all right and he had got hold of one of Johnny's old school books and made a good stab at imitating Johnny's handwriting. It was not a hard job to do that. Johnny never let himself get past the fourth grade and his handwriting was like a child would do.

Missus Crusper never bothered about the handwriting anyway, Your Honor. She was so glad to hear from Johnny she sent for everybody in the neighborhood and read them the letter. It must have sounded genuine because Jennie Twofer went home and told her old man that

Missus Crusper had got a letter from Johnny and her old man told his brother Fred who was a plain-clothes cop and Fred went around to see Missus Crusper and find out where Johnny was. Jim the mailman got hold of Fred first and they had a long talk and Fred went away without asking Missus Crusper anything.

Yes, my wife Ethel ses, that Jennie Twofer always was a two-face meddlesome old thing and nobody ever had any use for her. I ses look, Ethel, kindly do not knock our neighbors in public. I ses wait until we get back home and she ses all right but Jennie Twofer is two face just the same.

Your Honor, I ses, every week for over ten years old Missus Crusper got a letter from Johnny and he was always doing well although he seemed to move around a lot. He was in Arizona, California, Oregon and everywhere else. Jim the mailman made him a mining engineer so he could have a good excuse for moving around. On Missus Crusper's birthdays and on Christmas she always got a little present from him. Jim the mailman took care of that. She kept the letters in a box under her bed and she would read them to all her old friends when they called and brag about the way Johnny was doing and what a good boy he was to his mother. Your Honor, old chromos in our neighborhood whose sons were bums and who had a pretty good idea the letters were phony would set and listen to Missus Crusper read them and tell her Johnny surely was a wonderful man.

About a month ago the only legitimate letter that came to Missus Crusper since Johnny went away bobbed up in Jim the mailman's sack, I ses. It was a long thin envelope and Jim the mailman opened it and read it and then he touched a match to it and went on to Missus Crusper's house and delivered a letter to her from Johnny in Australia. This letter ses he was just closing a deal that would make him a millionaire and that he would then come home and bring her a diamond breastpin and never leave her again as long as he lived.

But Your Honor, I ses, Jim the mailman knew that it would be the last letter he would ever deliver to Missus Crusper because old Doc Steele told him the day before that she had only a few hours more to go and she died that night. Jim the mailman was setting by her bed. He ses that at the very last she tried to lean out the window and call Johnny.

Well I ses, some louse saw Jim the mailman burn that letter and turned him in to the Government and got him fired from his job but Jim could not do anything else but burn it because it was a letter from the warden of the San Quentin prison where Johnny had been a lifer for murder all those years, telling Missus Crusper her son had been killed by the guards when he was trying to escape and saying she could have his body if she wanted it.

Your Honor, I ses, I guess we have got plenty of gall coming to you with a thing like this when you are so busy. I ses my wife Ethel wanted me to go to some politicians about it but I told her the best we would get from politicians would be a pushing around and then she ses we better see you and here we are. But I ses it is only fair to tell you that if you do anything to help Jim the mailman we cannot do anything for you in return because we are just very little people and all we can do is say much obliged and God bless you and that is what everybody in our neighborhood would say.

Well, my wife Ethel ses, Jim the mailman has got to have his job back because I would hate to have anybody else bring me my mail. I ses Ethel baby, the only mail I ever knew you to get was a Valentine from Linky Moses four years ago and I told him he better not send you any more and she ses yes, that is the mail I mean.

The President of the United States ses Joe and Missus Turp think no more of it. You have come to the right place. I will take good care of the matter of Jim the mailman. Then he pushes a button on his desk and the man in the striped pants came in and the President ses tell them I will have two more for luncheon. The fellow ses who are they and the President ses my friends Joe and Missus Turp of Brooklyn and my wife Ethel ses it is a good job I wore my new hat.

We drove back home in the old bucket after we had something to eat and I got back to work the next day on time all right and a couple of days later I saw Jim the mailman around delivering mail so I knew he was okay too.

I never gave the trip to Washington any more thought and my wife did not say anything about it either for a couple of weeks then one night she woke me up out of a sound sleep by jabbing me in the back with her elbow and ses Joe, I have been thinking about something. I ses look Ethel, you do your thinking in the day time please and let me sleep. But she ses no, listen Joe. She ses if ever I go back to Washington again I will give that hick cop a piece of my mind because I have just this minute figured out what he meant when he said he had one of those too and sympathized with you.

RUNYON A LA CARTE

So You Won't Talk!

It is along about two o'clock of a nippy Tuesday morning, and I am sitting in Mindy's Restaurant on Broadway with Regret, the horse player, speaking of this and that, when who comes in but Ambrose Hammer, the newspaper scribe, and what is he carrying in one hand but a big bird cage, and what is in his bird cage but a green parrot.

Well, if anybody sits around Mindy's Restaurant long enough, they are bound to see some interesting and unusual scenes, but this is undoubtedly the first time that anybody cold sober ever witnesses a green parrot in there, and Mindy himself is by no means enthusiastic about this spectacle. In fact, as Ambrose Hammer places the cage on our table, and sits beside me, Mindy approaches us and says to Ambrose:

"Horse players, yes," Mindy says. "Wrong betters, yes. Dogs and song writers and actors, yes. But parrots," Mindy says, "no. Take it away," he says.

But Ambrose Hammer pays no attention to Mindy and starts ordering a few delicacies of the season from Schmalz, the waiter, and Mindy finally sticks his finger in the cage to scratch the parrot's head and goes cootch-cootch-cootch, and the next thing anybody knows, Mindy is sucking his finger and yelling bloody murder, as it seems the parrot starts munching on the finger as if it is a pretzel.

Mindy is quite vexed indeed and he says he will go out and borrow a Betsy off of Officer Gloon and blow the parrot's brains out, and he also says that if anybody will make it worth his while, he may blow Ambrose Hammer's brains out, too.

"If you commit such a deed," Ambrose says, "you will be arrested. I mean, blowing this parrot's brains out. This parrot is a material witness in a murder case."

Well, this statement puts a different phase on the matter, and Mindy goes away speaking to himself, but it is plain to be seen that his feelings are hurt as well as his finger, and personally, if I am Ambrose Hammer, I will not eat anything in Mindy's again unless I have somebody taste it first.

Naturally, I am very curious to know where Ambrose Hammer gets the parrot, as he is not such a character as makes a practice of associating with the birds and beasts of the forest, but of course I do not ask any questions, as the best you can get from asking questions along Broadway is a reputation for asking questions. And of course I am wondering what Ambrose Hammer means by saying this parrot is a material witness in a murder case, although I know that Ambrose is always mixing himself up in murder cases, even when they are really none of his put-in. In fact, Ambrose's hobby is murder cases.

He is a short, pudgy character of maybe thirty, with a round face and googly eyes, and he is what is called a dramatic critic on one of the morning blatters, and his dodge is to observe new plays such as people are always putting on in the theaters and to tell his readers what he thinks of these plays, although generally what Ambrose Hammer really thinks of them is unfit for publication.

In fact, Ambrose claims the new plays are what drive him to an interest in murder for relief. So he is always looking into crimes of this nature, especially if they are mysterious cases, and trying to solve these mysteries, and between doing this and telling what he thinks of the new plays, Ambrose finds his time occupied no little, and quite some.

He is a well-known character along Broadway, because he is always in and out, and up and down, and around and about, but to tell the truth, Ambrose is not so popular with the citizens around Mindy's, because they figure that a character who likes to solve murder mysteries must have a slight touch of copper in him which will cause him to start investigating other mysteries at any minute.

Furthermore, there is a strong knock out on Ambrose in many quarters because he is in love with Miss Dawn Astra, a very beautiful young Judy who is playing the part of a strip dancer in a musical show at the Summer Garden, and it is well known to one and all that Miss Dawn Astra is the sweet pea of a character by the name of Julius Smung, until Ambrose comes into her life, and that Julius' heart is slowly breaking over her.

This Julius Smung is a sterling young character of maybe twenty-two, who is in the taxicab business as a driver. He is the son of the late Wingy Smung, who has his taxi stand in front of Mindy's from 1922 down to the night in 1936 that he is checking up the pockets of a sailor in Central Park to see if the sailor has the right change for his taxi fare, and the sailor wakes up and strikes Wingy on the head with Wingy's own jack handle, producing concussion of the brain.

Well, when Wingy passes away, leaving behind him many sorrowing friends, his son Julius takes his old stand, and naturally all who know Wingy in life are anxious to see his son carry on his name, so they throw all the taxicab business they can to him, and Julius gets along very nicely.

He is a good-looking young character and quite energetic, and he is most courteous to one and all, except maybe sailors, consequently public sentiment is on his side when Ambrose Hammer moves in on him with Miss Dawn Astra, especially as Miss Dawn Astra is Julius Smung's sweet pea since they are children together over on Tenth Avenue.

Their romance is regarded as one of the most beautiful little romances ever seen in this town. In fact, there is some talk that Julius Smung and Miss Dawn Astra will one day get married, although it is agreed along Broadway that this may be carrying romance a little too far.

Then Ambrose Hammer observes Miss Dawn Astra playing the part of a strip dancer, and it is undoubtedly love at first sight on Ambrose's part, and he expresses his love by giving Miss Dawn Astra better write-ups in the blatter he works for than he ever gives Miss Katharine Cornell, or even Mr. Noel Coward. In fact, to read what Ambrose Hammer says about Miss Dawn Astra, you will think that she is a wonderful artist indeed, and maybe she is, at that.

Naturally, Miss Dawn Astra reciprocates Ambrose Hammer's love, because all the time she is Julius Smung's sweet pea, the best she ever gets is a free taxi ride now and then, and Julius seldom speaks of her as an artist. To tell the truth, Julius is always beefing about her playing the part of a strip dancer, as he claims it takes her too long to get her clothes back on when he is waiting outside the Summer Garden for her, and the chances are Ambrose Hammer is a pleasant change to Miss Dawn Astra as Ambrose does not care if she never gets her clothes on.

Anyway, Miss Dawn Astra starts going around and about with Ambrose Hammer, and Julius Smung is so downcast over this matter that he scarcely knows what he is doing. In fact, inside of three weeks, he runs through traffic lights twice on Fifth Avenue, and once he almost drives his taxi off the Queensboro Bridge with three passengers in it, although it comes out afterwards that Julius thinks the passengers may be newspaper scribes, and nobody has the heart to blame him for this incident.

There is much severe criticism of Ambrose Hammer among the citizens around Mindy's Restaurant, as they feel he is away out of line in moving in on Julius Smung's sweet pea, when any one of a hundred other Judys in this town will do him just as well and cause no suffering to anybody, but Ambrose pays no attention to this criticism.

Ambrose says he is very much in love with Miss Dawn Astra and he says that, besides, taxicab drivers get enough the best of it in this town as it is, although it is no secret that Ambrose never gets into a taxi after he moves in on Julius Smung without first taking a good look at the driver to make sure that he is not Julius.

Well, by the time it takes me to explain all this, Miss Dawn Astra comes into Mindy's, and I can see at once that Ambrose Hammer is not to blame for being in love with her, and neither is Julius Smung, for she is undoubtedly very choice indeed. She is one of these tall, limber Judys, with a nice expression in her eyes and a figure such as is bound to make anybody dearly love to see Miss Dawn Astra play the part of a strip dancer.

Naturally, the first thing that attracts Miss Dawn Astra's attention when she sits down at the table with us is the parrot in the cage, and she says to Ambrose, "Why, Ambrose," she says, "where does the parrot come from?"

"This parrot is a material witness," Ambrose says. "Through this parrot I will solve the mystery of the murder of the late Mr. Grafton Wilton."

Well, at this, Miss Dawn Astra seems to turn a trifle pale around the gills and she lets out a small gasp and says, "Grafton Wilton?" she says. "Murdered?" she says. "When and where and how?"

"Just a few hours ago," Ambrose says. "In his apartment on Park Avenue. With a blunt instrument. This parrot is in the room at the time. I arrive ten minutes after the police. There is a small leopard there, too, also a raccoon and a couple of monkeys and several dogs.

"The officers leave one of their number to take care of these creatures," Ambrose says. "He is glad to let me remove the parrot, because he does not care for birds. He does not realize the importance of this parrot. In fact," Ambrose says, "this officer is in favor of me removing all the live stock except the monkeys, which he plans to take home to his children, but," Ambrose says, "this parrot is all I require."

Well, I am somewhat surprised to hear this statement, as I am acquainted with Grafton Wilton, and in fact, he is well known to one and all along Broadway as a young character who likes to go about spending the money his papa makes out of manufacturing soap back down the years.

This Grafton Wilton is by no means an odious character, but he is considered somewhat unusual in many respects, and in fact, if his family does not happen to have about twenty million dollars, there is no doubt but what Grafton will be placed under observation long ago.

But of course nobody in this town is going to place anybody with a piece of twenty million under observation.

This Grafton Wilton is quite a nature lover and he is fond of walking into spots leading a wild animal of some description on a chain, or with a baboon sitting on his shoulder, and once he appears in the 9-9 Club carrying a young skunk in his arms, which creates some ado among the customers.

In fact, many citizens are inclined to censure Grafton for the skunk, but the way I look at it, a character who spends his money the way he does is entitled to come around with a boa constrictor in his pocket if he feels like it.

I am really somewhat depressed to hear of Grafton Wilton being murdered, and I am sitting there wondering who will replace him in the community, when all of a sudden Miss Dawn Astra says:

"I hate parrots," she says.

"So do I," I say. "Ambrose," I say, "why do you not bring us the leopard? I am very fond of leopards."

"Any way," Miss Dawn Astra says, "how can a parrot be a material witness to anything, especially such a thing as a murder?"

"Look," Ambrose says. "Whoever kills Grafton Wilton must be on very friendly terms with him, because every indication is that Grafton and the murderer sit around the apartment all evening, eating and drinking. And," Ambrose says, "anybody knows that Grafton is always a very solitary character and he seldom has anybody around him under any circumstances. So it is a cinch he is not entertaining a stranger in his apartment for hours.

"Grafton has two servants," Ambrose says. "A butler, and his wife. He permits them to take the day off to go to Jersey to visit relatives. Grafton and his visitor wait on themselves. A private elevator that the passenger operates runs to Grafton's apartment. No one around the building sees the visitor arrive or depart.

"In the course of the evening," Ambrose says, "the visitor strikes Grafton down with a terrific blow from some blunt instrument and leaves him on the floor, dead. The deceased has two black eyes and a badly lacerated nose. The servants find the body when they arrive home late tonight. The weapon is missing. There are no strange fingerprints anywhere around the apartment."

"It sounds like a very mysterious mystery, to be sure," I say. "Maybe it is a stick-up, and Grafton Wilton resists."

"No," Ambrose says, "there is no chance that robbery is the motive. There is a large sum of money in Grafton's pockets, and thousands of dollars' worth of valuables scattered around, and nothing is touched."

"But where does the parrot come in?" Miss Dawn Astra says.

"Well," Ambrose says, "if the murderer is well known to Grafton Wilton, the chances are his name is frequently mentioned by Grafton during the evening, in the presence of this parrot. Maybe it is Sam. Maybe it is Bill or Frank or Joe. It is bound to be the name of some male character," Ambrose says, "because no female can possibly strike such a powerful blow as causes the death of Grafton Wilton.

"Now then," Ambrose says, "parrots pick up names very quickly, and the chances are this parrot will speak the name he hears so often in the apartment, and then we will have a clue to the murderer.

"Maybe Grafton Wilton makes an outcry when he is struck down, such as 'Oh, Henry,' or, 'Oh, George.' This is bound to impress the name on the parrot's mind," Ambrose says.

Naturally, after hearing Ambrose's statement, the parrot becomes of more interest to me, and I examine the bird in the cage closely, but as far as I can see, it is like any other green parrot in the world, except that it strikes me as rather stupid.

It just sits there on the perch in the cage, rolling its eyes this way and that and now and then going awk-awk-awk, as parrots will do, in a low tone of voice, and of course nobody can make anything of these subdued remarks. Sometimes the parrot closes its eyes and seems to be sleeping, but it is only playing possum, and any time anybody gets close to the cage, it opens its eyes and makes ready for another finger, and it is plain to be seen that this is really a most sinister fowl.

"The poor thing is sleepy," Ambrose says. "I will now take it home with me. I must never let it out of my sight or hearing," he says, "as it may utter the name at any moment out of a clear sky, and I must be present when this comes off."

"But you promise to take me to the Ossified Club," Miss Dawn Astra says.

"Tut-tut!" Ambrose says. "Tut-tut-tut," he says. "My goodness, how can you think of frivolity when I have a big murder mystery to solve? Besides, I cannot go to the Ossified Club unless I take the parrot, and I am sure it will be greatly bored there. Come to think of it," Ambrose says, "I will be greatly bored myself. You run along home, and I will see you some other night."

Personally, I feel that Ambrose speaks rather crisply to Miss Dawn Astra, and I can see that she is somewhat offended as she departs, and I am by no means surprised the next day when Regret, the horse player, tells me that he sees somebody that looks very much like Miss Dawn Astra riding on the front seat of Julius Smung's taxicab as the sun is coming up over Fiftieth Street.

Naturally all the blatters make quite a fuss over the murder of Grafton Wilton, because it is without doubt one of the best murders for them that takes place in this town in a long time, what with the animals in the apartment, and all this and that, and the police are also somewhat excited about the matter until they discover there is no clue, and as far as they can discover, no motive.

Then the police suggest that maybe Grafton Wilton cools himself off somehow in a fit of despondency, although nobody can see how such a thing is possible, and anyway, nobody will believe that a character with an interest in twenty million is ever despondent.

Well, the next night Ambrose Hammer has to go to a theater to see the opening of another new play, and nothing will do but he must take the parrot in the cage to the theater with him, and as nobody is expecting a dramatic critic to bring a parrot with him to an opening, Ambrose escapes notice going in.

It seems that it is such an opening as always draws the best people, and furthermore it is a very serious play, and Ambrose sets the cage with the parrot in it on the floor between his legs, and everything is all right until the acting begins on the stage. Then all of a sudden the parrot starts going awk-awk-awk in a very loud tone of voice indeed, and flapping its wings and attracting general attention to Ambrose Hammer.

Well, Ambrose tries to soothe the parrot by saying shush-shush to it, but the parrot will not shush, and in fact it keeps on going awk-awk louder than ever, and presently there are slight complaints from the people around Ambrose, and finally the leading character in the play comes down off the stage and says he can see that Ambrose is trying to give him the bird in a subtle manner, and that he has a notion to punch Ambrose's nose for him.

The ushers request Ambrose to either check the parrot in the cloakroom or leave the theater, and Ambrose says he will leave. Ambrose says he already sees enough of the play to convince him that it is unworthy of his further attention, and he claims afterwards that as he goes up the aisle with the bird cage in his hand he is stopped by ten different theatergoers, male and female, who all whisper to him that they are sorry they do not bring parrots.

This incident attracts some little attention, and it seems that the editor of the blatter that Ambrose works for tells him that it is undignified for a dramatic critic to go to the theater with a parrot, so Ambrose comes into Mindy's with the parrot again and informs me that I must take charge of the parrot on nights when he has to go to the theater.

Ambrose says he will pay me well for this service, and as I am always willing to pick up a few dibbs, I do not object, although personally, I am by no means a parrot fan. Ambrose says I am to keep a notebook, so I can jot down anything the parrot says when it is with me, and when I ask Ambrose what it says to date, Ambrose admits that so far it does not say a thing but awk.

"In fact," Ambrose says, "I am commencing to wonder if the cat has got its tongue. It is the most noncommittal parrot I ever see in all my life."

So now I am the custodian of the parrot the next night Ambrose has to go to the theater, and every time the parrot opens its trap, I out with my notebook and jot down its remarks, but I only wind up with four pages of awks, and when I suggest to Ambrose that maybe the murderer's name is something that begins with *awk,* such as 'Awkins, he claims that I am nothing but a fool.

I can see Ambrose is somewhat on edge to make a comment of this nature, and I forgive him because I figure it may be because he is not seeing as much of Miss Dawn Astra as formerly, as it seems Miss Dawn Astra will not go around with the parrot, and Ambrose will not go around without it, so it is quite a situation.

I run into Miss Dawn Astra in the street a couple of times, and she always asks me if the parrot says anything as yet, and when I tell her nothing but awk, it seems to make her quite happy, so I judge she figures that Ambrose is bound to get tired of listening to nothing but awk and will return to her. I can see that Miss Dawn Astra is looking thin and worried, and thinks I, love is too sacred a proposition to let a parrot disturb it.

Well, the third night I am in charge of the parrot I leave it in my room in the hotel where I reside in West Forty-ninth Street, as I learn from Big Nig, the crap shooter, that a small game is in progress in a garage in Fifty-fourth Street, and the parrot does not act as if it is liable to say anything important in the next hour.

But when I return to the room after winning a sawbuck in two passes in the game, I am horrified to find the parrot is absent.

The cage is still there but the gate is open, and so is a window in the room, and it is plain to be seen that the parrot manages to unhook the fastening of the gate and make its escape, and personally I will be very much pleased if I do not remember about Ambrose Hammer and think how bad he will feel over losing the parrot.

So I hasten at once to a little bird store over in Eighth Avenue, where they have parrots by the peck, and I am fortunate to find the proprietor just closing up for the night and willing to sell me a green parrot for twelve dollars, which takes in the tenner I win in the crap game and my night's salary from Ambrose Hammer for looking after his parrot.

Personally, I do not see much difference between the parrot I buy and the one that gets away, and the proprietor of the bird store tells me that the new parrot is a pretty good talker when it feels like it and that, to tell the truth, it generally feels like it.

Well, I carry the new parrot back to my room in a little wooden cage that the proprietor says goes with it and put it in the big cage, and then I meet Ambrose Hammer at Mindy's Restaurant and tell him that the parrot says nothing worthy of note during the evening.

I am afraid Ambrose may notice that this is not the same old parrot, but he does not even glance at the bird, and I can see that Ambrose is lost in thought, and there is no doubt but what he is thinking of Miss Dawn Astra.

Up to this time the new parrot does not say as much as awk. It is sitting in the little swing in the cage rocking back and forth, and the chances are it is doing some thinking, too, because all of a sudden it lets out a yell and speaks as follows:

"Big heel! Big heel! Big heel!"

Well, at this, three characters at tables in different parts of the room approach Ambrose and wish to know what he means by letting his parrot insult them and it takes Ambrose several minutes to chill these beefs. In the meantime, he is trying to think which one of Grafton Wilton's acquaintances the parrot may have reference to, though he finally comes to the conclusion that there is no use trying to single out anyone, as Grafton Wilton has a great many acquaintances in his life.

But Ambrose is greatly pleased that the parrot at last displays a disposition to talk, and he says it will not be long now before the truth comes out, and that he is glad of it, because he wishes to renew his companionship with Miss Dawn Astra. He no sooner says this than the parrot lets go with a string of language that is by no means pure, and causes Ambrose Hammer himself to blush.

From now on, Ambrose is around and about with the parrot every night, and the parrot talks a blue streak at all times, though it never mentions any names, except bad names. In fact, it mentions so many bad names that the female characters who frequent the restaurants and night clubs where Ambrose takes the parrot commence complaining to the managements that they may as well stay home and listen to their husbands.

Of course I never tell Ambrose that the parrot he is taking around with him is not the parrot he thinks it is, because the way I look at it, he is getting more out of my parrot than he does out of the original, although I am willing to bet plenty that my parrot does not solve any murder mysteries. But I never consider Ambrose's theory sound from the beginning, anyway, and the chances are nobody else does, either. In fact, many citizens are commencing to speak of Ambrose Hammer as a cracky, and they do not like to see him come around with his parrot.

Now one night when Ambrose is to go to a theater to witness another new play and I am to have charge of the parrot for a while, he takes me to dinner with him at the 9-9 Club, which is a restaurant that is patronized by some of the highest-class parties, male and female, in this town.

As usual, Ambrose has the parrot with him in its cage, and although it is plain to be seen that the headwaiter does not welcome the parrot, he does not care to offend Ambrose, so he gives us a nice table against the wall, and as we sit down, Ambrose seems to notice a strange-looking young Judy who is at the next table all by herself.

She is all in black, and she has cold-looking black hair slicked down tight on her head and parted in the middle, and a cold eye, and a cold-looking, dead-white face, and Ambrose seems to think he knows her and half bows to her, but she never gives him a blow.

So Ambrose puts the birdcage on the settee between him and the cold-looking Judy and orders our dinner, and we sit there speaking of this and that, but I observe that now and then Ambrose takes a sneak-peek at her as if he is trying to remember who she is. She pays no attention to him whatever, and she does not pay any attention to the parrot alongside her, either, although everybody else in the 9-9 Club is looking our way and, the chances are, making remarks about the parrot.

Well, now what happens but the headwaiter brings a messenger boy over to our table, and this messenger boy has a note which is addressed to Ambrose Hammer, and Ambrose opens this note and reads it and then lets out a low moan and hands the note to me, and I also read it, as follows:

Dear Ambrose:

When you receive this Julius and I will be on our way to South America where we will be married and raise up a family. Ambrose I love Julius and will never be happy with anybody else. We are leaving so suddenly because we are afraid it may come out about Julius calling on Mr. Grafton the night of the murder to demand an apology from him for insulting me which I never tell you about Ambrose because I do not wish you to know about me often going to Mr. Grafton's place as you are funny that way. They have a big fight and Ambrose Julius is sorry he kills Mr. Wilton but it is really an accident as Julius does not know his own strength when he hits anybody.

Ambrose pardon me for taking your parrot but I tell Julius what you say about the parrot speaking the name of the murderer some day and it worries Julius. He says he hears parrots have long memories, and he is afraid it may remember his name although Julius only mentions it once when he is introducing himself to Mr. Wilton to demand the apology. I tell him he is thinking of elephants but he says it is best to be on the safe side so I take the parrot out of the hotel and you will find your parrot in the bottom of the East River Ambrose and thanks for everything.

Dawn

P.S. Ambrose kindly do not tell it around about Julius killing Mr. Wilton as we do not wish any publicity about this. D.

Well, Ambrose is sitting there as if he is practically stunned, and shaking his head this way and that, and I am feeling very sorry for him indeed, because I can understand what a shock it is to anybody to lose somebody they dearly love without notice.

Furthermore, I can see that presently Ambrose will be seeking explanations about the parrot matter, but for maybe five minutes Ambrose does not say a word, and then he speaks as follows:

"What really hurts," Ambrose says, "is to see my theory go wrong. Here I am going around thinking it is somebody in Grafton Wilton's own circle that commits this crime, and the murderer turns out to be nothing but a taxicab driver.

"Furthermore, I make a laughingstock of myself thinking a parrot will one day utter the name of the murderer. By the way," Ambrose says "what does this note say about the parrot?"

Well, I can see that this is where it all comes out, but just as I am about to hand him the note and start my own story, all of a sudden the parrot in the cage begins speaking in a loud tone of voice as follows:

"Hello, Polly," the parrot says. "Hello, Pretty Polly."

Now I often hear the parrot makes these remarks and I pay no attention to it, but Ambrose Hammer turns at once to the cold-looking Judy at the table next to him and bows to her most politely, and says to her like this:

"Of course," he says. "To be sure," he says. "Pretty Polly. Pretty Polly Oligant," he says. "I am not certain at first, but now I remember.

Well, well, well," Ambrose says. "Two years in Auburn, if I recall, for trying to put the shake on Grafton Wilton on a phony breach-of-promise matter in 1932, when he is still under age.

"Strange I forget it for a while," Ambrose says. "Strange I do not connect you with this thing marked *P*, that I pick up in the apartment the night of the murder. I think maybe I am protecting some female character of good repute."

And with this, Ambrose pulls a small gold cigarette case out of his pocket that he never mentions to me before and shows it to her.

"He ruins my life," the cold-looking Judy says. "The breach-of-promise suit is on the level, no matter what the jury says. How can you beat millions of dollars? There is no justice in this world," she says.

Her voice is so low that no one but Ambrose and me can hear her, and her cold eyes have a very strange expression to be sure as she says:

"I kill Grafton Wilton, all right," she says. "I am glad of it, too. I am just getting ready to go to the police and give myself up, anyway, so I may as well tell you. I am sick and tired of living with this thing hanging over me."

"I never figure a Judy," Ambrose says. "I do not see how a female can strike a blow hard enough to kill such a sturdy character as Grafton Wilton."

"Oh, that," she says. "I do not strike him a blow. I get into his apartment with a duplicate key that I have made from his lock, and I find him lying on the floor half conscious. I revive him, and he tells me a taxicab driver comes to his apartment and smashes him between the eyes with his fist when he opens the door, and Grafton claims he does not know why. Anyway," she says, "the blow does not do anything more serious to him than skin his nose a little and give him a couple of black eyes.

"Grafton is glad to see me," she says. "We sit around talking and eating and listening to the radio all evening. In fact," she says, "we have such an enjoyable time that it is five hours later before I have the heart and the opportunity to slip a little cyanide in a glass of wine on him."

"Well," I say, "the first thing we must do is to look up Miss Dawn Astra's address and notify her that she is all wrong about Julius doing the job. Maybe," I say, "she will feel so relieved that she will return to you, Ambrose."

"No," Ambrose says. "I can see that Miss Dawn Astra is not the one for me. If there is anything I cannot stand it is a female character who does not state the truth at all times, and Miss Dawn Astra utters a prevarication in this note when she says my parrot is at the bottom of the

East River, for here it is right here in this cage, and a wonderful bird it is, to be sure. Let us all now proceed to the police station, and I will then hasten to the office and write my story of this transaction, and never mind about the new play."

"Hello, Polly," the parrot says. "Pretty Polly."

A Light in France

IN THE SUMMER of 1936, a personality by the name of Blond Maurice is found buried in a pit of quicklime up in Sullivan County, or, anyway what is found is all that is left of Maury, consisting of a few odds and ends in the way of bones, and a pair of shoes which have Brown the shoemaker's name in them, and which Brown identifies as a pair of shoes he makes for Maury some months before, when Maury is in the money and is able to have his shoes made to order.

It is common gossip in all circles along Broadway that Maury is placed in this quicklime by certain parties who do not wish him well, and it is also the consensus of opinion that placing him there is by no means a bad idea, at that, as Maury is really quite a scamp and of no great credit to the community. In fact, when it comes out that there is nothing left of him but a pair of shoes, it is agreed by one and all that it is two shoes too many.

Well, knowing that Maury is quicklimed, it is naturally something of a surprise to me to come upon him in Mindy's restaurant one evening in the spring of 1943, partaking of cheese blintzes. At first I think I am seeing a ghost, but, of course, I know that ghosts never come in Mindy's, and, if they do, they never eat cheese blintzes, so I realize that it is nobody but Maury himself.

Consequently I step over to his table and give him a medium hello, and he looks up and gives me a medium hello right back, for, to tell the truth Maury and I are never bosom friends. In fact, I always give him plenty of the back of my neck because I learn long ago that it is best not to associate with such harum-scarum personalities unless, of course, you need them.

But naturally I am eager to hear of his experiences in the quicklime as I never before meet a guy who returns from being buried in this substance, so I draw up a chair and speak to him as follows:

"Well, Maury," I say, "where are you all this time that I do not see you around and about?"

"I am in a place called France," Maury says. "I leave there on account of the war. Perhaps you hear of the war?"

"Yes," I say, "I hear rumors of it from time to time."

"It is a great nuisance," Maury says.

"But, Maury," I say, "how do you come to go to a place where there is a war?"

"Oh," Maury says, "there is no war when I go there. The war is here in New York. This city is very unsettled at the time, what with the unpleasantness between my employer, the late Little Kishke, and Sammy Downtown developing cases for the medical examiner all over the layout. I am pleased to find on my return that law and order now prevail."

"But, Maury," I say, "how do you stand with reference to law and order?"

"I am in favor of both," Maury says.

"Oh, I am all right. Immediately upon my return, I call on the D.A. in Manhattan to see if he has anything he wishes me to plead guilty to, and he cannot find a thing, although he seems somewhat regretful, at that.

"Then," Maury says, "I go over to Brooklyn and call on the D.A. there, and he consults the books of Murder, Incorporated, and he states that all he can find entered under my name is that I am deceased, and that he hopes and trusts I will remain so. I am as clean as a whistle, and," Maury says, "maybe cleaner."

"Well," I say, "I am glad to hear this, Maury. I always know you are sound at bottom. By the way, do you run into Girondel on your travels? We hear that he is over there also. At least, he is absent quite a spell. Girondel is always a great one for going around and about in foreign lands."

"No," Maury says, "I do not see him there. But if you care to listen, I will now relate to you my adventures in France."

Well (Maury says), I go to France when things come up that convince me that I am not as popular as formerly with Sammy Downtown and his associates, and, furthermore, I am tired out and feel that I can use a little rest and peace.

And the reason I pick this France as a place to go to is because I take a fancy to the country when I am there once on a pleasure trip all over Europe as a guest of the late Drums Capello, who is in the importing business, and what he imports is such merchandise as morphine and heroin and sometimes a little opium.

But I wish to state that I have no part of Drums' play in this respect and no part of his fall when the Brush finally catches up with him. And, furthermore, I wish to state that I never approve of his enterprise in any way whatever, but I must say he is a fine host and takes me all over England and Germany, and introduces me to many of his friends and business associates, and you can have them.

Now, the exact spot in France to which I go is a sleepy little town on the seacoast, but I cannot reveal the name at this time as it is a military secret and, anyway, I am unable to pronounce it. The main drag of this town faces a small harbor and you can stand in front of any place of business along the stem and almost flip a dime into the water—if you happen to have a dime to spare.

It is an old fishing spot, and when I first go there, it is infested by fishermen with hay on their chins, and while most of them inhabit dinky little houses in the town, others live on farms about the size of napkins just outside the burg, and they seem to divide their time between chasing fish and cows. But it is quiet and peaceful there, and very restful after you get used to not hearing the Broadway traffic.

I reside in a tiny gaff that is called a hotel on the main street, and this gaff is run by a French bim by the name of Marie. In fact, all bims in France seem to be named Marie when they are not named Yvonne. I occasionally notice an old sack in the background who may be Marie's mamma or her aunt or some such, but Marie is strictly the boss of the trap and operates it in first-class style. She is the chief clerk and the headwaiter and she is also the bartender in the little smoky barroom that opens directly on the street, so, if the door is left open, you get herring with your cognac.

I know she makes the beds and dusts up the three tiny bedrooms in the joint, so you can see she is an all-around personality. She is maybe twenty years old, and I will not attempt to describe her except to say that if I am interested in the hugging and kissing department, I will most certainly take my business to Marie, especially as she speaks English, and you will not have to waste time with the sign language.

Well, it is very pleasant, to be sure, strolling around the little town talking to the fishermen or wandering out into the country and observing the agriculturists, who seem to be mostly female personalities who are all built in such a way that they will never be able to sit down in a washtub with comfort, and who really have very little glamor.

It is also very pleasant to nuzzle a dram or two in the cool of the evening at a little table in front of Marie's hotel and it is there I make the acquaintance of the only other roomer in the hotel. He is a fat old guy who is nobody but Thaddeus T. Blackman, a rich zillionaire from the city of New York and a lam-master from the Brush boys back home for over twenty years on an income-tax beef.

It seems that Thaddeus T. is mixed up in a large scandal about oil lands, and a grand jury hands out readers right and left among some of the best people in the U.S.A., although all they do is swindle the government, and it is a great shock to them to learn that this is against the law.

Anyway, Thaddeus T. starts running as soon as he gets wind of the beef and does not pause for breath until he arrives in this little town in France, and there he lives all these years. It seems the Brush cannot touch him there, and why this is I do not know, but I suppose it is because he is smart enough to take his zillions with him, and naturally this kind of moolouw is protection on land or sea.

He discusses his case with me once and gives me to understand that it is a bum beef as far as he is concerned and that he only takes the fall for others, but of course this is by no means an unfamiliar tale to me, and, as he never mentions why he does not try to chill the beef by paying the government the dough, I do not consider it tactful to bring the matter up.

He is up in the paint-cards in age when I meet him, being maybe close to seventy, and he is a fashion plate of the fashion of about 1922. Moreover, he seems to be a lonely old gee, though how anybody can be lonely with all his zillions is a great mystery to me. He always has a short briar pipe in his mouth and is generally lighting it with little wax matches, and, in fact, I never see a pipe man who is not generally lighting his pipe, and if ever I get time I will invent a pipe that stays lit and make a fortune.

Anyway, Thaddeus T. and I become good friends over the little table in front of the hotel, and then one day who shows up but an old pal of mine out of the city of Boston, Mass., who is also an absentee from a small charge of homicide in his home town.

He is called by the name of Mike the Mugger because it seems his occupation is reaching out of doorways on dark nights and taking passers-by by the neck and pulling them in close to him with one hand and examining into their pockets with the other hand, the idea of the hand around the neck being to keep them from complaining aloud until he is through with them.

Personally, I do not consider this occupation at all essential or even strictly ethical, but I always say every guy to his own taste and naturally I have to respect Mike as the very top guy in his profession who never makes a mistake except the one time he clasps a customer too tight and too long and becomes involved in this difficulty I mention.

He is about thirty-odd and is a nifty-drifty in his dress and very good company, except that he is seldom holding anything and is generally leaning on me. However, I am personally loaded at this time and I am not only pleased to okay Mike for Marie for the last of her three rooms, but I stake him to walk-about money, which is money for his pocket, and he is grateful to me in every respect.

Naturally, Mike joins out with Thaddeus T. and me in strolling here and there and in sitting at the little table in front of the hotel or in the barroom, talking and playing cards, and what we generally talk about, of course, is the good old U.S.A., which is a subject of great interest to all three of us.

A few fishermen and small merchants of the town are also usually in the barroom, and Marie is always behind the bar, and it is not long before I notice that both Thaddeus T. and Mike the Mugger are paying considerable attention to her. In fact, Mike tells me he is in love with her and is surprised that I am not in the same condition.

"But," Mike says, "of course I will never mention my love to Marie because I am undoubtedly a low-class personality with a tough beef against me and am unfit to associate with a nice lady saloon-keeper."

As far as I can see, Thaddeus T.'s interest in Marie is more fatherly than anything else, which is very nice if you like an old wolf for a father. He tells me he wishes he has her for his daughter because, he says, the one of his own back in the U.S.A. is a dingbat and so is her mamma, and from the way he carries on about them, I can see that Thaddeus T.'s former home life is far from being a plug for matrimony.

Now it comes on 1939 and with it the war, and Thaddeus T., who can gabble the frog language quite fluently and is always around on the Ear-ie finding out what is going on, tells me that the people of the town are pretty much worked up and that some of the guys are going away to join the army, but it makes little difference in our lives, as we seem to be outside the active war zone, and all we know about any actual fighting is what we hear.

We still sit out in front of the hotel in the afternoon and in the barroom at night, though I observe Marie now pays more attention to other customers than she does to us and is always chattering to them in a most excited manner, and Thaddeus T. says it is about the war. He says Marie is taking it to heart no little and quite some.

But it is not until the summer of 1940 that Thaddeus T. and me and even Mike really notice the war, because overnight the little town fills up with German soldiers and other German guys who are not soldiers but seem to be working gees, and it is plain to be seen that something big is doing. Thaddeous T. says he hears they are making a submarine base of the harbor because it is a very handy spot for the subs to sneak out of and knock off the British ships, and in fact after a while we see many subs and other shipping along the quays.

Anyway, the Germans pay very little attention to us at first except to examine our papers, and the officers who come into Marie's bar for drinks are quite polite and nod to us and sometimes talk to Thaddeus T., who speaks German better than he does French. Presently we are practically ignoring the presence of the Germans in our midst, although naturally Marie has no fancy for them whatever and is always making faces at them behind their backs and spitting on the ground when they pass, until I tell her that this is unladylike.

Well, on coming home one night from a little stroll, I hear a commotion in the kitchen, which is just off the barroom, and on entering I observe Marie wrestling with a big blubber in civilian clothes who is wearing a small scrubbly mustache and a derby hat and who has practically no neck whatever.

They are knocking kitchen utensils right and left, including a pot of spaghetti which I know Marie prepares for my dinner and which vexes me no little. Marie is sobbing and I can see that the blubber is out-wrestling her and in fact has a strangle hold on her that figures to win him the fall very shortly. I am standing there, admiring his technique in spite of my vexation over the sphaghetti, when Marie sees me and calls to me as follows:

"Please help me, Chauncey," which, as I forget to tell you before, is at this time my monicker, and I am then in possession of passports and other papers to prove same.

Naturally, I pay no attention to her, as I do not know on what terms she is wrestling the blubber, but finally I see she is in some distress, so I step forward and tap the bloke on the shoulder and say to him like this:

"I beg your pardon," I say, "but the strangle hold is illegal. If you are going to wrestle, you must observe the rules."

At this, the guy lets go of Marie and steps back and I say to her in English, "Who is this plumber?"

"He is Herr Klauber," Marie says back to me in English. "He is the head of the Gestapo in this district."

Well, then I get a good glaum at the gee and I see that he is nobody but the same Klauber that Drums Capello does business with in Hamburg the time I am Drums' guest only in those days he is not usually called by the name of Klauber. He is called the Vasserkopf, which is a way of saying "waterhead" in German, because he has an extra large sconce piece that is practically a deformity and as the Vasserkopf he is known far and wide on two continents, and especially here in New York where he once operates, as a very sure-footed merchant in morphine, heroin, opium and similar commodities.

Naturally, it is a great pleasure to me to behold a familiar puss in a strange place, even if it is only the Vasserkopf's puss, so I give him a sizable hello and speak to him as follows:

"Well, Vasser," I say, "this is an unexpected privilege, to be sure. There you are and here I am, and much water runs over the dam since last we met, and how are you anyway?"

"Who are you?" the Vasserkopf says in English and in a most unfriendly manner.

"Come, come, Vasser," I say. "Let us not waste time in shadow-boxing. Do you know our old pal Drums finally takes a fall in Milwaukee, Wis., for a sixer?"

Then the Vasserkopf comes close to me and speaks to me in a low voice like this: "Listen," he says, "it is in my mind to throw you in the jail house."

"Tut-tut, Vass," I say, "if you throw me in the jail house, I will be compelled to let out a bleat. I will be compelled to remember the time you ship the cargo of Santa Clauses out of Nuremburg and each Santa contains enough of the white to junk up half of the good old U.S.A. I hear your Fuehrer is a strait-laced gee, and what will he say if he hears one of his big coppers peddles junk and maybe uses it?"

I can see the Vasserkopf turns a little pale around the guzzle at this statement and he says: "Come outside. We will talk."

So I go outside the gaff with him, and we stand in the street in the darkness and have quite a chat and the Vasserkopf becomes more friendly and tells me that he is now a real high-muck-a-muck with the Gestapo and the greatest spy catcher in the racket. Then he wishes to know what I am doing in these parts, and I tell him quite frankly that I am there for my health and explain my ailment to him. I also tell him why Thaddeus T. and Mike the Mugger are there because I know that, as a former underworld personality, the Vasserkopf is apt to be understanding and sympathetic in such situations, especially when he knows my hole card is my knowledge of his background in junk.

"Now, Vass," I say, "all we wish is to be let alone, and if you can assist us in any way, I will personally be much obliged. What is more," I say, "I will see that you are well rewarded if a member of the Gestapo takes."

"Sure," the Vasserkopf says. "Only let us understand one thing right off the reel. The broad belongs to me. I am crazy about her. But there is talk today at headquarters of closing this place and putting her out of business because of her attitude, and because one of our officers becomes ill after drinking cognac in here last night.

"I will tell the dumb military he probably has a touch of ptomaine," he continues. "I will tell them I need this hotel as a listening post to find out what is going on among the people around here. I will advise them not to molest you, as you are neutrals, and it may make trouble with your government, although," the Vasserkopf says, "I can see that the only trouble your government may make will be for you. But the Reich is not interested in American lammeroos, and neither am I as long as you remember the dame is mine and see that I collect a hundred a week in your money. I can scarcely sleep nights thinking of her."

Now this seems to me to be a very reasonable proposition all the way around, except for the hundred a week. The way I look at it, the Vasserkopf is at least entitled to Marie for his trouble because, to tell the truth, it will be most inconvenient for Thaddeus T. and Mike the Mugger and me to leave this spot at the moment, as there is no other place we can go and no way of getting there if there is such a place.

So I shave the Vasserkopf to half a C every week, and then I go back into the hotel to find Marie in the bar with Thaddeus T. and Mike, and I can see that she is quite agitated by her recent experience with the Vasserkopf. I also learn from her that it is not his first visit.

"He is here several times before," Marie says. "He comes to me first with news of my brother who is a prisoner in a camp near Hamburg. Herr Klauber tells me he can make things easier for Henri and perhaps get him released. He comes again and again on different excuses. I am frightened because I fear his motive." Then all of a sudden Marie puts her fingers to her lips and says, "Hark!"

We hark, and I hear away off somewhere a sound that I know must come from a lot of planes, and as this sound grows louder and louder, and then dies away again, Marie says:

"English bombers," she says. "Every night they pass over here and go on up the coast to drop their bombs. They do not know what is going on here. Oh, if we can only show a light here to let them know this is a place to strike—this nest of snakes."

"A light?" I say. "Why, if you show a light around here, these squareheads will settle you in no time. Besides," I say, "it may get me and my friends in a jam, and we are Americans and very neutral. Let us not even think of showing a light and, Marie," I say, "kindly cease sizzling every time you serve a German, and, Mike, if you have any more Mickey Finns on your person, please take them yourself instead of dropping them in officers' drinks."

"Who? Me?" Mike the Mugger says.

Well, I see the Vasserkopf in the hotel almost every day after this talking to Marie, and he always give me an E-flat hello and I give him the same and, while I can see that Marie is afraid of him, she says he is now very polite to her and does not try to show her any more holds.

Of course, I do not tell Marie about my deal with the Vasserkopf and I do not tell Mike either, though I inform Thaddeus T., as I expect him to kick with some of the dough, and he says okay and that he is glad to learn that the Vasserkopf is on the take, only he thinks the half a C is enough without throwing in Marie. But he says a deal is a deal, and I can count on his co-operation.

From now on as far as we are concerned, everything seems to be almost the same as before there is any war whatever, except that we cannot go near the water front where the Germans are working and everything has to be blacked out good after dark, and you cannot as much as strike a match in the street, which is a great nuisance to Thaddeus T., as he is always striking matches. In fact, he almost gets his toupee blown off by sentries before he can break himself of the habit of striking matches outdoors at night.

I can see that the Vasserkopf must be keeping his agreement to front for us at headquarters, all right, and I am greasing him every week per our arrangement, but I find myself bored by the place, and I have a feeling that it is time for Mike the Mugger and maybe Thaddeus T., too, to leave, especially as the Vasserkopf accidentally drops a hint one day that he finds himself impeded in his progress with Marie by our constant presence in the hotel and that he thinks he is getting the short end of the deal. Finally, I have a conference with Thaddeus T. and state my views to him.

"Yes," Thaddeus T. says, "you are a hundred per cent right. But," he says, "leaving here is not a simple matter for us now. I am reliably informed that the military is likely to oppose our departure for the present, because the sub base here is a great secret and they do not care to run the risk of having us noise it about.

"In fact," he says, "I am told that they are sorry they do not chase us when they first come here, but now that they make this mistake, they are not going to make another by letting us depart, and other information that I hesitate to credit is that they may wind up clapping us in a detention camp somewhere."

"Thaddeus T.," I say, "I am an American and so is Mike and so are you, and our country is not concerned in this war. No one can hold us here against our wishes."

Well, at this, Thaddeus T. lets out a large laugh, and I can see his point and laugh with him, and then he informs me that for some days he is personally laying plans for our departure and that he buys a slightly tubercular motorboat from a certain personality and has it hidden at this very moment in a little cove about a mile up the coast and that all he now needs is a little petrol which is a way of saying gasoline, to run the boat with the three of us in it out to sea, where we will have the chance of being picked up.

Thaddeus T. explains to me that all the petrol in this vicinity is in the hands of the Germans, but he says that where there is a will, there is a way. Consequently, he makes arrangements with the same personality who sells him the boat for a supply of gasoline, and who is this personality but the Vasserkopf, and Thaddeus is paying him more per gill for the gas than the old Vass ever gets per ounce for his hop, and, as I am personally paying him regularly, I can see that he is getting his coming and going and, naturally, I have to admire his enterprise.

However, Thaddeus states that the Vasserkopf is really most co-operative in every respect, and that he is to deliver the gas at the hotel the following night, and moreover that he is going to escort us to the cove so we will not be molested by any sentries we may encounter in that vicinity, which I say is very nice of the Vasserkopf though I seem to remember that there are never any sentries in that vicinity anyway, as it is part of the coast that does not seem to interest the Germans in any manner.

Then I get to meditating more and more on the Vasserkopf and on what a big heart he has, to be sure, and as I am meditating I am also sauntering late the next evening in a roundabout way up the coast as I wish to confirm the presence of the boat in the cove because, of course, there is the possibility of it getting away after the Vasserkopf has it placed there.

My roundabout saunter carries me across the fields of the little farms beyond the town that in some places run almost down to the sea, and it is a route that the Germans are not apt to suspect as taking me on any considerable journey, even if they notice me sauntering, which I take care they do not.

Finally, I saunter through a field to a slight rise of ground that overlooks the little cove, and there is just enough daylight left by now for me to see a boat floating just offshore, and at this same moment, I am surprised to scent the odor of fresh-turned earth near at hand, and the reason I am surprised is because it is now winter and by no means plowing time.

Consequently, I look around and I am further surprised to observe on this rise a newly made trench in the ground of a size and shape that brings back many memories to me. So I saunter back in a more roundabout way still meditating no little and quite some on the Vasserkopf.

But, sure enough, he shows up this very night around nine o'clock after Marie closes her place, and he brings with him two five-gallon cans of gasoline which he delivers to Thaddeus T. in the bar where Thaddeus and me and Mike the Mugger are waiting to receive the gas. Then, after handing over the cans, the Vass goes looking for Marie, saying he wishes to speak to her before escorting us to the boat.

As soon as he leaves the bar, Mike the Mugger outs with his pocket-knife and stabs holes in two corners of the can and speaks as follows, "It smells like gasoline on the outside, but we smear the outside of cans with booze in the old bootleg days for the liquor smell when there is only water inside the cans. I hear the Vasserkopf is an old booter and he may remember the trick, and, besides, I do not trust him on general principles."

Now Mike lifts the can up as if it is no more than a demitasse and he holds it to his mouth so he can get a swig of the contents through one of the holes, when all of a sudden who comes into the bar all out of breath but Marie, and who is right behind her but the Vasserkopf and there is no doubt that Marie is greatly flustered, and the Vasserkopf is much perturbed.

"So," he says to me, "you are double-crossing me and are going to take this omelet with you, hey? Well, it is a good thing I walk in on her as she is packing a keister, and I am now arresting her as a dangerous spy."

Marie begins to weep and wail and to carry on as bims will do when they are flustered, and naturally Thaddeus T. and me and Mike the Mugger are quite perplexed by this situation and, in fact, Mike is so perplexed that he is still holding the can in his hands and his cheeks are bulged out on each side from the gasoline in his mouth as if he has the mumps.

I am about to say something to cool the Vasserkopf off, for, to tell the truth, up to this minute I have no idea Marie is going with us, though I can see from the way Thaddeus T. and Mike the Mugger look that it is undoubtedly their idea. And, before I can say anything, Mike steps up to the Vasserkopf and gives a huge ploo-oo-oo and spews his mouthful of gasoline right in the Vasserkopf's kisser and, as he gets his mouth clear, Mike says, "Why, you muzzler, it is somewhat watered, just as I suspect."

Well, naturally, the gasoline runs off the Vasserkopf's face and down over his clothes and he is standing there looking quite nonplused, and, as Mike the Mugger sees me gazing at him disapprovingly, he becomes embarrassed and self-conscious and, maybe to cover his confusion, he lifts the can of gasoline and holds it over the Vasserkopf's head, and the gas pours out and splashes off the old Vass' derby hat and splatters over his shoulders while he just stands there nonplused.

Thaddeus T. Blackman is leaning against the bar and, as usual, he is lighting his pipe with a little wax match and watching the Vasserkopf, and Marie has stopped crying and is laughing, and I am just standing there, when we again hear the sound of the planes high overhead and Thaddeus T. speaks as follows:

"A light you say, Marie?" he says. "A light for the English?"

Then he flips the lighted match on the Vasserkopf, whose clothes burst into flames at once and, almost as if they plan it all out beforehand, Mike jumps to the front door and opens it, and Thaddeus T. pushes the Vasserkopf, all ablaze out the door into the street and yells at him:

"Run for the water!" he yells. "Run, run, run!"

The Vasserkopf seems to see what he means and starts galloping lickity-split toward the water front with Thaddeus T. puffing along behind him and giving him a shove whenever he shows signs of lagging, and Mike the Mugger runs up behind the Vasserkopf and keeps throwing little spurts of gasoline on him by jerking the can at him and, from the way it burns on the Vasserkopf, I think Mike's statement of its dilution may be a slight exaggeration.

As he runs and burns, the Vasserkopf is letting out loud cries which bring soldiers from every which way, and presently they start shooting off their rifles in different directions. He is really quite a bonfire there in the darkness, and now I hear once more far overhead the drone of planes and I figure the English bombers see the light and turn back over the town.

All of a sudden, there is a whistling sound and then a big *ker-bloom,* and then more whistling and more *ker-blooms,* and there is no doubt in my mind that it is Katie-bar-the-door for the water front and the subs lying along the quays.

I can see the Vasserkopf still blazing and I can hear Thaddeus T. still urging him to run, and now the bombs are shellacking the surrounding buildings, and presently I hear, in between the blasts of the bombs, some rifle shots, and I know the soldiers are firing at Thaddeus T. and Mike the Mugger and maybe at the Vasserkopf, too, for making the light.

In fact by the glow shed by the Vasserkopf, I see old Thaddeus stumble and fall, and Mike the Mugger go down right afterward with his can of gasoline blazing over him, but the Vasserkopf continues on still in flames until he falls off the quay into the water and, the chances are, goes out with a zizz.

Well, when I think of Marie, I turn from these unusual scenes to the little hotel, but it is no longer there, because a bomb flattens it, too, and it is now nothing but a pile of miscellany. I do not have much time to look for Marie, as the German soldiers are all over the layout, trying to learn what happens, but I finally locate her with a big beam across her chest, and I can see that there is nothing I can do for her except kiss her and say goodby, and when I do this, she murmurs, "Thanks," but I am sure it is only for Thaddeus T. and Mike the Mugger and the light.

You will scarcely believe the difficulty I experience in getting away from this unpleasant situation and out of the country. In fact, I have only a vague recollection of my adventures now, but I will always remember very clearly how neatly I slip past four German soldiers sitting in the new-made trench on the rise of ground above the cove, with a machine gun covering the cove itself, and how I get in the boat and cut it loose and work it, with my hands for paddles, to open water, before they realize what is going on.

And I can never again have any respect for the memory of the Vasserkopf when I take to meditating on his unsportsmanlike conduct in trying to double-cinch a sure thing with a machine gun, although there are times before I am picked up at sea by an English destroyer that I find myself wishing that Mike the Mugger does not waste all the gasoline on the Vass, even if it is watered.

And this is all there is to the story (Maury says).

"But, Maury," I say, "do you not know that some remainders found in a pit of quicklime up in Sullivan County are supposed to be yours? They have on your shoes, which are identified by Brown the shoemaker. Are you ever in a quicklime pit in Sullivan County and, if so, what is it like?"

"Oh," Maury says, "I am in Sullivan County, all right, but never in a quicklime pit. I go to Sullivan County at the invitation of Girondel and the purpose of his invitation is to discuss ways and means of getting me straightened out with his chief, Sammy Downtown.

"But one day," Maury says, "Girondel invites me to a stroll in the woods with him and, while we are strolling, he is talking about the beauties of the landscape and calling my attention to the flowers and the birds, which is all very interesting, to be sure, but something tells me that Girondel is by no means the nature lover he seems.

"Finally," Maury says, "he strolls me to a spot in the deep, tangled wildwood, and all of a sudden I catch an odor of something I never scent but once before in my life but will never again forget, and that is the time we lay the late Bugs Wonder to rest in Greenvale Cemetery.

It is the odor of the fresh-turned earth from Bugs' last resting place.

"And as I catch this again in the woods," Maury says, "I realize that somebody does some digging around there lately, so I quietly give Girondel a boff over his pimple with a blackjack and flatten him like a welcome mat. Then I examine my surroundings and sure enough, there, hidden by the shrubbery, I find a deep fresh-made hole lined with quicklime, and I place Girondel in it and cover him up and leave him with my best wishes.

"But first," Maury says, "I change shoes with him because my own are badly worn and, besides, I know that if ever he is found the shoes will outlast the quicklime and be traced as mine, and I wish Girondel's connection to think I am no more. By the way," he says, "the odor I mention is the same I notice on the rise of ground at the cove in France which causes me to distrust the Vasserkopf. I guess I am just naturally allergic to the odor of new-made graves."

Old Em's Kentucky Home

ALL THIS REALLY begins the April day at the Jamaica race track when an assistant starter by the name of Plumbuff puts a twitch on Itchky Ironhat's fourteen-year-old race mare, Emaleen, who is known to one and all as Em for short.

A twitch is nothing but a rope loop that they wrap around a horse's upper lip and keep twisting with a stick to make the horse stand quiet at the starting gate and while I never have a twitch on my own lip and hope and trust that I never have same, I do not see anything wrong with putting twitches on horses' lips, especially the ones I am betting against as it generally keeps them so busy thinking of how it hurts that they sometimes forget about running.

However, it seems that Itchky Ironhat not only considers a twitch very painful to horses, but he also considers it undignified for such a horse as old Em, because while everybody else regards Em as strictly a porcupine, Itchky thinks she is the best horse in the world and loves her so dearly he cannot bear to see her in pain or made to look undignified. To tell the truth, it is common gossip that Itchky loves old Em more than he loves anything else whatever, including his ever-loving wife, Mousie.

In fact when Mousie tells him one day that the time comes for a showdown and that it is either her or old Em and Itchky says well, he guesses it is old Em, and Mousie packs up on him at once and returns to her trade as an artists' model many citizens who remember Mousie's shape think Itchky makes a bad deal, although some claim that the real reason Itchky decides in favor of Em against Mousie is not so much love as it is that Em never wishes for any large thick sirloin steaks such as Mousie adores.

Anyway, it seems that Itchky always goes to the trouble of personally requesting the assistant starters not to place twitches on Em's lip, even though he knows very well that she is by no means a bargain at the post and that she greatly enjoys nibbling assistant starters' ears off and when Plumbuff ignores his request it vexes Itchky no little.

The night after the race he calls on Plumbuff at his home in Jackson Heights and chides him quite some and he also gives him such a going-over that Plumbuff is compelled to take to his bed slightly indisposed for several weeks.

When the racing officials learn of the incident they call Itchky before them and address him in very severe terms. They ask him if he thinks old Em is Mrs. Man o' War, or what, that he expects great courtesy for her from assistant starters and they say they have half a mind to rule Itchky off the turf for life and old Em along with him. But Itchky states that he only acts in self-defense and that he can produce twenty witnesses who will testify that Plumbuff pulls a blunt instrument on him first.

The chances are Itchky can produce these witnesses, at that, as all he will have to do is go down to Mindy's restaurant on Broadway and summon the first twenty horse players he sees. Horse players hate and despise assistant starters because they feel that the assistants are always giving the horses they bet on the worst of the starts and naturally these horse players will deem it a privilege and a pleasure to perjure themselves in a case of this nature, especially for Itchky Ironhat, who is a popular character.

His right name is something in twelve letters, but he is called Itchky Ironhat because he always wears a black derby hat and generally he has it pulled down on his head until the brim is resting on his ears and as Itchky is a short, roly-poly guy with a fat puss he really looks a great deal like a corked jug.

Finally the racing officials say they will not rule Itchky or old Em off this time but that he must remove Em from the New York tracks and run her elsewhere and this is wonderful news to the assistant starters, who are awaiting the decision with interest.

They feel that they are all sure to wind up daffy if they have to always be deciding on whether to cater to old Em at the post or take a going-over from Itchky Ironhat and in fact they say the only thing that keeps them from going daffy on account of old Em long before this is that she does not go to the post often.

She is entered in more races than any horse that ever lives, but just before a race comes up Itchky generally starts figuring that maybe the track will not suit her, or that the race is too long, or maybe too short, or that it is not the right time of day or that old Em will not feel just like running that day, so he usually withdraws her at the last minute.

Sometimes the racing officials are a little tough with owners who wish to scratch horses from a race at the last minute, but they never argue a second with Itchky Ironhat. In fact, they often give three cheers when Em is taken out of a race, not only because she is so cross at the post but because she is so slow that she is always getting in the way of other horses and inconveniencing them more than somewhat.

It is the way Itchky thinks old Em feels that figures with him in taking her out of a race more than anything else, and to hear him talk you will think she comes right out and informs him how she feels every day. Indeed, Itchky converses with old Em as if she is a human being and he claims she can understand everything he says, though personally I do not believe any horse can understand a slightly Yiddish dialect such as Itchky employs.

She is a big bay mare with a sway-back and of course she is quite elderly for a horse, and especially a race horse, but Itchky says she does not look her years. She is as fat as a goose what with him feeding her candy, apples, cakes and ice cream, besides a little hay and grain, and she is wind-broken and a bleeder and has knobs on her knees the size of baseballs.

She has four bad ankles and in fact the only thing that is not the matter with her is tuberculosis and maybe anemia. It makes some horse owners shudder just to look at her, but in Itchky Ironhat's eyes old Em is more beautiful than Seabiscuit.

A guy by the name of Crowbar gives her to Itchky at the Woodbine track in Canada when she is just a two-year-old, rising three. This guy Crowbar buys her as a yearling out of a sale at Saratoga for fifty fish but becomes discouraged about her when he notices that she cannot keep up with a lead pony even when the pony is just walking.

On top of this she bows a tendon, so Crowbar is taking her out to shoot her to save the expense of shipping her and he is pretty sore at having to waste a cartridge on her when he meets up with Itchky Ironhat and Itchky asks what is coming off. When Crowbar explains, Itchky takes a closer look at Em and she gazes at him with such a sorrowful expression that Itchky's heart is touched.

He asks Crowbar to give her to him, although at this time Itchky is just doing the best he can around the tracks and has about as much use for a race horse as he has for a hearse, and naturally Crowbar is pleased to make the saving of a cartridge. So this is how Itchky becomes the owner of old Em and from now on he practically lives with her even after he marries Mousie, which is what starts Mousie to complaining, as it seems she does not care to be excluded from her home life by a horse.

It is no use trying to tell Itchky that Em is nothing but an old buzzard, because he keeps thinking of her as a stake horse and saying she is bound to win a large stake someday and he spends every dime he can get hold of in entering her in big races and on shipping her and feeding her and on jockey fees.

And all this is very surprising to be sure, as Itchky Ironhat is by no means a sucker when it comes to other horses and he makes a pretty good living hustling around the tracks. What is more, the way he can bring old Em back to the races every time she breaks down, which is about every other time she starts in a race, shows that Itchky is either a natural-born horse trainer or a horse hypnotist.

When he is very desperate for a little moolah, he will place Em in a cheap selling race and it is in spots such as this that she occasionally wins. But then Itchky always worries himself sick for fear somebody will claim her, the idea of a claiming race being that another owner can always claim a horse in such a race by putting up the price for which the horse is entered, which may be anywhere from a few hundred dollars on up, according to the conditions of the race and what the owner thinks his horse is worth.

Naturally, Itchky has to run old Em for as cheap a price as horses are ever run for her to win a race, but even then there is really no sense in him worrying about her being claimed as no owner with any brains wants such a lizard as old Em in his barn, and especially after what happens to a character by the name of One-Thumb Haverstraw.

This One Thumb is considered quite a joker and one day in Maryland he claims old Em out of a race for eight hundred boffoes just for a joke on Itchky, although personally I always figure the joke is on One Thumb when he gets her for this price.

Itchky is really greatly dejected over losing old Em and he goes to see One Thumb right after the race and tries to buy her back for two hundred dollars over the claiming price, but One Thumb is so pleased with his joke that he refuses to sell and then the most surprising things begin to occur to him.

A few nights later a ghost in a white sheet appears at his barn and frightens away all the colored parties who are working for him as stablehands and turns all of One Thumb's horses out of their stalls except old Em and chases them around the country until they are worn plumb out and are no good for racing for some weeks to come.

What is more, every time One Thumb himself steps into the open at night, a bullet whistles past him and finally one breezes through the seat of his pants and at this he hunts up Itchky Ironhat and returns old Em to him for four hundred less than the claiming price and considers it a great bargain at that, and nobody ever plays any more jokes on Itchky with old Em.

Now the night of the racing officials' decision, I am sitting in Mindy's restaurant enjoying some choice pot roast with potato pancakes when in comes Itchky Ironhat looking somewhat depressed and, as he takes a seat at my table, naturally I tell him I deeply regret hearing that he will no longer be permitted to run old Em in New York, and Itchky sighs and says:

"Well," he says, "it is a great loss to the racing public of this state, but I always wish to do something nice for old Em and this gives me the opportunity of doing it."

"What will be something nice for her, Itchky?" I say.

"Why," Itchky says, "I take her many places the past dozen years, but there is one place I never take her and that is her old home. You see, Em comes from the Bluegrass country of Kentucky and I get to thinking that the nicest thing I can do for her is to take her there and let her see the place where she is born."

"Itchky," I say, "how is the bank roll?"

"It is thin," Itchky says. "In fact, if you are thinking of a touch, it is practically invisible."

"I am not thinking of such a thing," I say. "What I am thinking of is it will cost a gob to ship old Em to Kentucky."

"Oh," Itchky says "I do not intend to ship her. I intend to take her there in person by motor truck and I am wondering if you will not like to go with us for company. Old Em loves company. After we let her see her old home we can drop her in a stake race at Churchill Downs and win a package."

Then Itchky explains to me that he acquires a truck that very afternoon from a vegetable peddler for the sum of sixty dollars and that he also gets a couple of wide, strong planks which he figures he can let down from the rear end of the truck like a runway so old Em can walk on them getting on and off the truck and that by driving by day and resting by night he can take her to the Bluegrass of Kentucky this way very nicely.

Now it is coming on time for the Kentucky Derby and if there is one thing I wish to see it is this event, and furthermore I never get around the country much and I figure that such a journey will be most educational to me so I tell Itchky he has a customer. But if I see the truck first I will certainly never think of trying to get anywhere in it, not even to the Polo Grounds.

Of course when Itchky tells me the truck costs him only sixty dollars, I am not looking for a fancy truck, but I have no idea it is going to be older than Henry Ford, or anyway Edsel, and not much bigger than a pushcart and with no top whatever, even over the seat.

The body of the truck is not long enough for old Em to stand in it spraddled out, the way horses love to stand, or her hind legs will be hanging out the rear end, so what Itchky does is to push her front legs back and her hind legs forward, so that all four feet are close together under her like she is standing on a dime.

Personally, I consider this an uncomfortable position all the way around for a horse but when Itchky and I get on the seat and Em finds she can rest her head on Itchky's shoulder, she seems quite happy, especially as Itchky talks to her most of the time.

It is no time after we start that we find old Em makes the truck top-heavy and in fact she almost falls overboard every time we take a curve and Itchky has to choke down to about two miles per hour until all of a sudden Em learns how to lean her weight to one side of the truck or the other on the curves and then Itchky can hit it up to the full speed of the truck, which is about ten miles per hour. I will say one thing for old Em, I never see a brighter horse in my life.

The first time we stop to take her off for the night, we find that the plank runway is all right for loading her because she can run up the boards like a squirrel but they have too much of a pitch for her to walk down them, so finally we drop the tail gate and get hold of the front end of the truck and lift it gently and let her slide down to the ground like she was on a toboggan and I always claim that old Em likes this better than any other part of the trip.

It seems to be a most surprising spectacle to one and all along our route to see a truck going past with a horse leaning this way and that to keep balanced and with forty per cent of her sticking out of one end of the truck and twenty per cent of her sticking out of the other end and we often attract many spectators when we stop. This is whenever we have a blowout, which is every now and then. Sometimes there is much comment among these spectators about old Em and as it is generally comment of an unfavorable nature, I am always having difficulty keeping Itchky from taking pops at spectators.

We sleep at night in the truck with old Em tied to the rear end and we use her spare blankets for covering as Em has more blankets than any other horse in the country and most of them are very fancy blankets, at that. It is not bad sleeping except when it rains and then Itchky takes all the blankets off us and puts them on Em and my overcoat, too, and we have to sit up under the truck and the way Itchky worries about Em catching cold is most distressing.

Sometimes when we are rolling along the road and Em is dozing on Itchky's shoulder, he talks to me instead of her, and I ask him if he knows just where to find Em's old home in the Bluegrass country.

"No," he says. "I do not know just where, but the record book gives the breeder of Em as the Tucky Farms and it must be a well-known breeding establishment to produce such a horse as Em, so we will have no trouble finding it. By the way," Itchky says, "Em comes of a very high-class family. She is by an important stallion by the name of Chris-tofer out of a mare called Love Always, but," he says, "the curious thing about it is I am never able to learn of another horse of his breed-ing in this country, though Christofer is once a good race horse in France."

Personally, I consider it a great thing for this country that there is only one horse bred like Em but naturally I do not mention such a thought to Itchky Ironhat, not only because I know it will displease him but because I am afraid old Em may overhear me and be greatly offended.

The road signs state that we are a few miles out of the city of Lexing-ton, Ky., and we know we are now down in the Bluegrass country, when we come upon a tall old guy leaning against a fence in front of a cute little white house. This old guy looks as if he may be a native of these parts as he is wearing a wide-brimmed soft hat and is chewing on a straw, so Itchky stops the truck and puts on a Southern accent and speaks to him as follows:

"Suh," Itchky says, "can you all direct me to a place called the Tucky Farms, suh?"

The tall old guy gazes at Itchky and then he gazes at me and finally he gazes at old Em and he never stops chewing on the straw and after a while he smiles and points and says:

"It is about three miles up that road," he says. "It is a big red brick house with some burned-down barns in the background, but friend," he says, "let me give you a piece of good advice. I do not know what your business is, but keep away from that place with anything that looks like a horse. Although," he says, "I am not sure that the object you have on your truck answers such a description."

Of course Itchky can see from this crack that the old guy is making fun of Em and he starts to sizzle all over and forgets his Southern ac-cent at once and says:

"You do not like my horse?"

"Oh, it is a horse, then?" the old guy says. "Well, the party who owns Tucky Farms is a trifle eccentric about horses. In fact, he is eccentric about everything, but horses most of all. He does not permit them on his premises. It is a sad case. You may meet a disagreeable reception if you go there with your so-called horse."

Then he turns and walks into the cute little white house and I have all I can do to keep Itchky from going after him and reprimanding him for speaking so disrespectfully of old Em, especially as the old guy keeps looking around at us and we can see that he is smiling more than somewhat.

Itchky drives on up the road a little ways and, just as the old guy says, we come upon a big red brick house and there is no doubt that this is the Tucky Farms because there is a faded sign over an arched gateway that so states. The house is all shuttered up and is on a small hill pretty well back from the road and not far from the house are the remainders of some buildings that look as if they burned down a long time ago and are never fixed up again or cleared away.

In fact, the grounds and the house itself all look as if they can stand a little attention and there is not a soul in sight and it is rather a dismal scene in every respect. The gate is closed, so I get down off the truck and open it and Itchky drives the truck in and right up to the front door of the house under a sort of porch with white pillars.

Now the truck makes a terrible racket and this racket seems to stir up a number of colored parties who appear from around in back of the house, along with a large white guy. This large guy is wearing corduroy pants and laced boots and a black mustache and he is also carrying a double-barreled shotgun and he speaks to Itchky in a fierce tone of voice as follows:

"Pigface," he says, "get out of here. Get out of here before you are hurt. What do you mean by driving in here with a load of dog meat such as this, anyway?"

He points a finger at old Em who has her head up and is snuffling the air and gazing about her with great interest, and right away Itchky climbs down off the seat of the truck and removes his derby and places it on the ground and takes off his coat and starts rolling up his sleeves.

"It is the last straw," Itchky Ironhat says. "I will first make this big ash can eat that cannon he is lugging and then I will beat his skull in. Nobody can refer to Emaleen as dog meat and live."

Now the front door of the house opens and out comes a thin character in a soiled white linen suit and at first he seems to be quite an old character as he has long white hair but when he gets closer I can see that he is not so very old at that, but he is very seedy-looking and his eyes have a loose expression. I can also see from the way the large guy and the colored parties step back that this is a character who packs some weight around here. His voice is low and hard as he speaks to Itchky Ironhat and says:

"What is this?" he says. "What name do I just hear you pronounce?"

"Emaleen," Itchky says. "It is the name of my race mare which you see before you. She is the greatest race mare in the world. The turf records say she is bred right here at this place and I bring her down here to see her old home, and everybody insults her. So this is Southern hospitality?" Itchky says.

The new character steps up to the truck and looks at old Em for quite a spell and all the time he is shaking his head and his lips are moving as if he is talking to himself, and finally he says to the large guy:

"Unload her," he says. "Unload her and take good care of her, Dobkins. I suppose you will have to send to one of the neighbors for some feed. Come in, gentlemen," he says to Itchky and me and he holds the front door of the house open. "My name is Salsbury," he says. "I am the owner of Tucky Farms and I apologize for my foreman's behavior but he is only following orders."

As we go into the house I can see that it is a very large house and I can also see that it must once be a very grand house because of the way it is furnished, but everything seems to be as run-down inside as it does outside and I can see that what this house needs is a good cleaning and straightening out.

In the meantime, Mr. Salsbury keeps asking Itchky Ironhat questions about old Em and when he hears how long Itchky has her and what he thinks of her and all this and that, he starts wiping his eyes with a handkerchief as if the story makes him very sad especially the part about why Itchky brings her to the Bluegrass.

Finally Mr. Salsbury leads us into a large room that seems to be a library and at one end of this room there is a painting taller than I am of a very beautiful Judy in a white dress and this is the only thing in the house that seems to be kept dusted up a little and Mr. Salsbury points at the painting and says:

"My wife, Emaleen, gentlemen. I name the horse you bring here after her long ago, because it is the first foal of her favorite mare and the first foal of a stallion I import from France."

"By Christofer, out of Love Always," Itchky Ironhat says.

"Yes," Mr. Salsbury says. "In those days, Tucky Farms is one of the great breeding and racing establishments of the Bluegrass. In those days, too, my wife is known far and wide for her fondness for horses and her kindness to them. She is the head of the humane society in Kentucky and the Emaleen Salsbury annual award of a thousand dollars for the kindest deed toward a horse brought to the attention of the society each year is famous.

"One night," Mr. Salsbury continues, "there is a fire in the barns and my wife gets out of bed and before anyone can stop her she rushes into the flames trying to save her beautiful mare, Love Always. They both perish, and," he says, "with them perishes the greatest happiness ever given a mortal on this earth."

By this time, Itchky Ironhat and I are feeling very sad, indeed, and in fact all the creases in Itchky's face are full of tears as Mr. Salsbury goes on to state that the only horses on the place that are saved are a few yearlings running in the pastures. He sends them all with a shipment a neighbor is taking to Saratoga to be disposed of there for whatever they will bring.

"Your mare Emaleen is one of those," he says. "I forget all about her at the time. Indeed," he says, "I forget everything but my unhappiness. I feel I never wish to see or hear of a horse again as long as I live and I withdraw myself completely from the world and all my former activities. But," he says, "your bringing the mare here awakens old fond memories and your story of how you cherish her makes me realize that this is exactly what my wife Emaleen will wish me to do. I see where I sadly neglect my duty to her memory. Why," he says, "I never even keep up the Emaleen Salsbury award."

Now he insists that we must remain there a while as his guests and Itchky Ironhat agrees, although I point out that it will be more sensible for us to move on to Louisville and get into action as quickly as possible because we are now practically out of funds. But Itchky takes a look at old Em and he says she is enjoying herself so much running around her old home and devouring grass that it will be a sin and a shame to take her away before it is absolutely necessary.

After a couple of days, I tell Itchky that I think absolutely necessary arrives, but Itchky says Mr. Salsbury now wishes to give a dinner in honor of old Em and he will not think of denying her this pleasure. And for the next week the house is overrun with colored parties, male and female, cleaning up the house and painting and cooking and dusting and I do not know what all else, and furthermore I hear there is a great to-do all through the Bluegrass country when the invitations to the dinner start going around, because this is the first time in over a dozen years that Mr. Salsbury has any truck whatever with his neighbors.

On the night of the dinner, one of the male colored parties tells me that he never before sees such a gathering of the high-toned citizens of the Bluegrass as are assembled in a big dining hall at a horseshoe-shaped table with an orchestra going and with flowers and flags and racing colors all around and about. In fact, the colored party says it is just like the old days at Tucky Farms when Mr. Salsbury's wife is alive, although he says he does not remember ever seeing such a character sitting alongside Mr. Salsbury at the table as Itchky Ironhat.

To tell the truth, Itchky Ironhat seemed to puzzle all the guests no little and it is plain to be seen that they are wondering who he is and why he is present, though Itchky is sharpened up with a fresh shave and has on a clean shirt and of course he is not wearing his derby hat. Personally, I am rather proud of Itchky's appearance but I can see that he seems to be overplaying his knife a little, especially against the mashed potatoes.

Mr. Salsbury is dressed in a white dinner jacket and his eyes are quiet and his hair is trimmed and his manner is most genteel in every way and when the guests are seated he gets to his feet and attracts their attention by tapping on a wineglass with a spoon. Then he speaks to them as follows:

"Friends and neighbors," he says. "I know you are all surprised at being invited here but you may be more surprised when you learn the reason. As most of you are aware, I am as one dead for years. Now I live again. I am going to restore Tucky Farms to all its old turf glory in breeding and racing, and," he says, "I am going to re-establish the Emaleen Salsbury award, with which you are familiar, and carry on again in every way as I am now certain my late beloved wife will wish."

Then he tells them the story of old Em and how Itchky Ironhat cares for her and loves her all these years and how he brings her to the Bluegrass just to see her old home, but of course he does not tell them that Itchky also plans to later drop her in a race at Churchill Downs, as it seems Itchky never mentions the matter to him.

Anyway, Mr. Salsbury says that the return of old Em awakens him as if from a bad dream and he can suddenly see how he is not doing right with respect to his wife's memory and while he is talking a tall old guy who is sitting next to me, and who turns out to be nobody but the guy who directs us to Tucky Farms, says to me like this:

"It is a miracle," he says. "I am his personal physician and I give him up long ago as a hopeless victim of melancholia. In fact, I am always expecting to hear of him dismissing himself from this world entirely. Well," the old guy says, "I always say medical science is not everything."

"My first step toward restoring Tucky Farms," Mr. Salsbury goes on, "is to purchase the old mare Emaleen from Mr. Itchky Ironhat here for the sum of three thousand dollars, which we agree upon this evening as a fair price. I will retire her of course for the rest of her days which I hope will be many."

With this he whips out a check and hands it to Itchky and naturally I am somewhat surprised at the sum mentioned because I figure if old Em is worth three G's War Admiral must be worth a jillion. However,

I am also greatly pleased because I can see where Itchky and I will have a nice taw for the races at Churchill Downs without having to bother about old Em winning one.

"Now," Mr. Salsbury says, "for our guest of honor."

Then two big doors at one end of the banquet hall open wide and there seems to be a little confusion outside and a snorting and a stamping as if a herd of wild horses is coming in and all of a sudden who appears in the doorway with her mane and tail braided with ribbons and her coat all slicked up but old Em and who is leading her in but the large guy who insults her and also Itchky on our arrival at Tucky Farms.

The guests begin applauding and the orchestra plays My Old Kentucky Home and it is a pleasant scene to be sure, but old Em seems quite unhappy about something as the large guy pulls her into the hollow of the horseshoe-shaped table, and the next thing anybody knows, Itchky Ironhat climbs over the table, knocking glasses and dishes every which way and flattens the large guy with a neat left hook in the presence of the best people of the Bluegrass country.

Naturally, this incident causes some comment and many of the guests are slightly shocked and there is considerable criticism of Itchky Ironhat for his lack of table manners. But then it is agreed by one and all present that Itchky is undoubtedly entitled to the Emaleen Salsbury kindness to horses award when I explain that what irks him is the fact that the large guy leads old Em in with a twitch on her lip.

Well, this is about all there is to the story, except that Itchky and I go over to Louisville the next day and remain there awaiting the Kentucky Derby and we have a wonderful time, to be sure, except that we do not seem to be able to win any bets on the horse races at Churchill Downs.

In fact, the day before the Derby, Itchky remarks that the bank roll is now lower than a turtle's vest buttons and when I express surprise that we toss off four G's in such a short period, Itchky says to me like this:

"Oh," he says, "it is not four G's. I send the Emaleen Salsbury kindness-to-horses award of one G to Mousie. I figure she is legally entitled to this for leaving me with Em. Otherwise, we will never get even the three and besides," Itchky says, "I love Mousie. In fact, I invite her to join me here and she agrees to come after I promise I will never as much as think of old Em again.

"By the way," Itchky says, "I call up Tucky Farms this morning and Mr. Salsbury brings old Em into his study and lets her hear my voice over the phone. Mr. Salsbury says she is greatly pleased. I give her your love, but of course not as much of yours as I give her of mine," he says.

"Thanks, Itchky," I say, and at this moment I am somewhat surprised to notice a metal ash tray removing Itchky's derby hat from his head and, gazing about, who do I observe standing in the doorway and now taking dead aim at Itchky with another tray but his ever-loving wife, Mousie.

Johnny One-Eye

THIS CAT I AM going to tell you about is a very small cat, and in fact it is only a few weeks old, consequently it is really nothing but an infant cat. To tell the truth, it is just a kitten.

It is gray and white and very dirty and its fur is all frowzled up, so it is a very miserable-looking little kitten to be sure the day it crawls through a broken basement window into an old house in East Fifty-third Street over near Third Avenue in the city of New York and goes from room to room saying merouw, merouw in a low, weak voice until it comes to a room at the head of the stairs on the second story where a guy by the name of Rudolph is sitting on the floor thinking of not much.

One reason Rudolph is sitting on the floor is because there is nothing else to sit on as this is an empty house that is all boarded up for years and there is no furniture whatever in it, and another reason is that Rudolph has a .38 slug in his side and really does not feel like doing much of anything but sitting. He is wearing a derby hat and his over-coat as it is in the wintertime and very cold and he has an automatic Betsy on the floor beside him and naturally he is surprised quite some when the little kitten comes merouwing into the room and he picks up the Betsy and points it at the door in case anyone he does not wish to see is with the kitten. But when he observes that it is all alone, Rudolph puts the Betsy down again and speaks to the kitten as follows:

"Hello, cat," he says.

Of course the kitten does not say anything in reply except merouw but it walks right up to Rudolph and climbs on his lap, although the chances are if it knows who Rudolph is it will hightail it out of there quicker than anybody can say scat. There is enough daylight coming through the chinks in the boards over the windows for Rudolph to see that the kitten's right eye is in bad shape, and in fact it is bulged half out of its head in a most distressing manner and it is plain to be seen that the sight is gone from this eye. It is also plain to be seen that the injury happens recently and Rudolph gazes at the kitten a while and starts to laugh and says like this:

"Well, cat," he says, "you seem to be scuffed up almost as much as I

am. We make a fine pair of invalids here together. What is your name,
cat?"

Naturally the kitten does not state its name but only goes merouw and
Rudolph says, "All right, I will call you Johnny. Yes," he says, "your
tag is now Johnny One-Eye."

Then he puts the kitten in under his overcoat and pretty soon it gets
warm and starts to purr and Rudolph says:

"Johnny," he says, "I will say one thing for you and that is you are
plenty game to be able to sing when you are hurt as bad as you are. It
is more than I can do."

But Johnny only goes merouw again and keeps on purring and by
and by it falls sound asleep under Rudolph's coat and Rudolph is wishing the pain in his side will let up long enough for him to do the same.

Well, I suppose you are saying to yourself, what is this Rudolph doing in an old empty house with a slug in his side, so I will explain that
the district attorney is responsible for this situation. It seems that the
D.A. appears before the grand jury and tells it that Rudolph is an ex-
tortion guy and a killer and I do not know what all else, though some
of these statements are without doubt a great injustice to Rudolph as,
up to the time the D.A. makes them, Rudolph does not kill anybody
of any consequence in years.

It is true that at one period of his life he is considered a little wild
but this is in the 1920's when everybody else is, too, and for seven or
eight years he is all settled down and is engaged in business organization work, which is very respectable work, indeed. He organizes quite
a number of businesses on a large scale and is doing very good for
himself. He is living quietly in a big hotel all alone, as Rudolph is by
no means a family guy, and he is highly spoken of by one and all when
the D.A. starts poking his nose into his affairs, claiming that Rudolph
has no right to be making money out of the businesses, even though
Rudolph gives these businesses plenty of first-class protection.

In fact, the D.A. claims that Rudolph is nothing but a racket guy
and a great knock to the community, and all this upsets Rudolph no
little when it comes to his ears in a roundabout way. So he calls up his
lawbooks and requests legal advice on the subject and lawbooks says
the best thing he can think of for Rudolph to do is to become as in-
conspicuous as possible right away but to please not mention to anyone
that he gives this advice.

Lawbooks says he understands the D.A. is requesting indictments
and is likely to get them and furthermore that he is rounding up certain parties that Rudolph is once associated with and trying to get them
to remember incidents in Rudolph's early career that may not be en-

tirely to his credit. Lawbooks says he hears that one of these parties is a guy by the name of Cute Freddy and that Freddy makes a deal with the D.A. to lay off of him if he tells everything he knows about Rudolph, so under the circumstances a long journey by Rudolph will be in the interest of everybody concerned.

So Rudolph decides to go on a journey but then he gets to thinking that maybe Freddy will remember a little matter that Rudolph long since dismisses from his mind and does not wish to have recalled again, which is the time he and Freddy do a job on a guy by the name of The Icelander in Troy years ago and he drops around to Freddy's house to remind him to be sure not to remember this.

But it seems that Freddy, who is an important guy in business organization work himself, though in a different part of the city than Rudolph, mistakes the purpose of Rudolph's visit and starts to out with his rooty-toot-toot and in order to protect himself it is necessary for Rudolph to take his Betsy and give Freddy a little tattooing. In fact, Rudolph practically crochets his monogram on Freddy's chest and leaves him exceptionally deceased.

But as Rudolph is departing from the neighborhood, who bobs up but a young guy by the name of Buttsy Fagan, who works for Freddy as a chauffeur and one thing and another, and who is also said to be able to put a slug through a keyhole at forty paces without touching the sides though I suppose it will have to be a pretty good-sized keyhole. Anyway, he takes a long-distance crack at Rudolph as Rudolph is rounding a corner but all Buttsy can see of Rudolph at the moment is a little piece of his left side and this is what Buttsy hits, although no one knows it at the time, except of course Rudolph who just keeps on departing.

Now this incident causes quite a stir in police circles, and the D.A. is very indignant over losing a valuable witness and when they are unable to locate Rudolph at once, a reward of five thousand dollars is offered for information leading to his capture alive or dead and some think they really mean dead. Indeed, it is publicly stated that it is not a good idea for anyone to take any chances with Rudolph as he is known to be armed and is such a character as will be sure to resent being captured, but they do not explain that this is only because Rudolph knows the D.A. wishes to place him in the old rocking chair at Sing Sing and that Rudolph is quite allergic to the idea.

Anyway, the cops go looking for Rudolph in Hot Springs and Miami and every other place except where he is, which is right in New York wandering around town with the slug in his side, knocking at the doors of old friends requesting assistance. But all the old friends do for him is to slam the doors in his face and forget they ever see him, as the D.A. is very tough on parties who assist guys he is looking for, claiming that this is something most illegal called harboring fugitives. Besides Rudolph is never any too popular at best with his old friends as he always plays pretty much of a lone duke and takes the big end of everything for his.

He cannot even consult a doctor about the slug in his side as he knows that nowadays the first thing a doctor will do about a guy with a gunshot wound is to report him to the cops, although Rudolph can remember when there is always a sure-footed doctor around who will consider it a privilege and a pleasure to treat him and keep his trap closed about it. But of course this is in the good old days and Rudolph can see they are gone forever. So he just does the best he can about the slug and goes on wandering here and there and around and about and the blats keep printing his picture and saying, where is Rudolph?

Where he is some of the time is in Central Park trying to get some sleep, but of course even the blats will consider it foolish to go looking for Rudolph there in such cold weather, as he is known as a guy who enjoys his comfort at all times. In fact, it is comfort that Rudolph misses more than anything as the slug is commencing to cause him great pain and naturally the pain turns Rudolph's thoughts to the author of same and he remembers that he once hears somebody say that Buttsy lives over in East Fifty-third Street.

So one night Rudolph decides to look Buttsy up and cause him a little pain in return and he is moseying through Fifty-third when he gets so weak he falls down on the sidewalk in front of the old house and rolls down a short flight of steps that lead from the street level to a little railed-in areaway and ground floor or basement door and before he stops rolling he brings up against the door itself and it creaks open inward as he bumps it. After he lays there a while Rudolph can see that the house is empty and he crawls on inside.

Then when he feels stronger, Rudolph makes his way upstairs because the basement is damp and mice keep trotting back and forth over him and eventually he winds up in the room where Johnny One-Eye finds him the following afternoon and the reason Rudolph settles down in this room is because it commands the stairs. Naturally, this is important to a guy in Rudolph's situation, though after he is sitting there for about fourteen hours before Johnny comes along he can see that he is not going to be much disturbed by traffic. But he considers it a very fine place, indeed, to remain planted until he is able to resume his search for Buttsy.

Well, after a while Johnny One-Eye wakes up and comes from under the coat and looks at Rudolph out of his good eye and Rudolph waggles his fingers and Johnny plays with them catching one finger in his front paws and biting it gently and this pleases Rudolph no little as he never before has any personal experience with a kitten. However, he remembers observing one when he is a boy down in Houston Street, so he takes a piece of paper out of his pocket and makes a little ball of it and rolls it along the floor and Johnny bounces after it very lively indeed. But Rudolph can see that the bad eye is getting worse and finally he says to Johnny like this:

"Johnny," he says, "I guess you must be suffering more than I am. I remember there are some pet shops over on Lexington Avenue not far from here and when it gets good and dark I am going to take you out and see if we can find a cat croaker to do something about your eye. Yes, Johnny," Rudolph says, "I will also get you something to eat. You must be starved."

Johnny One-Eye says merouw to this and keeps on playing with the paper ball but soon it comes on dark outside and inside, too, and in fact, it is so dark inside that Rudolph cannot see his hand before him. Then he puts his Betsy in a side pocket of his overcoat and picks up Johnny and goes downstairs, feeling his way in the dark and easing along a step at a time until he gets to the basement door. Naturally, Rudolph does not wish to strike any matches because he is afraid someone outside may see the light and get nosey.

By moving very slowly, Rudolph finally gets to Lexington Avenue and while he is going along he remembers the time he walks from 125th Street in Harlem down to 110th with six slugs in him and never feels as bad as he does now. He gets to thinking that maybe he is not the guy he used to be, which of course is very true as Rudolph is now forty-odd years of age and is fat around the middle and getting bald, and he also does some thinking about what a pleasure it will be to him to find this Buttsy and cause him the pain he is personally suffering.

There are not many people in the streets and those that are go hurrying along because it is so cold and none of them pay any attention to Rudolph or Johnny One-Eye either, even though Rudolph staggers a little now and then like a guy who is rummed up, although of course it is only weakness. The chances are he is also getting a little feverish and lightheaded because finally he stops a cop who is going along swinging his arms to keep warm and asks him if he knows where there is a pet shop and it is really most indiscreet of such a guy as Rudolph to be interviewing cops. But the cop just points up the street and goes on without looking twice at Rudolph and Rudolph laughs and pokes Johnny with a finger and says:

"No, Johnny One-Eye," he says, "the cop is not a dope for not recognizing Rudolph. Who can figure the hottest guy in forty-eight states to be going along a street with a little cat in his arms? Can you, Johnny?"

Johnny says merouw and pretty soon Rudolph comes to the pet shop the cop points out. Rudolph goes inside and says to the guy like this:

"Are you a cat croaker?" Rudolph says. "Do you know what to do about a little cat that has a hurt eye?"

"I am a kind of a vet," the guy says.

"Then take a glaum at Johnny One-Eye here and see what you can do for him," Rudolph says.

Then he hands Johnny over to the guy and the guy looks at Johnny a while and says:

"Mister," he says, "the best thing I can do for this cat is to put it out of its misery. You better let me give it something right now. It will just go to sleep and never know what happens."

Well, at this, Rudolph grabs Johnny One-Eye out of the guy's hands and puts him under his coat and drops a duke on the Betsy in his pocket as if he is afraid the guy will take Johnny away from him again and he says to the guy like this:

"No, no, no," Rudolph says. "I cannot bear to think of such a thing. What about some kind of an operation? I remember they take a bum lamp out of Joe the Goat at Bellevue one time and he is okay now."

"Nothing will do your cat any good," the guy says. "It is a goner. It will start having fits pretty soon and die sure. What is the idea of trying to save such a cat as this? It is no kind of a cat to begin with. It is just a cat. You can get a million like it for a nickel."

"No," Rudolph says, "this is not just a cat. This is Johnny One-Eye. He is my only friend in the world. He is the only living thing that ever comes pushing up against me warm and friendly and trusts me in my whole life. I feel sorry for him."

"I feel sorry for him, too," the guy says. "I always feel sorry for animals that get hurt and for people."

"I do not feel sorry for people," Rudolph says. "I only feel sorry for Johnny One-Eye. Give me some kind of stuff that Johnny will eat."

"Your cat wants milk," the guy says. "You can get some at the delicatessen store down at the corner. Mister," he says, "you look sick yourself. Can I do anything for you?"

But Rudolph only shakes his head and goes on out and down to the delicatessen joint where he buys a bottle of milk and this transaction reminds him that he is very short in the moo department. In fact, he can find only a five-dollar note in his pockets and he remembers that he has no way of getting any more when this runs out which is a very sad predicament indeed for a guy who is accustomed to plenty of moo at all times.

Then Rudolph returns to the old house and sits down on the floor again and gives Johnny One-Eye some of the milk in his derby hat as he neglects buying something for Johnny to drink out of. But Johnny offers no complaint. He laps up the milk and curls himself into a wad in Rudolph's lap and purrs.

Rudolph takes a swig of the milk himself but it makes him sick for by this time Rudolph is really far from being in the pink of condition. He not only has the pain in his side but he has a heavy cold which he probably catches from lying on the basement floor or maybe sleeping in the park and he is wheezing no little. He commences to worry that he may get too ill to continue looking for Buttsy, as he can see that if it is not for Buttsy he will not be in this situation, suffering the way he is, but on a long journey to some place.

He takes to going off into long stretches of a kind of stupor and every time he comes out of one of these stupors the first thing he does is to look around for Johnny One-Eye and Johnny is always right there either playing with the paper ball or purring in Rudolph's lap. He is a great comfort to Rudolph but after a while Rudolph notices that Johnny seems to be running out of zip and he also notices that he is running out of zip himself especially when he discovers that he is no longer able to get to his feet.

It is along in the late afternoon of the day following the night Rudolph goes out of the house that he hears someone coming up the stairs and naturally he picks up his Betsy and gets ready for action when he also hears a very small voice calling kitty, kitty, kitty, and he realizes that the party that is coming can be nobody but a child. In fact, a minute later a little pretty of maybe six years of age comes into the room all out of breath and says to Rudolph like this:

"How do you do?" she says. "Have you seen my kitty?"

Then she spots Johnny One-Eye in Rudolph's lap and runs over and sits down beside Rudolph and takes Johnny in her arms and at first Rudolph is inclined to resent this and has a notion to give her a good boffing but he is too weak to exert himself in such a manner.

"Who are you?" Rudolph says to the little pretty, "and," he says, "where do you live and how do you get in this house?"

"Why," she says, "I am Elsie, and I live down the street and I am looking everywhere for my kitty for three days and the door is open downstairs and I know kitty likes to go in doors that are open so I came to find her and here she is."

"I guess I forgot to close it last night," Rudolph says. "I seem to be very forgetful lately."

"What is your name?" Elsie asks, "and why are you sitting on the floor in the cold and where are all your chairs? Do you have any little girls like me and do you love them dearly?"

"No," Rudolph says. "By no means and not at all."

"Well," Elsie says, "I think you are a nice man for taking care of my kitty. Do you love kitty?"

"Look," Rudolph says, "his name is not kitty. His name is Johnny One-Eye because he has only one eye."

"I call her kitty," Elsie says. "But," she says, "Johnny One-Eye is a nice name too and if you like it best I will call her Johnny and I will leave her here with you to take care of always and I will come to see her every day. You see," she says, "if I take Johnny home Buttsy will only kick her again."

"Buttsy?" Rudolph says. "Do I hear you say Buttsy? Is his other name Fagan?"

"Why, yes," Elsie says. "Do you know him?"

"No," Rudolph says, "but I hear of him. What is he to you?"

"He is my new daddy," Elsie says. "My other one and my best one is dead and so my mamma makes Buttsy my new one. My mamma says Buttsy is her mistake. He is very mean. He kicks Johnny and hurts her eye and makes her run away. He kicks my mamma too. Buttsy kicks everybody and everything when he is mad and he is always mad."

"He is a louse to kick a little cat," Rudolph says.

"Yes," Elsie says, "that is what Mr. O'Toole says he is for kicking my mamma but my mamma says it is not a nice word and I am never to say it out loud."

"Who is Mr. O'Toole?" Rudolph says.

"He is the policeman," Elsie says. "He lives across the street from us and he is very nice to me. He says Buttsy is the word you say just now, not only for kicking my mamma but for taking her money when she brings it home from work and spending it so she cannot buy me nice things to wear. But do you know what?" Elsie says. "My mamma says some day Buttsy is going far away and then she will buy me lots of things and send me to school and make me a lady."

Then Elsie begins skipping around the room with Johnny One-Eye in her arms and singing I am going to be a lady, I am going to be a lady, until Rudolph has to tell her to pipe down because he is afraid somebody may hear her. And all the time Rudolph is thinking of Buttsy and regretting that he is unable to get on his pins and go out of the house.

"Now I must go home," Elsie says, "because this is a night Buttsy comes in for his supper and I have to be in bed before he gets there so I will not bother him. Buttsy does not like little girls. Buttsy does not like little kittens. Buttsy does not like little anythings. My mamma is afraid of Buttsy and so am I. But," she says, "I will leave Johnny here with you and come back tomorrow to see her."

"Listen, Elsie," Rudolph says, "does Mr. O'Toole come home tonight to his house for his supper, too?"

"Oh, yes," Elsie says. "He comes home every night. Sometimes when there is a night Buttsy is not coming in for his supper my mamma lets me go over to Mr. O'Toole's and I play with his dog Charley but you must never tell Buttsy this because he does not like O'Toole either. But this is a night Buttsy is coming and that is why my mamma tells me to get in early."

Now Rudolph takes an old letter out of his inside pocket and a pencil out of another pocket and he scribbles a few lines on the envelope and stretches himself out on the floor and begins groaning oh, oh, oh, and then he says to Elsie like this:

"Look, Elsie," he says, "you are a smart little kid and you pay strict attention to what I am going to say to you. Do not go to bed tonight until Buttsy gets in. Then," Rudolph says, "you tell him you come in this old house looking for your cat and that you hear somebody groaning like I do just now in the room at the head of the stairs and that you find a guy who says his name is Rudolph lying on the floor so sick he cannot move. Tell him the front door of the basement is open. But," Rudolph says, "you must not tell him that Rudolph tells you to say these things. Do you understand?"

"Oh," Elsie says, "do you want him to come here? He will kick Johnny again if he does."

"He will come here, but he will not kick Johnny," Rudolph says. "He will come here, or I am the worst guesser in the world. Tell him what I look like, Elsie. Maybe he will ask you if you see a gun. Tell him you do not see one. You do not see a gun, do you, Elsie?"

"No," Elsie says, "only the one in your hand when I come in but you put it under your coat. Buttsy has a gun and Mr. O'Toole has a gun but Buttsy says I am never, never to tell anybody about this or he will kick me the way he does my mamma."

"Well," Rudolph says, "you must not remember seeing mine, either. It is a secret between you and me and Johnny One-Eye. Now," he says, "if Buttsy leaves the house to come and see me, as I am pretty sure he will, you run over to Mr. O'Toole's house and give him this note, but do not tell Buttsy or your mamma either about the note. If Buttsy does not leave, it is my hard luck but you give the note to Mr. O'Toole anyway. Now tell me what you are to do, Elsie," Rudolph says, "so I can see if you have got everything correct."

"I am to go on home and wait for Buttsy," she says, "and I am to tell him Rudolph is lying on the floor of this dirty old house with a fat stomach and a big nose making noises and that he is very sick and the basement door is open and there is no gun if he asks me, and when Buttsy comes to see you I am to take this note to Mr. O'Toole but Buttsy and my mamma are not to know I have the note and if Buttsy does not leave I am to give it to Mr. O'Toole anyway and you are to stay here and take care of Johnny my kitten."

"That is swell," Rudolph says. "Now you run along."

So Elsie leaves and Rudolph sits up again against the wall because his side feels easier this way and Johnny One-Eye is in his lap purring very low and the dark comes on until it is blacker inside the room than in the middle of a tunnel and Rudolph feels that he is going into another stupor and he has a tough time fighting it off.

Afterward some of the neighbors claim they remember hearing a shot inside the house and then two more in quick succession and then all is quiet until a little later when Officer O'Toole and half a dozen other cops and an ambulance with a doctor come busting into the street and swarm into the joint with their guns out and their flashlights going. The first thing they find is Buttsy at the foot of the stairs with two bullet wounds close together in his throat, and naturally he is real dead.

Rudolph is still sitting against the wall with what seems to be a small bundle of bloody fur in his lap but which turns out to be what is left of this little cat I am telling you about, although nobody pays any attention to it at first. They are more interested in getting the come-alongs on Rudolph's wrists but before they move him he pulls his clothes aside and shows the doctor where the slug is in his side and the doctor takes one glaum and shakes his head and says:

"Gangrene," he says. "I think you have pneumonia, too, from the way you are blowing."

"I know," Rudolph says. "I know this morning. Not much chance, hey, croaker?"

"Not much," the doctor says.

"Well, cops," Rudolph says, "load me in. I do not suppose you want Johnny, seeing that he is dead."

"Johnny who?" one of the cops says.

"Johnny One-Eye," Rudolph says. "This little cat here in my lap. Buttsy shoots John's good eye out and takes most of his noodle with it.

I never see a more wonderful shot. Well, Johnny is better off but I feel sorry about him as he is my best friend down to the last."

Then he begins to laugh and the cop asks him what tickles him so much and Rudolph says:

"Oh," he says, "I am thinking of the joke on Buttsy. I am positive he will come looking for me, all right, not only because of the little altercation between Cute Freddy and me but because the chances are Buttsy is greatly embarrassed by not tilting me over the first time, as of course he never knows he wings me. Furthermore," Rudolph says, "and this is the best reason of all, Buttsy will realize that if I am in his neighborhood it is by no means a good sign for him, even if he hears I am sick.

"Well," Rudolph says, "I figure that with any kind of a square rattle I will have a better chance of nailing him that he has of nailing me, but that even if he happens to nail me, O'Toole will get my note in time to arrive here and nab Buttsy on the spot with his gun on him. And," Rudolph says, "I know it will be a great pleasure to the D.A. to settle Buttsy for having a gun on him.

"But," Rudolph says, "as soon as I hear Buttsy coming on the sneaksby up the stairs, I can see I am taking all the worst of it because I am now wheezing like a busted valve and you can hear me a block away except when I hold my breath, which is very difficult indeed, considering the way I am already greatly tuckered out. No," Rudolph says, "it does not look any too good for me as Butsy keeps coming up the stairs, as I can tell he is doing by a little faint creak in the boards now and then. I am in no shape to maneuver around the room and pretty soon he will be on the landing and then all he will have to do is to wait there until he hears me which he is bound to do unless I stop breathing altogether. Naturally," Rudolph says, "I do not care to risk a blast in the dark without knowing where he is as something tells me Buttsy is not a guy you can miss in safety.

"Well," Rudolph says "I notice several times before this that in the dark Johnny One-Eye's good glim shines like a big spark, so when I feel Buttsy is about to hit the landing, although of course I cannot see him, I flip Johnny's ball of paper across the room to the wall just opposite the door and tough as he must be feeling Johnny chases after it when he hears it light. I figure Buttsy will hear Johnny playing with the paper and see his eye shining and think it is me and take a pop at it and that his gun flash will give me a crack at him.

"It all works out just like I dope it," Rudolph says, "but," he says, "I never give Buttsy credit for being such a marksman as to be able to hit a cat's eye in the dark. If I know this, maybe I will never stick

Johnny out in front the way I do. It is a good thing I never give Buttsy a second shot. He is a lily. Yes," Rudolph says, "I can remember when I can use a guy like him."

"Buttsy is no account," the cop says. "He is a good riddance. He is the makings of a worse guy than you."

"Well," Rudolph says, "it is a good lesson to him for kicking a little cat."

Then they take Rudolph to a hospital and this is where I see him and piece out this story of Johnny One-Eye, and Officer O'Toole is at Rudolph's bedside keeping guard over him, and I remember that not long before Rudolph chalks out he looks at O'Toole and says to him like this:

"Copper," he says, "there is no chance of them outjuggling the kid on the reward moo, is there?"

"No," O'Toole says, "no chance. I keep the note you send me by Elsie saying she will tell me where you are. It is information leading to your capture just as the reward offer states. Rudolph," he says "it is a nice thing you do for Elsie and her mother, although," he says, "it is not nearly as nice as icing Buttsy for them."

"By the way, copper," Rudolph says, "there is the remainders of a pound note in my pants pocket when I am brought here. I want you to do me a favor. Get it from the desk and buy Elsie another cat and name it Johnny, will you?"

"Sure," O'Toole says. "Anything else?"

"Yes," Rudolph says, "be sure it has two good eyes."

Broadway Incident

ONE NIGHT Ambrose Hammer, the newspaper scribe, comes looking for me on Broadway and he insists that I partake of dinner with him at the Canary Club, stating that he wishes to talk to me. Naturally, I know that Ambrose must be in love again, and when he is in love he always wishes to have somebody around to listen to him tell about how much he is in love and about the way he is suffering, because Ambrose is such a guy as must have his suffering with his love. I know him when he first shows up on Broadway, which is a matter of maybe eight or ten years ago, but in all this time I seldom see him when he is not in love and suffering and especially suffering, and the reason he suffers is because he generally falls in love with some beautiful who does not care two snaps of her fingers about him and sometimes not even one snap.

In fact, it is the consensus of opinion along Broadway that Ambrose is always very careful to pick a beautiful who does not care any snaps of her fingers whatever about him because if he finds one who does care these snaps there will be not reason for him to suffer. Personally I consider Ambrose's love affairs a great bore but as the Canary Club is a very high-class gaff where the food department is really above par, I am pleased to go with him.

So there we are sitting on a leather settee against the wall in the Canary Club and I am juggling a big thick sirloin steak smothered in onions while Ambrose is telling me how much he loves a beautiful by the name of Hilda Hiffenbrower and how he is wishing he can marry her and live happily ever afterwards, but he is unable to complete this transaction because there is an ever-loving husband by the name of Herbert in the background from whom Hilda is separated but not divorced. And the way Ambrose tells it, Hilda cannot get a divorce because Herbert is just naturally a stinker and does not wish to see her happy with anybody else and will not let her have same.

Well, I happen to know Hilda better than Ambrose does. To tell the truth, I know her when her name is Mame something and she is dealing them off her arm in a little eating gaff on Seventh Avenue, which is before she goes in show business and changes her name to Hilda, and

I also know that the real reason Herbert will not give her this divorce is because she wants eight gallons of his heart's blood and both legs in the divorce settlement, but as Herbert has a good business head he is by no means agreeable to these terms, though I hear he is willing to compromise on one leg to get rid of Hilda.

Furthermore, I know that Hilda is never very sympathetic towards marriage in any manner, shape or form, as she has a few other husbands prior to this and dismisses them before they are in office very long, and I am willing to bet that she has an ice-cream cone where her heart is supposed to be. But of course I do not feel disposed to mention this matter to Ambrose Hammer, especially while I am enjoying his steak.

So I just go on eating and listening and Ambrose seems about ready to burst into tears as he tells me about his suffering because of his love for Hilda, when who comes into the Canary Club all dressed up in white tie and tails but a guy by the name of Brogan Wilmington, who is what is called a playwright by trade, a playwright being a guy who writes plays which are put on the stage for people to see.

As Ambrose is a dramatic critic, it is his duty to go and view these plays and to tell the readers of the blat for which he works what he thinks of them, and it seems that he tells them that the play written by this Brogan Wilmington is a twenty-two-karat smeller. In fact, it seems that Ambrose tells them it is without doubt the worst case of dramatic halitosis in the history of civilization and it is plain to be seen that Brogan Wilmington is somewhat vexed as he approaches our table and addresses Ambrose as follows:

"Ah," he says, "here you are."

"Yes," Ambrose says, "here I am, indeed."

"You do not care for my play?" Brogan Wilmington says.

"No," Ambrose says, "I loathe and despise it."

"Well," Brogan Wilmington says, "take this."

Then he lets go with his right and grazes Ambrose Hammer's chin but in doing so, Brogan Wilmington's coattails swing out behind him and across a portion of lobster Newburg that a beautiful at the next table is enjoying and in fact the swinging coattails wipe about half the portion off the plate onto the floor.

Before Brogan Wilmington can recover his balance, the beautiful picks up what is left of her lobster Newburg, plate and all, and clops Brogan on the pimple with it and knocks him plumb out onto the dance floor where many parties, male and female, are doing the rumba with great zest.

Naturally, Ambrose is slightly surprised at this incident, but as he is a gentleman at all times, even if he is a dramatic critic, he turns to the beautiful and says to her like this:

"Miss," Ambrose says, "or madam, I am obliged to you. Waiter," he says "bring this lovely creature another dash of lobster Newburg and put it on my check."

Then he resumes his conversation with me and thinks no more of the matter, because of course it is by no means a novelty for Ambrose Hammer to have playwrights throw punches at him, although generally it is actors and sometimes producers. In the meantime, the parties out on the dance floor find they cannot rumba with any convenience unless Brogan Wilmington is removed from their space, so a couple of waiters pick Brogan up and carry him away and Ambrose notices that the beautiful who slugs Brogan with the lobster Newburg now seems to be crying.

"Miss," Ambrose says, "or madam, dry your tears. Your fresh portion of lobster Newburg will be along presently."

"Oh," she says, "I am not crying about the loss of my lobster Newburg. I am crying because in my agitation I spill the little bottle of cyanide of potassium I bring in here with me and now I cannot commit suicide. Look at it all over my bag."

"Well," Ambrose says, "I am sorry, but I do not approve of anybody committing suicide in the Canary Club. It is owned by a friend of mine by the name of Joe Gloze and every Christmas he sends me a dozen expensive ties, besides permitting me to free-load here at will. A suicide in his club will be bad publicity for him. It may get around that death ensues because of the cooking. However, miss," Ambrose says, "or madam, if you are bound and determined to commit this suicide you may walk around the corner to a deadfall called El Parcheeso, which is Joe's rival, and I will follow you and observe your action in all its sad details and it will be a fine story for me."

Well, the beautiful seems to be thinking this proposition over and Ambrose is so occupied watching her think that he loses the thread of his story of his love for Hilda and seems to forget some of his suffering, too, and finally the beautiful turns to him and says:

"Sir, do you rumba?"

"Do I rumba?" Ambrose says. "Miss," he says, "or madam, you now behold the best rumba dancer in the Western Hemisphere, bar Havana. There is one guy there who can defeat me, although," Ambrose says, "it is a photo finish. Let us put it on."

So they get out on the floor and rumba quite a while and after that they samba some and then they conga and Ambrose can see that the beautiful has a very liberal education, indeed, along these lines. In fact, he can see that she rumbas and sambas and congas much better than any married beautiful should, because between a rumba and a samba she informs him that her name is Mrs. Brumby News and that she is the ever-loving wife of a doctor by the same name without the Mrs., who is much older than she is.

Finally they get all tuckered out from dancing and are sitting at the table talking of this and that and one thing and another, and I can tell from Mrs. News' conversation that she is far from being as intellectual as Professor Einstein and to tell the truth she does not seem right bright and Ambrose Hammer probably notices the same thing, but when it comes to beautifuls, Ambrose does not care if they are short fifteen letters reciting the alphabet. So he is really enjoying his chat with her and presently he asks her why she ever figures on knocking herself off and she relates a somewhat surprising story.

She states that her husband is always too busy trying to find out what is wrong with his patients to pay much attention to her and as she has no children but only a chow dog by the name of Pepe to occupy her time and as her maid can look after the dog better than she can, she takes to visiting this same Canary Club and similar traps seeking diversion.

She says that on one of these afternoons some months back she meets a fat blonde by the name of Mrs. Bidkar and they become great friends as they both like to gab and sip cocktails and sometimes pick up rumbas with stray guys as beautifuls will do when they are running around loose although it seems from what Mrs. News says that Mrs. Bidkar is by no means a beautiful but is really nothing but a bundle and a little smooth on the tooth in the matter of age. However, she is good company and Mrs. News says they find they have much in common including the cocktails and the rumbas.

It seems they both also like to play bridge and Mrs. Bidkar invites Mrs. News to her apartment, stating that she has several friends in every so often to play this bridge. So Mrs. News goes to the apartment which is in East Fifty-seventh Street and very nice, at that, and she discovers that the friends are all young and married beautifuls like herself. There are three of them and one has the name of Mrs. Smythe and another the name of Mrs. Brown but what the third one's name is Mrs. News says she does not remember as it is a long name, and anyway this one does not seem as well acquainted with Mrs. Bidkar as the others and does not have much to say.

Anyway, from now on they all play bridge in Mrs. Bidkar's apartment three or four afternoons a week and sip plenty of cocktails in between hands and a pleasant time is had by one and all, according

Broadway Incident

to Mrs. News. Then one day after playing bridge they are sitting around working on the cocktails and talking of different matters, when it comes out that they are all unhappy in their married lives. In fact, it comes out that they all hate their husbands no little and wish to be shed of them and Mrs. News states that the one who wishes this the most is Mrs. Bidkar.

Mrs. News says that Mrs. Bidkar declares she wishes her Olaf is dead so she can collect his life insurance and lead her own life in her own way, and then she starts asking the others if their husbands carry such insurance and it seems they do and finally Mrs. Bidkar says as if in a joke that it will be a good idea if they dispose of their husbands and put the insurance moo in a common pool. She says one may put more in the jackpot than another, but since it will scarcely be possible for them to dispose of five different husbands all at once the pool will give each a drawing account after it starts until the whole deal is carried out.

Well, it seems from the way Mrs. News tells it that Mrs. Bidkar keeps making quite a joke about the idea and the others join in, especially as they keep pecking away at the cocktails, and after a while it is a big laugh all the way around. Then Mrs. Bidkar suggests that to make it more of a joke they deal out the cards to see which is to be the first to dispose of her husband and the one who draws the nine of diamonds is to be it, and Mrs. News gets the nine.

So the party breaks up with everybody still laughing and joking with Mrs. News over winning the prize and she is laughing, too, but as she is leaving Mrs. Bidkar calls her back and hands her a little vial which she states contains cyanide of potassium and whispers that after Mrs. News thinks it over she will see that many a true word is said in jest and that perhaps she will wish to use the cyanide where it will do the most good. Then Mrs. News says before she can say aye, yes, or no, Mrs. Bidkar pushes her out the door and closes it, still laughing.

"So," Mrs. News says, "I come here to the Canary Club and I get to thinking what a great sin I am guilty of in participating in such a joke, even though my husband is really nothing but an old curmudgeon and is related to Clarence Closeclutch when it comes to money, and I become so remorseful that I decide to take the cyanide myself when I am interrupted by the good-looking gentleman striking you. By the way," she says, "do you know if he rumbas?"

Now this story seems rather interesting to me and I am expecting Ambrose Hammer to become greatly excited by it, because it sounds like a crime mystery and next to love Ambrose Hammer's greatest hobby is crime mystery. He often vexes the cops quite some by poking his nose into their investigations and trying to figure out who does what. To tell the truth, Ambrose's interest is sometimes so divided between love and crime that it is hard to tell whether he wishes to be Clark Gable or Sherlock Holmes, though the chances are he wishes to be both. But I can see that Ambrose is half asleep and when Mrs. News concludes her tale he speaks to her quite severely as follows:

"Madam," he says, "of course you are a victim of a gag. However," he says, "you are such a swell rumba dancer I will overlook your wasting my time with such a dreary recital. Let us shake it up a little more on the dance floor and then I must return to my office and write a Sunday article advising the sanitation authorities to suppress Brogan Wilmington's play before it contaminates the entire community. He is the guy you flatten with your lobster Newburg. He is not good-looking, either, and he cannot rumba a lick. I forget to mention it before." Ambrose says, "but I am Ambrose Hammer."

Mrs. News does not seem to know the name and this really cuts Ambrose deeply, so he is not sorry to see her depart. Then he goes to his office and I go home to bed, and the chances are neither of us will give the incident another thought if a guy by the name of Dr. Brumby News does not happen to drop dead in the Canary Club one night while in the act of committing the rumba with his wife.

Ambrose and I are sitting in Mindy's restaurant on Broadway when he reads an item in an early edition of a morning blat about this, and as Ambrose has a good memory for names he calls my attention to the item and states that the wife in question is undoubtedly the beautiful who tells us the unusual story.

"My goodness, Ambrose," I say, "do you suppose she gives the guy the business after all?"

"No," Ambrose says, "such an idea is foolish. It says here he undoubtedly dies of heart disease. He is sixty-three years old and at this age the price is logically thirty to one that a doctor will die of heart disease. Of course," Ambrose says, "if it is known that a doctor of sixty-three is engaging in the rumba, the price is one hundred to one."

"But Ambrose," I say, "maybe she knows the old guy's heart is weak and gets him to rumba figuring that it will belt him out quicker than cyanide."

"Well," Ambrose says, "it is a theory, of course, but I do not think there is anything in it. I think maybe she feels so sorry for her wicked thoughts about him that she tries to be nice to him and gets him to go out stepping with her, but with no sinister motives whatever. However, let us give this no further consideration. Doctors die of heart disease every day. Do I tell you that I see Hilda last night and that she believes she is nearer a settlement with Hiffenbrower? She is breakfasting with him at his hotel almost every morning and feels that he is softening up. Ah," Ambrose says, "how I long for the hour I can take her in my arms and call her my own dear little wife."

I am less interested in Hilda than ever at this moment, but I am compelled to listen for two hours to Ambrose tell about his love for her and about his suffering and I make up my mind to give him a miss until he gets over this one. Then about a week later he sends for me to come to his office saying he wishes me to go with him to see a new play, and while I am there waiting for Ambrose to finish some work, who comes in but Mrs. News. She is all in mourning and as soon as she sees Ambrose she begins to cry and she says to him like this:

"Oh Mr. Hammer," she says, "I do not kill my husband."

"Why," Ambrose says, "certainly not. By no means and not at all. But," Ambrose says, "it is most injudicious of you to permit him to rumba at his age."

"It is his own desire," Mrs. News says. "It is his method of punishing me for being late for dinner a few times. He is the most frightful rumba dancer that ever lives and he knows it is torture for me to dance with a bad rumba dancer, so he takes me out and rumbas me into a state approaching nervous exhaustion before he keels over himself. Mr. Hammer, I do not like to speak ill of the dead but my late husband really has a mean disposition. But," she says, "I do not kill him."

"Nobody says you do," Ambrose says.

"Yes," Mrs. News says, "somebody does. Do you remember me telling you about drawing the cards at Mrs. Bidkar's apartment to see who is to dispose of her husband first?"

"Oh," Ambrose says, "you mean the little joke they play on you? Yes," he says, "I remember."

"Well," Mrs. News says, "Mrs. Bidkar now says it is never a joke at all. She says it is all in earnest and claims I know it is all the time. She is around to see me last night and says I undoubtedly give my husband poison and that I must turn his insurance money in to the pool when I collect it. There is quite a lot of it. Over two hundred thousand dollars, Mr. Hammer."

"Look," Ambrose says, "this is just another of Mrs. Bidkar's little jokes. She seems to have quite a sense of humor."

"No," Mrs. News says, "it is no joke. She is very serious. She says unless I turn in the money she will expose me to the world and there will be a horrible scandal and I will go to jail and not be able to collect a cent of the insurance money. She just laughs when I tell her I spill the cyanide she gives me and says if I do, I probably get more poison somewhere else and use it and that she and the others are entitled to their share of the money just the same because she furnishes the idea. Mr. Hammer, you must remember seeing me spill the cyanide."

"Mrs. N.," Ambrose says, "does anyone tell you yet that you make a lovely widow? But no matter," he says. "Yes, I remember hearing you say you spill something but I do not look to see. Are you positive you do not do as Mrs. Bidkar suggests and get some other destructive substance and slip it to your husband by accident?"

Well, at this Mrs. News begins crying very loudly indeed, and Ambrose has to spend some time soothing her and I wish to state that when it comes to soothing a beautiful there are few better soothers than Ambrose Hammer on the island of Manhattan. Then when he gets her quieted down he says to her like this:

"Now," Ambrose says, "just leave everything to me. I am commencing to sniff something here. But," he says, "in the meantime remain friendly with Mrs. Bidkar. Let her think you are commencing to see things her own way. Maybe she will hold another drawing."

"Oh," Mrs. News says, "she has. She tells me the one whose name I cannot remember draws the nine of diamonds only the day before my husband departs this life. It is a long name with a kind of a foreign sound. Mrs. Bidkar says she has a lot of confidence in this one just on her looks although she does not know her intimately. I only wish I can think of the name. I have a dreadful time thinking of names. I remember yours when I happen to see it over an article in the paper the other day about Brogan Wilmington's play and then I remember, too that you mention that he is the good-looking gentleman in the Canary Club the night we meet. Mr. Hammer," she says, "you say some very mean things about his play."

"Well," Ambrose says, "I do not know about the propriety of a beautiful in widow's weeds attending the theater, but I happen to have a couple of skulls to Wilmington's play right here in my desk and I will give them to you and you can go and see for yourself that it really is most distressing. Probably you will see Wilmington himself standing in the lobby taking bows for no reason whatever, and I hope and trust you take another close glaum at him and you will see that he is not good-looking. And," Ambrose says, "I tell you once more he is a total bust at the rumba."

"Why," Mrs. News says, "I will be delighted to see his play. It may help break the monotony of being a widow, which is quite monotonous to be sure, even after a very short time. I almost miss poor Brummy in spite of his narrow views on punctuality for dinner, but please do something about Mrs. Bidkar."

Then she leaves us, and Ambrose and I gaze at the new play which

seems to me to be all right but which Ambrose says is a great insult to
the theater because Ambrose is very hard to please about plays, and
it is some days before I see him again. Naturally, I ask him if he does
anything about Mrs. News' case and Ambrose says:

"Yes," he says, "I prod around in it to some extent and I find it is
an attempt at blackmail, just as I suspect. It is a most ingenious setup,
at that. I look up Mrs. Smythe and Mrs. Brown and one is a chorus
gorgeous by the name of Beerbaum and the other is a clerk in a Broadway lingerie shop by the name of Cooney. Neither of them is ever
married as far as anybody knows. Mrs. Bidkar is originally out of Chicago and has a husband, but," Ambrose says, "nobody seems to know
who he is or where he is."

"But Ambrose," I say, "how can Mrs. Smythe and Mrs. Brown enter
into a deal to dispose of their husbands as Mrs. News states when they
have no husbands? Is this entirely honest?"

"Why," Ambrose says, "they are stooges. You see," he says, "Mrs.
Bidkar has a little moo and she rents this apartment and uses these
two as trimming. Her idea is to pick up dumb beautifuls such as Mrs.
News who are not too happy with their husbands and get them wedged
in on such a situation as develops here, and the other two help out."

"Ambrose," I say, "do you mean to tell me this Mrs. Bidkar is so
heartless as to plan to have these beautifuls she picks up chill their
husbands?"

"No," Ambrose says. "This is not her plan at all. She has no idea they
will actually do such a thing. But she does figure to maneuver them
into entering into the spirit of what she calls a joke just as she does
Mrs. News, the cocktails helping out no little. It all sounds very harmless to the married beautiful until Mrs. Bidkar comes around afterwards and threatens to tell the husband that his wife is a party to a
scheme of this nature. Naturally," Ambrose says, "such a wife is very
eager to settle with Mrs. Bidkar for whatever she can dig up."

"Why, Ambrose," I say, "it is nothing but a shakedown, which is very
old-fashioned stuff."

"Yes," Ambrose says, "it is a shake, all right. And," he says, "it
makes me very sad to learn from Mrs. Smythe and Mrs. Brown, who
work with Mrs. Bidkar in other cities, that many husbands must be
willing to believe anything of their ever-lovings, even murder, and that
the wives know it, because they always settle promptly with Mrs.
Bidkar. She is a smart old broad. It is a pity she is so nefarious. Mrs.
Smythe and Mrs. Brown are very grateful when they find I am not
going to put them in jail," Ambrose says. "I have their phone numbers."

"Well," I say, "now there is nothing left to be done but to clap this Mrs. Bidkar in the pokey and inform Mrs. News that she can quit worrying. Why, goodness gracious, Ambrose," I say, "Mrs. Bidkar is really a great menace to be at large in a community. She ought to be filed away for life."

"Yes," Ambrose says, "what you say is quite true, but if we put her in jail it will all come out in the blats and Mrs. News cannot afford such notoriety. It may bother her in collecting her insurance. Let us go and see Mrs. Bidkar and explain to her that the best thing she can do is to hit the grit out of town."

So we get in a taxicab and go to an address in East Fifty-seventh Street that turns out to be a high-toned apartment house, and Ambrose stakes the elevator guy to a deuce and the guy takes us up to the sixth floor without going to the trouble of announcing us on the house phone first and points to a door. Then Ambrose pushes the buzzer and presently a female character appears and gazes at us in a most hospitable manner.

She is short and is wearing a negligee that permits her to widen out freely all the way around and she has straw-colored hair and a large smile and while she is by no means a beautiful, still you cannot say she is a crow. In fact, I am somewhat surprised when Ambrose asks her if she is Mrs. Bidkar and she states that she is, as I am expecting a genuine old komoppo. We enter an elegantly furnished living room and she asks our business, and Ambrose says:

"Well, Mrs. B.," he says, "you almost get a good break when old Doc News drops dead after you stake his wife to the poison because it looks as if you have her where she can never wiggle off no matter what she says. But," Ambrose says "my friend Mrs. News is cute enough to seek my advice and counsel."

"Yes?" Mrs. Bidkar says. "And who are you?"

"Never mind," Ambrose says. "I am here to tell you that if you are present in these parts tomorrow morning you will find yourself in the canneroo."

At this, Mrs. Bidkar stops smiling and a very hard look indeed comes into her eyes and she says:

"Listen, guy, whoever you are," she says. "If you are a friend of Mrs. News you will tell her to get it on the line at once and save herself trouble. I may go to jail," she says, "but so will she and I can stand it better than she can because I am there before, and anyway the charge against me will not be poisoning my husband."

"Mrs. Bidkar," Ambrose says, "you know Mrs. News does not poison her husband."

"No?" Mrs. Bidkar says. "Who does, then? They cannot pin it on me because Mrs. News herself claims she spills the stuff I give her and which she thinks is cyanide but which is really nothing but water, so she must get something else to do the job. Her own statement lets me out. But if you take her story that she does not poison him at all, you must be dumber than she is, although," Mrs. Bidkar says, "I will never believe such a thing is possible."

"Water, hey?" Ambrose says. "Well, Mrs. Bidkar," he says, "I can see that you really believe Mrs. News is guilty of this poisoning so I will have to show you something. I have here," he says, "a little document from the medical examiner stating that an autopsy on the remains of the late Dr. Brumby News discloses no sign of poison whatever. You can confirm this by calling up the district attorney, who has the autopsy performed and who is still very angry at me for putting him to a lot of bother for nothing," Ambrose says.

"An autopsy?" Mrs. Bidkar says, taking the paper and reading it. "I see. Tomorrow morning, do you say? Well," she says, "you need not mind looking in again as I will be absent. Good day," she says.

Then Ambrose and I take our departure and when we are going along the street I suddenly think of something and I say to him like this:

"An autopsy, Ambrose?" I say. "Why, such an action indicates that you never entirely believe Mrs. News yourself, does it not?"

"Oh," Ambrose says, "I believe her, all right, but I always consider it a sound policy to look a little bit behind a beautiful's word on any proposition. Besides, cyanide has an odor and I do not remember noticing such an odor in the Canary Club and this makes me wonder somewhat about Mrs. News when I begin looking the situation over. But," Ambrose says, "of course Mrs. Bidkar clears this point up. Do you know what I am wondering right this minute? I am wondering what ever happens to Mrs. Bidkar's husband," he says.

Well, personally I do not consider this a matter worth thinking about, so I leave Ambrose at a corner and I do not see him again for weeks when we get together in the Canary Club for another dinner, and while we are sitting there who comes past our table without her mourning and looking very gorgeous indeed but Mrs. Brumby News.

When she sees Ambrose she stops and gives him a large good evening and Ambrose invites her to sit down and she does same but she states that she is on a meet with a friend and cannot remain with us long. She sits there chatting with Ambrose about this and that and he is so attentive that it reminds me of something and I say to him like this:

"Ambrose," I say, "I understand the course of your true love with

Hilda may soon be smoothed out. I hear Hiffenbrower is in a hospital and may not be with us much longer. Well," I say, "let me be the first to congratulate you."

Now Mrs. News looks up and says:

"Hilda?" she says. "Hiffenbrower?" she says. "Why, this is the name of the other girl at Mrs. Bidkar's I am never able to remember. Yes, Hilda Hiffenbrower."

Naturally, I am greatly surprised and I gaze at Ambrose and he nods and says:

"Yes," he says, "I know it from the day I begin my investigation, but," he says, "I am too greatly shocked and pained to mention the matter. She becomes acquainted with Mrs. Bidkar the same way Mrs. News does. Hilda is always quick to learn and personally I feel that Hiffenbrower makes a mistake in not canceling her out as the beneficiary of his insurance when they first separate. It is unfair to place great temptation before any beautiful and," Ambrose says, "especially Hilda.

"Well," he says, "Hiffenbrower is suffering from prolonged doses of powdered glass in his cereal but you are wrong about his condition. They are laying even money he beats it although of course his digestion may be slightly impaired. I hear the cops trace Hilda to South America. Oh, well," Ambrose says, "I am through with the beautifuls forever Mrs. N., do you care to push a rumba around with me?"

"No," Mrs. News says, "here comes my friend. I think you meet him before. In fact," she says, "you are responsible for us getting together by sending me to the theater on the free tickets that night."

And who is the friend but this Brogan Wilmington, the playwright, whose play is now running along quite successfully and making plenty of beesom in spite of what Ambrose states about it, and as Mrs. News gets up from the table to join him, Brogan Wilmington gazes at Ambrose and says to him like this:

"Bah," Brogan Wilmington says.

"Bah right back to you," Ambrose says, and then he begins going through his pockets looking for something.

"Now where do I put those phone numbers of Mrs. Smythe and Mrs. Brown?" Ambrose says.

The Idyll of Miss Sarah Brown

OF ALL THE high players this country ever sees, there is no doubt but that the guy they call The Sky is the highest. In fact, the reason he is called The Sky is because he goes so high when it comes to betting on any proposition whatever. He will bet all he has, and nobody can bet any more than this.

His right name is Obadiah Masterson, and he is originally out of a little town in southern Colorado where he learns to shoot craps, and play cards and one thing and another, and where his old man is a very well-known citizen, and something of a sport himself. In fact, The Sky tells me that when he finally cleans up all the loose scratch around his home town and decides he needs more room, his old man has a little private talk with him and says to him like this:

"Son," the old guy says, "you are now going out into the wide, wide world to make your own way, and it is a very good thing to do, as there are no more opportunities for you in this burg. I am only sorry," he says, "that I am not able to bank-roll you to a very large start, but," he says, "not having any potatoes to give you, I am now going to stake you to some very valuable advice, which I personally collect in my years of experience around and about, and I hope and trust you will always bear this advice in mind.

"Son," the old guy says, "no matter how far you travel, or how smart you get, always remember this: Some day, somewhere," he says, "a guy is going to come to you and show you a nice brand-new deck of cards on which the seal is never broken, and this guy is going to offer to bet you that the jack of spades will jump out of this deck and squirt cider in your ear. But, son," the old guy says, "do not bet him, for as sure as you do you are going to get an ear full of cider."

Well, The Sky remembers what his old man says, and he is always very cautious about betting on such propositions as the jack of spades jumping out of a sealed deck of cards and squirting cider in his ear, and so he makes few mistakes as he goes along. In fact, the only real mistake The Sky makes is when he hits St. Louis after leaving his old home town, and loses all his potatoes betting a guy St. Louis is the biggest town in the world.

Now of course this is before The Sky ever sees any bigger towns, and he is never much of a hand for reading up on matters such as this. In fact, the only reading The Sky ever does as he goes along through life is in these Gideon Bibles such as he finds in the hotel rooms where he lives, for The Sky never lives anywhere else but in hotel rooms for years.

He tells me that he reads many items of great interest in these Gideon Bibles, and furthermore The Sky says that several times these Gideon Bibles keep him from getting out of line such as the time he finds himself pretty much frozen-in over in Cincinnati, what with owing everybody in town except maybe the mayor from playing games of chance of one kind and another.

Well, The Sky says he sees no way of meeting these obligations and he is figuring the only thing he can do is to take a run-out powder, when he happens to read in one of these Gideon Bibles where it says like this:

"Better is it," the Gideon Bible says, "that thou shouldest not vow, than that thou shouldest vow and not pay."

Well, The Sky says he can see that there is no doubt whatever but that this means a guy shall not welsh, so he remains in Cincinnati until he manages to wiggle himself out of the situation, and from that day to this, The Sky never thinks of welshing.

He is maybe thirty years old, and is a tall guy with a round kisser, and big blue eyes, and he always looks as innocent as a little baby. But The Sky is by no means as innocent as he looks. In fact, The Sky is smarter than three Philadelphia lawyers, which makes him very smart, indeed, and he is well established as a high player in New Orleans, and Chicago, and Los Angeles, and wherever else there is any action in the way of card-playing or crap-shooting, or horse-racing, or betting on the baseball games, for The Sky is always moving around the country following the action.

But while The Sky will bet on anything whatever, he is more of a short-card player and a crap shooter than anything else, and furthermore he is a great hand for propositions, such as are always coming up among citizens who follow games of chance for a living. Many citizens prefer betting on propositions to anything you can think of, because they figure a proposition gives them a chance to out-smart somebody, and in fact I know citizens who will sit up all night making up propositions to offer other citizens the next day.

A proposition may be only a problem in cards, such as what is the price against a guy getting aces back-to-back, or how often a pair of deuces will win a hand in stud, and then again it may be some very daffy proposition, indeed, although the daffier any proposition seems to be, the more some citizens like it. And no one ever sees The Sky when he does not have some proposition of his own.

The first time he ever shows up around this town, he goes to a baseball game at the Polo Grounds with several prominent citizens, and while he is at the ball game, he buys himself a sack of Harry Stevens' peanuts, which he dumps in a side pocket of his coat. He is eating these peanuts all through the game, and after the game is over and he is walking across the field with the citizens he says to them like this:

"What price," The Sky says, "I cannot throw a peanut from second base to the home plate?"

Well, everybody knows that a peanut is too light for anybody to throw it this far, so Big Nig, the crap shooter, who always likes to have a little the best of it running for him, speaks as follows:

"You can have 3 to 1 from me, stranger," Big Nig says.

"Two C's against six," The Sky says, and then he stands on second base, and takes a peanut out of his pocket, and not only whips it to the home plate, but on into the lap of a fat guy who is still sitting in the grand stand putting the zing on Bill Terry for not taking Walker out of the box when Walker is getting a pasting from the other club.

Well, naturally, this is a most astonishing throw, indeed, but afterwards it comes out that The Sky throws a peanut loaded with lead, and of course it is not one of Harry Stevens' peanuts either, as Harry is not selling peanuts full of lead at a dime a bag, with the price of lead what it is.

It is only a few nights after this that The Sky states another most unusual proposition to a group of citizens sitting in Mindy's restaurant when he offers to bet a C note that he can go down into Mindy's cellar and catch a live rat with his bare hands and everybody is greatly astonished when Mindy himself steps up and takes the bet, for ordinarily Mindy will not bet you a nickel he is alive.

But it seems that Mindy knows that The Sky plants a tame rat in the cellar, and this rat knows The Sky and loves him dearly, and will let him catch it any time he wishes, and it also seems that Mindy knows that one of his dish washers happens upon this rat, and not knowing it is tame, knocks it flatter than a pancake. So when The Sky goes down into the cellar and starts trying to catch a rat with his bare hands, he is greatly surprised how inhospitable the rat turns out to be, because it is one of Mindy's personal rats, and Mindy is around afterwards saying he will lay plenty of 7 to 5 against even Strangler Lewis being able to catch one of his rats with his bare hands or with boxing gloves on.

I am only telling you all this to show you what a smart guy The Sky is, and I am only sorry I do not have time to tell you about many other very remarkable propositions that he thinks up outside of his regular business.

It is well-known to one and all that he is very honest in every respect, and that he hates and despises cheaters at cards, or dice, and furthermore The Sky never wishes to play with any the best of it himself, or anyway not much. He will never take the inside of any situation, as many gamblers love to do, such as owning a gambling house, and having the percentage run for him instead of against him, for always The Sky is strictly a player, because he says he will never care to settle down in one spot long enough to become the owner of anything.

In fact, in all the years The Sky is drifting around the country, nobody ever knows him to own anything except maybe a bank roll, and when he comes to Broadway the last time, which is the time I am now speaking of, he has a hundred G's in cash money, and an extra suit of clothes, and this is all he has in the world. He never owns such a thing as a house, or an automobile, or a piece of jewelry. He never owns a watch, because The Sky says time means nothing to him.

Of course some guys will figure a hundred G's comes under the head of owning something, but as far as The Sky is concerned, money is nothing but just something for him to play with and the dollars may as well be doughnuts as far as value goes with him. The only time The Sky ever thinks of money as money is when he is broke, and the only way he can tell he is broke is when he reaches into his pocket and finds nothing there but his fingers.

Then it is necessary for The Sky to go out and dig up some fresh scratch somewhere, and when it comes to digging up scratch, The Sky is practically supernatural. He can get more potatoes on the strength of a telegram to some place or other than John D. Rockefeller can get on collateral, for everybody knows The Sky's word is as good as wheat in the bin.

Now one Sunday evening The Sky is walking along Broadway, and at the corner of Forty-ninth Street he comes upon a little bunch of mission workers who are holding a religious meeting, such as mission workers love to do of a Sunday evening, the idea being that they may round up a few sinners here and there although personally I always claim the mission workers come out too early to catch any sinners on this part of Broadway. At such an hour the sinners are still in bed resting up from their sinning of the night before, so they will be in good shape for more sinning a little later on.

There are only four of these mission workers, and two of them are old guys, and one is an old doll, while the other is a young doll who is tootling on a cornet. And after a couple of ganders at this young doll,

The Sky is a goner, for this is one of the most beautiful young dolls anybody ever sees on Broadway, and especially as a mission worker. Her name is Miss Sarah Brown.

She is tall, and thin, and has a first-class shape, and her hair is a light brown, going on blond, and her eyes are like I do not know what, except that they are one-hundred-per-cent eyes in every respect. Furthermore, she is not a bad cornet player, if you like cornet players, although at this spot on Broadway she has to play against a scat band in a chop-suey joint near by, and this is tough competition, although at that many citizens believe Miss Sarah Brown will win by a large score if she only gets a little more support from one of the old guys with her who has a big bass drum, but does not pound it hearty enough.

Well, The Sky stands there listening to Miss Sarah Brown tootling on the cornet for quite a spell, and then he hears her make a speech in which she puts the blast on sin very good, and boosts religion quite some, and says if there are any souls around that need saving the owners of same may step forward at once. But no one steps forward, so The Sky comes over to Mindy's restaurant where many citizens are congregated, and starts telling us about Miss Sarah Brown. But of course we already know about Miss Sarah Brown, because she is so beautiful, and so good.

Furthermore, everybody feels somewhat sorry for Miss Sarah Brown, for while she is always tootling the cornet, and making speeches, and looking to save any souls that need saving, she never seems to find any souls to save, or at least her bunch of mission workers never gets any bigger. In fact, it gets smaller, as she starts out with a guy who plays a very fair sort of trombone, but this guy takes it on the lam one night with the trombone, which one and all consider a dirty trick.

Now from this time on, The Sky does not take any interest in anything but Miss Sarah Brown, and any night she is out on the corner with the other mission workers, you will see The Sky standing around looking at her, and naturally after a few weeks of this, Miss Sarah Brown must know The Sky is looking at her, or she is dumber than seems possible. And nobody ever figures Miss Sarah Brown dumb, as she is always on her toes, and seems plenty able to take care of herself, even on Broadway.

Sometimes after the street meeting is over, The Sky follows the mission workers to their headquarters in an old storeroom around in Forty-eighth Street where they generally hold an indoor session, and I hear The Sky drops many a large coarse note in the collection box while looking at Miss Sarah Brown, and there is no doubt these notes come in handy around the mission, as I hear business is by no means so good there.

It is called the Save-a-Soul Mission, and it is run mainly by Miss Sarah Brown's grandfather, an old guy with whiskers, by the name of Arvide Abernathy, but Miss Sarah Brown seems to do most of the work, including tootling the cornet, and visiting the poor people around and about, and all this and that, and many citizens claim it is a great shame that such a beautiful doll is wasting her time being good.

How The Sky ever becomes acquainted with Miss Sarah Brown is a very great mystery, but the next thing anybody knows, he is saying hello to her, and she is smiling at him out of her one-hundred-per-cent eyes, and one evening when I happen to be with The Sky we run into her walking along Forty-ninth Street and The Sky hauls off and stops her, and says it is a nice evening, which it is, at that. Then The Sky says to Miss Sarah Brown like this:

"Well," The Sky says, "how is the mission dodge going these days? Are you saving any souls?" he says.

Well, it seems from what Miss Sarah Brown says the soul-saving is very slow, indeed, these days.

"In fact," Miss Sarah Brown says, "I worry greatly about how few souls we seem to save. Sometimes I wonder if we are lacking in grace."

She goes on up the street, and The Sky stands looking after her, and he says to me like this:

"I wish I can think of some way to help this little doll," he says, "especially," he says, "in saving a few souls to build up her mob at the mission. I must speak to her again, and see if I can figure something out."

But The Sky does not get to speak to Miss Sarah Brown again, because somebody weighs in the sacks on him by telling her he is nothing but a professional gambler, and that he is a very undesirable character, and that his only interest in hanging around the mission is because she is a good-looking doll. So all of a sudden Miss Sarah Brown plays plenty of chill for The Sky. Furthermore, she sends him word that she does not care to accept any more of his potatoes in the collection box, because his potatoes are nothing but ill-gotten gains.

Well, naturally, this hurts The Sky's feelings no little, so he quits standing around looking at Miss Sarah Brown, and going to the mission, and takes to mingling again with the citizens in Mindy's, and showing some interest in the affairs of the community, especially the crap games.

Of course the crap games that are going on at this time are nothing much, because practically everybody in the world is broke, but there is a head-and-head game run by Nathan Detroit over a garage in Fifty-second Street where there is occasionally some action, and who shows up at this crap game early one evening but The Sky, although it seems he shows up there more to find company than anything else.

In fact, he only stands around watching the play, and talking with other guys who are also standing around and watching, and many of these guys are very high shots during the gold rush, although most of them are now as clean as a jaybird, and maybe cleaner. One of these guys is a guy by the name of Brandy Bottle Bates, who is known from coast to coast as a high player when he has anything to play with, and who is called Brandy Bottle Bates because it seems that years ago he is a great hand for belting a brandy bottle around.

This Brandy Bottle Bates is a big, black-looking guy, with a large beezer, and a head shaped like a pear, and he is considered a very immoral and wicked character, but he is a pretty slick gambler, and a fast man with a dollar when he is in the money.

Well, finally The Sky asks Brandy Bottle why he is not playing and Brandy laughs, and states as follows:

"Why," he says, "in the first place I have no potatoes, and in the second place I doubt if it will do me much good if I do have any potatoes the way I am going the past year. Why," Brandy Bottle says, "I cannot win a bet to save my soul."

Now this crack seems to give The Sky an idea, as he stands looking at Brandy Bottle very strangely, and while he is looking, Big Nig, the crap shooter, picks up the dice and hits three times hand-running, bing, bing, bing. The Big Nig comes out on a six and Brandy Bottle Bates speaks as follows:

"You see how my luck is," he says. "Here is Big Nig hotter than a stove, and here I am without a bob to follow him with, especially," Brandy says, "when he is looking for nothing but a six. Why," he says, "Nig can make sixes all night when he is hot. If he does not make this six, the way he is, I will be willing to turn square and quit gambling forever."

"Well, Brandy," The Sky says, "I will make you a proposition. I will lay you a G note Big Nig does not get his six. I will lay you a G note against nothing but your soul," he says. "I mean if Big Nig does not get his six, you are to turn square and join Miss Sarah Brown's mission for six months."

"Bet!" Brandy Bottle Bates says right away, meaning the proposition is on, although the chances are he does not quite understand the proposition. All Brandy understands is The Sky wishes to wager that Big Nig does not make his six, and Brandy Bottle Bates will be willing to bet his soul a couple of times over on Big Nig making his six, and figure he is getting the best of it, at that, as Brandy has great confidence in Nig.

Well, sure enough, Big Nig makes the six, so The Sky weeds Brandy Bottle Bates a G note, although everybody around is saying The Sky makes a terrible over-lay of the natural price in giving Brandy Bottle a G against his soul. Furthermore, everybody around figures the chances are The Sky only wishes to give Brandy an opportunity to get in action, and nobody figures The Sky is on the level about trying to win Brandy Bottle Bates' soul, especially as The Sky does not seem to wish to go any further after paying the bet.

He only stands there looking on and seeming somewhat depressed as Brandy Bottle goes into action on his own account with the G note, fading other guys around the table with cash money. But Brandy Bottle Bates seems to figure what is in The Sky's mind pretty well, because Brandy Bottle is a crafty old guy.

It finally comes his turn to handle the dice, and he hits a couple of times, and then he comes out on a four, and anybody will tell you that a four is a very tough point to make, even with a lead pencil. Then Brandy Bottle turns to The Sky and speaks to him as follows:

"Well, Sky," he says, "I will take the odds off you on this one. I know you do not want my dough," he says. "I know you only want my soul for Miss Sarah Brown, and," he says, "without wishing to be fresh about it, I know why you want it for her. I am young once myself," Brandy Bottle says. "And you know if I lose to you, I will be over there in Forty-eighth Street in an hour pounding on the door, for Brandy always settles.

"But, Sky," he says, "now I am in the money, and my price goes up. Will you lay me ten G's against my soul I do not make this four?"

"Bet!" The Sky says, and right away Brandy Bottle hits with a four.

Well, when word goes around that The Sky is up at Nathan Detroit's crap game trying to win Brandy Bottle Bates' soul for Miss Sarah Brown, the excitement is practically intense. Somebody telephones Mindy's, where a large number of citizens are sitting around arguing about this and that, and telling one another how much they will bet in support of their arguments, if only they have something to bet, and Mindy himself is almost killed in the rush for the door.

One of the first guys out of Mindy's and up to the crap game is Regret, the horse player, and as he comes in Brandy Bottle is looking for a nine, and The Sky is laying him twelve G's against his soul that he does not make this nine, for it seems Brandy Bottle's soul keeps getting more and more expensive.

Well, Regret wishes to bet his soul against a G that Brandy Bottle gets his nine and is greatly insulted when The Sky cannot figure his price any better than a double saw, but finally Regret accepts this price, and Brandy Bottle hits again.

Now many other citizens request a little action from The Sky, and if there is one thing The Sky cannot deny a citizen it is action, so he says he will lay them according to how he figures their word to join Miss Sarah Brown's mission if Brandy Bottle misses out, but about this time The Sky finds he has no more potatoes on him, being now around thirty-five G's loser, and he wishes to give markers.

But Brandy Bottle says that while ordinarily he will be pleased to extend The Sky this accommodation, he does not care to accept markers against his soul, so then The Sky has to leave the joint and go over to his hotel two or three blocks away, and get the night clerk to open his damper so The Sky can get the rest of his bank roll. In the meantime the crap game continues at Nathan Detroit's among the small operators, while the other citizens stand around and say that while they hear of many a daffy proposition in their time, this is the daffiest that ever comes to their attention, although Big Nig claims he hears of a daffier one, but cannot think what it is.

Big Nig claims that all gamblers are daffy anyway, and in fact he says if they are not daffy they will not be gamblers, and while he is arguing this matter back comes The Sky with fresh scratch, and Brandy Bottle Bates takes up where he leaves off, although Brandy says he is accepting the worst of it, as the dice have a chance to cool off.

Now the upshot of the whole business is that Brandy Bottle hits thirteen licks in a row and the last lick he makes is on a ten, and it is for twenty G's against his soul, with about a dozen other citizens getting anywhere from one to five C's against their souls, and complaining bitterly of the price.

And as Brandy Bottle makes his ten, I happen to look at The Sky and I see him watching Brandy with a very peculiar expression on his face, and furthermore I see The Sky's right hand creeping inside his coat where I know he always packs a Betsy in a shoulder holster, so I can see something is wrong somewhere.

But before I can figure out what it is, there is quite a fuss at the door, and loud talking, and a doll's voice, and all of a sudden in bobs nobody else but Miss Sarah Brown. It is plain to be seen that she is all steamed up about something.

She marches right up to the crap table where Brandy Bottle Bates and The Sky and the other citizens are standing, and one and all are feeling sorry for Dobber, the doorman, thinking of what Nathan Detroit is bound to say to him for letting her in. The dice are still lying on the table showing Brandy Bottle Bates' last throw, which cleans

The Sky and gives many citizens the first means they enjoy in several months.

Well, Miss Sarah Brown looks at The Sky, and The Sky looks at Miss Sarah Brown, and Miss Sarah Brown looks at the citizens around and about, and one and all are somewhat dumfounded, and nobody seems to be able to think of much to say, although The Sky finally speaks up as follows:

"Good evening," The Sky says. "It is a nice evening," he says. "I am trying to win a few souls for you around here, but," he says, "I seem to be about half out of luck."

"Well," Miss Sarah Brown says, looking at The Sky most severely out of her hundred-per-cent eyes, "you are taking too much upon yourself. I can win any souls I need myself. You better be thinking of your own soul. By the way," she says, "are you risking your own soul, or just your money?"

Well, of course up to this time The Sky is not risking anything but his potatoes, so he only shakes his head to Miss Sarah Brown's question, and looks somewhat disorganized.

"I know something about gambling," Miss Sarah Brown says, "especially about crap games. I ought to," she says. "It ruins my poor papa and my brother Joe. If you wish to gamble for souls, Mister Sky, gamble for your own soul."

Now Miss Sarah Brown opens a small black leather pocketbook she is carrying in one hand, and pulls out a two-dollar bill, and it is such a two-dollar bill as seems to have seen much service in its time, and holding up this deuce, Miss Sarah Brown speaks as follows:

"I will gamble with you, Mister Sky," she says. "I will gamble with you," she says, "on the same terms you gamble with these parties here. This two dollars against your soul, Mister Sky. It is all I have, but," she says, "it is more than your soul is worth."

Well, of course anybody can see that Miss Sarah Brown is doing this because she is very angry, and wishes to make The Sky look small, but right away The Sky's duke comes from inside his coat, and he picks up the dice and hands them to her and speaks as follows:

"Roll them," The Sky says, and Miss Sarah Brown snatches the dice out of his hand and gives them a quick sling on the table in such a way that anybody can see she is not a professional crap shooter, and not even an amateur crap shooter, for all amateur crap shooters first breathe on the dice and rattle them good, and make remarks to them, such as "Come on, baby!"

In fact, there is some criticism of Miss Sarah Brown afterwards on account of her haste, as many citizens are eager to string with her to hit, while others are just as anxious to bet she misses, and she does not give them a chance to get down.

Well, Scranton Slim is the stick guy, and he takes a gander at the dice as they hit up against the side of the table and bounce back, and then Slim hollers, "Winner, winner, winner," as stick guys love to do, and what is showing on the dice as big as life, but a six and a five, which makes eleven, no matter how you figure, so The Sky's soul belongs to Miss Sarah Brown.

She turns at once and pushes through the citizens around the table without even waiting to pick up the deuce she lays down when she grabs the dice. Afterwards a most obnoxious character by the name of Red Nose Regan tries to claim the deuce as a sleeper and gets the heave-o from Nathan Detroit, who becomes very indignant about this, stating that Red Nose is trying to give his joint a wrong rap.

Naturally, The Sky follows Miss Brown, and Dobber, the doorman, tells me that as they are waiting for him to unlock the door and let them out, Miss Sarah Brown turns on The Sky and speaks to him as follows:

"You are a fool," Miss Sarah Brown says.

Well, at this Dobber figures The Sky is bound to let one go, as this seems to be most insulting language, but instead of letting one go, The Sky only smiles at Miss Sarah Brown and says to her like this:

"Why," The Sky says, "Paul says 'If any man among you seemeth to be wise in the world, let him become a fool, that he may be wise.' I love you, Miss Sarah Brown," The Sky says.

Well, now, Dobber has a pretty fair sort of memory, and he says that Miss Sarah Brown tells The Sky that since he seems to know so much about the Bible, maybe he remembers the second verse of the Song of Solomon, but the chances are Dobber muffs the number of the verse, because I look the matter up in one of these Gideon Bibles, and the verse seems a little too much for Miss Sarah Brown, although of course you never can tell.

Anyway, this is about all there is to the story, except that Brandy Bottle Bates slides out during the confusion so quietly even Dobber scarcely remembers letting him out, and he takes most of The Sky's potatoes with him, but he soon gets batted in against the faro bank out in Chicago, and the last anybody hears of him he gets religion all over again, and is preaching out in San Jose, so The Sky always claims he beats Brandy for his soul, at that.

I see The Sky the other night at Forty-ninth Street and Broadway, and he is with quite a raft of mission workers, including Mrs. Sky, for it seems that the soul-saving business picks up wonderfully, and The

Sky is giving a big bass drum such a first-class whacking that the scat band in the chop-suey joint can scarcely be heard. Furthermore, The Sky is hollering between whacks, and I never see a guy look happier, especially when Mrs. Sky smiles at him out of her hundred-per-cent eyes. But I do not linger long, because The Sky gets a gander at me, and right away he begins hollering:

"I see before me a sinner of deepest dye," he hollers. "Oh, sinner, repent before it is too late. Join with us, sinner," he hollers, "and let us save your soul."

Naturally, this crack about me being a sinner embarrasses me no little, as it is by no means true, and it is a good thing for The Sky there is no copper in me, or I will go to Mrs. Sky, who is always bragging about how she wins The Sky's soul by outplaying him at his own game, and tell her the truth.

And the truth is that the dice with which she wins The Sky's soul, and which are the same dice with which Brandy Bottle Bates wins all his potatoes, are strictly phony, and that she gets into Nathan Detroit's just in time to keep The Sky from killing old Brandy Bottle.

The Melancholy Dane

IT IS A MATTER of maybe two years back that I run into Ambrose Hammer, the newspaper scribe, one evening on Broadway and he requests me to attend the theater with him, as Ambrose is what is called a dramatic critic and his racket is to witness all the new plays and write what he thinks about them in a morning blat.

I often hear the actors and the guys who write the plays talking about Ambrose in Mindy's restaurant when they get the last edition and read what he has to say, and as near as I can make out, they feel that he is nothing but a low criminal type because it seems that Ambrose practically murders one and all connected with any new play. So I say to him like this:

"No, Ambrose," I say, "I may happen to know the guy who writes the play you are going to see, or one of the actors, and as I understand it is always about nine to five that you will put the blister on a new play, I will be running the risk of hurting myself socially along Broadway. Furthermore," I say, "where is Miss Channelle Cooper who accompanies you to the new plays for the past six months hand-running?"

"Oh," Ambrose says, "you need not worry about the guy who writes this play, as his name is Shakespeare and he is dead quite a spell. You need not worry about any of the actors, either, as they are just a bunch of plumbers that no one ever hears of before, except maybe the leading one who has some slight notoriety. And, as for Miss Channelle Cooper, I do not know where she is at this particular moment and, not to give you a short answer, I do not give a D and an A and an M and an N."

"Why, Ambrose," I say, "the last time we meet, you tell me that you are on fire with love for Miss Channelle Cooper, although, of course," I say, "you are on fire with love for so many different broads since I know you that I am surprised you are not reduced to ashes long ago."

"Look," Ambrose says, "let us not discuss such a tender subject as Miss Cooper at this time or I am apt to break into tears and be in no mood to impartially perform my stern duty toward this play. All I know is she sends me a letter by messenger this morning, stating that she cannot see me tonight because her grandmother's diabetes is worse and she has to go to Yonkers to see her.

"And," Ambrose goes on, "I happen to know that in the first place her grandmother does not have diabetes but only a tumor, and in the second place she does not live in Yonkers but in Greenwich Village, and in the third place Miss Cooper is seen late this afternoon having tea at the Plaza with an eighteen-carat hambola by the name of Mansfield Sothern. I wonder," Ambrose says, "if the bim is ever born who can tell the truth?"

"No, Ambrose," I say, "or anyway not yet. But," I say, "I am surprised to hear Miss Cooper turns out unstable as she always strikes me as the reliable sort and very true to you, or at least as true as you can expect these days. In fact," I say, "I have it on good authority that she turns down Lefty Lyons, the slot-machine king, who offers to take charge of her career and buy a night club for her. But of course Mansfield Sothern is something else again. I often enjoy his comedy on the stage."

"He is a hunk of Smithfield who steals the names of two great actors to make one for himself," Ambrose says. "I will admit that he is sometimes endurable in musical comedy, if you close your eyes when he is on the boards and make believe he is somebody else, but, like all actors, he is egotistical enough to think he can play Hamlet. In fact," Ambrose says, "he is going to do it tonight and I can scarcely wait."

Well, I finally go to the theater with Ambrose and it is quite a high-toned occasion with nearly everybody in the old thirteen-and-odd because Mansfield Sothern has a big following in musical comedy and it seems that his determination to play Hamlet produces quite a sensation, though Ambrose claims that most of those present are members of Mansfield's personal claque from café society and he also claims that it is all nothing but a plot to make Mansfield seem important.

Personally, I am not a Shakespeare man, although I see several of his plays before and, to tell you the truth, I am never able to savvy them, though naturally I do not admit this in public as I do not wish to appear unintelligent. But I stick with Ambrose through the first act of this one and I observe that Mansfield Sothern is at least a right large Hamlet and has a voice that makes him sound as if he is talking from down in a coal mine, though what he is talking about is not clear to me and consequently does not arouse my interest.

So as Ambrose seems very thoughtful and paying no attention to me, I quietly take my departure and go to Mindy's where some hours later along in the early morning I notice Miss Channelle Cooper and this gee Mansfield Sothern reading Ambrose's column, and Mansfield is shedding tears on the paper until the printer's ink runs down into his bacon and eggs. Naturally, I go out and buy a paper at once to see what causes his distress and I find that Ambrose writes about the play as follows:

"After Mansfield Sothern's performance of Hamlet at the Todd Theater last night, there need no longer be controversy as to the authorship of the immortal drama. All we need do is examine the graves of Shakespeare and Bacon, and the one that has turned over is it."

Now I do not clap eyes on Ambrose Hammer again until the other evening when he enters Mindy's at dinnertime, walking with a cane and gimping slightly. Furthermore, he is no longer roly-poly, but quite thin and he gives me a huge hello and sits down at my table and speaks to me as follows:

"Well, well," Ambrose says, "this is indeed a coincidence. The last time we meet I take you to a theater and now I am going to take you again on my first night back in harness. How is the *gedemte brust* and the *latkas* you are devouring?"

"The *latkas* are all right, Ambrose," I say, "but the *brust* is strictly second run. The war conditions are such that we must now take what we can get, even when it comes to *brust*. I do not see you for a spell, Ambrose. Are you absent from the city and why are you packing the stick?"

"Why," Ambrose says, "I am overseas and I am wounded in North Africa. Do you mean to tell me I am not missed in these parts?"

"Well, Ambrose," I say, "now that you mention it, I do remember hearing you are mixed up in the war business, but we are so busy missing other personalities that we do not get around to missing you as yet. And as for going to the theater with you, I must pass, because the last time you steer me up against a most unenjoyable evening. By the way, Ambrose," I say, "I wonder what ever becomes of that bloke Mansfield Sothern and Miss Channelle Cooper. And what are you doing in North Africa, anyway?"

I am in North Africa (Ambrose says) risking my life for my paper as a war correspondent because one day my editor calls me into his office and speaks to me as follows:

"Hammer," he says, "kindly go to the front and send us back humaninterest stories about our soldiers. Our soldiers are what our readers are interested in. Please eat with them and sleep with them and tell us how they live and what they think about and how they talk and so forth and so on."

So I go to London, and from London, I go to North Africa on a transport, and on this voyage I endeavor to start following my instructions at once, but I find that eating with the soldiers has its disadvantages as they can eat much faster than I can because of their greater experience and I am always getting shut out on the choicer tidbits.

And when I ask one of them if I can sleep with him, he gives me a strange look, and afterward I have a feeling that I am the subject of gossip among these gees. Furthermore, when I try to listen in on their conversation to learn how they talk, some of them figure I am a stool pigeon for the officers and wish to dunk me in the ocean. It is by no means a soft touch to be a war correspondent who is supposed to find out how the soldiers live and how they talk and what they think about, and when I mention my difficulties to one of the officers, he says I may get closer to the boys if I enlist, but naturally I figure this will be carrying war correspondenting too far.

But I write these human-interest stories just the same and I think they are pretty good even if I do hear a guy in the censor's office call me the poor man's Quentin Reynolds, and I always mingle with the soldiers as much as possible to get their atmosphere and finally when they learn I am kindly disposed toward them and generally have plenty of cigarettes, they become quite friendly.

I am sorry I do not have time to tell you a great deal about my terrible personal experiences at the front, but I am putting them all in the book I am writing, and you can buy a copy of it later. In fact, I have enough terrible experiences for three books, only my publisher states that he thinks one book per war correspondent is sufficient for the North African campaign. He says that the way correspondents are writing books on North Africa with Sicily and Italy coming up, he does not figure his paper supply to last the war out.

I first arrive at a place called Algiers in North Africa and I find it is largely infested by Arabs and naturally I feel at home at once, as in my younger days in show business, when I am working for a booking office, I personally book a wonderful Arab acrobatic troop consisting of a real Arab by the name of Punchy, two guys by the name of O'Shea, and a waffle who is known as Little Oran, though her square monicker is really Magnolia Shapiro.

Consequently, I have great sentiment for Arabs, and the sights and scenes and smells of Algiers keep me thinking constantly of the good old days, especially the smells. But I will not tax your patience with the details of my stay in Algiers because, by the time I reach there, the war moves away off to a place called Tunisia and I am willing to let it stay there without my presence. Then, after a week my editor sends me a sharp message asking why I am not at the front getting human-interest stories instead of loitering in Algiers wasting my time on some tamale, although, as a matter of fact, I am not wasting my time. And how he learns about the tamale I have no idea, as she does not speak a word of English.

However, one way and another I proceed to a place called Bone and then I continue on from there one way and another, but mostly in a little consumptive car, in the general direction of Tunis, and as I go, I keep asking passing British and American soldiers where is the front. And they say the front is up front, and I keep going and in my travels I get very sick and tired of the war because the enemy is always dropping hot apples all over the landscape out of planes, and sprinkling the roads with bullets or throwing big shells that make the most uncouth noises around very carelessly indeed.

Naturally, this impedes and delays my progress some because, from time to time, I am compelled to pause and dismount from my little bucket and seek refuge from these missiles in holes in the earth, and, when I cannot find a hole, I seek the refuge by falling on my face on the ground. In fact, I fall so often on my face that I am commencing to fear I will wind up with a pug nose.

Part of the time J am traveling with another newspaper scribe by the name of Herbert something, but he goes to Foldsville on me soon after we leave Bone, with a case of heartburn caused by eating Army rations, which reminds me that I must speak to the F.B.I. about these rations some day as it is my opinion that the books of the guy who invents them should be looked over to see which side he is betting on.

Well, all the time I keep asking where is the front, and all the time the soldiers say the front is up front. But I do not seem to ever find the front and, in fact, I later learn from an old soldier that nobody ever finds the front because by the time they get to where it ought to be, the front is apt to be the rear or the middle, and it is all very confusing to be sure.

Early one morning, I arrive at what seems to be the ruins of a little town, and at the same moment, an enemy battery on a hill a couple of miles away starts throwing big biscuits into the town, although I do not see hide or hair of anyone there, and whether it is because they think some of our troops are in the town or just have a personal grudge against me, I never learn.

Anyway, all of a sudden something nudges my little wagon from under me and knocks it into pieces the size of confetti and at the same moment I feel a distinct sensation of pain in my Francesca. It comes to my mind that I am wounded and I lie there with what I know is blood running down the inside of my pants leg which gives me a most untidy feeling, indeed, and what is more, I am mentally depressed quite some as I am already behind with my copy and I can see where this will delay me further and cause my editor to become most peevish.

But there is nothing I can do about it, only to keep on lying there and to try to stop the blood as best I can and wait for something to happen and also to hope that my mishap does not inconvenience my editor too greatly.

It is coming on noon, and all around and about it is very quiet, and nothing whatever seems to be stirring anywhere when who appears but a big guy in our uniform, and he seems more surprised than somewhat when he observes me, as he speaks to me as follows:

"Goodness me!" he says. "What is this?"

"I am wounded," I say.

"Where?" he says.

"In the vestibule," I say.

Then he drops on one knee beside me and outs with a knife and cuts open my pants and looks at the wound, and as he gets to his feet, he says to me like this:

"Does it hurt?" he says. "Are you suffering greatly?"

"Sure I am," I say. "I am dying."

Now the guy laughs ha-ha-ha-ha, as if he just hears a good joke and he says, "Look at me Hammer," he says. "Do you not recognize me?"

Naturally I look and I can see that he is nobody but this Mansfield Sothern, the actor, and of course I am greatly pleased at the sight of him.

"Mansfield," I say, "I am never so glad to see an old friend in my life."

"What do you mean by old friend?" Mansfield says. "I am not your old friend. I am not even your new friend. Hammer," he says, "are you really in great pain?"

"Awful," I say. "Please get me to a doctor."

Well, at this, he laughs ha-ha-ha-ha again and says, "Hammer, all my professional life, I am hoping to one day see a dramatic critic suffer, and you have no idea what pleasure you are now giving me, but I think it only fair for you to suffer out loud with groans and one thing and another. Hammer," Mansfield says, "I am enjoying a privilege that any actor will give a squillion dollars to experience."

"Look, Mansfield," I say, "kindly cease your clowning and take me somewhere. I am in great agony."

"Ha-ha-ha-ha," Mansfield Sothern ha-has. "Hammer, I cannot get you to a doctor because the Jeremiahs seem to be between us and our lines. I fear they nab the rest of my patrol. It is only by good luck that I elude them myself and then, lo and behold, I find you. I do not think there are any of the enemy right around this spot at the moment and I am going to lug you into yonder building, but it is not because I take pity on you. It is only because I wish to keep you near me so I can see you suffer."

Then he picks me up in his arms and carries me inside the walls of what seems to be an old inn, though it has no roof and no windows or doors, and even the walls are a little shaky from much shellfire, and he puts me down on the floor and washes my wound with water from his canteen and puts sulfa powder on my wound and gives me some to swallow, and all the time he is talking a blue streak.

"Hammer," he says, "do you remember the night I give my performance of Hamlet and you knock my brains out? Well you are in no more agony now than I am then. I die ten thousand deaths when I read your criticism. Furthermore, you alienate the affections of Miss Channelle Cooper from me, because she thinks you are a great dramatic critic, and when you say I am a bad Hamlet, she believes you and cancels our engagement. She says she cannot bear the idea of being married to a bad Hamlet. Hammer," he says, "am I a bad Hamlet?"

"Mansfield," I say, "I now regret I cause you anguish."

"Mr. Sothern to you," Mansfield says. "Hammer," he says, "I hear you only see two acts of my Hamlet."

"That is true," I say. "I have to hasten back to my office to write my review."

"Why," he says, "how dare you pass on the merits of an artist on such brief observation? Does your mad jealousy of me over Miss Channelle Cooper cause you to forget you are a human being and make a hyena of you? Or are all dramatic critics just naturally hyenas, as I suspect?"

"Mansfield," I say, "while I admit to much admiration and, in fact, love for Miss Channelle Cooper, I never permit my emotions to bias my professional efforts. When I state you are a bad Hamlet, I state my honest conviction and, while I now suffer the tortures of the damned, I still state it."

"Hammer," Mansfield Sothern says, "listen to me and observe me closely because I am now going to run through the gravediggers' scene for you which you do not see me do, and you can tell me afterward if Barrymore or Leslie Howard or Maurice Evans ever gives a finer performance."

And with this, what does he do but pick up a big stone from the floor and strike a pose and speak as follows:

" 'Alas, poor Yorick! I knew him, Horatio; a fellow of infinite jest, of most excellent fancy; he hath borne me on his back a thousand times; and now, how abhorred in my imagination it is! my gorge rises at it. Here hung those lips that I have kissed I know not how oft. Where be your gibes now? your gambols? your songs? your flashes of merriment, that were wont to set the tables on a roar? Not one, now, to mock your own grinning? quite chapfallen? Now get you to my lady's chamber, and tell her, let her paint an inch thick, to this favour she must come; make her laugh at that. Pr'ythee, Horatio, tell me one thing.' "

Now Mansfield stops and looks at me and says: "Come, come, Hammer, you are Horatio. Throw me the line."

So I try to remember what Horatio remarks at this point in Hamlet and finally I say, " 'How is that, my lord?' "

"No, no," Mansfield says. "Not 'How is that?' but 'What's that?' And you presume to criticize me!"

"All right, Mansfield," I say. " 'What's that, my lord?' "

And Mansfield says, " 'Dost thou think Alexander looked o' this fashion i' the earth?' "

I say, " 'E'en so.' "

" 'And smelt so? pah!' " Mansfield says, and with this, he throws the stone to the floor, and at the same moment I hear another noise and, on looking around, what do I see in the doorway but two German officers covered with dust, and one of them says in English like this:

"What is going on here?"

Naturally, I am somewhat nonplused at the sight of these guys, but Mansfield Sothern does not seem to notice them and continues reciting in a loud voice.

"He is an actor in civil life," I say to the German. "He is now presenting his version of Hamlet to me."

" 'To what base uses we may return, Horatio!' " Mansfield Sothern says. " 'Why may not imagination trace the noble dust of Alexander—' "

" 'Till he finds it stopping a bunghole?' " the German cuts in, and then Mansfield looks at him and says:

" 'Find,' not 'finds,' " he says.

"Quite right," the German says. "Well, you are now prisoners. I will send some of my soldiers to pick you up immediately. Do not attempt to leave this place or you will be shot, as we have the town surrounded."

Then the two depart and Mansfield stops reciting at once and says, "Let us duffy out of here. It is growing dark outside, and I think we can make it. Are you still suffering first class, Hammer?"

"Yes," I say, "and I cannot walk an inch, either."

So Mansfield laughs ha-ha-ha and picks me up again as easy as if I am nothing but a bag of wind and carries me out through what seems to have been a back door to the joint, but before we go into the open, he throws himself face downward on the ground and tells me to pull myself on his back and hook my arms around his neck and hold on, and I do same. Then he starts crawling along like he is a turtle and I am its shell. Naturally, our progress is very slow, especially as we hear guys everywhere around us in the dark talking in German.

Every few yards, Mansfield has to stop to rest, and I roll off his back until he is ready to start again and, during one of these halts, he whispers, "Hammer, are you still suffering?"

"Yes," I say.

"Good," Mansfield says, and then he goes on crawling.

I do not know how far he crawls with me aboard him because I am getting a little groggy, but I do remember him whispering very softly to himself like this:

> " 'Imperious Caesar, dead and turn'd to clay,
>   Might stop a hole to keep the wind away.' "

Well, Mansfield crawls and crawls and crawls until he crawls himself and me right into a bunch of our guys, and the next thing I know is I wake up in a hospital, and who is sitting there beside me but Mansfield Sothern and, when he sees I am awake, he says like this:

" 'O, I die, Horatio.' "

"Mansfield," I say, "kindly cheese it and permit me to thank you for saving my life."

"Hammer," he says, "the pleasure is all mine. I am sustained on my long crawl (which they tell me is a new world record for crawling with a guy on the deck of the crawler) by the thought that I have on my back a dramatic critic who is suffering keenly every inch of the way.

"I suppose," he says, "that you hear I am decorated for rescuing you, but kindly keep it quiet, as the Actors' Guild will never forgive me for rescuing a critic. Also, Hammer, I am being sent home to organize overseas entertainment for my comrades, and naturally it will be along Shakespearean lines. Tell me, Hammer, do you observe your nurse as yet?"

And, with this, Mansfield points to a doll in uniform standing not far away, and I can see that it is nobody but Miss Channelle Cooper, and I can also see that she is hoping she is looking like Miss Florence Nightingale. When she notices I am awake, she starts toward my cot, but at her approach, Mansfield Sothern gets up and departs quite hastily without as much as saying boo to her and as she stands looking at him, tears come to her eyes and I can see that a coolness must still prevail between them.

Naturally, I am by no means displeased by this situation because the sight of Miss Channelle Cooper even in a nurse's uniform brings back fond memories to me and, in fact, I feel all my old love for her coming up inside me like a lump and, as she reaches my bedside, I can scarcely speak because of my emotion.

"You must be quiet, Ambrose," she says. "You know you are delirious for days and days, and in your delirium you say things about me that cause me much embarrassment. Does Mansfield happen to mention my name?"

"No," I say. "Forget him, Channelle. He is a cad as well as a bad Hamlet."

But the tears in her eyes increase, and suddenly she leaves me and I do not see her for some days afterward and, in fact, I do not even think of her because my editor is sending me messages wishing to know what I am doing in a hospital on his time and to get out of there at once, and what do I mean by putting a horse in my last expense account, which of course is an error in bookkeeping due to my haste in making out the account. What I intend putting in is a hearse as I figure that my editor will be too confused by such an unexpected item to dispute it.

So here I am back in the good old U.S.A. (Ambrose says) and now as I previously state I am going to take you to the theater again with me, and who are you going to see but our old friend Mansfield Sothern playing Hamlet once more!

Now this prospect by no means thrills me, but I am unable to think of a good out at once, so I accompany Ambrose, and when we arrive at the theater, we find the manager, who is a guy by the name of Thomas Bodkin, walking up and down in front of the joint and speaking in the most disparaging terms of actors, and customers are milling around the lobby and on the sidewalks outside.

They are going up to Thomas Bodkin and saying, "What is the matter, Bodkin?" and "When does the curtain go up?" and "Who do you think you are?" and all this and that, which only causes him to become very disrespectful indeed in his expressions about actors and, in fact, he is practically libelous, and it is several minutes before Ambrose and I can figure out the nature of his emotion.

Then we learn that what happens is that Mansfield Sothern collapses in his dressing room a few minutes before the curtain is to rise, and the gaff is all sold out, it is naturally a terrible predicament for Thomas Bodkin, as he may have to refund the money, and thinking of this has Thomas on the verge of a collapse himself.

"Hammer," he says to Ambrose, "you will do me a favor if you will go backstage and see if you can find out what is eating this hamdonny. I am afraid to trust myself to even look at him at the moment."

So Ambrose and I go around to the stage entrance and up to Mansfield Sothern's dressing room, and there is Mansfield sprawled in a chair
in his Hamlet make-up, while his dresser, an old stovelid by the name
of Crichton, is swabbing Mansfield's brow with a towel and speaking
soothing words to him in a Southern accent.

"Why, Mansfield," Ambrose says, "what seems to ail you that you
keep an eager audience waiting and put Thomas Bodkin in a condition
bordering on hysteria?"

"I cannot go on," Mansfield says. "My heart is too heavy. I just learn
of your return and, as I am sitting here thinking of how you must make
plenty of hay-hay with Miss Channelle Cooper when you are lying there
under her loving care in North Africa and telling her what a bad Hamlet I am, I am overcome with grief. Ambrose," he says, "is there any
hope of you being crippled for life?"

"No," Ambrose says. "Come, come, Mansfield," he says. "Pull yourself together. Think of your career and of poor Thomas Bodkin and
the box-office receipts. Remember the ancient tradition of the theater:
The show must go on—although, personally, I do not always see why."

"I cannot," Mansfield says. "Her face will rise before me, and my
words will choke me as I think of her in another's arms. Ambrose, I am
in bad shape, but I am man enough to congratulate you. I hope and
trust you will always be happy with Miss Channelle Cooper, even if
you are a dramatic critic. But I cannot go on in my present state of
mind. I am too melancholy even for Hamlet."

"Oh," Ambrose says, "do not worry about Miss Channelle Cooper.
She loves you dearly. The last time I see her, I request her to be my
ever-loving wife when this cruel war is over, but she says it can never be,
as she loves only you. I say all right; if she wishes to love a bad Hamlet
instead of a good correspondent, to go ahead. And then," Ambrose says,
"Miss Channelle Cooper speaks to me as follows:

" 'No, Ambrose,' she says. 'He is not a bad Hamlet. A better judge
than you says he is a fine Hamlet. Professor Bierbauer, the great dramatic coach of Heidelberg, now a colonel in the German army, tells me
he witnesses a performance by Mansfield in a ruined tavern in a town
near the front, that, under the conditions, is the most magnificent effort
of the kind he ever views.'

"It seems," Ambrose says, "that the professor is wounded and captured by our guys when they retake the town, and, at the moment Miss
Channelle Cooper is addressing me, he is one of her patients in a
near-by ward, where I have no doubt he gets quite an earful on your history and her love. Where are you going, Mansfield?"

"Why," Mansfield says, "I am going around the corner to send a cablegram to Miss Channelle Cooper, telling her I reciprocate her love and also requesting her to get Professor Bierbauer's opinion in writing for my scrapbook."

Well, I wait up in Mindy's restaurant with Mansfield to get the last editions containing the reviews of the critics and, naturally, the first review we turn to is Ambrose Hammer's, and at Mansfield's request I read it aloud as follows:

" 'Mansfield Sothern's inspired performance of Hamlet at the Todd Theater last night leads up to the hope that in this sterling young actor we have a new dramatic force of the power in Shakespearean roles of all the mighty figures of another day, perhaps including even the immortal Edwin Booth.' "

"Well, Mansfield," I say, when I finish, "I think Ambrose now pays you off in full on your account with him, including saving his life, what with giving you Miss Channelle Cooper and this wonderful boost, which, undoubtedly, establishes your future in the theater."

"Humph!" Mansfield says. "It seems a fair appraisal, at that, and I will send a clipping to Miss Channelle Cooper at once, but," he says, "there is undoubtedly a streak of venom left in Ambrose Hammer. Else, why does he ring in Booth?"

Barbecue

ONE AFTERNOON in an early November, I am sitting in Chesty Charles' little Sharkskin Grill on Biscayne Boulevard in the city of Miami, Florida, chatting of this and that with a guy by the name of High-C Homer, who is called by this name because he loves to sing songs in a real high voice.

In fact, Homer tells me that when he is much younger he wishes to become a singer by trade and tries out one amateur night at the old Colonial Theater in New York but he says professional jealousy is very strong at the time and somebody in the audience pegs a turnip at him while he is singing Sweet Alice, Ben Bolt and hits him on the Adam's apple and affects his vocal cords so his voice is never again good enough for the stage, but all right for back rooms.

Anyway, when he sees there is no hope for him in a musical career, Homer has to find something else to do and what he does is the best he can, which is one thing and another, and he is explaining to me in the Sharkskin Grill that even doing the best he can, he is not doing so good when in comes a fuzz by the name of Finnegan, a fuzz being a way of saying a plain-clothes copper, who steps up to Homer and speaks to him as follows:

"Homer, the chief of police will consider it a favor if you will kindly bid us farewell."

"Why?" Homer says. "What is his idea?"

"Does the chief have to have one?" Finnegan asks.

"No," Homer says, "by no means and not at all. I am just wondering."

"Well," Finnegan says, "when he first mentions your name he requests me to bring you in because it seems a large touch comes off in West Palm Tuesday night and right away the chief thinks of you. But," Finnegan says, "I remember seeing you in the police station all night Tuseday night trying to square that traffic violation, so you cannot also be in West Palm and when I speak of this to the chief he says all right but to suggest your departure anyway. You may thank me if you wish."

"Thanks," Homer says. "Do you mind telling me the details of the touch to which you refer?"

"Oh," Finnegan says, "it is a pay-off swindle. They beat an old sim-kin from Iowa for fifty thousand tears of blood."

"A fifty-er?" Homer says. "My goodness, this is important moo. But, Finnegan," he says, "I am not in the pay-off world and I do not see how anybody can associate me with such incidents. I am an operator on the race courses and quite upright and legitimate."

"Well," Finnegan says, "if you call skinning marks on those phony tip sheets you peddle legitimate, maybe you are legit, but perhaps the chief looks through the files on you. I seem to be able to remember some things myself."

"Never mind," Homer says. "Tell the cheese of police goodby for me, Finnegan, and the same to you."

Then Homer thinks a while and finally he guesses he will go over to Tampa and he invites me to accompany him and as it is quite a while before the races start in Miami and I have nothing on my mind at the moment and the fuzz also gives me some severe looks, I accept the invitation.

So Homer goes to a parking lot not far away where he keeps an old bucket parked and presently we are rolling along the Tamiami Trail headed west, and as we journey along Homer sings several songs to me that sound very soothing but all the time he seems to be in deep thought and finally he sighs and says to me like this:

"Well," Homer says, "fifty thou is undoubtedly a splendid tally but I am glad I am not in on it. Honesty is the best policy, to be sure. There are no handholds on a wrong dollar. The way of the transgressor is hard. But," he says, "if it is the guys I think it is, they at least owe me the courtesy of a refusal to participate because of past favors rendered. I never hear a word from them."

Then Homer begins singing again and I get to thinking that it is really most remarkable that there are still marks in this world for the pay-off, as the pay-off is really a very old-fashioned dodge in which the marks are convinced that they are being let in on crooked horse races and are permitted to win a while in an astonishing manner, but when they commence asking about being paid off they are told they must first prove they will be able to settle if they happen to lose.

So the marks generally send to their banks and get the cash money to prove this, as the pay-off guy never picks marks who do not have cash money in banks, and the next thing anybody knows the money disappears and so do the pay-off guys. Furthermore, the marks seldom squawk, as the pay-off guys are cute enough to pick marks who cannot afford to let it become noised about that they are trying to make a few dishonest dibs, though it is well known to one and all that when such a mark does squawk it is the loudest squawk ever heard on land or sea.

There is no doubt that the pay-off requires great perseverance and much preparation and expense, but personally I do not approve of this method of making a living, as it calls for much deceit.

Now the Tamiami Trail is a road that runs from Miami toward Tampa and vice versa through the Everglades, and the Everglades is a big stretch of flat country that makes you feel very lonesome indeed after the sun goes down. And soon after dusk it comes on to blow and after a while it is quite a high breeze and, in fact, the wind is picking up our old can in one place and setting it down in another yards away and this makes riding in it a trifle bumpy.

Furthermore, it begins raining more than somewhat and it is darker than a yard down a bear's throat except when it lightnings and I tell Homer it may be a good idea to pull up and wait until the storm blows over. Homer says he quite agrees with me and that in fact he is looking for a gaff he knows of which ought to be somewhere along about where we are at the moment, and I tell him he better find it very shortly as it does not look as if the old rattle-and-jar can hold the road much longer.

Finally we notice some streaks of light through the dark and the rain off to one side of the road and Homer says this must be the spot and he turns the car in that direction and we come on a long, low frame building which I can see seems to be some kind of a jook, which is a sort of a roadhouse where refreshments are sold and dancing goes on and I do not know what all else.

Homer runs his old pail as close as possible to the side of the building where the other cars are parked and we get out and he locates a door that figures to open outward and we pull on it together with the wind pushing against us for several minutes before we can pull it wide enough to ease inside. And there we are in a long, narrow room with a number of tables scattered around in it and a small bar and an old piano on one side and with big gas lamps swinging back and forth from the ceiling as the wind shakes the building.

There are maybe half a dozen guys in the joint sitting at the tables and behind the bar is a short, stocky-built female party of maybe half past thirty-eight, to give her a few hours the best of it. She is by no means fashionably dressed and, in fact, she has on a short-sleeved ragged sweater and her brown hair with streaks of gray in it is flying every which way about her head and she is far from beautiful. In fact, she is strictly a blouwzola, but when Homer sees her he seems greatly pleased and he walks up to the bar and speaks to her as follows:

"Hello, Barbecue," he says. "Big wind outside."

"Big wind inside now," she says. "Well, Homer," she says, "what line of larceny are you engaged in this season?"

"Look, Barbecue," Homer says, "why do you always speak of larceny to me when I come to pay you a social call? It hurts my feelings, especially," he says, "when I am now as honest as the day is long."

"The days are getting shorter," this Barbecue says. "Homer," she says, "I never ask you to pay me any social calls. In fact, it seems to me that when you are here a year ago I tell you to please remain away forever. It is the time you persuade me to bet forty dollars of my hard-earned funds on some catfish in a race at Hialeah stating you know something, and it is not in yet. It is also the time I miss a tenner from my damper after you go, Homer," she says. "I am always hearing strange things about you from the cops who come around asking questions whenever you are in this part of the country, and besides," she says, "you remind me of gloomy days. But," she says, "I will not turn a dog out on such a night. Sit down, Homer, and keep quiet and do not try to talk me into anything," she says.

So we go to a table and sit down and Homer seems very sad and finally I say to him:

"Homer," I say, "what is the idea of this old komoppo speaking to you in such a discourteous manner? Who is she and how well do you know her?"

"I know her well," Homer says. "She is no komoppo. In fact, I think she is quite handsome if you look at her from a certain angle. She is once my wife. Her name is Sadie but everybody calls her Barbecue since she opens this drum because she specializes in barbecued spare-ribs, which is a very tasty morsel, indeed. She divorces me years ago because she claims my way of life is not substantial. But," Homer says, "I still love her. Every time I see her I love her more than ever. I hear she does very nicely here, too. I am always hoping to win her back again, but she seems somewhat hostile this evening. Can I always pick winners?" Homer says.

Naturally, I am somewhat surprised to learn that Homer High-C is ever married and I am more surprised that he seems to be carrying the torch for such a looking pancake as this Barbecue. Personally I will just as soon carry one for a crocodile, but, of course, I do not mention these sentiments to Homer. On the contrary I express my deepest sympathy for him and about now Homer notices two guys sitting at a table in a corner away back in the rear of the room and gives them a hello. It is not a large hello and, in fact, it is a very small hello and they hello him back just as small and maybe smaller and Homer lowers his voice to a whisper and says to me like this:

"The big guy is Dandy Jock McQueen out of St. Louis," he says. "The little guy is Johnny Aquitania. They are very rapid guys in every way, shape, manner and form."

"What is their business?" I say.

"They have a pay-off background," Homer says. "Now I can understand the touch Finnegan the fuzz speaks of because these parties are connected with a pay-off store which operates out of Tampa. Yes," Homer says, "it will be a privilege and a pleasure to me to get a glaum at the contents of the little brown suitcase under the table there. I will almost guarantee it contains the beesom they take off the marks in West Palm and they are undoubtedly on their way back to Tampa with it."

I am looking the guys over when there is a noise at the front door and in comes a guy and a pretty thing and the guy is dragging what seems to be a big bull fiddle in a zippered-up canvas case behind him, a bull fiddle being a large musical instrument about six feet long which is sometimes called a bass viol and which is played with great zest by musicians in orchestras. In fact, I recognize the guy as a party by the name of Juliano who has an orchestra of his own in a night trap in Miami where I go occasionally though I do not know him personally and I do not remember him playing a bull fiddle, either. What I remember him playing is a clarinet and very hot, too.

He is a young guy and the pretty with him is also young and she is wearing a long raincoat and has a felt hat pulled down to her eyes but I can see enough of her face to judge that she is quite a lovely object to behold, if you like blondes, and I like blondes. They sit down at a table not far from Homer and me and Juliano lays the bull-fiddle case down on the floor beside him and they both glance around in a way that causes me to figure that they are somewhat agitated.

But naturally I also figure their agitation comes of their experience in the storm outside and I am thinking that they make a fine-looking young couple together when I happen to observe the bull-fiddle case more closely and I say to Homer like this:

"Homer," I say, "I think there is something in the bull-fiddle case that is not a bull fiddle."

"Why?" Homer says.

"Because," I say, "it is something too limp for a bull fiddle and I notice it pulls heavy for a bull fiddle when the guy drags it in. Besides," I say, "you do not lay a bull fiddle flat on the floor. What you do with a bull fiddle is to stand it up against the wall."

Well, at this, Homer takes a good glaum himself at the bull-fiddle case and finally he says:

"No," he says, "it is not a bull fiddle in the bull-fiddle case. It is a body. I see a finger sticking out of a place where the zipper comes open a little. But," he says, "I cannot tell from the finger whether it is a male or a female body."

"Homer," I say, "why do you suppose they are carrying a body around in a bull-fiddle case?"

"Oh," Homer says, "perhaps it is just a hobby. Anyway," he says, "it is a live body because the finger just wiggles."

Well, I can see the finger for myself and sure enough, it is wiggling though not very much and I have a notion to go over and ask Juliano and the pretty what is the idea of a body in the bull-fiddle case, only I am afraid they may think I am inquisitive. Then Juliano seems to notice that Homer and I are glauming the bull-fiddle case though he does not seem to observe the finger himself and in fact by this time the finger disappears from view. But presently Juliano says something to the pretty and they get up and go out the front door again, this Juliano dragging the bull-fiddle case after him.

We can hear their car starting even above the wind but they are not gone more than five minutes before they are back again but without the bull-fiddle case and Juliano stops at the bar and remarks to Barbecue that the breeze is too strong for them to think of continuing their journey.

They sit down at their table again and Homer whispers to me that their going out is just a stall to plant the bull-fiddle case in their car because the chances are our gazing at it makes Juliano nervous and he also tells me not to stare at them any more as it is most impolite. So I pay no more attention to them and neither does Homer and they pay no more attention to us, which makes it even, but continue talking to each other very earnestly with their heads close together and finally Homer whispers to me like this:

"I am commencing to be a little curious about the bull-fiddle case," Homer says. "Follow me," he says, "but," he says, "make it nonchalant."

Then he gets up but instead of going toward the front he saunters in the direction of the back end of the room and as I tail him I can see that Homer is somewhat familiar with these premises. He leads the way into a kitchen where an old colored guy with a bald head is cooking meat on a revolving spit over a charcoal brazier and producing very savory odors, indeed, and then on into a small room opening off the kitchen which I can see is a sort of storeroom. It is full of sacks and boxes and there are vegetables and other truck hanging from the rafters including a middling-sized dressed pig and Homer points to this pig and says:

"Barbecue personally raises them and butchers them for her business," he says. "She is really a smart broad," he says. "Do you wonder I love her?"

Now Homer goes out a door of the storeroom into the wind and I go with him and he moves around the parked cars fumbling in each one in the dark until he finds what he is looking for, which is the bull-fiddle case. It is jammed in the back seat of a big limousine and Homer lifts it out and drags it into the storeroom where he unzippers the case from top to bottom and what falls out of it but a little tiny gray-haired guy with a little tiny gray mustache who is in dinner clothes and whose hands are tied in front of him with cords.

His feet are also tied and he has a gag in his mouth, and naturally Homer and I are greatly surprised at this spectacle and Homer says to the guy like this:

"What is the idea of putting yourself in a bull-fiddle case?" he says.

But the guy just rolls his eyes and it is plain to be seen that he cannot speak with the gag in his mouth, so Homer outs with his pocket knife and cuts all the cords and lifts the guy to his feet and says:

"Come, come," he says. "Please explain this hiding in a bull-fiddle case, will you? It is not dignified for a party of your years."

"They put me in it," the little guy finally says. "My wife Dimples and Juliano. She hits me over the head with a blunt instrument when I am not looking and when I regain consciousness I am tucked in this bull-fiddle case. I have a terrible headache. They think I am dead and are driving out into the Glades to cast my remains into a swamp. I hear them discussing the matter when I revive in the bull-fiddle case. My name is Greebins."

"Tut, tut," Homer says. "This sounds most unconstitutional. What is their idea?"

"Dimples is in love with Juliano," Greebins says. "She wishes to get rid of me so she can acquire my money and marry Juliano and live happily ever afterward. Well," he says, "I cannot blame her. I am nearly three times her age and by no means vivacious, and Dimples enjoys laughter and music and the rumba."

"Well," Homer says, "now you can step in and confront them and they will think they are seeing a ghost and after we scare them half to death we will turn them over to the law, although," he says, "personally I am opposed to doing the law any favors."

"No," Greebins says. "I will not confront them now. It will be too great a shock to Dimples. She is a nervous little thing. Let us consider this situation."

Then he sits down on a box and I suggest to Homer that while we are doing this considering, Juliano may miss us from the scene inside and become uneasy and take it into his head to see if his bull-fiddle case is still where he places it and not finding it, he and the pretty may fan off and we will have nothing to consider and Homer says this is undoubtedly true and that we must not waste too much time.

At this moment, the old colored guy comes into the storeroom and removes the dressed pig from its hook on the rafter, probably with the idea of lugging it into the kitchen and carving it up, but Homer stops him and takes the pig himself and puts it in the bull-fiddle case and zippers it up tight. Then Homer goes out into the wind again dragging the bull-fiddle case and when he returns he says:

"Now," he says, "we can consider at our leisure. I put the bull-fiddle case back in their car, pig and all, so if they investigate they will find everything in order."

"Why," Greebins says, "you are really a genius. You settle the whole problem. If I confront them now it will not only be a great shock to Dimples' nervous system but they will flee in dismay and I may never see her again. But if we let them go on their way and dispose of this bull-fiddle case in a swamp thinking I am still in it, they will not know I am still alive until Dimples tries to collect my money. Then," he says, "when she finds she is unable to do this while I am alive, she will return to me because Dimples cannot do without money and Juliano does not have a quarter. Of course," Greebins says, "it is somewhat humiliating to use a pig as a stand-in. I will prefer a lamb."

"Greebins," Homer says, "do you mean to state that you will take her back after all this? Why?"

"I love her," Greebins says.

"Ah," Homer says. "I see your point. Well," he says, "you remain out of sight in the kitchen until the storm passes and they leave and we will drive you back to Miami where you can await developments. That is," Homer says, "if my car is not blown there already."

So Homer and I go back to the large room and nobody seems to notice our return any more than they do our departure and it may be because one and all now have something else to think about, which is the way the building is shaking in the wind. In fact, everyone is just sitting still looking somewhat perturbed and there is no conversation and finally Barbecue speaks up and says like this:

"Listen," Barbecue says, "is this a wake, or what? Homer," she says, "sing something, will you? I will play for you."

Then she goes over to the old piano and begins playing and what she plays is Sweet Alice, Ben Bolt, and Homer sings as follows:

"Oh, don't you remember,
Sweet Alice, Ben Bolt,
Dah-dah, de, dah-dah,
Dah, de dah."

"Homer," Barbecue says, "a little less of the dah-de-dah stuff and more words."

"I do not remember the words," Homer says. "I do not sing this song in years. Not since I used to sing it to you. Barbecue," he says, "you know I still love you. What about you and me trying it again?"

"Homer," she says, "you are not really a bad guy at heart and I like you, but," she says, "you are loaded with larceny and I fear you always will be. Come back a year from today and if you can tell me you live 100 per cent on the square during this period, there is a chance for you."

Well, all of a sudden there is quite a crash and the roof over the rear of the room caves in, and it caves in over the spot where the piano is located, too, and Homer pulls Barbecue off the stool and out of the way just in time and all of us go to the front part of the joint where a piece of the roof still holds, including this Juliano and the pretty, who is sobbing and carrying on in such a manner that I can see she is indeed highstrung. Personally, I flatten out on the floor and the others soon follow my example and now there is nothing else to do but to lie there and to hope and trust that the rest of the gaff does not go.

Finally when daylight comes on, the wind dies down and the sun shines and we can look around and see what happens and it is something of a mess, to be sure, though not as bad as you will expect. The parked cars outside the building seem to be pushed around no little, but I can see that at least one of them is not damaged, as I observe Juliano and the pretty departing lickity-split with the bull-fiddle case bouncing up and down in the back of the car, they are going so rapidly. And what becomes of them I do not know and, furthermore, I do not care, as I consider them most unworthy characters, indeed, though from what I see of the pretty I judge Greebins calls the turn in figuring her to come back to him when she discovers the true situation about his money.

Now I remember that the guys Homer High-C mentions as Dandy Jock McQueen and Johnny Aquitania never seem to be among us after the roof caves in, so I go to the spot where they are sitting the last time I see them and I behold them under a pile of rubbage, lying quite still, and I tell Homer that I fear these parties are no more.

"Yes," Homer says, "I know this several hours ago. You do not notice it, but during the confusion I crawl over there figuring to help them, only to find I am too late. It is very sad. I also secure the little brown suitcase while I am about it. Just as I suspect, it is full of the soft. It is all in neat stacks. I can tell by feeling around in it in the dark. I have a wonderful sense of feeling for banknotes. Yes," he says, "it contains plenty of moo. I am most fortunate."

"Why, Homer," I say, "you do not intend keeping it, do you? It seems to me," I say, "that there is a law requiring you to turn this property over to the heirs of the deceased."

"Can this be true?" Homer says. "Well," he says, "such a course will only lead to legal complications and take a lot of time. I am going to South America and establish a home and live there honestly on these funds for a year from date to keep my promise to Barbecue. Then I will return and we will resume our happiness where we leave off. Do I tell you she kisses me for yanking her away from the piano and saving her life? But, come," Homer says, "let us find our friend Greebins and return to Miami."

Well, as we are making ready to depart Barbecue comes up to Homer and puts her arms around him and gives him a large hug and says to him like this:

"Be strong, Homer," she says. "Think of me when you feel temptation and never do the least little thing out of line, because," she says, "it may come to my ears and cancel my promise. Return to me pure and we will finish our lives together in great happiness. I am going to trust you once more, Homer," she says.

"Barbecue," Homer says, "wild horses will not be able to drag me from the straight and narrow path from now on, and," he says, "this even goes for race horses, too."

Then he points the car for Miami and we are off, with Barbecue and the old colored guy waving us farewell, and I observe that tears are running down Homer's cheeks and splashing on the little brown suitcase which is resting in his lap, so I can see that he is deeply touched.

So I suggest to Homer that we go to the Sharkskin Grill and have a few drinks and maybe they will cheer Greebins up too, and Homer thinks the drinks a good idea even if they do not cheer Greebins up, and presently we are lined up in front of the Sharkskin Grill bar having these drinks when who comes in but Finnegan, the fuzz, and he walks up to Homer and says:

"Hello," he says. "I am very glad to see you again, Homer, although it seems to me I tell you to take it on the lammeroo out of here just yesterday. Or am I mistaken?"

"No," Homer says, "you are not mistaken. I go, but I am driven back by the big storm."

"What big storm?" Finnegan says. "Do you mean the slight squall over the Glades? Look, Homer," he says, "you must not speak of such a minor disturbance as a big storm. The chamber of commerce will disapprove of your statement as a knock to our weather, which is wonderful at all times. Anyway," he says, "I repeat I am glad to see you because I now have a definite order for your arrest."

"Copper," Homer says, "I tell you again I am not in the pay-off department. I have nothing whatever to do with the West Palm matter. You may arrest me if you choose but I will immediately summon a lawbooks and sue you for false imprisonment."

"Well, I choose," Finnegan says. "Come with me."

Now all this time Homer is carrying the little brown suitcase and in fact he never loosens his clutch on it for a minute.

And at this point Greebins, who does not say much more than yes or no for several hours, steps up to Homer and taps him on the shoulder and speaks as follows:

"Brother," Greebins says, "I am trying to think of where I see you before ever since I stand out in the kitchen last night and hear you sing Sweet Alice, Ben Bolt. It just this very instant comes to me. It is years ago at the Colonial Theater and you appear on the stage and sing the same song. You are really terrible both times, but," he says, "this is neither here nor there. I peg a vegetable at you from the Colonial audience and score a bull's-eye under your chin. It is the only unconventional conduct of which I am ever guilty and I wish now to make you a belated apology."

"Ah," Homer says. "So you are the one? Do you realize," he says, "that you ruin my whole life? If it is not for your destroying my musical career with your vegetable I will probably still be married to Barbecue and partaking of her profits and never come in contact with such scurvy characters as this copper."

I am greatly surprised to note that Homer High-C appears to be laboring under strong emotion because he is usually quite calm, no matter what. In fact, he appears to be losing control of himself for the moment. Suddenly he swings this little brown suitcase around his head like Hubbell taking a windup and belts Greebins over the pimple with it, almost knocking him loose from his little gray mustache. It is a blow of such great force that it not only flattens Greebins but it breaks open the suitcase and a number of fat packages of banknotes spill out over the floor and Finnegan picks up one of these packages and observes that the band around it has the name of a Des Moines bank on it.

"Well, well," Finnegan says. "Well, well, well, well. Des Moines, eh? Iowa, eh? The West Palm swag, eh? Homer," he says, "how fortunate for me you boff this little old gee with such a weapon as your suitcase, although, Homer," he says, "it strikes me as most unsportsmanlike considering the difference in your ages. But if I do not see this money with my own eyes, I will never suspect you of being mixed up in the West Palm skulduggery, especially when I know you are right here in this city when it comes off. I will get promoted for this, I hope," he says.

"Wait a minute," Homer says. "What do you mean you will never suspect me? Do you not just put the arm on me for it? Do you not just state you have an order for my arrest?"

"Oh," Finnegan says, "the arrest order is for something entirely different, Homer. I am wondering why you keep beefing about the pay-off thing when I do not even dream of connecting you with it. The chief gets a call today from a biscuit by the name of Barbecue who runs an eating joint out on the Trail and who states that she can prove by the eye-witness testimony of a colored party who works for her that you rob her of a pig. Come on, Homer."

Little Pinks

ONE NIGHT IN the Canary Club, Case Ables, the bookmaker, slaps a red-headed chorus Judy who is called Your Highness across the mouth and knocks her down a flight of stairs and he uses only his bare hand, at that.

It is agreed by one and all that Case Ables is a little out of line in this situation as he is a big fat guy who outweighs Your Highness maybe a hundred and eighty pounds, but it is also agreed that if some Judy in the city of New York must be knocked down a flight of stairs it may as well be Your Highness, for she is without doubt a great pain in the neck.

And, of course, Case Ables is slightly vexed at the moment as he is just after spending plenty of moolouw in the Canary Club and when it comes on the closing hour for the drum he wishes to go somewhere else and have jolly times and he also wishes to take Your Highness with him for company and so forth, and she refuses to go.

To tell the truth, if Case Ables only thinks to ask somebody in advance he will learn that Your Highness always refuses to go out with anybody for company or anything else, unless she is sure they are in the high income-tax brackets and of excellent social position, and naturally the social position lets Case out.

In fact, the reason she is called Your Highness and is considered such a pain in the neck is because she plays the frost for all who are not well established as practically zillionaires, and she makes no bones of stating that her angle is to find a character of means who is not entirely repulsive and marry him, and when somebody asks her what about love, she says well, what about it, and, of course, there is no answer to this.

Personally, I consider Your Highness' attitude slightly unromantic, especially for a Judy who is only about twenty-two years old, but many citizens claim that it displays great intelligence, although they all admit they are glad she can never have them in mind for her purpose.

In fact, Joe Gloze, the owner of the Canary Club, states that as far as he is concerned he will just as soon marry a fire plug as Your Highness as he says he figures a fire plug will not be so cold and hard in case of a clinch. But, of course, Joe Gloze admits he is only guessing both ways.

However, no one can deny that Your Highness does very good for herself by specializing in characters of means. They are always taking her nice places and she has fine clothes and fur wraps and other odds and ends such as these characters dearly love to bestow upon chorus Judys for the asking, and Your Highness is not at all tongue-tied when it comes to asking.

Furthermore, she has quite a personal following of these characters and always brings trade to any joint in which she is working, so she gets a good salary although all she has to do is to walk around with the rest of the chorus and look beautiful, which is really no effort at all for Your Highness. In fact, many citizens say that if she is not the most beautiful Judy that ever hits Broadway, she is at least in there somewhere scrambling along close up.

The price is 8 to 5 anywhere along Broadway that Your Highness will sooner or later marry the United States Mint, or maybe the Bank of England, and 20 to 1 that she will make either of them sick of her in two weeks when she winds up in a heap at the foot of the stairs from Case Ables' slap. I remember she has on a red dress and what with this and her red hair she reminds me more than somewhat of a woodpecker that someone knocks out of a tree with a rock.

Well, while she is lying there, a bus boy in the Canary Club by the name of Little Pinks, who has a very large nose and a short forehead and who does not weigh more than ninety pounds, apron and all, runs down the stairs and begins carrying on in a way that is most distressing to hear, especially to Case Ables, as Little Pinks keeps yelling that Case is a murderer and a no-good and I do not know what all else.

So naturally Case has to go down the stairs and give Little Pinks a few good clops on the chops because such talk is practically vilification of character and by no means pleasing to Case Ables. But the more clops Little Pinks gets the louder he yells and as a scene of this nature is by no means beneficial to an establishment such as the Canary Club, Joe Gloze and two of his captains of waiters go down and assist Case in the clopping, so after a while Little Pinks is very well clopped indeed.

It comes out that Little Pinks is a great admirer of Your Highness, but it is agreed that even so he is going too far in speaking so freely of Case Ables. In fact, after some discussion it is the consensus of opinion that a bus boy has no right to admire anybody and consequently Little Pinks is in great disfavor with one and all, especially when it comes out that his admiration of Your Highness is from a distance and that he never more than says good evening to her in his life and even then she does not answer unless she feels like it. And of course, everybody who knows Your Highness knows that she will very seldom feel like answering a bus boy.

It becomes plain to all that Your Highness probably never knows Little Pinks is alive, yet it seems that whenever she goes to work in a night club, Little Pinks always gets himself a bussing job there, just so he can be near her and see her. When this information is made public it is generally agreed that Little Pinks is slightly eccentric and, furthermore, when Joe Gloze gets to figuring that if Pinks is so busy admiring Your Highness he must be neglecting his bussing, he gives Little Pinks a few more clops for luck.

Well, finally it also comes out that Your Highness' spine is injured so she will never walk again and Case Ables feels so sorry about this that he talks some of paying her hospital expenses, but Joe Gloze convinces him that it will be setting a bad precedent in these situations. In fact, Joe Gloze says it may start his chorus Judys to falling down the stairs of their own free will just to get in hospitals.

There is also a rumor around that Your Highness has a right to sue Case Ables for damages, but as Case soon has thirty-four witnesses, including the cop on the beat, who are willing to swear she attacks him first and that she is undoubtedly under the influence of something at the time, nothing comes of this rumor. In fact, everybody forgets the incident as quickly as possible except Your Highness and maybe Little Pinks, who is bound to remember if only because Joe Gloze gives him the heevus from his job in the Canary Club.

Now all this is some years ago and it comes on a winter when things are pretty tough for one and all and I judge they must be especially tough for bus boys as I meet Little Pinks on Broadway one cold day and he is thinner than an old dime and does not have enough clothes on to make a bathrobe for a mouse. His toes are leaking out of his shoes and he is as blue as a toad from the cold and I stake him to four bits out of the goodness of my heart. Then I ask him if he ever sees Your Highness and he says to me like this:

"Sure, I see her," Little Pinks says. "I see her all the time. In fact, Your Highness lives in the same place I do which is in a basement over in West Fifty-second Street near Tenth Avenue. I am the only one who does see her nowadays as all her former friends give her the brush-off after she is hurt. She is in the hospital nearly a year and," he says, "she has to sell all her possessions to pay the expenses. She does not have one penny when I take her to my place to live."

"How is she now?" I say.

"She is cold," Little Pinks says. "Always so cold. There is not much heat in our basement and this is one reason why Your Highness is always slightly irritable. But," he says, "it keeps me so busy hustling around trying to get a few dibs to keep up the installments on the wheel chair I buy her and for food and magazines that I cannot afford a better place. Your Highness must have her magazines so she can keep up with what the society people are doing. They cost quite a lot," he says.

"Are you married to her?" I say.

"Oh, my goodness, no," Pinks says. "Do you suppose Your Highness will marry anybody like me? She is too proud to think of such a thing. She is just letting me take care of her until she can get well and marry somebody with a lot of sugar. That is always her dream," he says. "When she is in good humor she talks about how she will reward me some day.

"But," Little Pinks says, "she is not often in good humor lately because she is so cold. She says she wants to go to Miami where it is warm and where there are society people like she sees in the magazines. She says she will get a chance to meet guys with money there. Yes," he says, "I think I will take her to Miami."

"Well, Pinks," I say, "that will be fine, but how are you going to get her there? It looks to me as if you may be a little short of what it takes."

"Why," Little Pinks says, "I will push her there in her wheel chair."

"Pinks," I say, "I guess you are a case for Bellevue. It is thirteen hundred miles to Miami."

"How far is thirteen hundred miles?" Little Pinks says.

"Pinks," I say, "thirteen hundred miles is thirteen hundred miles. That is how far it is. You can no more push somebody in a wheel chair such a distance than you can roll a peanut from here to Chicago with your nose."

"Well," he says, "I must try because Your Highness cannot stand the cold much longer. Now I must hurry home to cook the dinner, and," he says, "tonight is the night I do the washing. Your Highness does not like to be without clean clothes, especially lingerie. I am a good cook and launderer now and nobody can dust and sweep or wait on an invalid better than I can. Your Highness takes a lot of waiting on," he says. "I used to forget things but now she keeps a long cane at her chair to remind me when I forget."

"Pinks," I say, "everybody knows his own business best, but what is the idea of your working and slaving for a cold, selfish little broad such as Your Highness if you are not married to her and are not even going to get married to her? What is your percentage?" I say.

"Why," Little Pinks says, "I love her."

And with this he goes on down the street and I can see that he shrinks a lot since I last see him and in fact he is now so small that I look for him to fall out of the hole in the seat of his pants any minute.

Well, it comes on the winter of 1938 and I am in Chesty Charles' little grill on Biscayne Boulevard in the city of Miami thinking of very little when I notice that the character who is doing porter work around the joint seems to be nobody but Little Pinks although he is without doubt greatly altered. So I ask Chesty if this is not who the porter is and Chesty says to me like this:

"All I know," Chesty says, "is that he is a little stirry. He comes to me with a screeve from some old friends of mine in the canneroo at Raiford. He is just after doing a three-er and it seems to leave some impression on him. He talks to himself a lot. Yes," Chesty says, "he is without doubt stir-crazy."

After a while, when the porter does not seem to have anything on his hands, I walk over to him and slap him on the back and speak to him as follows:

"Hello, Pinks," I say. "How is everything?"

He turns around and looks at me a minute and I can see that it is Little Pinks all right and then he says:

"Oh, hello."

"Do you remember me?" I say.

"Sure," Little Pinks says. "You give me four bits on Broadway cne day. It is a cold day."

"How is Your Highness?" I say.

At this, Little Pinks puts his finger on his lips and says shush and then he takes me by the arm and leads me out the back door of the grill into a sort of areaway where they keep the garbage cans and he motions me to sit down on one can and he sits on the other and says like this:

"It is now over four years ago," he says, "since I bring Your Highness down here."

"Wait a minute, Pinks," I say. "You state you bring her. How do you bring her?"

"I push her in her wheel chair," he says.

"You push her in her wheel chair thirteen hundred miles?" I say. "Pinks, do you think you are kidding somebody?"

"Wait till I tell the story," he says. "It is thirteen hundred miles. It does not seem like a block to me now. But let me tell it all."

It is not so difficult as it may sound to push a wheel chair from New York City to Miami (Little Pinks says) with such a tiny thing as Your Highness in the chair as by the time we start she does not weigh much more than a bag of popcorn and besides it is a very nice wheel chair with rubber tires and ball-bearing wheels and rolls very easy, to be sure.

In fact, the only tough part of the journey is from the basement in West Fifty-second Street to the ferry that takes us across the river to the Jersey side. After that we thumb our way along, with Your Highness doing the thumbing and we get many a lift in empty trucks, although the drivers are generally greatly surprised, indeed, at the spectacle of a Judy in a wheel chair asking for a ride.

But it is seldom an empty comes along without stopping for us and usually the driver has to get off and help lift Your Highness, chair and all, into the truck and block the wheels so the chair will not roll out on the bumps and sometimes Your Highness is so bossy about the job that she gets the drivers to asking her who she thinks she is.

She likes the open trucks best and often passes up closed vans that offer a lift to wait for one without a top so she can sit in her chair and watch the scenery on all sides and pretend she is somebody big like a queen. When she is in one of those open trucks she nearly always pretends she is Cleopatra in her royal barge scooting along the Nile which is an idea she gets from some movie and while I do not mind her pretending to be Cleopatra or anybody else I can see that her conversation often makes the truck drivers very nervous.

Once in the state of South Carolina when I am pushing the chair along a road we are stopped by an automobile containing three characters who are very hard-looking, indeed, and one of these characters outs with a large Betsy and requests us to hold up our hands. Then one of the others fan me to see if I have any funds or valuables, and the third character looks Your Highness over and they are surprised and slightly annoyed to find only eighty-six cents on us all told.

So they start questioning us and when I tell them all about Your Highness and me, they are more surprised than ever and one of them picks Your Highness up out of her wheel chair and puts her in the automobile. They make me get in after her and then they tie a rope to the wheel chair and tow it quite a distance behind the automobile, traveling very slow, so as not to yank the chair around too much.

They let us go at a crossroads where they say they must branch off to get to a town off the main highway where they wish to rob a bank and, furthermore, they give me a pound note for my pocket and one of them who listens to Your Highness more than anyone else says that what I really deserve is a gold medal although he does not state why.

Another time in Georgia, I somehow lose the highway and hit a road that goes nowhere but into a swamp and the next thing we know we are in the midst of a bunch of five stove lids in striped clothes and it turns out that they are escaped convicts and are very desperate guys.

Personally, I figure we are going to have a lot of trouble with these

parties, but right away Your Highness puts them to work fixing up a
camp for us for the night and ordering them around until one of them
tells me he will be glad to return to the prison and give himself up,
especially as every time one of the stove lids gets close enough to Your
Highness' chair she reaches out and gives him a good belt with her cane.

It takes us about two weeks to get to Miami between her thumbing
and my pushing and we live very good on the way. Sometimes I mooch
a dookey at a kitchen door but Your Highness does not care much for
Southern cooking and prefers canned goods such as I am able to obtain
by climbing in the windows of country stores at night. Once I enter a
henroost and sneeze a pullet when Your Highness thinks she feels in a
mood for a little chicken à la king, but the pullet turns out to be very
tough and Your Highness is most critical, indeed.

However, she cheers up no little and quite some when she feels the
sun and sees the ocean in Miami. In fact, she is so cheerful that she
forgets to remind me of anything with her cane for one whole day and
has only a few cross words for me. The first thing I do is to find a
room for her in a small rooming house on Miami Beach and the next
thing I do is get myself a job bussing in a restaurant not far from
the rooming house.

Then every morning before I go to work, I push her in her wheel
chair over to a big hotel on the beach that is called the Roney Plaza and
she sits there on the sidewalks all day long watching the people walking
up and down and here and there and to and fro and, the chances are,
trying to flirt with any guy that she figures has as much as nine dollars
in his pockets, for Your Highness never for a minute forgets her dream
of marrying someone with money and social position, but, anyway,
money.

Well, to tell the truth, Your Highness is now not as beautiful as
formerly, though I never before admit it to anybody. In fact, she is so
thin she is almost a shadow and her face is drawn down to the size
of a nickel and there is no more glint in her hair and she is by no means
such a looking Judy as will attract the attention of guys, especially as
the shape that once draws them her way in herds is no longer on public
view.

But Your Highness does not realize the change in her appearance
and when she finds that the only ones who smile at her and stop and
talk to her as she is sitting there are kindhearted old Judys, and that
guys never rap to her at all, she becomes somewhat impatient and one
day she speaks to me as follows:

"Pinks," she said, "I know what is wrong. I do not have any jewelry.
I notice that anybody who has a lot of jewelry on always attracts plenty

of attention even if they are as ugly as anything. Pinks, you get me a lot of jewelry," she says.

"Well, Your Highness," I say, "this is quite an order to be sure. I do not know how I am going to get you any jewelry. I am wondering right now about the room rent."

"Oh," she says, "you can get it. You get those groceries and that chicken when you want them. Pinks, I must have a lot of jewelry. I must, I must, I must."

Then she gets mad at me and the way Your Highness gets mad at me is to never say a word but just sit looking sad and it almost breaks my heart when she does this. In fact, I can scarcely sleep when she is mad at me, so instead of trying I spend the next few nights looking around a little and casing a few big houses in which I figure there is bound to be plenty of jewelry.

One night I enter one of these houses by way of a loose window and make my way very quietly to a bedroom in which I can see somebody is sleeping and there on a bureau in plain sight is a whole hatful of jewelry. In fact, there is a big square-cut diamond ring and a batch of diamond bracelets and a large diamond clip, so I figure that the party sleeping in the bedroom is some Judy and that she wears this jewelry earlier in the evening and is careless enough not to put it away in a safe place when she is going to bed.

Anyway, I remove the jewelry and present it the next morning to Your Highness and she is quite pleased with it, although she states that the square-cut diamond is not of first-class color and that the mountings of the bracelets are old-fashioned and cheap. However, she says they will do very well and she puts all the jewelry on and sits looking at herself in a mirror for half an hour. She never asks me where I get it or how. One thing about Your Highness, she never wishes to know where anybody gets anything or how as long as she gets it herself.

I push her in her chair over to the Roney as usual and when I go for her late in the afternoon she is smiling and happy and says that just as she figures the jewelry attracts plenty of attention to her, although she admits she does not get much of a tumble from any young guys who look as if they may be worth getting a tumble from.

"But," Your Highness says, "they will come later. This afternoon a very fine-looking old party who says he is Dr. Quincey, of Chicago, and his wife talk to me an hour. She is old, too, but nice. Pinks, I think they are rich and maybe they will introduce me to people. Maybe they have a son. They are much interested in my jewelry."

Well, about an hour later I can understand this interest because a gendarme comes around to the rooming house and calls me out and tells me I am under arrest charged with the burglary of the home of Dr. Quincey, of Chicago, of sixty thousand dollars' worth of swag, and while I am naturally somewhat perturbed by this announcement, I can see that what Your Highness knows about the value of jewelry is not much.

The gendarme takes me to the police station and into a room where several other coppers are waiting and also an old guy with a beard that they tell me is this Dr. Quincey and I am quite surprised to see him smile at me and to observe that he does not seem to be anywhere near as indignant as I will be myself upon beholding a guy who knocks me off for my valuables.

In fact, it is Dr. Quincey who starts questioning me instead of the cops and what he questions me most about is Your Highness and finally I tell him the whole story about us from start to finish including the part about where I finally enter his house and remove the jewelry and when I speak of this the cops are all in favor of immediately placing me in the jailhouse without any more dickering and then sending out and arresting Your Highness, too, and recovering the jewelry.

"One moment, gentlemen," this Dr. Quincey says. "I have a long talk with the girl today and observe her closely. She is extremely ill. There is no doubt of that. She is not only extremely ill but," he says, "she has strange delusions of grandeur."

"Is that bad, Doc?" I say.

"Never mind," he says. "I am not willing to condone this young fellow's crime, but let us suspend action on him temporarily. Say nothing to the girl and let her keep on wearing the jewelry a while longer under surveillance and let Pinks remain at liberty in the meantime if he promises to give himself up when you send for him and accept punishment afterward."

"What do you mean afterward?" I say.

"Never mind," he says. "We will let you know later. Do you agree?"

Well, naturally I am glad to agree to anything whatever if it is going to keep me out of the pokey but the coppers are by no means so eager. They say I have all the earmarks of a guy who will breeze off out of their reach as soon as they take their hands off me, but the old guy has them send me out of the room and has a long talk with them in private and then they tell me I can go until they want me.

Of course I do not tell Your Highness what comes off and she goes on wearing the jewelry every day and taking great pleasure in same but I notice that one of the coppers I see in the room is always around somewhere close in plain clothes, so I judge they are taking no chances on the jewelry evaporating.

In fact, sometimes the copper talks to Your Highness and as he is a young guy and by no means bad-looking, and is always hanging around, she commences to figure that maybe he has a crush on her and she plays plenty of swell for him.

When I come to get her when he is around, she gives me a large bawling out for this and that and lets on that I am just a guy working for her, although of course he knows very well who I am. Then the copper happens to let it out that he is married and after that he cannot get close enough to her to hand her a grapefruit.

Your Highness tells me that Dr. Quincey and his wife are around to see her often and she says that sometimes she thinks that maybe the old Doctor likes her pretty well himself. In fact, she says she thinks Dr. Quincey has plenty of gall to look at her the way he does right in front of his wife and I say maybe he is only admiring her jewelry.

Now for several days Your Highness is very thoughtful and has little to say and it seems to me that she is getting so she is not much more than a shadow in her chair. Her eyes are as big as dinner plates and once I think she is crying which is a great surprise to me as I never before see her shed a tear. Then one afternoon I go to the Roney Plaza to get her and I find her watching the sunset instead of the people and after a while she looks at tme and smiles and says:

"Come close to me, Little Pinks."

It is one of the few times she ever calls me Little Pinks. Generally it is just Pinks and it is not often she smiles at me, either. So I go up to the side of her chair but only figuring that the chances are she wishes to get me close enough to give me a belt with her cane for something I forget to remember and she says:

"Kneel down, Little Pinks."

Well, of course, this is an unusual request, especially in such a place, but if there is one thing I am accustomed to from Your Highness it is unusual requests, so I kneel down in front of her chair and she reaches out with her cane but instead of belting me she taps me on the shoulder with it and says:

"Rise up, Sir Little Pinks, my brave and true knight. Rise up and may God bless you forever and always."

Naturally I figure this is something else Your Highness gets from a movie or maybe out of a book and I am wondering what the idea is when I see that there are real tears running down her cheeks and she holds out her thin arms to me and says:

"Kiss me, Little Pinks."

So I kiss her for the first and only time in my life and she holds me tight to her breast a moment and slowly whispers:

"Little Pinks, I love you."

Now I feel her arms loosen and her poor little body slips down farther in the chair and I do not need Dr. Quincey who happens along just then to tell me Your Highness is dead. He says she lasts longer than he expects from the first time he ever sees her.

I get her buried out here in a little cemetery in the sun where she will never be cold again and then I go to the police station and give myself up and cop a plea of guilty to robbery and take two to ten years. I am now out on parole (Little Pinks says) and this is all there is to the story.

"Pinks," I say, "I am indeed very sorry for you."

"Sorry for me?" Little Pinks says. "Say," he says, "I am sorry for you. You never kiss Your Highness and hear her say she loves you."

Well, it is a couple of weeks before I am in Chesty's drum again and I do not see Little Pinks around, so I ask Chesty what becomes of his porter and Chesty says to me like this:

"Why," he says, "they pick him up again for violating his parole and send him back to Raiford. I do not know how or why he violates it because I never think to ask, but," he says, "that guy is better off there because he surely is off his nut."

So I call up a guy I know by the name of Smiddy who works in the sheriff's office and ask him if he can remember anything about a character by the name of something that sounds like Pinks.

"Wait until I look in the record," Smiddy says. "Pinks, Pinks, Pinks," he keeps saying, so I figure he is going through a book. "Say," he says, "here is a guy by the name of Pincus who is grabbed for parole violation. Maybe he is your guy. I remember him now myself. It is a most unusual case."

"What is most unusual about it?" I say.

"Why," Smiddy says, "this Pincus makes his way into the hotel room of a winter tourist by the name of Ables and for no reason anybody can figure out he ties Ables to his bed at the point of a Betsy and bangs him across the back with a baseball bat until he permanently injures the poor guy's spine. Do you know what I think?" Smiddy says.

"No," I say, "what do you think?"

"I think this Pincus is daffy," Smiddy says. "But," he says, "of course we cannot have our winter tourists treated like Mr. Ables."

Palm Beach Santa Claus

———————◆■◆◆————————

IT IS THE afternoon of a hot day in the city of West Palm Beach, Florida, and a guy by the name of Fatso Zimpf is standing on a street corner thinking of very little and throwing so much shade that a couple of small stove lids are sitting on the curb at his feet keeping cool, for this Fatso weighs three hundred pounds if he weighs a karat and as he is only about five feet eight inches tall he is really quite a tub of blubber and casts a very wide shadow.

At that, he is somewhat undernourished at this time and in fact is maybe fifteen or twenty pounds underweight as he does not partake of food for two days, and if the small stove lids know how hungry he is the chances are they will not be sitting so close to him. To tell the truth, Fatso is so hungry that his stomach is wondering if his throat is on a vacation and what is more he does not have as much as one thin dime in his pants pocket to relieve his predicament.

This Fatso is a horse player by trade and he is en route to Miami to participate in the winter meetings at Tropical Park and Hialeah, and he leaves New York City with just enough money to get him as far as West Palm Beach by bus, but with nothing over for food and drink on the journey. However, he does not regret having to leave the bus at West Palm Beach as his strength is slowly dwindling from hunger and he figures he may be able to get something to eat there.

Besides, the bus people are talking of charging him excess fare because it seems that Fatso laps over on both sides in one seat so much that they claim it is just the same as if he has three seats, and other passengers are complaining and the journey is by no means a pleasure trip for Fatso.

Well, while Fatso is standing there on the corner all of a sudden a big red roadster pulls up in the street in front of him with a good-looking tanned young guy in a sport shirt driving it and a skinny Judy sitting in the seat next to him and the skinny Judy motions for Fatso to come out to the car.

At first Fatso does not pay any attention to her because he does not wish to move around and take his shade away from the small stove lids, as he can see that they are very comfortable, and when it comes to children no kinder-hearted guy than Fatso ever lived no matter if they are slightly colored children. In fact, Fatso is enduring no little suffering from the heat, standing there just because he is too kindhearted to move.

The skinny Judy in the roadster keeps motioning to him and then she cries "Hey, you!" in a loud tone so finally Fatso goes out in the street to the car figuring that maybe she wishes to ask him the way to some place although of course Fatso does not know the way to any place in these parts, and he can see that she is not a bad-looking Judy, though not young, and that she has yellow hair tied back with a fancy handkerchief and a blue sweater and blue slacks and a lot of bracelets on her arms and rings on her fingers.

Fatso can see that this is a party who must be in the money and he can also see that she has haid blue eyes and a bossy way about her because as he goes up to the side of the car with the small stove lids following in his shade she speaks to him in a voice that seems to scratch on her tonsils coming up, as follows:

"Look here," she says, "are you out of a job?"

Now this Fatso is always very courteous to all female characters even when he can see that they are nothing but mountain lions and he bows and says:

"Well," he says, "not to give you a short answer, ma'am, but who wants to know?"

"I do," the skinny Judy says. "I am Mrs. Manwaring Mimm."

"I am Elmore Zimpf," Fatso says, though up to this time he never before mentions his first name in public for fear of arousing criticism.

"Never mind who you are," Mrs. Mimm says. "Do you want a job or are you on relief?"

Naturally, Fatso does not want a job, for jobs are what he is keeping away from all his life and furthermore he does not care for Mrs. Mimm's manner and he is about to back away from this situation when he gets to thinking how hungry he is. So he asks her what kind of a job she is thinking of and she says to him like this:

"I want you for my Santa Claus," she says. "I am giving my annual Christmas Eve party at my place in Palm Beach tomorrow night and as soon as I see you I say to the count here that you are the very one for my Santa Claus. My Santa Claus suit will just fit you," she says. "We always have to stuff it up with pillows for my butler Sparks and he never looks natural."

At this Fatso remembers that Christmas is indeed close at hand and naturally this makes him think of Mindy's restaurant on Broadway and the way they cook turkey there with dressing and cranberry sauce and with mashed potatoes and turnips or maybe baked squash to come along and thinking of these matters causes him to sigh heavily and to forget where he is for the moment until he is aroused by hearing the young guy driving the car speak as follows:

"This fat bum is dead from the neck up, Margaret," he says. "You better find someone else."

"No," she says, "I must have this one. Why, Gregorio, he will be a sensational Santa Claus. See here," she says to Fatso, "I will give you fifty dollars."

Well, on hearing the young guy speak of him as a fat bum, Fatso's thoughts return to West Palm Beach at once and he takes a good look at the young guy and he can now see that he has a piece of a mustache on his upper lip and that there is something about him that is quite familiar.

However, Fatso cannot place him as anybody he knows so he figures it is just the type that makes him seem familiar because of course there are thousands of good-looking tanned young guys with pieces of mustaches on their upper lips running around Florida at this season of the year, but he is greatly displeased with this particular young guy for calling him a fat bum.

In fact, Fatso is insulted because while he does not mind being called fat or even a bum he does not care to be called both at the same time because it sounds unrefined. He is figuring that maybe it will be an excellent idea to reach over and tag this young guy one on the chops, when he remembers hearing Mrs. Mimm mention fifty dollars.

So he takes this matter up with her to make certain his ears do not deceive him and sure enough she is willing to give him half a C to be her Santa Claus with two boffoes in advance so he can get across Lake Worth to an address she gives him without walking, provided he will proceed there at once, and Fatso accepts these terms and dismisses the small stove lids from his shade with a nickel apiece and the chances are they figure he is Santa Claus already.

Now this is how Fatso Zimpf comes to be at Pink Waters which is the name of Mrs. Manwaring Mimm's estate in Palm Beach and this estate is about the size of Central Park and faces on the ocean and has many palm trees and fountains and statuary and a swimming pool and a house that reminds Fatso of Rockefeller Center, and with enough servants running around to form a union.

Fatso reports to the butler Sparks and it turns out that this Sparks is very glad to see him when he learns that Fatso is to be Santa Claus because it seems that Sparks always considers it most undignified for a high-class butler to go around being Santa Claus with pillows stuffed down his pants.

Furthermore, it turns out that Sparks is a horse player at heart and when he finds that Fatso is familiar with the gee-gees he becomes very friendly to be sure and supplies him with plenty of information and scandal about one and all in the best circles of Palm Beach and several surrounding spots.

He explains to Fatso that Pink Waters is one of the biggest estates in these parts and that Mrs. Manwaring Mimm is richer than six feet down in Iowa, with money that she gets off her papa, who makes it out of the oil dodge years back, and that she marries any time she feels like it and that she feels like it three times so far and is now feeling like it again. In fact, Sparks tells Fatso that she is now feeling like marrying a young guy by the name of Johnny Relf who also has plenty of dough or will have when his parents kindly pass away.

Sparks says that personally he does not approve of this marriage because there is a slight disparity in age between the parties concerned. He says Johnny is only in his middle twenties and not too bright for his years, at that, while Mrs. Mimm is two face-liftings old that he knows of, but he says she is such a determined character that he does not think it advisable for him to mention his disapproval of her plan.

Then Fatso remembers the young guy in the roadster with Mrs. Mimm and he asks Sparks is this the party she is going to marry and Sparks says:

"Oh, no," he says. "That is Count Gregorio Ferrone of an old Italian noble family. Mrs. Mimm meets him in New York last summer and brings him here to Pink Waters as a house guest. I understand," Sparks says, "that he is about to contract a marriage that will be most advantageous to him. I do not think," he says "that the count is in funds to any extent."

"He is very impolite," Fatso says. "He does not talk much like a foreigner to me. He calls me a fat bum without any accent. Personally," Fatso says, "I mark him N.G."

"Well," Sparks says, "to tell you the truth I second the motion. The count is indeed a little brusque at times, especially," he says, "with the servants. He claims he lives in this country off and on for years so perhaps he loses his accent. Mrs. Mimm does not really seem to know much about him."

Then Sparks tells Fatso that he is not expected to do anything at all until it comes time for him to be Santa Claus the next night so Fatso wanders around and about and admires the sights and scenes of Palm

Beach and finally he strolls along the ocean sands and there in a lonely spot what does he behold but a beautiful young Judy of maybe eighteen crying as if her heart will break.

Now if there is one thing Fatso cannot stand it is the sight of a female character in distress, so he steps up to her and taps her on the shoulder and says to her like this:

"Little miss," he says, "are you in trouble?"

"Yes, I am," she says; "who are you?"

"Why," Fatso says, "I am Santa Claus."

"Oh, no," she says. "There is no Santa Claus. I know it better now than anybody else in this world. Anyway," she says, "if you are Santa Claus where are your whiskers?"

Then Fatso explains about how he is to be Santa Claus for Mrs. Mimm the next night and as soon as he mentions Mrs. Mimm's name the beautiful young Judy stars crying harder than ever.

"Mrs. Mimm is the whole trouble," she says. "Mrs. Mimm steals my Johnny away from me and now I must marry Count Gregorio. I hate him even if he is a count. Mrs. Mimm is an old thing and I want my Johnny."

She continues her crying and Fatso stands there putting two and two together and he can see that he comes upon another angle of the situation that Sparks the butler describes to him.

"Tut-tut," he says. "They tell me Johnny is a lightweight. Dry your tears and think no more of the matter."

Well at this she stops crying and gazes at Fatso who observes that her eyes are a soft brown and he also observes that she has a shape that is worthy of mention, for Fatso is very observing even if he is fat, and finally she says:

"Of course Johnny is a lightweight," she says. "Everybody knows that. In fact," she says, "everybody knows he is a complete nitwit, but," she says, "what difference does that make? I love him. He is awfully good-looking and lots of fun. I love him a zillion dollars' worth. If you are Santa Claus," she says, "you give me my Johnny for my Christmas present instead of the speedboat my papa is getting me. I want my Johnny. I hope Mrs. Mimm drops dead."

Now there are more tears and Fatso keeps patting her on the shoulder and saying now, now, now, and there, there, there, and finally she quiets down and he is able to get a better idea of her story. It is a simple love story such as Fatso often hears before, because a fat guy is always hearing love stories though he never has any to tell himself.

It seems that she and this Johnny have a big quarrel one night in New York because she wishes to go to the Stork Club and he wishes to go to El Morocco and harsh words are exchanged and they part in bitter anger and the next thing she knows he is in Palm Beach and Mrs. Mimm is taking dead aim at him and then this Count Gregorio Ferrone comes along and her papa and mamma decide that it will be a great idea for her to marry him and give them an excuse to have a villa in Italy.

Well, it seems that she agrees to do same while she is still sored up at Johnny but when her papa and mamma take her to their own home in Palm Beach for the winter and she learns the situation between Johnny and Mrs. Mimm is quite serious, she regrets her decision and spends all her time wandering along the sands by herself.

In fact, she says if Fatso does not happen along this particular day the chances are her remainders will now be floating out to sea, because she learns from a jeweler on Worth Avenue that Johnny just buys a square-cut diamond ring the size of a bath rug and that she knows it must be Mrs. Mimm's Christmas present and to tell the truth she hears that Mrs. Mimm picks it out herself and tips the jeweler off to promote Johnny into buying this ring. Furthermore, she hears that Mrs. Mimm is going to announce her engagement to Johnny at the Christmas party.

"And," she says, "I will have to be there to hear it because Count Gregorio is her house guest and my papa and mamma are going and it will be considered very peculiar if I fail to be present. Anyway," she says, "I will hate to have anyone know I am so downcast about Johnny and why I am telling you I cannot think except you are fat and have a kind face."

By this time Fatso is becoming somewhat impatient with tears, so he changes the subject and asks her who she is and she says her name is Betty Lou Marvel and that her papa is nobody but Junius X. Marvel, the big automobile guy.

She says everybody in Palm Beach is afraid of Mrs. Mimm because she can think up very strange things to say about anybody she does not like and that nobody dast stay away from her parties if they are invited, especially her Christmas party. Betty Lou says it is years since anybody has a private Christmas in Palm Beach because Mrs. Mimm makes them bring all their presents to her party and has them given away there by her own Santa Claus and Betty Lou says she is glad they cannot take her speedboat there, and so is Fatso when he comes to think it over.

"Well, little miss," Fatso finally says, "kindly give Count Gregorio no more thought. I am personally giving him much consideration ever since he calls me a fat bum and I will take care of him. But," he says,

"I do not see what I can do about your Johnny and Mrs. Mimm and if he is such a numskull as to prefer her to you maybe you are better off without him. Merry Christmas, little miss," he says.

"Merry Christmas, Santa Claus," Betty Lou says, and then Fatso goes on strolling along the sands wishing he is younger and two hundred pounds lighter.

Well, it comes on Christmas Eve and Pink Waters is all lighted up like Palisades Park with a Christmas tree as tall as a church steeple in the middle of the patio and all the fountains going with colored lights squirting on the water and two orchestras playing one after the other and long tables spread out in the open. In fact, it is as beautiful a scene as anybody could wish to see and very Christmasy-looking except it is quite hot.

When the guests are assembling, Fatso is taken in his Santa Claus suit into the library of the house which opens out into the patio by Sparks the butler and given a little final coaching there.

It seems that the first part of the party is for the neighbors' children and the second part is for the grownups, male and female, and on the Christmas tree in the patio and stacked up at the foot of the tree are many packages containing the presents for the little ones and Sparks explains that it is the duty of Fatso as Santa Claus to distribute these packages.

On a table in the library is a pile of small packages and Sparks says that after he distributes the packages to the children in the patio, Fatso is to return to the library and put these small packages in his Santa Claus bag and go out and stand under the tree again and take the small packages out of the bag one by one and call off the names written on them and hand them out to the parties they are meant for.

"You be very careful with these small packages," Sparks says. "They contain presents from husbands to their ever-loving wives and vice versa and from one sweet pea to another, and so forth and so on. The chances are there are many valuable gewgaws in these packages," he says.

Then Sparks leaves Fatso alone in the library while he goes out to see if everything is ready for the appearance of Santa Claus and Fatso can observe him through the tall French window that opens on the patio, bustling about through the gay scene, and with nothing else to do until Sparks' return, Fatso takes to examining the small packages and thinking to himself that if he has the money the contents represent the chances are he will be able to retire from horse playing and perhaps find some beautiful young Judy like Betty Lou to love him.

He observes Betty Lou in the patio with the young guy that he now knows as Count Gregorio and he can see that she seems somewhat depressed and then he notices Mrs. Mimm with a tall blond young guy at her heels that he figures must be the Johnny Relf that Betty Lou is crying about and Fatso thinks to himself that from his looks this Johnny must indeed be something of a waste ball.

Finally Sparks returns and says everything is all set and out into the patio goes Fatso jingling a lot of sleigh bells and beaming on one and all and the orchestras play and the little children let out shrill cries of joy. There is no doubt but what Fatso is a wonderful success as Santa Claus with the little children and many of them wish to shake hands with him but after an hour of standing under the tree picking up packages and calling off names, Fatso commences to get a little weary.

Moreover, he commences to get a trifle vexed with the little ones, especially when some of them insist on pulling his whiskers and small boys start kicking him on the ankles to see if he is alive and by and by Fatso is thinking that maybe President Roosevelt is right about the redistribution of wealth.

In fact, Fatso finally becomes so vexed that he takes to quietly stepping on a few little toesies here and there accidentally on purpose and the childish cries of pain are enough to break anybody's heart and probably many of these children stop believing in Santa Claus.

Well, he finally gets rid of all the little children and they are taken away by their nurses and only the grownups are left and it is a gay gathering to be sure with one and all in evening dress and drinking champagne and dancing, and Fatso retires to the library again and when Sparks comes in to help him load up with the small packages, Fatso says to him like this:

"Sparksy," he says, "who is the most jealous married guy present at this party?"

"Why," Sparks says, "that is an easy one. The most jealous married guy at this party or anywhere else in the world is undoubtedly old Joel Brokebaugh. He is an old walrus who is married to a young mouse, and," Sparks says, "he thinks that every guy who says good morning to Mrs. Brokebaugh is after her, although," he says, "this idea will make you laugh yourself sick when you see her.

"She is undoubtedly a very low score for looks," Sparks says. "Furthermore," he says, "she has no more spirit than a gooseberry. Old Brokebaugh is so stingy he will not let her buy a new hat or a new dress more than once every few years although he has millions. He does not wish her to dress up for fear some guy may notice her. Personally," Sparks say, "I think old Brokebaugh is touched in the wind for figuring anybody else will ever want his wife, but he has a violent temper and often causes scenes and some say he even carries a pistol in his pocket at all times."

"Brokebaugh, eh?" Fatso says.

"Yes," Sparks says. "They are sitting together under the coconut palm by the big fountain, though why they come to a Christmas party nobody knows because they never give each other anything in the way of presents and take no part in the festivities. Everybody feels sorry for Mrs. Brokebaugh, but," Sparks says, "I say what she needs is some spunk."

Well, Fatso again goes out into the patio with his bag full of the small packages and by this time what with the champagne and the dancing and the spirit of the occasion and all this and that, everybody is in a lively mood and they give Fatso a big cheer and no one is any gayer than Mrs. Mimm.

In fact, she is practically hilarious and she gives Fatso a large smile as he goes past her and he can see that she is pleased with his efforts and he can also see that she still has this Johnny with her and that Johnny looks no brighter than before, if as bright, and then Fatso spots the couple Sparks speaks of under the coconut palm and he is somewhat surprised to note that Sparks slightly overrates Mrs. Brokebaugh's appearance.

Even from a distance Fatso can see that she is a zero for looks but he can also see that the old guy with her seems to be about as described by Sparks, only more so. He is a tall, thin old guy with a red face and a bald head and eyes like a shark and Fatso observes that the servants tiptoe going past him.

Well, Fatso gets under the tree and starts calling out names once more and giving out packages and there is now great excitement and many oohs and ahs in female voices on all sides and finally he gets down to just a few packages and calls out the name of Johnny Relf and right away afterward the name of Miss Betty Lou Marvel and in fact Fatso calls them so close together that they meet under the tree though all they do is exchange cruel glances.

Fatso does not say anything whatever to this Johnny as he gives him his package, because Fatso feels that he already does enough talking in words of one syllable to the children, but when Miss Betty Lou steps up he gives her a smile and says:

"Merry Christmas, little miss."

"Merry Christmas, Santa Claus," she says, "but I still do not believe in you."

Then she starts walking away opening her package as she goes and all of a sudden she lets out a cry and starts running toward Johnny Relf but by now Johnny opens his own package, too, and starts running toward Betty Lou.

So they meet practically head-on and start taking holds on each other in the presence of one and all, because it seems that Betty Lou's present is a large square-cut diamond ring with a card in the box which states that it is to my beloved from Johnny and that his present is a pair of big black pearl studs with a card saying they are with all my heart to Johnny from Betty Lou.

Of course nobody bothers to look into the matter at the moment, but when somebody does so later on it is considered something of a coincidence that the writing on the two cards is exactly the same and not very neat, but one and all figure it is just an act of Providence and let it go at that, especially as an act of Providence is regarded as quite a compliment to Palm Beach.

In fact, at this particular moment nobody is paying much attention to anything much but the great happiness of Betty Lou and Johnny, except Mrs. Mimm and she is watching Fatso with keen interest, though Fatso is unaware of her attention as he walks over to where Mrs. Brokebaugh is sitting and hands her a package instead of calling out her name.

Then Fatso returns to the house figuring to get his Santa Claus suit off and collect his wages from Sparks and vanish from these parts before anybody learns that he writes these cards when he is alone in the library and swaps them for cards that will give the ring to Mrs. Mimm from Johnny and the black pearls to Johnny from Mrs. Mimm, in both cases with love.

While he is walking through a long hallway, all of a sudden Fatso gets a feeling that he is being followed, and looking around he observes Mrs. Mimm close behind him. There is something about Mrs. Mimm that causes Fatso to walk a little faster and then he notes that Mrs. Mimm is walking quite a little faster than he is.

So Fatso dodges into an open doorway that he hopes and trusts may lead him elsewhere but he forgets that when he goes through doors it is usually advisable for him to turn sideways because of his great width. He goes at this door frontways and the next thing he knows there he is stuck right in the middle of the doorway and then he becomes conscious of great discomfort to the southward as it seems that Mrs. Mimm is forgetting she is a lady and is kicking him severely and it also seems that these evening shoes that the Judys wear nowadays with their bare toes sticking out in front are capable of inflicting greater pain when used for kicking than just ordinary shoes.

In the meantime, it appears that there is some commotion in the patio because Mrs. Brokebaugh is so startled at getting any Christmas present at all that she cannot open the package Fatso gives her so old Mr. Brokebaugh opens it for her and finds a gold vanity case with a card that reads as follows:

"To my sweetest sweet from Gregorio."

Well, of course old Mr. Brokebaugh has no way of knowing that this is Count Gregorio's present to Betty Lou and that Fatso does not even change the card but only rubs out Betty Lou's name on it and puts down Mrs. Brokebaugh's, though naturally old Mr. Brokebaugh knows who Gregorio is.

In fact, he can see Gregorio at this very moment standing near by feeling of his little mustache and looking greatly bewildered at the scene that is still going on at intervals between Betty Lou and Johnny, and all of a sudden old Mr. Brokebaugh lets out a yell and jumps up and pulls a pistol out of his pocket and starts full tilt at the count speaking in a loud tone, as follows:

"So," he says, "you are making a play for my wife, are you, scoundrel?"

Well, of course Count Gregorio has no idea what old Mr. Brokebaugh is talking about, but he has eyes in his head and he can see that Mr. Brokebaugh is making a dead set for him and that he is hotter than a firecracker and he can also see the pistol and from the way the count turns and starts running it is plain to be seen that whatever he may be, he is no sucker.

He knocks over three debutantes and a banker worth ten million dollars making for the patio wall and trying to keep trees and bushes between him and old Mr. Brokebaugh as he goes and all this time old Mr. Brokebaugh is running after him and with surprising speed for a guy his age and waving the pistol and requesting the count to stand still and be shot.

He never gets a really fair crack at the count except when Gregorio is going over the wall and then old Mr. Brokebaugh lets fly twice and misses both times and the sound of this shooting probably saves Fatso many more contusions as it brings Mrs. Mimm running into the patio to find out what is going on and in her absense Fatso wiggles on through the doorway.

So Fatso shakes the sands of Palm Beach from his feet regretting only that he never gets a chance to ask Betty Lou if she now believes in Santa Claus and he goes on down to Miami and a year later he relates the above circumstances to me one day when we are sitting in the rocking chairs on the veranda of the Hotel McAllister hoping to catch somebody going to the races with a couple of spare seats in their car, for things are by no means dinkum with Fatso and me at the moment.

"You see," Fatso says, "tomorrow is Christmas again and this is what reminds me of these matters at this time."

"So it is, Fatso," I say. "It is strange how time flies. But, Fatso," I say, "are you not most severe on Count Gregorio in not only knocking him out of a chance to pick up a few boffoes by marriage but in almost getting him plugged by a jealous husband?"

"No," Fatso says. "By no means. You must always remember he calls me a fat bum. Besides," he says, "old Brokebaugh just spares me the humiliation of denouncing Gregorio as a former bus boy in Vincenti's wop restaurant in West Fiftieth Street and still wanted for robbing the damper of thirty-six dollars.

"I will never forgive myself if I am compelled to holler copper on anybody whatsoever," Fatso says, "but," he says, "of course I will do so as a last resort to prevent Gregorio from marrying Betty Lou. It comes to me all of a sudden why his face is familiar when I am strolling on the sands the time I meet Betty Lou. I never forget a face."

Well, at this moment a big limousine stops in front of the hotel and a small-sized lively Judy all dressed up and sparkling with jewelry hops out of the car and runs up the veranda steps with three good-looking tanned young guys with little mustaches running after her and she is laughing and gay and looks like plenty in the bank, and I am greatly surprised when she skips up to Fatso and gives him a pat on the arm and says like this:

"Merry Christmas, Santa Claus!"

Then she is gone as quick as she comes and the young guys with her and she is still laughing and Fatso is gazing at a fifty-dollar note in his hand with great pleasure and he says:

"She is from Palm Beach," he says. "Anytime anybody from Palm Beach recognizes me they stake me to something because they remember that Mrs. Mimm never pays me the fifty she promises me for being her Santa Claus. I understand," Fatso says, "that it is a public scandal in Palm Beach."

"Is this one Betty Lou?" I ask.

"Oh, no," Fatso says. "She is Mrs. Brokebaugh. I recall now I hear that ever since she gets the Christmas present that she thinks to this very day is from Count Gregorio, she decides she is a natural-born charmer and blossoms out into a life of gaiety, and," Fatso says, "they tell me her husband cannot do a thing about it. Well, Merry Christmas to you."

"Merry Christmas, Fatso," I say.

Cleo

———◆◆◆◆———

ONE PLEASANT spring day at the Bowie race track, there comes to me a guy by the name of Fat-Fat, who is a horse player by trade and who is called by this name because he is not only fat but he is double fat. In fact, he is very fat indeed. He has a paper in his hand and he seems greatly pleased and he says to me like this:

"Well," he says, "The Beard wants me. Yes," he says, "Uncle Sam at last calls me to join the colors. I have here a summons to report to my draft board in New York City. I understand you are seeking means of transportation there and I will be pleased to have you accompany me in my car as my guest. Why," Fat-Fat says, "I can scarcely wait to get my uniform. It is long my ambition to serve my country and besides," he says, "when Cleo my fiancée sees me as a soldier maybe she will speak to me again after giving me the back of her neck for all these months."

So there I am speeding through Delaware with Fat-Fat in his big, open automobile for at this time he is quite strong in the funds department what with putting over several nice parlays at Bowie and my presence is without doubt a great comfort to him as Fat-Fat always likes to have someone to converse with. But it seems to me he can do just as well alone, as when Fat-Fat gets sunk down behind the wheel all his chins pile up around his neck and he is never able to turn his head one way or the other to see who he is conversing with or how they are taking it. In fact, he just talks straight ahead.

He never talks about anything whatsoever but this Cleo he is in love with, but as most of his words get lost among his chins I never hear half of what he says so I do not try to answer him and anyway Fat-Fat does not care whether you answer him or not as long as you do not try to change the subject from Cleo.

She is a brown-haired pretty who has a dancing background and at the time I am speaking of she is working for Buddy DeSylva in a show by the name of Panama Hattie and she is regarded as one of the prettiest of all the pretties in the show. To tell the truth, she is regarded by some as a gorgeous and it is generally conceded that she is by no means an intellectual, or anyway not offensively so.

I am not very well acquainted with her but Fat-Fat tells me that she is a hard-working and conscientious pretty and that after the show is over at night she hastens right to her home in the Bronx and I have no doubt this is very true, although I also hear from other sources that she generally routes herself to the Bronx by way of the Stork Club, Leon and Eddie's, La Martinique and similar detours.

Well, as we go buzzing along, suddenly we behold an interesting spectacle at the side of the road. A cow is lying on the ground quite still and a little calf is standing beside it on very wobbly pins going mah-ah-ah, like that, and a guy in overalls and a dirty shirt, who is without doubt a Jasper, is also standing there looking most depressed, and seeing all this, Fat-Fat stops the car and gets out and views the situation a while and the following conversation ensues:

"Hello," Fat-Fat says. "What comes off?"

"A truck kills my cow," the Jasper says. "I see it disappearing over the hill just as I come up."

"Why," Fat-Fat says, "this is quite pitiful. What about the midget here?" he says, pointing to the calf. "Why is it making such a row? Does it get hit too? I see many a cow in my time," Fat-Fat says, "but never before do I see a midget one."

"Look, Fat-Fat," I say, "this is not a midget. This is a baby cow that is called a calf and a fine specimen it is, too, and it is bawling because its mamma is lying here cold in death. It is now an orphan."

"Well," Fat-Fat says, "I never see such a sawed-off cow before so naturally I think it is a midget cow. I never realize there are baby cows. I always figure they come full-size. Look at its big, soft brown eyes. Who do they remind you of?"

I look at the calf's eyes but they do not remind me of anybody's except a calf's and I so state to Fat-Fat who is now squatted down petting the calf and gazing into its eyes while the calf is still going mah-ah-ah.

"They are Cleo's eyes," Fat-Fat says. "I never see such a resemblance. Mister," he says to the Jasper, "is this a boy baby cow or a girl baby cow?"

"Why," the Jasper says, "it is a cow calf so it must be a girl. If it is a boy it will be a bull calf and not a cow calf at all. Now," he says, "I must lug this calf nearly two miles to my home back here in the woods. I do not see how they wander so far away in the first place."

"Why not shoo it along ahead of you?" I say. "Or maybe we can find a piece of string and you can pull it."

"No," the Jasper says, "I will have to carry it. It is too young and it is already plumb tuckered out from walking. This is a terrible blow to me as the cow is my sole possession in the way of livestock and she supplies milk for my children. She is a Jersey and a wonderful milker. Now," he says, "I have no means of getting milk for my children or for this calf either."

"Mister," Fat-Fat says, "will you sell this baby cow to me? I will give you a hundred dollars for it. It will make a wonderful present for Cleo my fiancée and something to remember me by when I am in the Army serving my country, and," he says, "more than anything else she is sure to consider it a most touching gesture when she learns I buy a baby cow just because its eyes remind me of her. Cleo is really very sentimental."

Well, at this I remonstrate with Fat-Fat and try to explain to him that such a purchase is most ill-advised. But Fat-Fat will not listen to me, and the upshot of it is he gives the Jasper the hundred dollars, and the Jasper, who is practically stunned by the transaction, lifts the calf into the back seat of the car and tells Fat-Fat he must feed it milk out of a bottle for a spell.

So away we go with the calf lying down in the seat and going mah-ah-ah, but presently Fat-Fat finds he cannot keep looking around at the calf on account of his chins preventing him from turning his head and he makes me do the driving while he gets in the back seat with the calf and before long he is calling it Cleo and I can see that this is now the calf's name.

We stop at the first town we come to and Fat-Fat buys a baby's nursing bottle with a nipple on it at a drugstore and then he buys some milk and gets a guy in a hamburger joint to warm it up and he feeds Cleo in a way that is astonishing to behold. I never know before that Fat-Fat is so handy in this respect but he tells me he often performs a similar service for his baby brother and his baby sister, too, when he is a kid over on Tenth Avenue. By the time we reach New York City, I can see that Fat-Fat is greatly devoted to Cleo the calf and I can also see that Cleo the calf thinks very well of Fat-Fat, which is not surprising considering he is the source of her warm milk.

We pull up in front of Mindy's restaurant on Broadway around the dinner hour when the place is well filled with customers and Fat-Fat lifts Cleo the calf out of the car and carries her inside in his arms and naturally it is quite a surprise to one and all to observe this spectacle, especially when Fat-Fat sits down at a table in a booth and puts Cleo on the settee opposite him. In fact, there is so much commotion that Mindy himself appears and when he sees Cleo the calf he does not even shake hands with Fat-Fat and tell him he is glad to see him back but says to him like this:

"Wrong bettors, yes," Mindy says. "Actors and newspapermen and song writers, yes. But," Mindy says, "calfs, no. You cannot keep these cattle in my gaff, Fat-Fat."

"This is Cleo, Mindy," Fat-Fat says.

"Cleo?" Mindy says. "Ha-ha-ha-ha," he says. "Cleo just leaves here for the theater full of goulash with the guy with the one eye-glass she is running around with while you are absent. I think he is a nobleman refugee. Everybody is a nobleman refugee nowadays. I do not like his looks. But," Mindy says, "this is neither here nor there nor elsewhere. You must take this thing out of here, especially," he says, "as calfs are very seldom house broke."

Well, at this, Cleo the calf goes mah-ah-ah and who comes up but Ambrose Hammer, the newspaper scribe, who speaks to Mindy as follows:

"See here, Mindy," he says, "you serve veal in here, do you not?"

"The very best," Mindy says. "Veal stew, veal chops, veal tenderloin and wiener schnitzel, which is a veal."

"It all comes from a calf," Ambrose says. "You also serve calves' liver, do you not?"

"None better," Mindy says. "It is very good for nimmicks."

"You mean anemics," Ambrose says. "Kindly do not distort the English language, Mindy. Now," he says, "what is the difference between permitting the by-products of the calf in here and the calf itself? You are being very unreasonable, if you ask me."

Naturally, Mindy is somewhat nonplused by this argument, especially as he wishes to remain on friendly terms with Ambrose Hammer because sometimes Ambrose mentions the joint in his column, which is very nice publicity indeed, and besides by this time everybody in the place is interested in Cleo the calf and all the pretties are coming up and addressing her in baby language and Mindy can see that she is quite an attraction.

"Well," he says, "I will have to think this situation over."

So he retires to the kitchen and Fat-Fat and I have our dinner and Cleo the calf has her milk out of the bottle and Ambrose Hammer sits down with us and listens with great interst to Fat-Fat's story of how he comes to buy Cleo the calf because of her eyes and why he calls her Cleo and all this and that. In fact, Ambrose is so interested that he goes to his office and writes a very fine story about Fat-Fat and Cleo the calf and also about Cleo the pretty, but of course we do not know this until the blat Ambrose works for comes out the next morning.

In the meantime, Fat-Fat takes Cleo the calf around to the hotel in West Forty-ninth Street where he always lives in New York, figuring to register her there and then go looking for Cleo the pretty and have a reunion and one thing and another with her. But he has great difficulty convincing the night clerk that Cleo the calf is acceptable as a lodger because it seems that just a couple of weeks previously the clerk admits a guest with a boa constrictor and this boa constrictor escapes during the night and goes visiting in other rooms and causes so much unrest in the hotel that the clerk does not get a wink of sleep throughout his watch.

However, Fat-Fat is an old patron of the hotel and besides he stakes the clerk to a sawsky, so he gets his old room and by this time he is pretty well tuckered out himself so he decides to get a good night's sleep before looking for Cleo the pretty and while Cleo the calf goes mah-ah-ah most of the night, it does not seem to disturb the other guests and does not bother the clerk at all, as it seems he is raised on a farm and is accustomed to such sounds in the night.

Well, soon after daylight the next morning the hotel is surrounded by reporters and photographers from the afternoon blats because it seems Ambrose Hammer makes Fat-Fat and Cleo the calf sound very interesting, indeed, but it also seems that even before they get there Cleo the pretty has Fat-Fat on the phone and that she is sizzling about Fat-Fat telling Ambrose the calf's eyes remind him of hers and claiming that this is just the same thing as comparing her to a cow.

"Furthermore," Fat-Fat says when he is telling me about this incident later in the day, "she informs me that I am nothing but a tub of lard and that if I ever as much as look at her again she will call the cops. She says anyway she is now in love with a very high-class guy by the name of Henri something and is going to marry him. When I tell her I buy Cleo the calf as a present for her she spurns my token in words I am never before aware she even knows.

"I also have other bad news," Fat-Fat says. "I am rejected today by the doctors for the Army. They say I am too corpulent. They give me the elbow without even permitting me to remove my garments. Now I cannot even serve my country. On top of everything else, I blow a good bet on Air Brigade in the fourth at Jamaica. I am most despondent," Fat-Fat says. "But," he says, "I am now very glad I buy Cleo the calf or I will have nothing whatever to console myself with. I can always gaze into her eyes and remind myself of my lost love."

For a couple of days the hotel receives so much publicity in connection with Cleo the calf that the management is greatly pleased with her presence but when the blats stop talking about her she gets to be quite a bore, and they request Fat-Fat to remove her, especially as guys from the health department commence coming around and stating that it is setting a bad precedent to other hotels to have a calf as a guest.

So Fat-Fat has to get rid of Cleo the calf or find another place to live and by this time he is very fond of her, indeed, and cannot bear the idea of parting from her. Finally he finds a spot over on Eleventh Avenue along in the Fifties not far from the North River docks where an old bundle by the name of Mrs. Squamm runs a small fleabag and who is very glad to have Fat-Fat and Cleo the calf. In fact, Mrs. Squamm states that she often longs for a touch of rural atmosphere over on Eleventh Avenue and feels that Cleo the calf will provide same.

Furthermore, right next door to Mrs. Squamm's little fleabag there is a fenced-in vacant lot covering half a block which is once occupied by a house that burns down years ago leaving nothing but a big hole in the ground in the center of the lot that is formerly the cellar, and Fat-Fat can see that this lot will be very handy for Cleo the calf to romp about in when she gets older, especially as Mrs. Squamm's kitchen where Cleo the calf sleeps opens right into the lot.

Now the summer passes by and I do not see Fat-Fat for some time although I hear of him hustling and bustling about the race courses at his trade as a horse player, and then one night I run into him in front of Mindy's and ask him how Cleo the calf is.

"Why," Fat-Fat says, "she is fine and growing like a weed. I play with her every day, wrestling and rolling about on the floor with her to strengthen her muscles and also to reduce my own weight. I never give up hope of being permitted to serve my country in the Army. She runs about the lot next door when I am at the track and is enjoying herself in a way that is a pleasure to behold. But," Fat-Fat says, "I am sorry to say that there has come up some friction between Cleo the calf and a bunch of small kids who also wish to use the lot as a playground. She detests them."

"What about the other Cleo?" I ask.

At this, the tears start rolling down Fat-Fat's cheeks and he is unable to speak, so I can see he is deeply affected and naturally I am very sorry for him, especially as I hear rumors along Broadway that Cleo the pretty seems to be crazy about this Henri. In fact, I observe them one night together in the Stork Club holding hands and gazing into each other's eyes in such a way that I can see it must be love.

Personally, I cannot blame her much as this Henri is a good-looking guy with a small mustache and is very well dressed except for a monocle and alongside of him Fat-Fat is naturally nothing but a plater compared to a stake horse, but of course looks are not everything. To tell the truth, they are only about eighty per cent. I make a few inquiries about Henri but nobody seems to have any line on him except that he is undoubtedly a foreign guy and seems to have plenty of beesom but at this time there are so many foreign guys in New York with plenty of beesom that no one ever bothers to find out who they are or where they are from, or whatever.

Well, one night in the late fall, Fat-Fat calls me up at Mindy's and requests me to come over to Mrs. Squamm's house and keep him company, stating that he is not feeling well and does not wish to go out. He also states that Mrs. Squamm goes to bed early and Cleo the calf is sleeping out in the lot because she is now so big she takes up too much room in the kitchen, and that he is low in his mind and lonesome. So I go there and am playing him a little pinochle and permitting him to win to cheer him up when along towards midnight there comes a knock at the door and when Fat-Fat opens it who rushes in but a big guy and a couple of smaller guys and the big guy displays a badge in his hand and speaks like this:

"Jubble is the name," he says. "Federal Bureau of Investigation. Where are they?"

"Where are who?" Fat-Fat says.

"Kindly do not stall," Jubble says. "One of my guys hears her give this house address to the taxi jockey as they drive away from the Stork Club. They leave the cab, which is now in our custody, waiting down the street a block off and walk here and the jockey says he sees them climb over the fence into the lot next door, and as we do not observe hide nor hair of them in the lot they must be in this house because there is no other house around close. Come, come," he says, "speak up."

Now all of a sudden we hear Cleo the calf's voice out in the lot going mah-ah-ah as if she is in distress and Fat-Fat runs out the back door of the kitchen and into the lot and Jubble and his guys run after him and so do I. The street lights outside the fence throw a dim light all over the lot but Cleo the calf is not to be seen although we can still hear her. So Fat-Fat follows the sound of her voice until it brings him to the hole in the ground that is once a cellar and as the voice seems to come from this hole, Jubble and his guys all turn flashlights into the hole and we observe a somewhat unusual scene.

Cleo the calf and Cleo the pretty and Henri the foreign guy are all down in the hole and Cleo the calf is chasing Cleo the pretty and Henri back and forth in this space which is about the size and depth of a long, narrow room, in a most surprising manner and going mah-ah-ah in a tone that indicates she is greatly vexed, and I can see that Cleo the calf is much more developed since I last notice her and in fact she is quite large.

Now and then Henri tries to climb up one side of the hole, digging his fingers in the dirt wail and Cleo the calf immediately butts him vigorously from behind and knocks him down. Once while we are gazing at this scene, Cleo the pretty also tries to climb the wall and Cleo the calf butts her in the same place she does Henri and just as vigorously and Cleo the pretty is sobbing and Henri is using the most ungenteel language and Cleo the calf keeps going mah-ah-ah so there is really some little confusion, and on viewing all this, Fat-Fat becomes slightly indignant and speaks as follows:

"See here, now," Fat-Fat says, "you must not be playing tag with Cleo the calf at such an hour in a hole in the ground. She is supposed to be getting her rest."

Well, even in the confusion I notice that the hole that is once a cellar looks as if somebody recently clears it out and does a lot of digging as if to make it deeper as there is much fresh earth around and about and there are steps dug in one wall as if to enable whoever does the digging to climb in and out and I also notice that there are light boards across the hole like a flat roof, and it is plain to be seen that these boards give way under some kind of weight in the middle so I figure this is where Cleo the calf and Cleo the pretty and Henri drop through into the hole. Furthermore, Jubble seems to notice this, too, because he says:

"Why," he says, "this is really most ingenious. I must tell our chief, Mr. Hoover, about this spy trap. Maybe we can build a few in Washington."

"What makes it a spy trap?" I say.

"It traps this Henri guy, does it not?" Jubble says. "And he is a spy. He is Henri la Porte, alias Muller, the most dangerous secret agent and saboteur in the world. We are tailing him for months. Johnson," he says to one of his guys, "jump down in there and put the handcuffs on him, although," he says, "maybe you better wait until somebody surrounds the animal that is pursuing him."

At this, Fat-Fat drops down into the hole and puts his arms around Cleo the calf and calls her pet names and quiets her down and then this Johnson follows him into the hole and applies the darbolas to Henri's wrists and all the time Henri is putting up quite a bleat and saying he will see his ambassador and maybe the President, and Cleo the pretty is sitting on the ground down in the hole crying as if her heart will break.

We finally get them all out of the hole but Cleo the calf and go back to Mrs. Squamm's house and on the way I ask Fat-Fat if he notices the way the old cellar is fixed up and he says he does and that he is greatly bewildered by same but that it is best not to speak of this matter until we see what is what. He says there is undoubtedly more here than meets the eye, and about now a tall guy I do not see before comes into the house with still another guy that I can see is a taxicab jockey and the tall guy whispers something to Jubble and Jubble says like this:

"Fine," he says. "I am glad you put it in a safe place. Well," he says, gazing at Cleo the pretty who is still crying no little, "I must also put this beautiful under arrest as an accomplice, although," he says, "it is by no means the established policy of our chief, Mr. Hoover, to molest beautifuls."

Now of course here is a predicament to be sure, because anybody can see that being arrested as an accomplice to a saboteur will present Cleo the pretty in an unfavorable light before her public and Cleo the pretty begins to cry louder than ever and she looks at Fat-Fat and speaks to him as follows:

"Irving," she says, "save me."

"Why," Fat-Fat says to Jubble, "what do you mean she is an accomplice? She is my fiancée and my personal assistant. I have her stool this Henri guy into the lot so we can trap him in exactly the manner you observe, although," Fat-Fat says, "of course I do not know he is as great a scapegrace as you state. I figure he is just a fiancée thief and it is my intention to give him a going-over and this marvelous here is in on the play."

"Oh," Jubble says, "I beg your pardon, Miss. I beg everybody's pardon. Why," he says, "you may get a medal for this. Now I must hasten to my office and leave my lads to follow with the prisoner. But," he says, "we must keep this capture quiet until we round up any others who may be connected with Henri."

As Jubble departs and while I am still thinking of what an exaggeration Fat-Fat is guilty of, and am also still wondering about the cellar, Cleo the pretty throws herself into Fat-Fat's arms and kisses him and says:

"Irving," she says, "forgive me for everything, I never really love anybody but you."

"Why," Fat-Fat says, "I forgive you, all right, but how do you come to be in this lot out here in the first place, not to mention being down in the hole?"

"Oh," Cleo the pretty says, "I am going away and I get to thinking of you, and I remember your address here, because I always keep track of you, and I induce Henri to make a stop. He is putting me aboard a ship that sails for South America at midnight and he is going to join me there later and we are to be married. I want to see you for the last time, but Henri has the cab stop before we reach your door. I can see now he must suspect we are being followed.

"We walk the rest of the way," Cleo the pretty says, "but Henri is evidently still suspicious as he boosts me over the fence into the lot and follows after me and tells me we must wait there a while and what do I see in the lot but a terrible animal and for no reason this animal becomes angry and chases us around until we run across what looks like solid ground but which gives way under our feet and drops us into the hole. It is a dreadful experience, Irving," she says.

"I do not understand it," Fat-Fat says. "It is not in keeping with Cleo the calf's character to display such temper. I guess she realizes Henri is a wrongie."

"Irving," Cleo the pretty says, "you must not think Henri is as bad as these parties state. He is very kind to me and gives me a perfectly huge basket of fruits and flowers and candies for my going-away present. I leave it in the cab and, Irving," she says, "I trust you will recover it for me."

At this, the tall guy who comes in last and who seems to be questioning the taxicab jockey, steps over to Cleo the pretty and taps her on the shoulder and says:

"Sister," he says, "Henri is not putting you on a boat for South America. He is putting you on one that is going to Egypt and is loaded with war supplies. And in the basket of stuff he gives you for a present is a time bomb that will sink the ship and you with it inside of twelve hours."

"Why," Cleo the pretty says, "maybe he is a rascal after all. But," she says, "it is a beautiful basket."

Afterwards I hear this same tall guy talking to Henri in another room and he says to Henri like this:

"Muller," he says, "how do you ever come to join out with a dumb broad such as this?"

"Why," Henri says, "I need a dumb one for my purpose. But I am dumber than she is. If I do not let her talk me into making this stop for a farewell to the blubberhead I will have her aboard the Zoozoo and my work will be accomplished."

But of course I do not mention this conversation to Fat-Fat or to Cleo the pretty either as I fear it may cast a slight cloud over their happiness.

"Well," Fat-Fat says, when the guys finally leave with Henri, "everything turns out for the best. But," he says, "I am still puzzled as to how such a gentle little thing comes to commit this violent assault. Maybe I do wrong in teaching her to butt," he says.

Then Fat-Fat and Cleo the pretty kiss and hug again and their pleasure in this proceeding is really beautiful to behold and later Cleo the pretty tells me in confidence that what makes her realize that she truly loves Fat-Fat is that when she sees Cleo the calf in the lot and remembers the rumors that come to her ears of how Fat-Fat adores this creature, a terrible wave of jealousy comes over her and she cannot resist giving Cleo the calf a good kick in the slats. And Cleo the pretty says this kick is undoubtedly what stirs Cleo the calf to a passion and causes her to run them into the hole.

I drop over to Mrs. Squamm's a few days later and Fat-Fat and Cleo the pretty and Mrs. Squamm are having something to eat in the kitchen and Cleo the calf is standing half in and half out of the doorway watching them and I give them all a huge hello including Cleo the calf and sit down and Fat-Fat says to me like this:

"Well," he says, "Mrs. Squamm finds out about the cellar for me. It seems the little kids of the neighborhood who are disputing with Cleo the calf for possession of the lot see a movie about big-game hunters in Africa or some such place and observe how they trap lions and tigers and elephants and all this and that and they are pretending among themselves as kids will do that Cleo the calf is a tiger and they make a trap of the cellar similar to something they see in the movies to snare her. Mrs. Squamm says it is called a pitfall. She thinks they are playing they are Frank Bucks. My gracious," Fat-Fat says, "when I am a kid, Jesse James is plenty good enough for me."

"Well," I say, "no doubt you will soon be passing about the neighborhood distributing a few bootses in the pantses?"

"By no means," Fat-Fat says. "Let us say no more about this incident as I am receiving great credit for personally trapping Henri and in fact I am to be rewarded with a job in the service of the Beard. They are going to send me to a school and make an undercover guy of me to run down other secret agents and saboteurs and such. So I will get to serve my country after all."

"Congratulations, Fat-Fat," I say. "And what is to become of Cleo the pretty here and also of Cleo the calf?"

"Oh," Fat-Fat says, "I am buying a little farm up the Hudson. We are going to live there and raise a lot of little Cleos on both sides."

Then he and Cleo the pretty begin hugging and kissing again and Mrs. Squamm laughs heartily and Cleo the calf goes moo-oo-oo, like that, so I can see her voice is commencing to change no little.

The Lacework Kid

———————◆◆●◆◆———————

NOW, OF COURSE, the war makes itself felt along Broadway no little and quite some and in fact it is a most disturbing element at times as it brings many strangers to the city who crowd Mindy's restaurant to the doors and often compel the old-time regular customers to stand in line waiting for tables, which is a very great hardship, indeed.

It does no good to complain to Mindy about this situation as he is making so much money he is practically insolent and he only asks you if you do not know there is a war going on, and besides Mindy is generally waiting for a table himself.

Well, one evening I am fortunate enough to out-cute everyone else for a chair that is the only vacant chair at a little table for two and the other chair is occupied by a soldier, and who is this soldier but a guy by the name of The Lacework Kid who is eating as if Hitler is coming up Broadway.

Now The Lacework Kid, who is generally called Lace for short, is a personality who is maybe thirty years old but looks younger and is a card player by trade. Furthermore he is considered one of the best that ever riffles a deck. In fact, he comes by his monicker because someone once remarks that his work with the card is as delicate as lace, although personally I consider this an understatement.

He comes from the city of Providence which is in Rhode Island, and of course it is well known to one and all that for generations Providence produces wonderful card players, and in his childhood The Lacework Kid has the advantage of studying under the best minds there, and afterwards improves his education in this respect by much travel.

Before the war he is a great hand for riding the tubs and makes regular trips back and forth across the Atlantic Ocean because a guy in his line can always find more customers on the boats than anywhere else and can also do very good for himself by winning the pools on the ship's daily run if he can make the proper connections to get the information on the run in advance.

I only wish you can see The Lacework Kid before the war when he is at the height of his career. He is maybe five feet nine and very slender and has brown eyes and wavy brown hair and a face like a choirboy and a gentle voice.

He wears the best clothes money can buy and they are always of soft quiet materials and his linen is always white and his shoes black. He wears no jewelry showing, but he carries a little gold watch in his pants pocket that stands him a G-er in Paris and a gold cigarette box that sets him back a gob in the same place.

He has long slim white hands like a society broad and in fact there is no doubt that his hands are the secret of The Lacework Kid's success at his trade of card playing as they are fast and flexible and have youth in them, and youth is one thing a good card player must have, because age stiffens fingers up more than somewhat. But of course age is a draw-back in everything in this wicked old world.

It is really a beautiful sight to watch The Lacework Kid handle a deck of cards because he makes the pasteboards just float together when he is shuffling and causes them to fall as light as flecks of foam when he is dealing. His specialty is a game called bridge when he is riding the tubs and he is seldom without customers because in the first place he does not look like a guy who can play bridge very well and in the second place he does not appear to be such a personality as the signs in the smoking rooms on the boats refer to when they say "Beware of Card Sharks." In fact The Lacework Kid generally tries to get a chair right under one of these signs to show that it cannot possibly mean him.

I see The Lacework Kid a few years before this night in Mindy's when he just gets in on a German liner and he has a guy by the name of Schultz with him and is entertaining this Schultz royally because it seems Schultz is the smoking room steward on the liner and is The Lace-work Kid's connection in winning the pools and in introducing bridge customers to him and putting him away with them as a rich young American zillionaire and as the trip nets Lace two thou on the pools alone he feels quite grateful to Schultz.

But of course this is before there is any war and later when I see him the unpleasantness is on and no liners are running and Lace tells me his trade is the greatest economic casualty of the whole war, and he is won-dering if there is any use trying to ride the submarines back and forth looking for customers.

And now here he is again as large as life and in fact slightly larger as I can see he puts on a little weight and he looks very good in his uni-form and has a red ribbon on his chest, so I say to him like this:

"Lace," I say, "it is indeed a pleasure to run into you and I can see by your uniform that you are in the war business and by your ribbon that you distinguish yourself in some manner. Perhaps you are decorated for dealing the general a nice hand off the bottom?"

Well, at this, The Lacework Kid gives me a most severe look and says:

"It is a Good Conduct Medal. I get it for being a fine soldier. I may get an even better award for an experience I will now relate to you."

I will omit the details of my early career in the Army (The Lacework Kid says) except to tell you that my comrades know me only as Sergeant Fortescue Melville Michael O'Shay, my mamma getting the first two names out of a novel she is reading at the time I am born, and my papa's papa bringing the last two over from Ireland.

Furthermore, they know nothing of my background and while there are occasions when I am greatly tempted to make assessments against them out of my great store of knowledge when they are playing such trifling games as blackjack, I resist the urge and confine myself strictly to the matter in hand, which is the war.

I am the waist gunner in a Flying Fortress on a raid over Germany one pleasant afternoon when our ship is so severely jostled by antiaircraft shells that we are compelled to bail out and no sooner do I land than up comes three German soldiers with rifles in their dukes.

They points these rifles at me in a most disquieting manner and while I only know a word or two of the German language I can see that I am their prisoner and the next thing I know I am in a prison camp where I find my comrades and also several hundred other gees who seem to be British and one thing and another.

It is not a large camp and in fact I learn that it is just a sort of temporary detention spot for prisoners who are rounded up in this particular section of the country and that they are usually transferred to a larger gaff after a while. It is located in a hilly country not far from the Swiss border and you can see high mountains in the distance that I am told are the Alps.

But even with the view it is by no means a desirable place. The life in this camp is most monotonous and the cuisine is worse, which is a terrible disappointment to me as I am rather fond of German cooking, and particularly adore the apple strudel of this race, and the chow they give us makes me more violently anti-Nazi than ever and also gives me indigestion. To tell the truth, I spend most of my time trying to figure a way to escape though they tell me that if I am patient I will sooner or later be exchanged for a German prisoner.

There is a company of maybe a hundred German soldiers guarding the camp and I am only there a few hours before I learn that the officer who is in charge of the joint is a captain by the name of Kunz, and that he is also sometimes called The Butcher because it seems that in the early days of the war he is in command of an outfit in Poland and thinks nothing of killing people right and left for no reason whatever except he enjoys seeing them die.

But it seems he finally gets himself in bad with his boss and is sent to this little out-of-the-way prison camp as a lesson to him and he runs the place like the tough warden of a stir back home though he does not show up much in person around the camp and in fact I never see him myself until the time I am going to tell you about.

One afternoon a German sergeant comes into the prison yard where I am taking a little exercise and beckons me off to one side and I am somewhat surprised to observe that the sergeant is nobody but Schultz the steward, who speaks to me in a low voice as follows:

"Hello, Lace," he says. "How is everything?"

"Schultz," I say, "everything stinks."

"Lace," he says, "what do you know about something American that is called gin rummy?"

"Gin rummy?" I say. "Why I know it is supposed to be a card game but as a matter of fact it is nothing but a diversion for idiots."

"Are you a gin rummy man?" Schultz says. "I mean do you play the game?"

"Schultz," I say, "nearly everybody in the United States of America plays gin rummy. The little children in the street play it. Old broads play it. I understand there is a trained ape in the Bronx Zoo that plays it very nicely and I am not surprised, because," I say, "I can teach any dumb animal to play gin rummy if I can get it to hold ten cards."

"Well," Schultz says, "what I am getting at is do you play it as well as you play bridge and in the same way? What I must know is are you a mechanic at gin? I mean if necessary?"

Well naturally I am slightly vexed by this question as I consider it an insult to my integrity as well as a reflection upon my card playing to even hint that I do anything in cards except outplay my opponent through my superior skill. To tell the truth, I feel it is just the same as asking Joe Louis if he uses the difference in his gloves when he is meeting a chump.

"Schultz," I say, "you are undoubtedly a scoundrel to always be thinking in terms of larceny. I never swindle anybody at anything despite any rumors to the contrary that you may hear. And I never hear of any swindles in gin rummy except planting a guy who is supposed to have a piece of your opponent's play alongside him to tip off his cards to you.

"But," I say, "I consider this a low form of thievery. However,

Schultz," I say, "I will be guilty of false modesty if I do not admit to you that like all gin players I think I am the best. In fact, I know of but one who can beat me consistently at gin and that is Kidneyfoot, the waiter in Mindy's, but then he teaches me the game and naturally figures to top me slightly."

Well, then this Schultz unfolds a very strange tale to me. He says that when Captain Kunz is in the United States for some years before the war as an attaché of the German embassy in Washington, he learns the game of gin rummy and it becomes a great passion with him.

It seems from what Schultz says that after Kunz returns to Germany, he misses his gin rummy no little as the game is practically unknown in his country where card players generally favor pinochle or maybe klabriasch. It seems that Kunz tries to teach some of his countrymen how to play gin but has little success and anyway the war comes on and promoting an American game will be deemed unpatriotic, so he has to cease his efforts in this direction.

But he cannot stop thinking of gin, so he finally invents a sort of solitaire gin and plays it constantly all by himself, but it is most unsatisfactory and when he hears of American prisoners arriving in his camp, he sends for Schultz and asks him to canvass us and see if there are any gin-rummy players in the crowd. And in looking us over, Schultz spots me.

"Now," Schultz says, "I build you up to the captain as the champion gin player of the United States, and he finally tells me the other night that he wishes to play you if it can be done in secret, as of course it will be very bad for morale if it gets out that the commandant of a prison camp engages in card games with a prisoner. The captain is rich and likes to play for high stakes, too," Schultz says.

"Look, Schultz," I say, "I do not have any moolouw with me here. All my potatoes are planted in a jug in England and I do not suppose the captain will accept notes of hand payable there."

"Listen," Schultz says, dropping his voice to a whisper, "I tell all my fellow soldiers here about your gin playing and how you are so clever you can make a jack jump out of a deck and sing Chattanooga Choo-Choo if necessary, and we all agree to pool our resources to provide you with a taw. We can raise maybe fifty thousand marks. But," Schultz says, "you must not breathe a word of this to your comrades. The captain must think they are the ones who are backing you. You will receive twenty-five per cent of your winnings, and I will personally guarantee your end."

Naturally, I figure Schultz is giving me the old rol-de-dol-dol for some reason because it does not make sense that an officer in the German army will wish to play an American prisoner gin rummy, but then I remember that gin players will do anything to play gin and I figure that maybe the captain is like the old faro bank player who is warned as he is going into a gambling house to beware of the bank game there because it is crooked and who says:

"Yes, I know it is, but what am I going to do? It is the only game in town."

Well, of course this is an ancient story to you and you will kindly forgive me for springing it at this time, but I am trying to explain the psychology of this captain as I see it. Anyway, I tell Schultz to go ahead and arrange the game and in the meantime I get a deck of cards and practice to refresh my memory.

Now, one night Schultz shows up at my quarters and tells me to come with him and he says it in such a stern voice and acts so mysterious that everyone figures I am being taken out to be shot and to tell you the truth I am not so sure myself that this is not the case. But when we get away from the other prisoners, Schultz is quite nice to me.

He takes me outside the gates of the prison camp and we walk along a road about a mile when we come to a small house set back from the road in a grove of trees and Schultz stops in front of this house and speaks to me as follows:

"Lace," he says, "in the course of your playing with the captain kindly do not refer to our people as krauts, pretzels, beerheads, Heinies, Boches, sausages, wienies or by the titles of any other members of the vegetable or animal kingdom, and do not tell him what you Americans are going to do to us. It will only make for an unfriendly atmosphere, and his replies may distract you from your gin. He understands English, so please be discreet in every respect."

Then he hands me a roll of German marks a steeplechase horse will be unable to hurdle and leads the way into the house, and by this time I figure out what the scamus is. I figure that Schultz pegs me for a bleater, and the captain is going to try to get some information out of me and, in fact, I am looking for a touch of the old third degree from the Gestapo.

But on entering the house, which seems to be very plainly furnished, the only person present is a big guy in uniform with a lot of gongs on his chest, which is a way of saying medals, and whose head is shaved like Eric von Stroheim's in a Nazi picture. He is sitting at a table in front of a burning fireplace fooling with a deck of cards.

Schultz introduces me to him, but the guy only nods and motions me to sit down at the table opposite him and tosses the deck of cards to me. I examine the backs carefully to see if they are marked, but they seem strictly kosher in every way, and then I say to Captain Kunz like this:

"Captain," I say, "let us understand one thing. I am a noncommissioned officer, and you outrank me from hell to breakfast time, but in this game you must not take advantage of your rank in any way, shape, manner or form, to intimidate me. We will play New York rules, with gins and undercuts to count twenty each and blitzes double."

Kunz nods and motions me to cut the cards for the deal, and he wins it and away we go. We play three games at once and as soon as both of us are on all three games, we start another frame of three, with Schultz keeping score, and it is not long before we have as many as three frames or nine games going at once, which makes a very fast contest, indeed. We are playing for a hundred marks a game or three hundred marks across, which Schultz tells me is about a hundred and twenty dollars in my money, the way the Germans figure their marks.

I will not attempt to describe gin rummy in detail as you can call up any insane asylum and get any patient on the phone and learn all about it in no time, as all lunatics are bound to be gin players, and in fact the chances are it is gin rummy that makes them lunatics. Furthermore, I will not bore you with my philosophy of the game, but I say it is ninety-five per cent luck and five per cent play, and the five per cent is the good card player's strength in the pinches, if there are any pinches.

The cards in gin rummy run hot and cold the same as the dice in a crap game. It is by no means necessary to go to Harvard to learn to play gin and in fact a moron is apt to play it better than Einstein. If you get the tickets in gin, you are a genius, and if you do not get them, you are a bum. When they do not come, you can only sit and suffer, and the aggravation of waiting on cards that never arrive will give you stomach ulcers in no time.

Well, I can see at once that Captain Kunz plays as good a game of gin as anybody can play and he also has good regulation dialogue, such as "This is the worst hand I ever see in my life," and "I only need one little card from the draw to get down," and so forth and so on, but he delivers his dialogue in German and then Schultz translates it for me as it seems the captain does not care to address me direct in English, which I consider very snobbish of him.

About the only word he says I can understand is *frischer* when he picks up a bad hand and wishes to know if I am agreeable to a fresh deal, which is a courtesy a gin player sometimes extends if he also has a bad hand, though personally I am opposed to *frischers*. In fact, when I get a bad hand, I play the Pittsburgh Muddle system on Kunz, which is to pick up every card he discards whether I need it or not and then throw it back at him when my hand improves, the idea being to confuse your opponent and make him hold cards that gum up his hand.

Well, I get my rushes right away and win the first frame and am going so strong on the second that Kunz gets up and peels his coat down to a pair of pink suspenders and 10 minutes later he drops the suspenders off his shoulders and opens his waist band. In the meantime, Schultz kibitzes the captain on one hand and me on the next, and of course a kibitzer is entitled to present his views on a play after it is over, and Schultz is undoubtedly a real kibitzer and becomes quite excited at times in his comment.

However, once he is very bitter in his criticism of a play that costs the captain a game, and Kunz turns on him like a wolf and bawls him out and scares Schultz silly. But later the captain apologizes because as a gin player he is bound to respect the right of a kibitzer.

I keep waiting for Kunz to slip in questions to me about our Air Forces and one thing and another, but he never makes a remark that is not in connection with the game and finally I can see that my suspicions are unfounded and that he is nothing but a gin player after all.

Well, daylight is coming through the windows of the house when the captain says we must knock off playing, and Schultz must hurry me back to camp, and I am somewhat startled to realize that I am four hundred marks loser, which I whip out and pay immediately. Furthermore, Schultz is terribly depressed by this situation and all the way back to the camp he keeps telling me how I disappoint him in not winning and asking me what becomes of my mechanics, and finally I get sore and speak to him as follows:

"Schultz," I say, "the guy is not only better than a raw hand at gin but he also outlucks me. And I tell you I do not know of any mechanics in gin rummy and if you do not care to trust to my superior skill to finally prevail, you can call it all off now."

Then Schultz cools down a little and says maybe I will do better next time, but I judge his disappointment is communicated to the other German soldiers as they seem very crusty with me all day though my greatest trouble is standing off the questions of my own gang about my absence.

Well, Schultz is around after me again that night to take me to the house in the grove, and in fact every night for a month handrunning I play the captain and it is not long before I am beating him like breaking sticks. And every night the captain pays off like a slot machine and every day I turn my dough over to Schultz and he pays me twenty-five per cent and then distributes the balance among the guys in his syndicate.

Naturally, I stand first-class with all the Jerries who are in on the play and they also become more pleasant toward my comrades, and finally I tell these comrades what is going on and while they are greatly amused I can see that they are also greatly relieved, because it seems they are troubled by my nightly absences from the camp and are glad to learn that it is only for the purpose of playing gin with the enemy.

At the end of the month and basing my estimate on around ten thousand marks I have stashed away, I figure I am forty thousand marks winner on Kunz. Then one night I beat him for a thousand marks and he does not whip it out as usual but says something in German to Schultz, and Schultz tells me the captain says he forgets his wallet somewhere, and I say all right, but that it is only fair for him to give me a scratch for the dough.

Schultz translates this to the captain, who looks very angry and seems to be highly insulted, but finally he outs with a notebook and scribbles an I.O.U., because, of course, at this stage of my life I am not trusting anyone and especially a Nazi.

He settles the next night before we start playing, but he takes a good bath this time and gives me the finger again, and while he comes alive the following night, this continues to happen again and again, and something tells me that Kunz is troubled with the shorts. When I mention this suspicion to Schultz, he seems a trifle uneasy and finally he says:

"Well, Lace," he says, "I fear you are right. I fear our good captain is in over his head. To tell the truth, your game is commencing to bore me and the other soldiers of the Fatherland no little because the captain borrows money from us every day, which is a terrible thing for a high officer to do to the soldiers of his command and, while you win it back for us promptly, we now fear he will never replace the principal."

"Why, Schultz," I say, "do you not tell me that the captain is richer than six feet down in Mississippi mud?"

"Yes," Schultz says, "and he keeps talking of his properties in Berlin, but we are nonetheless uneasy. And the worst thing about it is that your twenty-five per cent is eating up all the funds in circulation. It is a vicious circle. Lace," Schultz says, "can you spare me a couple of thou? I must send something to my frau and I will repay you when the boats get running again."

"Schultz," I say, "your story smacks of corn because I do not believe you have a wife and, if you do have one, you will never be sending her money. But," I say, "I will advance you a thousand marks for old times' sake on your marker."

So I weed him the thousand and accept his Kathleen Mavourneen, which is a promise to pay that may be for years and may be forever, and the reason I do this is because I am by no means certain that Schultz may not incite his fellow soldiers to gang up and deprive me of my hard-earned twenty-five per cent by force, if he can find out where I have it carefully buried. To tell the truth, I do not repose great confidence in Schultz.

Well, that night I beat Kunz for twelve hundred marks, and he pays me five hundred on account, and as Schultz and I are getting ready to leave, he says something in German to Schultz, and when we are on our way back to camp, Schultz tells me he has to return to the house and see the captain, and then I really commence to worry because I fear the two may get their heads together and plot against my well-being.

But as far as Captain Kunz is concerned, my worry is groundless as along toward noon of this same day, we hear a rumor that he commits suicide by shooting himself smack-dab through the head and this causes so much excitement that our guards forget to lock us in that night or even to watch us carefully, and all of us Americans and some of the British walk out of the gates and scatter over the countryside, and most of us reach safety in Switzerland, and I afterwards hear there is quite a scandal in German circles about the matter.

But before we go, I have a slight chat with Schultz and say to him like this:

"Schultz," I say, "tell me all."

"Well," Schultz says, "I know that when the captain asks me to return to the house after taking you back to camp, he wishes to borrow the money I get from you to play you again tonight, because when I tell him yesterday I am personally broke and cannot advance him any more, he is the one who suggests I approach you for a touch and in fact he threatens to make trouble for me over certain matters that transpire in Poland if I fail to do so.

"So," Schultz says, "when I reach the house, I first peer through a window into the living room and see the captain still sitting at the table with the deck of cards you use spread out before him as if he is examining them, and all of a sudden, I am seized with a terrible fury at the thought that he is waiting there to take my money to gamble it away frivolously, and an impulse that I cannot restrain causes me to out with my pistol and give it to him through the window and also through the onion.

"And," Schultz says, "I will always remember how the blood drips down off the table and splatters over the nine of diamonds that is lying on the floor and under your chair and how it comes to my mind that the nine of diamonds is considered a very unlucky card indeed and how fortunetellers say it is a sign of death. It is a great coincidence," Schultz says, "considering the number of times you catch the captain with big counts in his hands when he is waiting for that very nine."

"Ah," I say, "I figure you have something to do with his demise."

"But," Schultz says, "as far as anyone but you and me know, it is suicide because I also have the presence of mind to fire one shot from his pistol which is the same make as mine, and leave it in his hand. It is suicide because of despondency, which his superior officers say is probably because he learns of his impending purge."

"Schultz," I say, "you are bound to come to a bad end, but now goodby."

"Goodby," Schultz says. "Oh, yes," he says. "Maybe I ought to state that I am also prompted to my act by the fear that the captain will finally find the nine of diamonds on the floor, that you forget to retrieve when you leave him this morning."

"What do you mean, Schultz?" I say.

"Goodby," Schultz says.

And this is all there is to the story (The Lacework Kid says).

"Well, Lace," I say, "it is all very exciting, and it must be nice to be back on Broadway as free as the birds and with all that moolouw you collect as your twenty-five per cent in your pants pockets."

"Oh," Lace says, "I do not return with a white quarter. You see I use all my end to bribe Schultz and the rest of the German soldiers to leave the doors and gates unlocked that night and to be looking the other way when we depart."

Then The Lacework Kid leaves, and I am sitting there finishing my boiled yellow pike, which is a very tasty dish, indeed, and thinking about the captain's blood dripping on the nine of diamonds, when who comes up but old Kidneyfoot the waiter, who is called by this name because he walks as if he has kidneys in both feet and who points to Lace going out the door and says to me like this:

"Well," Kidneyfoot says, "there goes a great artist. He is one of the finest card players I ever see except in gin rummy. It is strange how this simple game baffles all good card players. In fact," Kidneyfoot says, "The Lacework Kid is a rank sucker at gin until I instruct him in one small maneuver that gives you a great advantage, which is to drop any one card to the floor accidentally on purpose."